BIBLIOMANCER

Book One of WOLFMAN WARLOCK
A COMPLETIONIST CHRONICLES Series

Written by
JAMES HUNTER and DAKOTA KROUT

MOUNTAINDALE
PRESS

TABLE OF CONTENTS

ACKNOWLEDGMENTS

JAMES

I'd like to thank all of the readers and fans who have supported me, year after year, book after book because without you folks none of this would be possible. Huge thanks to my wife and business partner, Jeanette, who has believed in me from the get go, and to our two wonderful kids, Lucy and Sam, who push me every day to be a better person. Thank you to all the beta readers, editors, and proofreaders who made this book possible—they slogged through the rough, ugly, messy first drafts so that no one else ever had to. And, of course, a huge thanks to Dakota, Danielle, and all the people at Mountaindale for the phenomenal work they put into this book. In particular, I'd like to say thank you to Dakota for letting me play around in his sandbox; co-authoring this book was an absolute blast and I can only say that all of the bad parts are my fault and all of the awesome stuff is Dakota bringing both the thunder and the puns.

DAKOTA

It was an amazing opportunity to work on this project with James Hunter. Not only do I feel that I as an author have grown from this experience, I truly believe that we made an awesome book together. Thank you to everyone who made this happen, from our wives—who are incredibly supportive—to our fans who are reading and reviewing this. A special thank you to those that support us outside of our books, especially my patrons: Justin Williams, Samuel Landrie, William Merrick, Brayden Wallach, John Grover, Dominic Q Roddan, Keifer Gibbs, and Ethan.

CHAPTER ONE

There was something waiting for him behind this door. He knew it, and he knew that he had to enter. Still, Sam King lingered on the steps.

His hands were sweaty; the suitcase was oddly heavy as he stared at the double doors of dark wood and frosted glass. Behind him, an engine purred, and tires crunched as his Uber driver pulled away, stranding him there with no other options. No escape. He licked his lips and glanced up—*anything* to put off the inevitable for just a second longer. The house was a massive thing—three stories of gray brick, peaked gables, and gleaming, oversized windows all trimmed in white marble. He hadn't seen the estate in more than a year, and after spending so much time locked away in his tiny dorm room, everything about this place felt... *excessive.*

He took a deep breath, holding it as he steeled himself for the pain and awkwardness certain to come. Finally—when he felt like his lungs would explode—he exhaled, turned the ornate silver knob, and pushed his way into a foyer that was bigger than his entire dorm room had been.

"*Surprise!*" came a chorus of voices, ringing off the vaulted ceilings.

It was even worse than expected! He *hated* surprise parties, but thankfully, he wasn't 'surprised' this time around. Sam's dad, in his infinite kindness, had 'accidentally' tipped him off the week before, so he wasn't walking into this thing blind. The entry room was packed with bodies, all of them wearing sports coats, tennis sweaters, or luxurious summer dresses.

A sea of teeth shined out at him from artificially tanned faces, which looked far too smooth and wrinkle-free to ever be natural. A horde of silver and gold balloons dotted the ceiling, crowding around the crystal chandelier while a multitude of ribbons hung limply from the ceiling. A brightly lettered banner was strung across the far wall: *Congratulations! You Did It!*

There was a polite cheer, followed by raised champagne glasses and a short toast in his honor—which, frankly, he barely listened to. When the half-heard platitudes and well-wishes finally came to an end, Sam plastered a very large, very *fake* smile in place. His cheeks dimpled while he swept his gaze across the crowd of assembled home invaders. Some of those faces were welcome.

His mother with her kind eyes and blonde hair, streaked with gray. His dad, solidly built, shoulders broad, decked out in blue jeans and a black polo. His little sister, Jenna—only sixteen and a major pain in the neck—was going through a goth phase, evident by the all black attire and white makeup. A couple of his dad's coworkers—site foremen and architects mostly—who were more like uncles to Sam than his actual uncle.

Most of the faces, however, weren't *nearly* so welcome. Sam spotted several of the 'neighbors', all dressed in clothes that could pay rent for a month in most cities, as well as a handful of his old 'friends', though he used the term in the loosest possible sense. He'd grown up with these kids, sure. In fact, Jack and Becky had been drifting in and out of his life since elementary school.

But in all reality, he had about as much in common with most of them as the Trekkie community had with the Star Wars fandom. He pushed away his worry and crippling anxiety. His parents were sweet, and they'd meant the best for him, so he could grin and bear the awkwardness. This was *his* day, he reminded himself. Though he didn't much care for parties, he had worked hard and *deserved* to celebrate!

"Thank you all so much," he forced the words out, fighting desperately to sound genuine. "It's so good to see everyone again, and I'm just so overwhelmed that you all took the time to be here. I really can't say thank you enough."

Another polite round of applause followed, the kind of golf claps you might hear on the putting green. His dad's voice cut through the crowd like a shark carving through white-capped waves, "Well, don't just stand there. Let's get this party started!"

"It's good to see you, kid." He slung a broad arm around Sam's shoulders, pulling him into a lopsided hug. He said the words softly; they were meant for Sam's ears alone. The rest of the crowd was dispersing from the foyer, ushered deeper into the house by his mother to where there would be a veritable feast set and ready to eat.

"Sorry about all this," his dad whispered conspiratorially as they watched the crowd shuffle away. "I tried to talk your mom out of it, but you know how she is. Gets an idea stuck in her head, and not even an act of God can change her mind."

Sam shrugged. "It's okay. I understand. I don't mind. Really. This was nice of you guys. I'm just glad to be home. More importantly, I'm *so~o~o* glad to be done with school."

The last four years had been a blur of classes, late nights, term papers, gallons of coffee, and endless tests. But not anymore. Adult life would have its own challenges, he knew, but at least they would be *different* challenges. He was sick to death of being in limbo, stranded in that twilight space where he wasn't *quite* an adult but he wasn't *quite* a child either.

"At least for *now*." His father offered him an evil grin. "A little birdie might've told me you're thinking about law school. Never thought we'd have a *lawyer* in the family, but that'll give me a good excuse to get in some trouble."

Sam felt like cringing, but he suppressed the urge, not wanting to ruin the good mood. "I don't even want to *think* about post-grad stuff. Not for a good, long while."

Never was a much more accurate statement, though Sam kept that piece of info firmly to himself. He'd spent four years slogging through a degree he didn't like—Business Management with a minor in Economics—there was no chance that law school was in his future, no matter how practical that might be. He'd sat through a handful of pre-law classes, and he'd hated every single minute of them. Boring, tedious, and unfulfilling. He would step in and help run the family business, but it wouldn't be as a lawyer.

"Well, that's fair enough." His dad dropped the subject and his arm at the same time. "You take as much time off as you want. You've earned it. In case I don't say it enough, I just wanted to tell you how proud I am of you."

"Anyway." His Dad faltered for a moment before clearing his throat and glancing away. He continued after a moment, "Why don't you go drop your stuff off in your room, then come and get a bite to eat. Your mom booked Fat Dave's for the catering. We've got enough barbeque, smoked ribs, and pulled pork in there to feed an army of hungry college kids."

"Will do," Sam replied, finally excited for *something* in the party. His dad patted him on the shoulder then sauntered off, bare feet slapping on the expensive marble floors. His dad hated shoes almost as much as he loved a good pair of sweatpants. Those were his *true* roots showing through like the glimmer of gold in a predawn morning. Though his parents had money, a lot of it, little things like that were constant reminders that they hadn't started off that way.

The patriarch disappeared around the corner, swallowed by the murmur of voices drifting over from the dining room.

Sam left his suitcase right where it was, and instead of beelining for his room, he decided to take a detour out into the backyard. A little fresh air wouldn't hurt. Plus, he could reorganize his thoughts before dealing with the random assortment of people invading his home like a horde of barbeque-eating, tennis-sweater-wearing, Beverly Hills Mongols. Sam somehow managed to sneak his way past the crowds, taking the well-familiar back hallways.

Unfortunately, when he slipped out through the garage, he found the backyard occupied as well—and this was the group he'd been hoping to avoid the most—his 'friends'. Jack and Becky had migrated out here and were congregating on the lounge chairs lining the tile-edged pool. They weren't alone. There was black-haired Olivia Rutherford, the daughter of Big Jim, who owned twenty or more car dealerships in Orange County, Carter Hawthorne, the son of an oil magnate, and Isabella Paige, the daughter of a real-estate mogul. The worst was Barron Calloway, star quarterback and son of a US Senator. He was in the pool, shirt off, arms draped on the concrete with red-headed Isabella curled up next to him.

"Well, look at what we have *here*." Barron instantly had a broad smile splitting his face, though it never quite reached his eyes. "It's *Sammy*! Back from the Peace Corps or wherever it was you went."

"It was *college*," Olivia explained unnecessarily, ashing a cigarette dangling between two long-nailed fingers. "Didn't you bothering to read the invitation?"

She turned her smoky gaze on Sam. "What was it, Berkeley?"

More than anything else, Sam wished he'd gone to his room, but he couldn't just turn around now and disappear back through the garage. He had too much pride for that. Though he didn't like these people, some part of him also wanted to impress them. They'd spent the past four years leeching off family trust funds, scions of the generational wealthy who would never need to work a day if they didn't want. But not Sam. He'd worked his entire life to be different, to earn his grades, to put in the effort, to make his own way just like his parents had before him. He'd always been an outsider, and his time away at school had only widened that gap.

Sam wanted to show them that their opinions didn't matter anymore. So, he held his ground. "Yep, Berkeley. Finally finished up my degree."

Barron rolled his eyes and gave an exaggerated sigh. "Peace Corps, college, *whatever.* Both are equally worthless. I mean, not to take anything away from you, but what's the point of going to college? You're just going to work in your dad's business, and it's not like he isn't going to give you a job. What's the point of having rich parents if you don't embrace nepotism like the *rest* of us?"

"Oh, stop it, Barron." Isabella slapped him lightly on the bare shoulder, a cross between irritation and flirtation. "You know Sam's not like the rest of us, and that's better than okay."

"Besides," Becky interjected, eyeing Sam from beneath the brim of a wide Prada sun hat with a pink bow wrapped around the front, "college looks like it did him some good. Had quite the growth spurt, didn't you?"

"Eh. I bet I could still give him an atomic wedgie without breaking a sweat." Barron nonchalantly sized Sam up, earning a round of jeering cackles.

Sam felt a flush creep into his cheeks, equal parts shame and embarrassment. He wanted to shoot back some quippy reply—*I'd just like to see you try, dude*—but his mind froze, and his mouth refused to obey him. He'd envisioned this moment more than a few times in his head, daydreaming about how he'd come back home and confront these people who'd made his life so miserable, but this wasn't going at all how he'd expected. He'd been gone for *four years*! He shouldn't have cared what these people thought of him... but he did.

He cared a *lot* more than he wanted to admit, and that was the worst part of all. Sam cleared his throat, his face burning like a bonfire.

"It's *so* great to see you guys," he mumbled half-heartedly before turning away, any measure of pride he had shriveling inside his chest like a dead flower. Shoving his way back through the garage door, he called over his shoulder, "I'll be right back. Forgot to ask my dad about something. Thanks for coming."

He heard the soft whisper of laughter behind him. Mortified, he slunk away, refusing to look back again. Sam retrieved his suitcase from the entry hall, bypassing the rest of the partygoers, and made it to his room without further incident, a miracle of miracles. Safe in his sanctuary, he quietly shut the door behind him and took a few deep breaths. He let the shame and guilt fade, the knots in his shoulders melting away in the process.

Sam didn't want to be rude, but maybe he'd just batten down the hatches and weather out the rest of the party here in his room. He dropped his bag and promptly flopped down on the mattress before easing himself up on his elbows. His bed was a king-sized monstrosity on a heavy, oak frame that seemed like it belonged in the room of someone thirty years his senior, but it was *his* mattress. Somehow being in his own bed banished thoughts of his frenemies, the surprise party, and everything else.

He let out a sigh of relief. Finally, he felt like he was home. His bedroom was more or less in the same shape as he'd left it; though it looked like the maid had probably been through a time or two since everything was neat and tidy, the floor meticulously vacuumed, not a spot of dust to be seen on a ledge or shelf.

The room was significantly larger than the one he'd had on campus. Expensive, dark wood bookcases lined one wall, the shelves filled to the brim with books—mostly fantasy, though there was a spattering of classic sci-fi novels like *Ender's Game* and *Dune*—and a treasure trove of D&D manuals and campaign books. Most of those, sadly, were unused. Sure, he'd flipped through the pages more times than he could count, reading over the various classes and eating through the game mechanics, but he'd never had the friends to play them. One of the greatest ironies of D&D was that, for a nerdy game, it required *so* many other people.

He also had a fair number of MMO game manuals, plus some of the high-gloss concept art books that companies like Imagine Quest, Frontflip, or StormShard Studios regularly published.

Sam had more of those pictures plastered across his bedroom walls—posters from some of his all-time favorite MMOs: Masterwind Chronicles, World of Alphastorm, Celestial Conquest Online. He felt a twinge of guilt as his gaze slid over the posters; it had been too long since he'd logged any hours online. He'd been a gamer most of his young adult life, but these last few years of college had left an abysmal amount of time for anything that wasn't studying, studying, or more studying. His thoughts flashed to Rachel 'DizzySparrow' Poulson, Caleb 'StormMachine' Tucker, Sean 'Potatoad' Bowman, and Jacob 'MajesticRhino' Watson. His old crew.

Idly, he wondered how they were, if they were still gaming together. Once he got back from his trip and settled into something resembling a normal routine, he'd have to dive back in for a while—maybe see if he could track some of those guys down. Speaking of his trip...

His eyes locked on the glossy pictures decorating the walls by his desk: the gleaming glass spires of Notre Dame, rebuilt into a modern masterpiece of art and beauty; the neon lights of Amsterdam glittering like the fireworks in a velvet night; the broad stoic face of Big Ben presiding over the River Thames like some stately monarch. He felt a surge of exhilaration. He'd traveled to Canada and Mexico a handful of times with his parents, but that was pretty much the extent of his worldly jet-setting. His parents might've been rich, but they were surprisingly frugal with things like that, and his dad was quite the homebody.

But all of that was going to change. Assuming that everything was on track, he'd be spending his summer backpacking through Europe—a graduation gift from his parents. He absolutely couldn't *wait* to leave all this behind, even if it was only for a little while.

CHAPTER TWO

A sharp *knock-knock-knock* on the door pulled Sam from his hazy thoughts of far off places.

"Yeah, come on in." He pushed himself upright so that he was sitting on the edge of the mattress with his legs trailing over the edge, his shoes brushing the brown carpet.

His dad poked his head in, a knowing grin on his weathered face. "You got a minute, champ?" He was grasping the door, and his fingers were drumming restlessly against the white-painted wood.

"Yeah, of course."

"Just wanted to stop in and make sure you're okay. I know this," he waved toward the door as he pushed his way in, closing it softly behind him with a *click*, "isn't really your whole thing. The party stuff, I mean. I also caught you talking to that brain-dead bunch in the backyard."

The older man grimaced and ran a hand through his short-cropped hair, which was a perpetual holdover from his Marine Corps days. "They're not bad kids, but I swear to all that is holy that there's not a living brain cell between the whole lot of them. It's not their fault; their parents have to own most of the responsibility for their current status as leeches, but good *lord*, I've never seen a more spoiled or entitled group of people in my life."

Sam shrugged helplessly, trying not to agree *too* readily. "They're not all bad."

"No, definitely not," his dad replied, shaking his head. "Wasn't trying to say that. I just know you don't really, you know, fit in very well with that bunch. You never really have. Frankly, there are few things in my life that I'm prouder of than the fact that you *don't* fit in with those knuckleheads. Your mom and me, we always worried about that. We were afraid you'd just coast along, but you going to college? Knocking it right out of the park like that? Well, I think that's one fear I won't have to worry about anymore. You did good, kid."

Sam blushed and looked away. "Thanks. Still, it's really gonna be good to get away and see some of the world. I mean Berkeley was cool, sure, but a lot of it was the *same*—if that makes sense. Like the scenery changed, but it was the same people I've been around my entire life. The same kind of environment in a lot of ways, and I can't wait to get out of here for a while."

His father glanced down, shuffling on nervous feet. "Yeah. About that. Your mother and I have been thinking. Talking a little..."

The man faltered, clearly searching for the right words. "Look, the thing is, I know you had your heart set on Europe, but we've been thinking it might not be such a good idea."

Sam's stomach lurched and dropped, worry rising up into the back of his throat. "*Seriously?*"

His father finally looked up; lips pressed into a thin line. "It's complicated. We had another idea, but it's a little hard to explain. It would probably be easier if I just showed you, but to do that, we'll need to take a ride. Don't suppose you want to blow this popsicle stand early?"

"If you stop speaking in clichés from the eighties, I mean..." Feeling a numb sort of detachment, Sam stood and followed his dad out of the house, not even bothering to say goodbye to the party guests.

The drive over from the house was a tense, uneasy thing. Sam worked furiously to get his dad to divulge some details, *any* details about what was going on, where they were going, and especially *why*. Normally, his dad couldn't keep a secret to save his life, but suddenly, he was about as talkative as a brick wall and just as revealing. They lived in Orange County but on the outskirts of the city, a handful of miles from San Clemente. His dad wouldn't let him know where they were going, but they were headed north toward Anaheim, crawling through the traffic on I-5.

Sam couldn't even begin to fathom what ominous thing might await them in Anaheim. He crawled through every memory, every conversation he'd had with his parents over the past few months and came up with absolutely nothing that made sense. Then—because he had nothing better to do since his dad was giving him the silent treatment—he thought back to the news. Had there been some sort of terror attack recently over in Europe? Something that might've convinced his parents not to send him on his backpacking expedition? Rumors of war? An outbreak of swine flu? There was tension overseas, but then there was *always* tension overseas. Honestly, he couldn't think of anything that fit.

Eventually, he just settled back into the leather passenger seat of the Beamer, flicked on the tunes, and resigned himself to whatever was in store. After another twenty minutes, they pulled off the five, weaving through the wide city streets before turning into a nondescript office park with a manned guard shack and a formidable gate. Other than the presence of the guard—a beefy guy who looked like he ate nails and punks for breakfast—the complex beyond could've belonged in just about any city in America.

The office building was four stories tall, boxy and white, with rows and rows of reflective windows. To Sam, it seemed like the kind of place someone might go to get their taxes done. What business could they possibly have in a place like this? He squinted as the guard at the shack pressed a button, opening the gate and waving them through with a thick-fingered hand. As the car lurched into motion, Sam could finally make out the signage on the building.

In bold letters, tattooed across the white stucco was the name of the company: *Elon's Electronics, a Division of Space-Y.* Sam, of course, had heard of Space-Y, which was a subsidiary company run by President Musk. He couldn't even fathom the idea that there was *anyone* who hadn't heard of Space-Y and its brilliant but eccentric founder, but... none of this was adding up inside his head.

The more pieces of the puzzle he found, the more bizarre the picture became. The only thing his mind could come up with was that his parents had decided to launch him into space. Which was an insane conclusion, obviously, but every other scenario seemed equally absurd. He had to admit, getting launched into space sounded pretty fun.

His dad pulled the Beamer into a wide space, marked off with fresh, white paint, that had a sign reading *Reserved for VIP Customers.* The next spot over was also occupied... by his mother's car, a sleek Audi in slate gray—or at least it was a car *exactly* like his mother's car, though Sam supposed it could possibly belong to someone else. He'd never bothered to learn the license plate number, and there were no other distinguishing marks, no bumper stickers or decals. But what were the odds?

"Come on," his dad said as he killed the engine. Now, the old man was clearly suppressing a smile. Something tremendously unorthodox was going on here, but Sam was starting to get the feeling that it wasn't bad. Not necessarily. Sam got out of the car, the locks chirping softly as he closed the door, and headed up a short concrete walk, which ended at a set of mirrored-glass doors which showed his reflection but nothing beyond. His dad pulled open the door and gestured toward the yawning opening with one hand. "After you, kid."

Sam headed toward the uninviting entryway, apprehension mounting with every step. He wasn't even remotely ready for when his mom popped out from behind a planter in the office lobby, yelling 'surprise' as she waved her hands frantically in the air. There were more balloons decorating the office interior, but thankfully, the place was devoid of the rest of the party guests—all of them must've been abandoned back at the house, which was fine by Sam but still shocking given his mother's normal attitude about guests.

"Surprise, *surprise*, surprise, sweetie-pie!" his mom squealed, nearly dancing across the floor toward him in sheer excitement. "This time, it's for *real!*"

The entryway door swung shut with a *whoosh*, and his dad ambled up beside him, clapping a callused hand—a working man's hand, despite the money—down on Sam's shoulder. He wasn't even *trying* to hide exactly how pleased with himself he was.

"I almost lost it." He beamed at Sam's mom. "You should've seen his face when I told him there was a problem with the trip—poor kid looked like I planted a knife in his guts. I almost spilled the beans right there, but I'm glad I held out. Totally worth it. Look at his face! Still confused. So good."

Sam raised his hands, head spinning like a merry-go-round. "Okay. Will someone please tell me what in the *heck* is going on?"

"We're sending you to space! *Oof*." His dad grunted as a pointy finger jabbed him in the ribs.

"We are *not*. This is your *real* surprise," his mom replied, folding her hands together. "I knew *someone* may have let the cat out of the bag about the first party, so I decided to throw two parties."

She shot a sideways glance at Sam's dad, then waggled her eyebrows at Sam. "A false party to throw you off the scent, but this is the one I knew you'd actually like."

She stepped to one side and motioned toward a counter at the far side of the lobby. Behind the desk was a smiling receptionist of maybe thirty, wearing a neat, white suit, her red hair tied up in a tight bun at the back of her head. On the wall behind the service counter was a sleek chrome sign, the lines sharp and precise, which simply said: *Eternium.*

The cogs inside Sam's head slowly clanked to life, the mystery resolving itself slowly but surely. Eternium was the brand new, ultra-deep dive MMO that released... *today.* No way. No *way!* The whole internet had been buzzing with speculation. Speculation Sam had largely ignored since *one,* he was working through finals and *two,* rumor was the earliest version of the game cost an arm and a leg. He'd watched the video trailers, of course—he didn't know anyone who hadn't—but he never thought he'd have a chance to play. At least not in the first round of gamers.

"Yep." His dad's grin somehow—almost impossibly— grew even wider. "Your mom and I, we knew you had your heart set on that trip, but then a buddy of mine mentioned that this game was coming out, and knowing you, well..."

He shrugged. "Well, we thought maybe it would be better than backpacking around Europe. It just seemed so perfect. I mean, the game launches today, on the day you were due home. The slots were going so *fast,* so we had to make an executive decision. Didn't even have time to talk to you about it."

The man sheepishly paused, rubbing the back of his neck with one hand. "We just pulled the trigger and went for it."

"*And*," his mom broke in, "you'll actually get an even *longer* break than you thought! Wendy, here—who is just lovely, by the way—was explaining to your father and me about something called *Time Dilation*. Sounds very complicated and fancy. I'm still not entirely sure how it's supposed to work, but from the sound of things, a three-month trip inside Eternium will feel like six months to you."

She faltered for a beat, searching his face for any sign of a reaction. Sam was quiet. Still. She winced and wiggled uncertainly before finishing weakly, "I... *we* hope you don't hate it."

Sam rushed her without a word, throwing his arms out and pulling her in against him. He'd grown a lot since leaving for college, putting on half a foot in height and nearly fifty pounds—most of it muscle—and his mother seemed smaller than she ever had before. A frail and fragile thing, but still, he hugged her tightly. "I *love* it, Mom."

It took a moment, but he finally ended up releasing her. Sam turned and almost tackled his dad. "This is the best gift *ever*! I think you guys might know me even better than I know myself."

It was true. Despite the fact that Sam's dad had been a football star in high school, he'd never pushed for Sam do the sports thing, especially not when it became clear that he'd rather be gaming with his friends online. In middle school, both of his parents had even signed up for World of Alphastorm accounts so they could 'game together as a family'—his mom's words. They were both *terrible*. His dad just couldn't seem to get a handle on the controls, and his mom spent most of her time running into corners, then accidentally blowing herself up with fireballs, but they'd tried.

He could see the visible relief on his mom's face as she sighed deeply. "Oh good. I'm so glad you like it, honey. I was a little worried that maybe you'd outgrown these games, but your father assured me this would be better than anything else we could give you."

"Welcome, Sam," the woman behind the counter said, standing. She smiled, her teeth white and unnaturally even. "We are so pleased to have you with us, and as one of the first people to ever play Eternium—and in a DIVE pod, no less—you're in for a world of fun. If you're ready to go, we're all set up and waiting for you. Your parents filled out most of the paperwork already, so we'll just need to have you sign some forms and get a blood draw and a few vitals, but then your adventure awaits."

CHAPTER THREE

His parents may have filled out most of the paperwork, but getting to the whole *adventure* thing was quite a bit more involved than Wendy had initially let on. The nurse—or maybe administrator, Sam wasn't sure what she actually was—had run him through a bevy of tests, most of them extremely uncomfortable and rather invasive. There were blood draws, MRIs, a short psychological examination, and a standard physical, which included a two-mile run with adhesive pads clinging to his chest monitoring every beep of his heart.

He had no idea what Eternium was going to be like, but if this was what it took just to get *in*, Sam had to imagine it was going to be unlike anything he'd ever experienced before. Just... hopefully in a good way. This felt more like joining the military.

Now, Sam found himself lying flat in a sleek, white capsule—the space a little claustrophobic—as a strange headset lowered down onto his head. It wasn't a full helmet like some of the simpler VR headsets he'd seen around for years but rather a simple, woven band with a gem attached to the middle. The gem itself was about the size of a dime, gleamed like a diamond, and glowed with a faint, otherworldly light. The odd band settled onto his temples, the gem resting gently above the bridge of his nose.

Honestly, Sam wasn't sure what to expect next, but it wasn't the thin line of text that appeared in the air above him. The message was simple and straightforward:

*Do you want **power***? Yes/No*

Huh. That was an odd question. Not whether he wanted to *continue* but whether he wanted *power*. Sam thought about it, turning the question over and over in his mind. *Did he want power?* He'd never really dwelled on the idea before. He wanted to get good grades—but he'd done that. He wanted to have fun and to enjoy life. He was working on that right now. Someday, Sam wanted a girlfriend and maybe to start a family, though that seemed like a hazy event far, far, far off in the distance, but the idea of actually wanting *power* was a new concept for his young college mind. He noticed there was an asterisk, which connected to a hyperlink.

Sam wanted to get into the game, no doubt about it, but after spending hours and hours in preparation, he wasn't in a blind rush. So, curious, he mentally selected the option. The prompt vanished, replaced by a wall of text.

Power is a weird thing. Some people are content to live the life mapped out for them, others not so much. Select no, and you're still going into the deep end, but you'll find the world of Eternium a kinder place. Run an inn, work your way up as a Tailor, maybe even unlock the path to Master Craftsman! Choose power, and you have the chance to change the world through force. Wield the elements. Slay the monster. Even become the monster, if you aren't careful. But stay on your toes because power comes with a price. Prepare for major discomfort and maximum effort!

After reading over the short description, Sam exited back to the initial prompt, which stared at him like a giant eye, unblinkingly waiting for him to make a decision. This decision sounded like it had some far-reaching implications for the next several months of his life. Although the idea of running an inn or being a Master Craftsman had a certain appeal, Sam knew he had his whole life to deal with the status quo, but how many chances would he get to wield the elements or shake the foundations of the world? Not many.

Now, he decided, was the time to adventure. "Yes. I want power."

Good choice. Now, do you know what is about to happen? Have you read the terms and conditions*?

Sam noticed there was another hyperlink next to *terms and conditions* and decided it would probably be a wise choice to at least give it a gander. Immediately, a block of script a mile long appeared in the air before him, packed with jargon and legalese so dense even someone with a legit law degree would have a tough time wading through the thick of things. Instead of really reading through the intimidating wall, he scanned over the headings, gaze bouncing along, looking for anything that sent up a red flag. Already, this was giving him a headache, but every pre-law class he'd ever taken insisted he read it to the end.

So far, everything was pretty mundane. Besides, this was just a video game—even if it was a really advanced one. He glanced at the slider. He was only a quarter of the way done. *Booo!* What was the worst that could happen? He scrolled all the way to the bottom without really looking at the rest, then headed back to the question and selected 'Yes' once more. The words flashed a brilliant scarlet.

Ah, so close, yet so far away. Okay. Prepare for pain. Also fun! Probably. Hopefully? We'll see, I guess. Yes / Yes

Well, that wasn't ominous or anything. With an intro like that, maybe he should've finished reading those ToS after all...

"Hey, is that right?" Sam called out, hoping the nurse would be able to hear him, but no reply came. "Hello? This says prepare for pain? That's gotta be a typo, right? Someone? Anyone?"

He raised a hand to beat on the lid, but then a roiling liquid poured onto his face, filling his mouth, funneling into his nose. He coughed, hacked, but the liquid—oddly goopy and gelatinous—made it nearly impossible to move. Yep. Definitely should have read those ToS all the way to the end. He was already regretting his choice. He tried to hold his breath but couldn't, and as he breathed in... air rushed into his lungs.

In the span of an eyeblink, the pod was gone, and he found himself in a blank, white room, utterly featureless save for the words hanging in the air in front of him like a storm cloud:

Welcome to Eternium! There is no saved data for your profile. Would you like to make a new character? Yes / No

Well, he was here to chew gum and play Eternium, and he seemed to have left his gum with a different body. Easy answer.

Great! You will only be able to have a single character profile at any given time while in Eternium—no alternates, sorry about that—so choose wisely! If you start a new character at a later time, all progress with the current character will be lost forever, including skills, items, and any gold which is on your character, though gold can be transferred through a secure, in-world banking account!

Would you like to select an available starting class or undergo tests and trials to see what the right choice is for you? These tests may unlock different or even unique *classes based on your ability. But be warned! Taking the tests and showing* low *aptitudes may* reduce *the number of available classes! You can exit these tests at any time! Start Game / Take Tests.*

Sam glowered. More *tests*. He didn't want to take any more tests; he wanted to play the game. Some small part of him demanded he just select the 'Start Game' option and dip his toes into the waters. After all, he could always come back and recreate a new character later if he needed to.

But... he'd skipped over the ToS and was already deeply regretting that decision. Plus, he'd been gaming long enough to know that earning a potentially unique class—especially right out the gate before almost anyone else was on the server—could have some *huge* long-term benefits. Since he'd be in the DIVE pod for six in-game months, some added long-term perks definitely wouldn't go amiss. As annoying as the idea of more tests was, starting off on the right foot would be worth whatever hardships or minor delays came with it. So, reluctantly, he reached out a hand and selected the 'Take Tests' options.

The air around him shimmered, and suddenly, he was standing in a cavernous hallway. The walls were a rough, reddish stone, eight or nine feet across and pockmarked from time and the relentless onslaught of the elements. *Wow.* The graphics were absolutely amazing. Uncanny, actually. He raised his hands, examining his fingers which were indistinguishable from the real things. There was a soft sigh of wind, the sound gentle in his ears, followed by a cool breeze brushing across his cheek. The cave was rather cold, which was another surprise, and the air smelled faintly of sea salt and ocean spray. He slowly tread over to one of the walls, trailing his digits across the surface of the stone.

Grit. Nuance. Texture. Heat. Every sensation was there. Orange County was beautiful, but the beaches down in San Diego were some of the best in the world; his family had often trekked down south during the summer months to soak up the sun and sand and surf. One of Sam's favorite spots in all of California was the Cabrillo National Monument, nestled at the tip of the Point Loma Peninsula, due south of Ocean Beach and just west of Coronado. It wasn't a flashy place, nor were there many beachgoers. Instead, there was a small visitor center and a long-standing monument to Juan Rodriquez Cabrillo, who was the first European explorer to set foot on the West Coast of the United States.

A stone lighthouse overlooked the expansive waters of the Pacific, but the real treasure of Cabrillo National Monument was a mysterious cave, tucked away near the waterline. Sam had found it with his sister. They'd edged past the tidepools then carefully picked their way down the Bluff Trail, which terminated at a set of stone steps that hugged the edge of a rather steep cliff face. At the bottom, hidden from prying eyes, was a beautiful cave gouged into the rock. Getting in was only possible at low tide, but the view inside was to *die* for. Literally, if you stayed there until high tide.

It was one of Sam's favorite places in all of California, and this odd hallway reminded him of it. The same porous walls. The same sea-salt smells. He glanced down and found fine, white sand beneath booted feet. Sam smiled and shook his head. Already this game had blown his expectations out of the water, and he was only in the testing phase!

The air in front of him shimmered and danced, a single word materializing before his eyes: *RUN!*

Huh, that was crazy. Why would he run? This place was absolutely awesome. Truthfully, he wanted to explore deeper into the cave, see if maybe there was loot or some other cool things hiding in the nooks and crannies of the rocks. There was a *thump* behind him, the ground trembling beneath his feet. Slowly, he turned, moving as though he were stranded in molasses. Rolling toward him like a runaway semi was an action-movie-sized boulder, easily ten feet tall by eight feet wide, which took up every available inch of tunnel space.

Suddenly, the '*Run*' prompt made a whole lot of sense. With a yelp, he spun and took off, legs pumping beneath him. Too late. He didn't make it five feet. Fear and pain in equal measures flashed through his body as the boulder bulldozed him, crushing his frail form like a Styrofoam cup beneath a truck tire.

CHAPTER FOUR

Sam came to an eyeblink later, a scream tearing free from his throat before trailing off in confusion. The moment of pain was gone and so was the giant boulder that had crushed him seconds before. His heart thundered in his chest as he stared around with wild-eyed terror; this whole place was different. The cavern had vanished, the entire landscape replaced by a hauntingly familiar hallway—checkered linoleum underfoot, orange and blue lockers running off to either side, halogen lights overhead. Oh no.

The rolling stone had been bad—abrupt and traumatic—but this was even *worse* than a quick, grisly death beneath a massive, Hollywood boulder. This... this was the *ultimate* trauma—high school.

Sam shuddered as he scanned those lockers. He hadn't visited the halls of Laguna Hills Unified since he'd picked up his diploma five years ago, and if he never went back, it would still be too soon. Yet here he was, the lights flickering like some bad horror movie, which was exactly what this felt like. Despite that, Sam had to admit that the graphics were absolutely the bee's knees, though he couldn't even *begin* to fathom how the game had known about any of this. Seriously. He'd taken a brief psych exam before entering, and he supposed it had access to most of his public records—like where he graduated from high school, say—but the detail here couldn't be coded in the few hours he'd been on site.

However the game was generating this content was beyond his imagining, but it was obviously on the bleeding edge of technological advancement. There was no prompt this time, nothing telling him what to do, but he couldn't just stand around indefinitely. After a few more seconds of indecision, he set off toward the right, heading for what should be the exit... assuming this place mirrored the real-world version of Laguna Hills Unified.

He blew through a hallway intersection—the right branch heading toward the science wing, the left leading to the English department—bearing straight and toward the exit. He'd gone another ten feet when he heard a clatter and a grunt of pain drifting out from a door, which stood slightly ajar. A thin slice of light cut across the floor like a straight razor. The bathroom. He gulped but padded forward, angling toward the restroom. More grunts and the muffled sound of voices were clearer now but still not quite clear enough to make out.

He paused outside the door, crouched on his toes, trying to figure out what to do here. Just move on, or stick his nose in business that was probably better left alone? A word appeared in the air before him.

Decide.

Of course. The smart thing to do was move along, find the next prompt, complete it, and ignore whatever was going on behind that propped open door. Except he couldn't. He'd grown *a lot* in college, even took a couple of judo classes so that he wouldn't ever be on the receiving end of a wedgie or a swirly whirly, but high school Sam had been a different story entirely. He'd been almost everyone's punching bag. Too rich to hang with the townie kids. Not rich enough to really fit in with the preps. Just smart enough to be a nerd but not nearly smart enough to run with the real nerds. Not particularly athletic or big or outgoing.

He'd worked hard over the past couple of years to put *that* Sam as far in the rearview mirror as feasibly possible, but he couldn't let some other poor kid go through that. Not if he could help. New and improved Sam? He could help; he *would* help. Course decided, Sam shoved his way inside the restroom, urinals and stalls marching off along the left wall, porcelain sinks and cheap mirrors on the right. He was ready for almost anything except what he actually found.

Himself. Or, at least, himself as he'd been five or six years ago. Surrounding young, fresh-faced Sam were a bunch of jocks in letter jackets, led by none other than Barron Calloway. The same smug Barron Calloway who'd been at his graduation party—who was probably still hanging out in the pool, smoking cigarettes and drinking beers. The bullies pressed in, encircling young Sam like a noose, and as they did, they changed. Shoulders swelled, jackets ripped along the seams, arms lengthened, and skin turned an ashy shade of pale green.

They looked like *trolls.* Though trolls in letter jackets and expensive blue jeans. Sam briefly considered turning and bolting... but no. Not this time. He'd let Barron get under his skin at the party, but he wasn't going to let that happen again. Sam had waited *years* to show these jerks he wasn't scared of them anymore. Yeah, maybe these weren't really the bullies who'd tormented him for most of his young life, but they were close enough to count.

Sam let the door slam behind him, the sound bouncing off the tile walls. Almost as one, the newly evolved trolls turned on him, beady black eyes fixing on him, glimmering with barely concealed joy. They were looking for a fight, and they'd finally found one. Sam did his best to keep his tone light but firm. "Leave him alone."

"Will do," Troll Calloway grunted, showing off a pair of jutting lower fangs. "We'll take a piece out of *you* instead!"

Troll Calloway broke into a loping, gorilla-like gait, his knuckles scraping along the floor as he moved. Sam knew he should be scared out of his mind, but instead, he felt a jolt of excitement. He adjusted his posture, knees slightly bent, head centered over his body, feet spread shoulder-width apart. The creature closed with unnatural speed, arms outstretched, its hands now as big as dinner plates. Sam shot inside Barron's guard, one hand latching on to the lapel of the troll's letter jacket—pulling the deformed creature down and off balance—while his other arm wrapped around the thing's head. Sam spun his torso clockwise, jerking down, dragging Troll Calloway up and over his hip in a common judo throw.

He'd never actually used a throw against a real opponent, but he grinned like a madman as the troll left the ground, flipping through the air in a sharp arc. Before his nightmarish bully landed, the creature in his hands simply dissolved, turning to smoke which drifted into the air and resolved into a new prompt:

Survive.

The high school disappeared just as quickly as it had come, and now, Sam found himself in a rugged jungle, stretching out around him in every direction. The ground beneath him was loamy—almost spongy—and covered in thick patches of twisted vegetation and a gnarled blanket of creeping tree roots. Enormous, moss-covered trunks reached *up, up, up,* and intermixed among them were palm trees with massive fronds and a thousand other types of trees that Sam couldn't name. The leafy canopy completely blocked out the sky, save for a few errant sunbeams, and the air was hot and sticky—far more humid even than southern California.

All around him were the sounds of a rainforest—the hoot of monkeys, the chirping cry of colorful songbirds, the soft rustle of a breeze through the high leaves. There was a *snap-crack* as something big pushed its way through the foliage, followed by an odd gurgling noise that he couldn't quite place. He turned, searching the tangle off to the left. Another *crack* in the deep brush and a purple-black blob the size of a minivan rolled into the open. The thing defied explanation—Sam didn't even have a frame of reference for what he was seeing.

Spoiled Jell-O given sentience maybe? If he were playing a D&D campaign, he'd say this was a Dungeon Slime, but it didn't look like any kind of Slime he'd ever heard of.

It had no face. No mouth. Floating inside it, suspended like little pieces of fruit in Aunt Jane's Thanksgiving cranberry Jell-O salad, was a mishmash of bones: skulls, femurs, rib cages—not just bones from humans but from pretty much everything. It had a small army of rudimentary limbs, formed from the bones within, but none of those limbs seemed especially functional. With another gurgle, it lurched forward, moving at a swift trot, though nothing close to a run, its strange limbs waggling manically like one of those wacky, waving-arm, inflatable, flailing tube-men. On a purely surface level, this thing seemed far less formidable and dangerous than the troll-bullies from the high school, but Sam had learned his lesson from the first test.

Run meant *run*. *Decide* meant *decide*. *Survive* meant *survive*. In this case, it *also* meant run—survive, but *book it*.

Since this thing was part of the 'survive' portion of the test, then clearly it was a serious threat. Sam had no weapon, and he doubted very much that his rudimentary skills in judo would work well against a gelatinous blob that probably outweighed him by a thousand pounds and had no proper limbs. Judo was about leverage, and in a fight against that thing, Sam would have none. So instead, he turned and jogged away, making his way deeper into the dense bush. Survive didn't necessarily mean *kill*, so maybe he could just run out the clock.

So it went for what felt like the next several hours. Where was the dang clock, anyway? Sam kept moving, always moving, tripping his way over exposed roots, forging past gently burbling brooks, and trudging through thorny vines that scratched at his skin and ripped at his clothes. The jungle shifted and changed as he moved, but there was no discernible way out; the blob of goo and bones kept on his trail like a bloodhound determined to bring down its prey. The creature never moved any faster, but it also never moved any slower. It was an implacable hunter, and Sam was soon sore, tired, and hungry.

There was no defeating something like that thing, so he pressed on. He didn't have access to food or water, but there were berries and other strange fruits dotting heavy tree boughs. By hour eight or so, his stomach was growling in protest and his throat burned. The creature was maybe a few hundred feet back, working to get through a deadfall of downed trees, so Sam risked plucking a handful of the berries and plopping them into his mouth. The flavor was brilliant, like the sweetest raspberries he'd ever tasted. Then he dipped his mouth into a small stream, no bigger than his thigh. The water, like the berries, was crisp and refreshing, curing his raging thirst in an instant.

Another *crack* and *blub* brought his head back up; the overgrown Slime had cleared the trees. Sam turned and jogged off, picking up the pace. He made it all of a hundred feet before a railroad spike of pain doubled him over. It dropped him to his knees while bright barbs of fire radiated out from his belly. When he tried to gain his feet, his legs simply refused to cooperate.

Sam glanced back over his shoulder to find the creature steadily gaining ground on his position. He fought to stand once again, but when it became utterly obvious that it wasn't going to happen, he gritted his teeth and proceeded to crawl away from the encroaching monster. He was pulling himself hand over hand, digging in with his knees and toes, but he wasn't fast enough. Not even close.

"Wow, this game is the absolute *worst*," Sam growled an instant before the gelatinous bone creep steam-rolled right over the top of him, the purple fluid eating at his skin like acid as he was pulled up inside the monster. No longer able to speak, he could only think, *"Yep, the absolute worst. Why in the world would someone make a game like this?"*

But despite everything, he wasn't quite ready to call it quits. He'd already come this far, after all, so he steeled his resolve even as the slime devoured him. Sometime later, he opened his eyes to find the monster was nowhere to be seen, and the jungle had been swapped out for a classroom. Happily not high school again, thank the lord. This time, it was the comforting and familiar seating of a lower-level college class. Unlike many of the higher-level classes—which were smaller and more traditional—this room had stadium-style seating to accommodate large freshmen groups a hundred or more strong. At the front was a wooden podium, though there was no instructor in sight, and behind that was an honest-to-goodness chalkboard.

Written across the board in an elegant script were three words:

Do Your Best!

The moment Sam finished scanning the scrawled text, a paper test booklet appeared on the wooden fold-out desk in front of him, the pages filled with a host of questions. There was a sharpened pencil beside the booklet, ready and waiting to be used. Well now, this wasn't exactly *fun,* but at least this was something Sam understood. Compared to being crushed alive by a huge boulder, facing down thuggish nightmare bullies, or being poisoned then slowly consumed by a giant, man-eating slug, this actually seemed pretty snazzy.

Sam broke the seal on the booklet and dove in with the reckless abandon of a kid fresh out of college, his head stuffed full of useless facts that had few real-world applications. He tore through the English section, answering questions about similes and metaphors, killing the reading comprehension portion, and then writing an entire long-form essay on classic literature. Next came mathematics, followed by a section of world history, astronomy—which was odd—biology and general anatomy, basic psychology, and even politics and religion.

Whenever he finished one section, it simply disappeared, whisking his answers away with it, until the booklet stared at him with empty pages. There were a few sections of the test he'd struggled through, but overall, he felt more confident about this portion of the trial than any other he'd slogged his way through. Which made sense, considering he'd *died* in two out of three trials so far. Finally, after what felt like ages—his mind foggy, his back sore, his stomach grumbling even more—the next prompt appeared.

Time is up! Select 'Proceed' to begin the next test.

He didn't know what would be next, but as long as it was better than the jungle-blob-survival-marathon, he'd do alright. Sam reached out and tapped 'proceed.' In an eyeblink, the world shifted around him as he was whisked away to the next area. This time, the room didn't change, only his location in it. Instead of being in a seat near the back of the auditorium-style classroom, he was now front and center, standing behind the wooden podium with a sheaf of notes neatly arrayed before him. Though the room itself hadn't changed, there was *one* rather disconcerting addition—the seats were now filled with people.

A sea of eager faces stared at him expectantly. The notes in front of him wriggled on the edges, dark, bold text appearing on the page with his next set of instructions.

Explain the Fundamentals of Trigonometry.

Of all the sections on the test, the mathematics portions had easily been his worst area; naturally, that was the thing he had to explain. The fact that he was *borderline* terrified of public speaking certainly didn't help the situation any. If Sam were honest with himself, this might actually have been worse than the Jungle Slime, though for *very* different reasons.

He hadn't given up then, and despite the fact that he was rapidly losing patience with this process—this was a game and one that was supposed to be fun—he wasn't ready to throw in the towel. Not quite. So, against every instinct in his body, he carefully straightened the papers on his lectern, cleared his throat, and spent the next hour muddling his way through the single worst lecture ever given on trig. By the end, he felt like a train wreck—his voice hoarse, his palms sweaty, his nerves shot. Yep, he was definitely not having fun. Not even remotely. He'd rarely experienced a bigger surge of relief than when *that* trial lapsed and the auditorium dissolved, reforming into...

The same stony passageway from the very first trial. The same rough-hewn walls. The same gritty sand underfoot. The scent of salt and seawater tickling at his nose. Except, now the hallway had a fork. Down one path were his mom and dad, both of them smiling as they waved encouragingly. Down the other path was his sister, hands planted on hips, a scowl on her goth-black lips. Sitting beside her was their German Shepard, Max, his doggy tongue lolling out from the side of his mouth. In front of Sam was a lever, and hanging from it was a sign that read:

Save One.

There was a thud and a crunch as the Indiana Jones boulder dropped from the air, rattling the ground with its landing. Sam glanced down at the lever, horror dawning on him as he realized just what this test wanted from him. This time around, the boulder wasn't going to crush him; it was going to obliterate either his parents *or* his sister and dog. The lever in front of him was essentially a railway track switch, and he was the one who got to decide who lived and who died.

"No," he muttered, shaking his head. "Nope. I've done enough, and I'm not doing *any*more."

Without a second thought, he broke into a headlong sprint toward the boulder, which was now rolling toward his parents. He zipped between his mom and dad, long legs eating up the distance in no time. The boulder hit him like a wrecking ball, accompanied by a brief flash of pain, and then he was back. Respawned right where he'd started a moment before. The cavernous hallway with its switch and sign, parents smiling at him while his sister scowled and Max wagged his fluffy tail.

The game was going to *make* him choose; it was testing his moral limits. Instinctively, he knew there was no way to move forward, not without pulling that lever and consigning one of the groups to death. That just wasn't something he was prepared to do.

"I'm *done!*" he yelled at the air around him. "I want to end the trials. This isn't what I came for. This isn't fun anymore. This whole thing was never fun, but this? This is too much. Please take me back."

The boulder dropped with a *thud* and crunched across the sandy gravel on the floor. For a second, Sam envisioned a superhero confronting a great evil in a time loop over and over again, suffering a horrific death each time. He just hoped that wasn't what he'd signed up for. He grimaced, bracing himself to die again, and took off for the boulder once more.

CHAPTER FIVE

Sam didn't die as he expected. It was a strange feeling, being alive when you weren't *supposed* to be. Something that was very hard to describe, but he felt that most people would somehow understand. The whole world had stopped, frozen, the boulder mere inches away from crushing him beneath its immense weight and apparently-not-unstoppable momentum.

His parents were still there, as was his sister and doggo, but someone had pressed the pause button on everyone but Sam. There was a sharp *ding-ding-ding* followed immediately by a message appearing in the air like a mirage in the deep desert.

Well, you didn't finish all the trials, but hey, you know what you want and you're sticking to your guns—good for you! Plus, you really tried. You were pretty close. Farther than anyone else has made it... though this is day one, so that's not a super huge achievement. But hey, take your wins where you can get them! Based on the results of your trials, new starting classes have been unlocked! Your basic stats will be adjusted based on the result of each test after you choose a class!

Title unlocked: High Five, I Tried! This title will cause NPCs to have pity on you because dang it, you're a good person and you tried! Effect: Randomly, an NPC might gift you with a small trinket. It could be a crust of bread, a tidbit of information, or even an invaluable object. -5% prices at good or neutral aligned shops.

Please note that all title effects are active at the same time, but the title you have equipped will be the only one that others can see without analysis abilities. The maximum number of titles you can have at any given time is ten.

The world swam around him, blurring on the edges as he was transported to a new room, absolutely packed with people. Not any ol' people but *him*. Fifty iterations of Sam in various attire and poses, all standing in neat, orderly rows. As he moved, they moved, mimicking his every motion. He lifted an arm, and so did they. When he smiled, a clone army of himself beamed back in return. Alright! Now *this* was what he'd come for!

Slowly, Sam moved into the rows, examining the uncanny doppelgangers.

There were versions of him with bulging muscles, heavy armor, and all manner of weapons. Versions with him in leathers, others where he held beakers and flasks. Class names hung above each head like faint storm clouds, colored with ghostly light. He ignored the Barbarians and heavy-hitting melee warriors. The thing was, classes like those would have a huge advantage in early gameplay. Chances were, a Ranger or a Warrior class would go in, ready to kick butt and take names—immediately effective.

But he was going to be in a DIVE pod for three freaking months, and with the time compression, that would feel like six months. *Six months* of near constant play, in the game for twenty-four hours a day. Although math was his worst suit by far, he'd just given a lecture on trig, so it wasn't hard to come up with a roughly estimated projection of the amount of time he'd be in Eternium. Two-thousand one-hundred sixty real-life hours or four-thousand three-hundred twenty hours if he were accounting for compression. That was a metric butt-ton of game time.

If he played things right, he could end up being one of the most powerful players in the meta, especially if some of these options were restricted or rare classes. A magic class would be as weak as single-ply toilet paper early on, but later... later, he would have a tremendous edge. So, he ignored the brawlers, bypassing them without a second thought, focusing instead on the glowing versions of himself, most of them clad in robes. He examined one that might have been a generic priest but passed it over. He was here to adventure, to quest and had *no* desire to play a pure support class.

At least not exclusively. He had no problem laying down some team buffs, but he wanted to slay. Healing was for people who were afraid to make *other* people bleed! He ordered the group of... *himself,* "Combat magic classes."

The figures shifted and whirled, the columns and rows rearranging themselves until only five figures stood before him, all highlighted with an ethereal glow. One looked like a druid build—decked out in furs and soft leathers—another was clearly a summoner, what with the stately black robes sewn with mystic sigils and a trio of little gremlin-looking creatures marching around him in a circle.

That might be an interesting option, though the idea of lurking at the rear behind a wall of puppets waiting for his minions to do the heavy lifting didn't sound all that fun. Sam looked over each before moving on to a class called *Aeolus Sorcerer,* which was a subclass of the Mage branch. This, now... this looked promising. Using the Tool Tips icon loitering in the corner of his vision, he pulled up more info.

Aeolus Sorcerer. A subclass of Mage that has mastery over the forces of wind and air. The Aeolus Sorcerer intuitively understands magic—it is a part of him that is as natural as breathing. Those choosing this class have Mana pools unlocked by default. They also naturally learn new class-compatible spells every third level without any training from an outside source. Although they have some defensive capabilities, Aeolus

Sorcerers tend to lean toward combat-oriented spellcraft; making excellent field Mages.

Overall, their spells are less powerful than those of a basic Mage at the same level, but the spells can cost less than half the Mana. The Aeolus Sorcerer gains four characteristic points to spend per three levels and one point of intelligence and wisdom on every <u>even</u> level. They gain two free skill points to spend per level. Intelligence, wisdom, and dexterity are the suggested characteristics for this class. Do you want to start the 'game' as an Aeolus Sorcerer?

Bingo. This was the one; he could feel it. Since *Eternium* was so new and a tightly guarded secret, there was really nothing out about the gameplay or overall mechanics, but based on Sam's past experience with MMOs, this looked exactly like the kind of class he wanted. Adventure-oriented, action-based, good gameplay up front with the potential for high power later on. Most importantly of all? It looked like it would be *fun*! He had no intention of being a pro-gamer or making his living as a live streamer; eventually, he would return to the real world and help his dad and mom run the family business.

But until then? He just wanted to have a blast. This was it. The trials had been terrible, but this was *definitely* worth the pain.

Congrats! You have accepted the subclass Aeolus Sorcerer. Professions unlock at level five. You have four characteristic points to spend. Please note, your starting characteristics have already been modified due to your trials, real-life capabilities, and class selection. Please allocate your remaining points now.

With a thought, Sam pulled up his character sheet. There were ten stats to choose from: strength, dexterity, constitution, intelligence, wisdom, charisma, luck, karmic luck, and perception. As a former gamer, most of those terms seemed pretty self-explanatory; in a game this new, strange, and immersive, however, he didn't want to take anything for granted and run the risk of being wrong. After all, most people didn't know that D&D Sorcerers used charisma instead of intelligence as their primary trait for spellcasting. What if this turned out to be similar? So, instead of simply bypassing those details, he used the Tool Tips feature again to get a bead on what everything did.

Strength, it seemed, was the stat which determined how much he could carry and how hard he could hit with weapons or his fists. Dexterity was the explosive speed he could muster, his ability to contort his body, and how well he could do complicated tasks like picking locks, crafting goods, or using ranged weapons—a trait that would likely come in handy as a ranged spellcaster.

Constitution determined how healthy he was, how much stamina he had, and his overall resistances to poison and disease. It also determined his physical appearance and made it harder to be knocked around at higher levels. Good for tanks and warriors especially. That was probably the least important trait for Sam, considering he planned to hit hard at range. A little extra health probably wouldn't hurt, though. No point in being unnecessarily squishy if he could avoid it, especially if he was going to play solo for any length of time.

As expected, intelligence determined how much Mana he had at any given time in addition to how well he could understand complicated concepts like spells or engineering. The most interesting Tool Tip was the entry for wisdom. Apparently, wisdom determined how fast his Mana *regenerated* as well as an esoteric statement that wisdom would 'help determine if he *should* do something'. It would also let him combine various concepts, working with his intelligence to make new and improved things.

The problem was, he couldn't really get his mind around that notion. How in the world would having an altered wisdom score help him to understand whether he *should* do something? It wasn't like the game could actually make him wiser, yet that seemed to be the implication.

Only time would tell how that mechanic actually worked.

Charisma, as in various MMOs he'd played, determined how people would interact with him and his ability to get good prices buying or selling. It would also impact his ability to lead or convince others to do things with or for him. As a social outcast, he expected to have a low charisma score but was pleasantly surprised to find he had a thirteen, which wasn't too shabby at all considering his highest score, intelligence, was at a seventeen. He wasn't sure that made sense, but he'd take any edge he could get.

Luck was something that affected all the other stats on an unstated level, as well as his chances of finding rare items or loot without specifically looking for them. As in real life, he seemed to be abnormally lucky with a base score of fifteen. Karmic luck wasn't explained even a little bit, but if Sam had to gamble, he'd say it was probably how a player's alignment was tracked. He'd played games where a single good or bad decision could have a drastic outcome on almost any given storyline, so maybe this was similar.

Finally, perception was the ability to spot details. This was everything that came from sensory input and would increase how well he experienced and interacted with the world. He noted that he had somehow scored an incredibly low *five* in perception, which seemed even more shocking than that his charisma score was so high. People had accused him once or twice of being absent-minded, but a *five*? Really? He wasn't *that* absent-minded and unobservant, was he? Couldn't be. But there it was, staring him right in the face like an accusatory finger.

Right below the perception was a note on the side that caught his attention.

*Be warned! Increasing perception will enhance how much pain players actually feel, as well as all other sensations! Eternium is not responsible for damage to player's mental state. For more information please read the capsule handbook included in your order!

On the plus side, you have the perception of a burnt piece of toast, so you shouldn't have too much to worry about! I would watch out for rotten food and poison if I were you, though. Also, steer clear of those Rogue classes, because a Mage-based class with a perception of five will be a bigger mark than Big Mark—a robust Innkeeper who happens to be named Mark, and guess what? Big Mark has way~y~y higher perception than you.

Well. That was super insulting. Guess it was just part of the flavor of the game. Dismissing the message, Sam surveyed his current stats, mulling over just which scores he should increase.

Characteristic: Raw score (Modifier)

Strength: 12 (1.12)
Dexterity: 13 (1.13)
Constitution: 11 (1.11)
Intelligence: 17 (1.17)
Wisdom: 16 (1.16)
Charisma: 13 (1.13)

Perception: 5 (0.05)
Luck: 15 (1.15)
Karmic Luck: 2

The whole system seemed a little wonky to him, especially the raw score versus the modified score and what practical effects that had, but after spending a little more time poring over the Tool Tips, examining the stats and their relationships to each other, he earned another pop up that seemed to lay everything out nice and neat:

Growth in Eternium is difficult when you are doing nothing! Unlike other systems, each day will be a struggle to survive, especially at the start of your journey. Because of the difficulty, the rewards will certainly be worth your effort! Since this system is somewhat unorthodox, please note that a modifier of 'one' is considered a normal, healthy, adult human. Because you're a book-smart, brain-dead college kid with a pampered upbringing and no real-world experience, your perception score has been negatively impacted to a high degree!

Each point allocated will increase your modifier by one one-hundredth of a point. An exception to this is when you gain your first ten points in any category. At this point, your score will increase to 'one point one' in that category. Moving forward, each time a category increases to the next multiple of fifty, the base score will increase by 'one'. At fifty points, your modifier will be plus 'two'. At one hundred points, the modifier will be plus 'three'. For example, a character with forty-nine points in a category will have a modifier of 1.49, which is forty-nine percent stronger than an average human! Then if they reach fifty points in the category, they will jump to a modifier of 2.0!

The discrepancy in strength is intended to push you to develop as fast as possible. Skill in the areas you focus on will

quickly allow you to reach higher than others of the same level,
even if you have similar stats! You can earn skill points and
characteristic points through your actions, so work hard! You will
need to be as powerful as possible when the first major update
comes into effect. That is... if you want to survive!

Huh, the developers on this game sure had a flair for the
ominous and slightly creepy flavor text. Putting that aside, Sam
had a pretty good idea of exactly what he should do. Hitting fifty
points in a given category sounded like the real goal, since that
would maximize the point multiplier, giving the greatest overall
boosts, but he really needed to bring up his perception stat,
which had a negative value multiplier. With a point-zero-five
modifier, he was liable to be as gullible as a toddler and miss
pretty much everything that wasn't directly hitting him in the face
like a baseball bat.

After a moment, he decided to drop two of his four
points into perception, so he was *slightly* more perceptive than a
shiny potato; then he added another point to wisdom, bringing it
up to seventeen. His last point he dropped into dexterity since
that was the lowest of his three class-essential character traits.

With his points distributed, he finally input a name. He
could, in theory, start a new character if he botched things too
badly—though he didn't relish the idea of redoing the tests—but
he really didn't want to get stuck with a stupid gamertag for the
next three months. How bad would it be to have a lame name
like PwnerBwner_69 for the rest of his days? So, instead, he
chose his own name, Sam_K, and was pleasantly surprised when
it went through.

But then again, these were young days. The game had
only been active for less than twenty-four hours, and only those
with quite a bit of money to throw around were likely on at this
point. Moreover, most of the players on the server would

probably be going with funny names like Shadow_Stalker, GlitterGurl, ExcitedPear, or Kangaroar!

His chosen name populated followed by the slightly insulting title he'd earned.

Name: Sam_K 'High Five, I Tried!'

Class: Aeolus Sorcerer

Profession: Locked

Level: 1 Exp: 0 Exp to next level: 1000

Hit Points: 70/70 (60+(10)*)

Mana: 212.5/212.5 (12.5 per point of intelligence)

Mana regen: 4.25/sec (.25 per point of wisdom)

Stamina: 65/65 (50+(10)**+(5)***)

*10 points for each point in Constitution, once it has increased above 10.

**5 points for each point in Strength, once it has increased above 10.

***5 points for each point in Constitution, once it has increased above 10.

Characteristic: Raw score (Modifier)

Strength: 12 (1.12)

Dexterity: 14 (1.14)

Constitution: 11 (1.11)

Intelligence: 17 (1.17)

Wisdom: 17 (1.17)

Charisma: 13 (1.13)

Perception: 7 (0.07)

Luck: 15 (1.15)

Karmic Luck: 2

Skills and Spells

Wind Blade (Novice I): Select an enemy target to attack, inflicting 3n damage, where n = skill level. (Air-aligned magic) Range: Ten meters. Cost: 5n. Cooldown: 1.5 seconds; hand gestures must be completed to cast.

Instinctual Casting (Novice I): As a Sorcerer, you automatically have an innate knowledge of spellcasting. You are able to cast any spell that is at the same rank as this ability for an increased (variable) Mana cost. Passive, no cost.

Cool. So right off the bat, Sam would be able to sling magic, and with the Instinctual Casting ability, it looked like he wouldn't even be required to do much training. At this point, he had no money or armor, but he did have one outstanding skill point—though it looked like he wouldn't be able to do anything with that until the second level—which was probably for the best. He didn't know enough about the gameplay yet or the overall meta to make an informed decision about what to use those points for, though the Tool Tips did provide a little bit of context.

Most skills and spells started at 'novice' and would get progressively better as they were used. When the level passed 'nine', the skill would be upgraded to a zero of the next rank. From lowest to highest, the ranks were: Novice, Beginner, Apprentice, Student, Journeyman, Expert, Master, Grandmaster, and Sage. Which meant that he had a *long* way to go before he was anywhere close to mastering even a single skill. Eh, that was fine. A game like this wouldn't really be enjoyable or hold his interest if he could max out his character in the first week. Better if he had to work at it for a while.

Looking forward to the adventure to come, he accepted all changes, and the world dissolved around him.

Chapter Six

An opalescent light engulfed Sam, suffusing his body with energy and power, and inside an eyeblink, he'd spawned in the square of a massive, medieval city. The breath caught in his throat, eyes bulging as he surveyed the cityscape. The ground underfoot was a bone-white mosaic of some complicated, geometric pattern, and directly at its center was an enormous marble fountain, spraying water into crystal clear air like the spout of some enormous whale. Cobblestone streets branched off from the town square, carving their way between shops sporting peaked roofs and wooden shutters, which were thrown wide in the crispy light of mid-morning.

The city was alive with the hustle and bustle of activity, men and women cutting across the square, the low hum of idle chatter filling the air. Unlike many of the MMOs he'd played over the years, the residents of this city—whatever this city was—were all human; not a Dwarf, Elf, or Half-Orc to be seen, which Sam thought was a little sad. He hadn't really considered it during the character creation process—he'd been too overwhelmed by the potential class options—but there had been no race selector option. Which was too bad. He usually played a non-human race just for the sake of doing things a little differently.

Despite the sea of pure humanity, however, there was a tremendous amount of variation. There were hulking warriors in heavy armor etched in silver or gold, leather-clad Rangers sporting bows on their backs and short swords at the hip, and plain-looking folks in linen outfits or the cloth and leather garb of a village peasant.

A woman wearing elaborate and colorful petticoats strolled by, a parasol raised above her head, while a mercenary in a conical helmet and segmented lorica armor skulked off in the opposite direction. Sam squinted at a short man in itchy-looking, brown robes—a cleric of some sort, perhaps—and noticed that the man's face was just a little blurry around the edges.

Huh. Weird. He focused on some of the other passersby and noticed the same thing—just a little blur to each face. The edges and outlines of buildings were just a little fuzzy, too. He'd had glasses his whole life, though these days he wore contacts. It was a weak prescription in the grand scheme of things, and this felt a little like stumbling through the house at night when he forgot to put his glasses on. Doable but uncomfortable and more than a little inconvenient.

Honestly, he couldn't believe his weak prescription had followed him through to the other side... Or had it? Then it dawned on him. His low perception. What if his negative score had actually given him *bad* eyesight, making it genuinely harder to perceive things clearly? That was an interesting thought. Suddenly, he was glad he'd invested those two extra points into perception; else he likely would've been as blind as his Grandma Tessa, who couldn't tell the difference between Sam and a golden retriever at ten feet. Yep, he'd definitely need to get his score up and see if it made a tangible difference.

But there would be time for that later. For now, he was excited to get started on his epic summer vacation. Where to even start, though?

Hands on hips, he took in the square, searching for some kind of prompt, an exclamation point free-floating above some NPCs head, or a quest alert which would tell him what to do. Nothing. There was no clear indication of what way he was supposed to go. As shocking, strange, and downright intrusive as the test had been, this city was far more jarring in its own way. It wasn't necessarily the strangeness of the place—because in a lot of ways, it was just the way he'd envisioned it being—but the sheer scope of the place was both daunting and impressive.

"I need to turn up the render distance." Sam's face soured at the obvious effect his low stat was having on him. The city was laid out in an orderly grid of streets, shops, and houses, and though he couldn't see everything, he had to guess that this city was easily big enough to accommodate a population of fifty thousand or more. Probably *a lot* more, considering how much of the city he couldn't see.

"Hey. You there," someone called, the voice female and brushed over with a slight cockney accent. Sam turned until he spotted a rather buxom woman with blonde hair worked into a single, tight braid, which she had draped over one shoulder.

"Me?" Sam hooked his thumb at his chest while glancing left and right.

"Well, who else, love?" She was heading his way, her colorful skirts swishing around her legs as she moved. "Been hollering at ya for a good thirty seconds, I have. You just stood there spinning like a buffoon who's soft in the head."

Sam frowned. No, that couldn't be right. He'd heard the gentle hum of conversation, but surely, he would've noticed someone literally *yelling* at him for thirty seconds. Unless... his terrible perception was at work again. He sighed, already realizing he'd made a few tactical errors and he'd only just barely started.

The big woman, now just a handful of feet away, snapped her fingers. "Hello there. Ya just drifted off a bit again, love."

She frowned, then canted her head to one side. "But bless yer little heart, it surely looks like yer trying. Plus you're new, so I guess I can cut ya some slack. Anywho, welcome to Ardania, capital city of the 'newly returned to the world' human Kingdom! Though..."

She paused, scratching at her chin. "*New* is a bit deceptive, isn't it then? Been about two hundred years, I suppose."

"I'm sorry." Sam held up his hands to slow her verbal deluge. "Who are you exactly?"

"Why, I'm Kathleen, of course," she replied as though that should be self-evident. "You, love, look like a little, lost kitten—doesn't know its nose from its tail. I take it yer one of them Travelers, then?"

Sam stood slacked jawed for a moment, then nodded.

"Well, ya certainly look the part, poor thing. I'm on my way to the market—need to pick up some turnips for a stew—and I saw ya standing there. Not sure what I can do, but might be I can point ya in the right direction at least. Get ya on yer way, as it were. So, what's yer class then, love?"

"Um, I'm an Aeolus Sorcerer. A spellcaster."

Kathleen snorted and rolled her eyes. "Of course ya are, and I'm the Queen of High Magic."

She guffawed, fluttered her eyelashes, and dipped him a small curtsy. "It's a pleasure to meet ya, high lord magic pants."

"What?" Sam felt like someone had sucker punched him in the gut. "I don't understand what's happening here. You asked me my class, and I told you."

"Aye, ya told me, love. Sorcerer, ya said." Kathleen rolled her eyes.

"Right. Yes, that's exactly right. Aeolus Sorcerer," he reconfirmed, as though she might simply have misheard him the first time around.

This time she full-on laughed at him, clutching her sides. As her bout of mirth subsided, she finally asked, "Are ya havin' a go at me, love? The only Mages in Ardania come from the Noble lines, and even they are a mighty rare sight. Why, I don't rightly reckon I've ever actually seen a real spellcaster up close. Now, if you're done having fun at my expense, tell me yer real class, and I'll point ya in the right direction. But try to be quick about it, love. I have errands to run yet today. If yer a warrior class, it's the guards you'll be wanting, and if yer Ranger or Rogue class, there's a dexterity training course over in Westham, not far from the Green Eye Tavern."

Sam smiled and spread his arms. "I don't know what to say. I'm a Sorcerer—it's a Mage subclass, I think."

The grin slowly slipped from her face as she crossed her arms. "Well, go on, let's see a bit of magic then."

Sam stood slack-jawed for a long beat. He didn't even know what in the heck to do about that. He felt like the woman, who was obviously a non-player character—or NPC—should just recognize his inherent Mage-*ness*. He hadn't even considered the notion that he'd have to prove himself right out of the gate. Was magic in this world really *that* rare? It seemed unlikely, preposterous almost, but there was no other solution that seemed to fit. Whatever. This was fine. *All fine!* As a Sorcerer, he had the ability of Instinctual Casting, so in *theory,* he should just be able to execute his Wind Blade spell.

"Alright, I will," he said, pushing up the sleeves of his robes—wait, he was wearing *robes?* When had that happened? Gah! This perception thing would be the death of him.

Focus! he scolded himself. *Keep your mind on the magic.*

Wind Blade did a fair amount of damage, so he wanted to be careful where he unleashed his potentially-deadly spellcraft. Taking aim at an NPC—or even hitting one by accident—could land him in a jail cell before he ever even got playing. He focused on a nearby sign hanging from a wooden pole which jutted from the side of a stone-fronted building. *Aristo-Cut Fine Tailors.* Sitting in the glass windows were old-fashioned mannequins decked out in fine silks, lush velvets, and supple leathers. Looked like the kind of store where a rich Noble might shop.

Sam took a deep breath, focusing his intention, and suddenly, knowledge bloomed inside his head like a flower unfurling in the springtime sun. Power blazed in his center—his Core—and energy surged along his limbs as his hands flew through a complex series of gestures. Sam's fingers flexed and curled in ways that didn't seem natural. He felt the power rush out of his outthrust palms, leaving him feeling just a little empty on the inside... but there was no visible sign of the magic. No blue light or crackling thunder. But Sam *knew* the spell landed since the sign suspended from the pole by a steel chain swung as though someone had given it a good smack.

Feeling a surge of pride, he broke out into a smile and rounded on the woman, one hand gesturing toward the slightly swaying sign. "See that. Magic."

Kathleen cocked an eyebrow, lips pressed into a thin line. "The swaying sign there, love?"

"Yeah," he said, bobbing his head. "That was me. I made it sway like that."

"That was the *wind*, love. Are ya sure you're not some sort of jester, maybe? Or perhaps ya have an interpretive dance class? Yer jazz hands were rather impressive, I'll admit."

Sam felt like he might explode from the shame. "Those weren't jazz hands, ma'am. Those were arcane hand *gestures*, and yes, the wind made the sign move, but I made the wind. That's my class, I'm a Wind Mage."

Finally, she sighed and gave him advice, though she sounded utterly skeptical, "Okay, love. You're a Wind Mage. Fine. You tell yerself whatever ya like. Don't suppose I can talk sense into ya, but if you're really convinced in yer mind, then it's the Mage's College you'll be wanting. Assuming ya really are a natural Mage, you'll be needing to get registered, which will cost ya some serious gold."

"But if ya *truly* have the skill and the coin," she continued, "ya might just be something special someday. I've never been to the College myself—they wouldn't want a commoner like me slumming around their *refined* grounds—but it's far to the east. Big, circular tower that ya can't miss if ya wanted to." She paused, grasping the end of her braid with one hand and giving it a light tug.

"Yer probably fuzzy in the head, but ya seem like a sweet boy. Here, take this." She dipped her other hand into a pouch and pulled free a crude paper map of the city. "I'm thinking you'll be needing it more than me. Good luck, love."

Kathleen dipped her head a final time, then turned and swished her way down a connecting street, quickly lost to the crowd. Sam glanced down at the paper, which wasn't much of a map, though it did give a general overview of the city and marked out some key landmarks, including the College, which was depicted as a long, thin tower. As he studied the crude drawing, his first prompt finally appeared.

Quest alert! Baby steps: Travel to the Mage's College and learn some basic information about using your abilities. Reward: Neophyte's Robe, Exp: 500. Accept/Decline.

Sam accepted without a thought, rolled up the map, and set off toward the east. His first encounter with an *Eternium* native hadn't exactly gone off without a hitch, but that was okay. He had a class—and a rare one from the sounds of it—his first quest, and a simple map to help guide the way. Things were looking up and were bound to get better once he figured out what he was doing and how the system worked. It was only a matter of time. Time, at least, was the one thing he had a lot of on his hands. Plus, he was going to go learn a bunch of magic. How cool was *that?*

CHAPTER SEVEN

Sam made his way down the grid-like streets of the city before finally winding up in the marketplace proper, which was everything he'd dreamed it would be. There was one oddity. His perception was *clearly* messing with him. The scent of grilling meat, musky perfume, and the odor of unwashed bodies touched his nose... and vanished as if he had just entered a clean room at a hospital. What had been colorful pennants—for an *instant* before becoming gray and muted, limp cloth—fluttered in the air, suspended from rope lines crisscrossing the streets.

Those lines held a secondary purpose too—supporting the paper lanterns that swayed gently in the breeze. There were shops everywhere, selling just about everything he could ever hope to buy. From swords to armor to books, parchment, and rare crafting ingredients. Hasty, open-air stalls dotted alleyways and formed little islands in the flow of traffic, while street peddlers wove through the ebb and flow of potential shoppers, attempting to hawk their wares on anyone with a few coins to rub together.

Although Sam may have looked poor to the casual observer, he was anything but. While undergoing the host of tests needed for his DIVE pod experience, his parents had kindly informed Sam that they'd made a sizeable deposit into his player account, which the techs explained would be transferred into the game as soon as he spawned.

It seemed strange that a game like this would be pay to play—especially considering just how expensive it was to get access in the first place—but that was just the way things were. Truthfully, with how *immersive* the experience was, Sam could easily envision gamers all over the world lining up in droves to throw fistfuls of money at the maker of Eternium.

Sam counted himself among that number. His parents had dropped a whooping *fifty grand* into his player account; which, at the ten to one ratio, translated into five thousand in-game gold. It was a lot of money, though he'd have to pace himself since that amount would need to last his entire stay inside the game. He was starting out with some serious advantages—he knew that—but if he wanted to win and have a competitive build, it was still wise to be frugal and discerning with just how he spent his limited supply of coin.

He bought a steaming turkey leg, dripping with grease and juice, and made his way past an oddly shaped building—the angles were wrong, the doors disjointed, not a window in sight—which turned out to be a bardic college. Eventually, the enormous, circular tower Kathleen had mentioned came into view like a phantom taking form on the horizon. The tower domineered much of the skyline this far east; as far as Sam could tell, it was perfectly circular and about fifty feet tall. Truthfully, it was a rather *unimpressive* sight. The building shifted color every minute or so, changing endlessly from red to purple to blue then back to purple, which was kind of cool.

Other than that? Eh. Big shrug. To Sam, it looked like an unadorned soup can tucked away in some dusty back corner of the pantry. The rest of the city was stunning, and he'd assumed this place would be even more so. A vision of a certain school for wizards cavorted through his head—stately and graceful with its arched bridges, conical towers, and tooth-like crenellations—but this was a far cry from that.

Even if its physical appearance was rather lackluster, just like when dating someone, it was what was *inside* that really mattered. He trotted through the portcullis in the outer defensive wall, which encircled the entire tower. Inside was a large courtyard, though it was just about as boring and unremarkable as the tower itself. In this particular part of the courtyard, there were a few trees with stone benches positioned beneath for the contemplative soul, but... there was no art, no epic statues of wizards in battle, no real forms of self-expression at all. It looked less like a college of the arcane and more like a stuffy, middle-ages IRS building—an establishment dedicated to upholding stuffy laws and the endless minutiae of a grand bureaucracy.

But Sam *knew*, on a gut level, that he had to be wrong. He'd played a ton of MMOs and RPGs in his years, and though the Mages' Guild typically had some kind of formal hierarchy, it was never outright *boring*. Usually, the Mage-based quest lines were some of the funniest in any game he'd ever played. Since magic in the world of Eternium was so rare, the quest lines were probably a *hundred times* cooler. This was probably one of those *don't-judge-a-book-by-its-cover* things. Had to be. Pretty please?

There were several small pockets of people loitering around the courtyard, talking in hushed voices. They were all decked out in robes, though the quality of the gear was all over the place—ranging from plain, brown robes to elaborate, black robes trimmed in gold or silver and glowing with mystic sigils of power.

At least, Sam *assumed* they were mystic sigils of power. None of them wore the plain, linen robes of a starter player, and suddenly, Sam felt more out of place than he had at the graduation party. Was there some kind of dress code no one had informed him of? If so, should he have picked up fancy Mage gear before trekking over here?

As he watched, one Mage lifted a hand and muttered some unheard spell. The next instant, the whole tower flashed, changing from red to a deep purple color. A group on the other side of the courtyard—these dressed in red robes, accented with orange, gold, and shifting runes that glowed like hot embers—visibly scowled. Sam wasn't sure what the significance of that was, but the group that had cast the spell looked awfully proud of themselves, smug satisfaction radiating off them in waves.

Sam skirted away from the purple group, angling toward a boxy, wooden door which led into the tower. The reds seemed extraordinarily grumpy, and the purples seemed like they might be looking for a fight—a new guy like Sam would be the perfect target for a bunch of mystical bullies. That was something he was hoping to avoid if at all possible. The idea of having to wade through even more jerks inside a *videogame* just seemed ridiculous. He was here to kill monsters, get some epic loot, level up, and have the time of his life.

So, it would be a hard pass on the college drama. He'd made it most of the way to the door when a voice cut through the relative silence of the courtyard like a hot knife passing through a pat of butter. That voice did *not* sound at all happy or amused. "You there! What in the love of The Accords do you think you're doing here, hmm?"

Sam faltered, reluctantly turning to face a stern-faced Mage wearing sand-colored robes edged in gold, who was storming across the courtyard like an angry rodeo bull. He was tall, at least six feet, broad across the chest and shoulders with brown hair that flowed down to his shoulders. His jawline looked sharp enough to cut glass. Sam instantly thought of Barron Calloway, even though the two only had a passing resemblance to one another. As the man got closer, Sam realized he didn't really look like Barron at all, though his bearing was the same. Entitled. Condescending. *Powerful.*

Gulp.

"This is the *esteemed* Mage's College," the man barked, planting himself in front of Sam to bar his way forward. "Not some *hostel* for traveling vagrants to beg at. I'm not sure where you're *supposed* to be, but it's not here. So why don't you turn around and scuttle back the way you've come, peasant. I'm sure the city guards would be more than happy to show you how to swing around a stick or take a punch to the face."

The man sneered as he spoke of the guards, and a round of snide snickers broke out across the grounds. Wow. Rude to the max.

Instead of lashing out, Sam smiled and bit back an acrid reply. After all, he *did* look more than a little out of place next to all the finely dressed men and women standing around the courtyard. Men and women who were all now staring daggers at him as though he'd just tracked mud onto the *good* Persian rug. Sam wasn't quite sure how to feel or act. He'd never fit in with his 'peer group', but he'd never felt more like an outsider than he did right then. An outcast. A leper. One thing was for certain, however; he was an adult, a college graduate, and he wasn't about to let a few nasty looks scare him away.

"No, good sir, you've got it all wrong!" Sam replied, raising his hands in protest and trying to placate the man. "I'm not *begging*. You see, I *am* supposed to be here. I have a ques–"

"Not likely," the man shot back, cutting Sam off with a scowl. "These esteemed grounds are not for your kind. This is a place of learning. Of knowledge. Of *magic*. Commoners do not walk the halls of such an institution as this, and you have neither the bearing of an aristocrat nor the..."

He paused, lips pursed into a thin line as his gaze roved over Sam's lackluster appearance, "*Demeanor* of a wealthy Traveler. I *very much* doubt you have the funds required to learn even the simplest of spells, and that doesn't even cover the licensure fee."

"Wait, so is this a shakedown, or is it all some giant... pay to play... thing?"

"I think, perhaps, you are finally starting to understand the rudiments of the conversation, you vagabond. So leave. Now. Before I punish you. Severely." His eyes glinted with a feverish light that gave Sam pause.

"Whatever, jerk," Sam grumbled, offering the man his back. "If that's the way it is, I'll just skip over this dumb tutorial. It's not like I really need whatever you scammers are selling. My class allows me to learn magic naturally on my own, so I don't need this."

An unnatural hush fell over the courtyard, and Sam just assumed it was because everyone was reeling from the totally sick burn he'd just laid down, but when he glanced back over one shoulder, he lost a little bit of his swagger. Everyone was staring at him like he'd sprouted a second head and turned into a dragon while simultaneously threatening to scorch the College from high orbit.

"You don't just *learn* magic, you uneducated *swine*," the jerk whispered, his voice nevertheless carrying over the courtyard. "That's not how this *works*. Not how *any* of this works. You and your kind can't even begin to comprehend the sheer responsibility and dedication required of a licensed Mage! We practitioners of the arcane arts can create and shape the elements—we are the heralds of all knowledge and the brotherhood of secret arts. Our ways can *only* be learned in our vaulted halls of academia!"

"Nope." Sam shook his head. "I can totally learn magic without you. Already know some."

He thrust one hand out, taking aim at one of the few scraggly trees in the area, then unleashed an invisible Wind Blade which sheared through the wooden limb with a near-silent *swish*. The branch dropped, clattering on the cobblestones. The noise was soft, but in the silence that followed, it seemed as loud as a ringing bell. Worse, every single eye was fixed on the branch.

"So, like I said," Sam added, crossing his arms, "I *don't* need you guys. I was just doing this because I got a quest prompt, but if this is the way you run the Guild—or College or whatever it is—then I'm *gone*."

The guy's face had gone ghostly white, and he stammered for a moment, clearly surprised. "Everyone, block the entrance. He can't be allowed to leave."

Sam froze, unsure what in the world was happening as a horde of Mages in colorful robes stormed toward the gate he'd entered through a moment before, forming into orderly battle ranks.

"Now," the man's voice took on a dark edge, and he stepped heavily in front of Sam, "explain yourself *at once*."

Sam rolled his eyes so hard he thought they might just fly out of his skull. "That's what I've been trying to do since I got here, ya walnut! I'm an *Aeolus Sorcerer,* and I already have both Instinctual Casting and Wind Blade; plus, I learn class-specific spells naturally every third level without any training. Maybe if you had just *listened* in the first place, we wouldn't be having any issues, but I'm done with your College. I don't want to be a part of any group that treats other people this way. So please get out of my way."

"Well, *that* simply isn't an option." The man folded his arms. The color was back in his face, and if anything, he looked even more pleased and self-assured than before. "Since you already know a Mage-class spell, you are now *required* by Kingdom decree to register with the College and sign The Accords, which govern our kind and preserve our Society."

"The Accords?"

"They are the only thing that protects us from Rogue Mages and keeps powerful spellcasters out of politics and governmental positions."

"You've got to be kidding me." Sam started rubbing at the bridge of his nose. "Not ten seconds ago you were trying to kick me out, and now, you won't let me leave unless I sign up with your College?"

The man looked grim as the grave. "It is the way of our kind. If you have even so much as a single Mage spell, you are required to sign. At *your* expense, I might add."

"You're crazy," Sam replied flatly. "What if I just say no, huh? Are you going to kill me? Lock me up? What?"

"Refuse, and we will mark you as a Rogue Mage and place a bounty on your head so large that you will never know a day of peace. Moreover, since you claim to be an actual Mage class, you will be expected not only to sign The Accords but to become a full member of the College. This means mandatory training, College-issued assignments, and a pre-approved course load."

Sam glanced at the guy, then at the line of Mages cutting off his only potential exit. He was a level one caster with exactly one spell—a spell he'd only ever used twice. If he made a stand here, there was no way he would walk out of the courtyard alive, and even after respawn, he'd be stuck with a powerful and obviously vindictive enemy.

He'd been treated poorly—and that was putting things mildly—but at the same time, he'd come to join the College, and now, he had his chance. Sam wanted to storm off in a huff, but that was more out of pride than anything else. Chances were that the smart thing to do here, the pragmatic thing to do... was to put the insult behind him and move on.

Finally, after mulling it over for a minute, Sam nodded. "Fine. You guys aren't giving me a lot of options here. I guess I'll join. Where do I go, and who do I need to talk to?"

The Mage broke into a huge, malevolent grin. "You are already talking to him. I am Octavius Igenitor, Peak Student in charge of new Initiate processing."

He glanced at the fallen tree branch. "You will pay for that and for everything else as well. Now, come; we have a *lot* of paperwork to do."

Wait, *this* guy was going to be in charge of him? Sam gulped and felt like dissolving into the earth. Oh no. He felt like an unfortunate toad who just leaped from a sizzling hot frying pan directly into the wizard-conjured fire.

CHAPTER EIGHT

Sam dropped into a wooden chair, already feeling exhausted from the day even though he hadn't really done *anything*. Dealing with all the administrative stuff had been both mentally taxing and emotionally draining, even if physically he was feeling fine.

Apparently, Octavius Ignitor—Stone Mage, Peak Student, and the human equivalent of rancid milk—wasn't kidding when he said Sam would 'pay'. That wasn't just in the figurative, evil villain sort of way; the guy had meant it quite literally. Not only did Sam get slapped with a twenty-five-gold fine for the 'property damage'—which seemed like a bit of a stretch for *trimming* a tree branch—but he had to pay for about a thousand other things. *Everything* in the college cost an arm and a leg; Sam had no idea how regular players were supposed to deal with the heavy fees associated with a Mage class.

He was starting to suspect the reason magic was so incredibly rare in Eternium was that the Mage's College had a virtual chokehold on the industry and was pricing out the competition. Heck, just the bare bones step of becoming a 'Licensed Mage' cost one hundred gold, the equivalent of a *thousand dollars*, and there was simply *no* option to be an 'Unlicensed' Mage.

Refuse to pay their fee and sign their Accords and they would slap the Rogue Mage label on your head and let bounty hunters kill you on repeat until you caved. Worse, membership didn't actually get you any tangible benefits. Just the opposite. The College took a steep percentage of all quest rewards, and members didn't even get so much as a discount on classes or items. According to the 'all-knowing' Octavius, initiates were paying for the *privilege* of association.

So worth. Much magic. Very association. Wow. That was just the tip of the arcane iceberg. The classes were even more outrageously priced than the entry fee. Many of the basic courses ran at fifty gold a pop—a hefty five-hundred dollars—while some of the rare, high-level courses could cost anywhere between one thousand and ten thousand gold.

It seemed *Mage's College* was an apt name since this placed charged actual college prices for their services—though graduates didn't even walk away with a slip of paper for their trouble. On its face, it was an ugly, mean-spirited system, and Sam was surprised a game company would have the gall to design a Guild which would no-doubt be universally hated by players everywhere.

Hopefully, they'd fix things in future patches, but until then, this was the only way to go. Sam really didn't want to start over as some run-of-the-mill tank or fighter, and he *did* have the money to spend. So, reluctantly, he paid the registration fee and signed up for his classes; many of them were 'suggestions', though they were very *forceful* suggestions. At the outset, he picked up *Mana manipulation and Mana Coalescence*—with a guided meditation module, of course—*Mage Shields and You: The Art of Defensive Magic*, and *Here Comes the Boom: Basics of Offensive Spell Casters*.

Those were the required courses for someone who hoped to grind their way up the ranks. Truth-be-told, they all sounded like practical classes that had some good, common-sense applications, but because Sam was actually interested in playing the game—*i.e.* Dungeon Crawls, adventuring, and not just sitting around the stuffy College—he also opted into an elective called *Field Monster Manual*, which was one of the cheaper courses available. The current session was covering the Wolfmen, their language, culture, and practices, which sounded both interesting and potentially useful since the Wolfmen seemed to be the primary baddies in the game.

Sam pushed all those thoughts from his head as one of his new teachers took to the podium at the front of the small classroom. There was only a double fistful of students, and all of them were newbs just like him—though there was only one other Traveler present. Most of these 'players' were actually NPCs, all of them from Noble families with a lot of money to toss around.

They would need a lot of money since this was one of the most expensive classes around at a mind-boggling *one thousand gold*—one-fifth of his total three-month budget—but according to Octavius, this was the single most important class he would take while at the College. It was the foundation for all magic, the cornerstone upon which everything else would be built around.

Mana Manipulation and Mana Coalescence.

The teacher was a petite woman named Mage Akora, who looked like she might be in her late forties or early fifties, though rumor was she was actually *much* older. She had a mousy face, a rather large nose, and streaks of silver lining her brown hair. She couldn't have stood much taller than five feet or weighed more than a hundred pounds soaking wet, yet in her deeply purple robes, she radiated power and authority—a teacher who knew her business and would accept no nonsense from bright-eyed youngsters learning magic for the first time. Being fresh out of College, Sam knew her type well and expected her to be a good teacher, though probably not a kind—or especially patient—one.

"Attention," she called out, her voice clipped, her words precise. "Welcome to Mana Manipulation and Mana

Coalescence. As most of you know, this is perhaps the single most important class you will ever take, and that is because it will teach you the fundamentals and core philosophy behind controlling your magical potential. You see, the truth is, everyone in the room—even those who have never cast a single spell in their lives—have access to what we call a Mana pool and Mana channels. The Mana pool is the seat of your power, the well of energy that drives the very forces of creation.

"Think of your Mana pool as a vast reservoir, while your Mana channels are the minor tributaries which branch off from that reservoir. Those tributaries carry the power out and away from your center so that it may be used in practical ways—a farmer irrigating her crops, someone washing dishes in a house far away, a child fetching water for a bath. So it is with you. But this vast reservoir of power can be dangerous to those who do not understand its proper use."

"If one of you," her gaze seemed to linger on Sam, "were to cast a spell without directing that rush of power through the *appropriate* channels, it could cause great damage. Everything from exhaustion to pain to fits of severe nausea. In some ways, it would be like the reservoir flooding its banks, all of that water rushing around without anywhere to go, destroying anything in its path indiscriminately.

"Fortunately for you lot, I can teach you the proper way to both access your Mana pool and how to safely direct that energy, which will broaden your Mana channels over time, allowing you to do far more with magic than most of the unwashed masses could ever *dream* possible. I could walk you through more of the history and theory revolving around Mana manipulation, but frankly, I have found the single best way to learn is through a hands-on guided meditation, of which I am a

Master. First, I want all of you to close your eyes and locate your Mana pool deep within your center."

Sam did as he was instructed, pressing his eyes shut tightly and delving deeply inside himself, searching out the rolling mass of power which burned and shifted like a kaleidoscope inside him. As he drew closer to that energy, the shifting colors and blurring lines began to take form, resolving into a chaotic bundle of blues and whites which churned like a hurricane about to make landfall. Sam just stared at the image in his mind's eye, awed by the power of this magic. Somewhere, a voice cut through his focus, though it sounded muffled and hazy, as though he was hearing it through hundreds of feet of water.

"Good," Mage Akora said, "I see a handful of you have found it, but the rest are having some difficulty. Please, all of you, open yourself and allow me to guide you."

As she finished speaking, a prompt appeared, which Sam accepted with only half a thought, still fixated on the sight of all that power burbling and swirling inside his chest.

Mage Akora used skill 'Guided Meditation' on you! Accept? Yes / No

Time seemed to slide by at half speed, but finally, Mage Akora spoke again, "Excellent, there now. All of you have managed to locate your Mana Pool, but that is only the first step. What you will need to do now—and what you must practice *every single day*—is condensing your Mana pool while cycling it through your spell channels. As you watch your energy, I want each of you to envision that ball of arcane energy *shrinking, condensing*, forcing it down and back in onto itself. Forge it into an orb that spins like a top, twirling, twirling, twirling. You need only to envision it... impose your will... and it will be so."

Sam licked his lips, a fine sheen of perspiration building on his forehead, then followed her instructions. Slowly and diligently, Sam reached his thoughts toward the ball of gale-force winds. Immediately, the bundle of chaotic, formless energy responded, the edges smoothing, the sides rounding into something that more closely resembled a sphere. *Oh my god, it's working*, he thought with a surge of pride and excitement. Spurred on by his minute success, he pushed even harder, working the energy like a lump of clay, rolling, pushing, and pressing it between the palms of mental-hands until it was a perfectly round ball, like a marble containing a blizzard within.

With that done, he began to rotate the ball, urging it to spin even as he bore down, pressing the energy back into itself so the ball shrank in size. After what felt like *years* of concerted effort, the ball finally stopped compressing. It was roughly half the size it'd been before, and now, no matter how much pressure Sam applied, the energy wouldn't budge so much as a millimeter. A thunderous headache began into throb in his brain, hot agony curling around the sides of his skull like ram's horns.

Being trained by a Master of a craft has greatly increased your speed of comprehension!

Skill gained: Coalescence (Beginner 0). You have taken the first steps on the path of the mind! By collecting your Mana in an orderly form, you will be able to pack more Mana into a single usage with far greater effect. +1% spell efficiency and +2% Mana regeneration per skill level. Wisdom +1. Increase your wisdom to coalesce your Mana to a higher degree. (Maximum 50% spell efficiency.)

As this is your first time gaining spell efficiency, here is a short explanation. Spell efficiency allows you to lessen the Mana cost of any action that requires Mana by packing Mana into the spell more densely. Spell efficiency, therefore, is a different way to say 'decreased Mana cost'.

"Very good," the teacher droned from a million miles away, "but that was only the first step of two. Learning to shape and condense your Mana pool, without learning to channel it naturally, is a recipe for disaster. Some of you may have problems with this next part, but never fear—that is the reason this class is a month-long endeavor. More time to build your Mana pool and perfect your core."

"In this next exercise, you are going to carefully grasp some of your Mana and pull it oh-so-gently away from the pool, but be sure to keep it attached. Your Mana should be a bit like a string. Once you have a thread of energy, start pulling it along the tunnels. Just walk and pull. Walk and pull. The more Mana you bring along on each pass, the better your overall bonus will be in the end."

So far, her advice had been sound, so Sam followed suit, reaching out with nimble mental fingers and grasping a hair-fine strand of power, stretching it out like playdoh until he had a strand as thick as his pinky finger. He found the exercise surprisingly easy, even though Mage Akora had indicated that it might be a somewhat difficult process, but then so far, all of his magical abilities had been easy to use, almost second nature, which he thought probably had something to do with his Instinctual Casting ability. Maybe it didn't just affect spells but *every* aspect related to spellcasting.

If so, that meant he might-well have a significant advantage over some of the other spell-slingers running around Eternium.

With the strand of energy in hand, he set out to stretch that burning energy along his Mana channels. He felt as though he were trekking through a dark cave system filled with a thousand twists, turns, and dead ends, but floating before him was a soft ball of white light like an ethereal Will-O-Wisp, guiding him through the dark tangles of an overgrown forest. Somehow, he knew that the little ball of light was actually Mage Akora, and though Sam had no idea where he was going, she seemed to be traversing the passages of his mind with frightening ease and familiarity.

The whole while, the tether of Mana followed after him like a lost puppy. Twist after twist, turn after turn, more than a few switchbacks—which completely threw off his sense of direction—then finally, the ball of light rounded a corner, and Sam found himself staring at the ball of Mana he'd left behind a few minutes ago.

"No, you are not lost," Mage Akora whispered into his mind, though Sam couldn't tell if her voice came from outside his body or inside his head. The noise echoed in stereo, making him suspect the answer might've been both. "We are back to where we've begun, but you'll notice there is a thin strand of Mana jutting off from the far side of your Mana pool. We have successfully navigated your prime channel, and it is time to reconnect to the source, completing the loop. Now, finish the process."

With a thought, Sam slid forward and directed the tether of Mana in his hand to connect with the pool. As soon as the glowing blue thread made contact with the sphere, his Mana began to pulse and thrum in time with the rock-steady beating of his heart.

Being trained by a Master of a craft has greatly increased your speed of comprehension!

Skill gained: Mana manipulation (Beginner 0). Where others are content to throw unseemly amounts of power into a spell—swiftly fueling their own destruction—you use a lighter touch. -30% Mana. +1% Mana and +1% spell efficiency per skill level. (Maximum 25% efficiency). Intelligence +1.

Sam read and reread the message, confusion quickly mounting as he did some rough math in his head. Yep, the numbers checked out—minus thirty percent Mana definitely seemed like a *bad* thing, not a good thing.

"Wait a minute." He opened his eyes. He wobbled in his seat for a heartbeat as the world reeled around him. He was light-headed, woozy, and exhausted to his core. Pun not intended. He shook away the fog in his brain and pressed on. "This doesn't make any sense. According to the last update, *Mana manipulation*, I've actually *lost* a bunch of Mana. Like... a *lot*. I thought this was supposed to help make me better at magic and *increase* my overall Mana pool."

The professor offered him a crooked smile and a shake of her head, a mischievous gleam in her eyes. "Such is the ignorance of the young and untrained. You must not have taken the recommended *Mage's College Overview Primer*, young man. If you *had,* you would know full-well that you won't start increasing your overall Mana pool size until you obtain Student Rank, and if you should somehow make it to the Sage level, this skill can actually bolster your pool by *seventy* percent. You should feel privileged, however. You'll notice that you've jumped all the way past the Novice Stage and directly into the Beginner ranks—just *one* of the many perks of having a Master such as myself educate you."

"This class will continue for the next four weeks," she continued, now speaking to everyone, "where I will be running you through a variety of techniques and exercises, all designed to drain your Mana, compress your Mana pool, and simultaneously stretch your channels. Assuming you all show up and pay attention to my instruction, I fully expect all of you to be *at least* Apprentice rank zero, which is no small feat. That also means you will have two channels open, which should be quite useful as you complete your other courses. Now, if there are no *further* questions?"

Her hard gaze said in no uncertain terms that there had *better not be* any more questions. "Then class is dismissed."

CHAPTER NINE

By the time Sam was finished with classes, registration, and all the other administrative red tape of his first day at the College, he felt as wrung out as an old dishtowel. Which was crazy because he hadn't really done all that much in the grand scheme of things—he hadn't killed any mobs, stormed any castles, or saved any damsels in distress. Technically, he'd finished the *Baby Steps Quest,* earning himself upgraded Neophyte's Robes and an extra one-hundred experience, but that wasn't anything to write home about.

Sure, he'd walked around the city for a while and done a little magic, but a typical day on the Berkeley campus was far more strenuous than this had been. He wasn't even close to leveling up yet. He'd gained a whopping five hundred experience points so far, which put him about halfway to level two. So, pretty much nothing there to account for his exhaustion. Sam reckoned it had something to do with the testing prior to spawning. Well, that and his time with Mage Akora. Although the class had been little more than a guided meditation session, compressing his core and widening his channels had been *taxing.*

The sun had set into the horizon a few hours back, and though Sam wanted to head back out into town—go explore a little more, maybe meet a few more Travelers and find someplace to crash—he decided against it. He had a big morning coming up, and an *unfortunately* early one at that. At seven AM he had an appointment before the College bigwigs to sign 'The Accords' and become an officially licensed Mage. Yay! Another one-hundred gold gone in the blink of an eye. Once he was done with that, he had a pair of classes back-to-back at noon and two—Mage Shield and Basics of Offensive Spell Casters—which had both cost a pretty penny as well.

Thankfully, he could afford the hefty price tag. Once he signed The Accords and completed a few more classes, he'd finally be able to get out on his own for a while. He planned to do some questing and play the game the way he wanted to. So far, the College was basically a train wreck, but it would all pay off in the long run. Sam was *sure* of it.

So, instead of heading back into the city and finding a proper inn, he metaphorically bit the bullet and decided to stay on the college grounds. The cost of the room was steep, one gold a night, but he figured he was paying for the convenience of not having to trek all the way across the city every day. Plus, this was something he'd more or less expected. On-campus housing was always a racket, so why would this be any different? He smiled as he rounded a corner and found his room straight ahead: a plain wooden door with an odd glyph gouged into the wood.

Home sweet home. Sam fished a small stone about the size of a quarter from his pocket. The stone itself was perfectly smooth, tar-black, polished to a bright sheen, and worked with a burning symbol that mirrored the glyph on the door. He held the rock up, pressing it against the ward-locked room; there was a *click* as some mechanism gave way, and the door swung inward on silent hinges.

Like much of the rest of the college, the room's interior was rather... *unimpressive* was probably too mild a word. *Underwhelming? Lackluster?* Hard to put his finger on it exactly. But one word he could most definitely decide upon was *small.* The room was about the size of a storage closet and even more claustrophobic than his dorm had been.

There was a cot—not a twin bed but an honest to god camping cot—on a weathered wooden frame, topped by a thin canvas mattress and a green woolen blanket. There wasn't even a pillow. Beside the bed was a compact wooden nightstand with a brass oil lamp, a chipped porcelain bowl, and a pitcher of water. *Clearly,* the College was putting its best foot forward to impress the new recruits.

Sam rolled his eyes and sighed, feeling even more defeated than he had during his time in the jungle being relentlessly pursued by a man-eating slug the size of a minivan. That had been worse *by far,* of course, but then the test was *supposed* to be awful. This though? This was supposed to be the fun, *cool* part of the game. So far, Sam was wildly indifferent. If this was the tutorial for all spellcasters, this game was going to tank for *sure.*

"No," he muttered to himself, shaking off his disgruntlement. "No point in whining about things. Maybe I can't change my circumstances, but I can change my attitude about it! Chin up, ol' chap, it's going to get better! Besides, I just need to sleep here, not live here."

With that settled, he unloaded his few meager possessions, splashed a little water onto his face from the pitcher. Lukewarm, he felt silly to have expected anything different. Sam collapsed onto the intentionally comfortless cot, thinking about how backpacking in Europe might have been the way to go after all. Since there was no pillow, he balled up his starter robes and jammed them under his head. Sam expected to have a hard time drifting off, what with the 'mattress' feeling like concrete, but he hadn't closed his eyes for more than a moment before it was time to wake up. He couldn't remember falling asleep, nor did he recall tossing and turning even once in the night. Out like a light.

When Sam sat up and swung his legs out over the edge of the bed, he expected to get hit with some kind of *Well Rested* bonus, but he actually felt *terrible*–like someone had beat him about the head and shoulders with a baseball bat. That didn't seem even *remotely* right. Ugh. If he wanted to get a bite to eat before signing The Accords and starting his day, he really needed to get moving. So, even though he felt sore and sleepy, he hauled himself from the painfully thin mattress, geared up, and slipped out of the room.

His stomach let out a gurgle of sharp hunger, so he stopped by the College cafeteria. Sam picked up a bowl of tasteless gruel which did nothing for his tongue but filled the hole gnawing through his center. Although, upon further reflection, Sam decided it was a distinct possibility that the food was actually *excellent* and that it was just his terrible perception at work again.

Either way, in no possible set of circumstances could it have been called an *enjoyable* breakfast. He scarfed the food down as quickly as possible, grimacing the whole time. He then dropped the bowl off with the kitchen staff and wound his way through the strange and twisted hallways, working his way toward the rendezvous spot with Octavius. Navigating the hallways was a tricky bit of business, as he'd come to find out.

For one, the hallways all looked strikingly similar–no art to set them apart, no landmarks to help him get his bearing–and two, thanks to something called 'spatial magic', the laws of physics didn't hold true in this place. Corridors didn't connect in a way that made logical sense, and space *literally* folded in on itself. This had the effect of making the interior of the College a hundred times larger than the exterior would suggest, but to the discerning eye, there was a set of runes worked into each archway or doorframe, which acted as rudimentary instructions—assuming the Traveler knew how to decipher them.

Guess who *didn't* have a discerning eye. Lousy low perception... the runic database was quite massive, and most of it was incomprehensible to Sam, but Octavius had carefully pointed out a number of different symbols—including one for the grand entrance hall, which was where they were to meet.

The symbol was an oblong circle, intersected by a variety of odd lines—like bike spokes—with a crescent-shaped mark jutting out from the top of one spoke. Sam turned left four times, then doubled back, retracing his steps by taking four rights. In theory, he should've arrived back by the cafeteria, but instead, he found himself standing in a circular chamber with high, vaulted ceilings and fluted pillars arranged in a circle.

"I can't decide if I love or hate this place," he muttered under his breath. This was *easily* the most interesting room he'd seen inside the Mage's College so far. Sam was there for only a few heartbeats before the *click-clacking* of boots on tile floors drifted through the air, followed in short order by a shimmer of electric-blue light.

Octavius Igenitor seemingly materialized out of thin air, even though Sam knew that was simply one of the many tricks of spatial magic. The Peak Student in charge of new Initiate processing looked as disgruntled as ever, a sneer perpetually worked into the lines of his face, his well-coiffed hair swept back and away from his forehead. He'd helped Sam get situated yesterday, but it was obvious the man had a serious axe to grind; it was *equally* obvious that he was looking to grind said axe against Sam's skull.

Any slip-up on Sam's part would be met with strict and terrible repercussions, Sam was sure. In the grand scheme of things, Octavius was a *nobody*, but in a very small realm, he had the power of a dictator. Unfortunately, Sam happened to fall inside that small realm. Sam had known guys like Octavius all his life, and the best way to deal with them was to either avoid them entirely, or if that simply wasn't an option, then ensure they had no reason to cause trouble.

"You're here," Octavius stated the obvious while folding his hands behind his back. "Oh, *goody.*"

His tone said that things weren't good at all and that he was in fact deeply disappointed that Sam was on time. Abyss, to Sam's ears, the man sounded disappointed that he had even survived the night. Maybe the pain in his head when he woke up was from less *natural* causes than he had thought.

"Well, there's no time to waste, *Neophyte.* The Archmage and the rest of the Council will already be assembled. It would be unwise to keep them waiting for long." He turned, then paused and glanced over one shoulder at Sam. "Also. Take heed, Neophyte. It would be *equally* unwise to show the Archmage or the Council any of the *disrespect* you've shown me thus far. If you insult them or embarrass me in any way, I *swear* you will suffer in ways you can't even begin to comprehend. Now, attend me."

He offered Sam his back and marched through an archway on the right of the chamber. Sam wanted to throw his shoe at the back of Octavius' stupid, ego-swollen head, but he bit his tongue, kept his shoes firmly on his feet, and reluctantly trailed after his direct 'superior'. He didn't like the guy, not even a *little*, but he didn't have to like everyone. Sooner or later, he'd be a licensed Mage and fully equipped for the world of adventure, and then he could beat feet and put Octavius and his bad attitude firmly in the rearview mirror. Until then, he just had to play along.

The Peak Student led him unwaveringly through passageway after passageway, corridor after corridor, taking turns seemingly at random until they finally stepped out into another chamber that was easily the strangest place Sam had seen since entering Eternium. The oversized room was spherically shaped and so large that it couldn't conceivably fit inside the tower proper, not without some serious arcane prestidigitation. Half the room was covered in stadium-style benches, allowing spectators a perfect view of whatever happened on the main floor. Speaking of spectators, there were a bunch of them filling out a few rows of the stands—less than he thought there should be but still more than he expected in the first place.

Another series of seats—these far fewer in number and far cushier looking—were on a platform in the center of the room. These seats were also occupied, and the Mages in those chairs almost glowed with power and authority, dressed in formal regalia which was as bright and ostentatious as a peacock's plumage. A single throne-like chair, larger and grander than the rest, was filled by an enormously obese man with cruel, piggy eyes who sported dazzling, multi-colored robes and a curled staff that looked a little like a shepherd's crook— though one made of pure gold and encrusted with jewels.

All of those details, however, were eclipsed by the true centerpiece of the room—a gigantic glass tube, larger than the largest redwoods in the Sequoia National Park, extended from floor to ceiling. Curiously, the tube narrowed in the middle as though it were some massive hourglass, and in the center, where the glass would have met, a book hung suspended in midair.

The tome was just floating there, radiating light and power like a small, personal star. Colored lights raced through the tubes, condensing into tiny beams of energy that shot into— and were apparently absorbed by—the strange book. Looking at the tube, book, and the assembled Mages, Sam couldn't help but feel *deeply* uncertain about all of this.

It was nothing Sam could point to exactly, no tangible item, but the hairs on the back of his neck stood at attention all the same, and a thoroughly unpleasant tingle raced along his spine. There was something subtly *off* about this whole display— especially the stony faces and lifeless gazes of the council members arrayed on their platform.

There was nothing Sam could do about it now, though. He'd already come too far, and if he didn't sign The Accords, he'd get slapped with the label Rogue Mage and his days as a magic-user would be done for. He'd have to go back to the drawing board and play as a Ranger or a Fighter, and that didn't even account for all the money he'd already spent at the College. This was weird, and he didn't like it, but for now, this was his future.

Ahead of him, Octavius cleared his throat and shot a glare at Sam strong enough to strip paint. Octavius tilted his head and pointed at the steps beside him with one finger. Sam nodded, feeling oddly numb, and joined him.

"Most esteemed Council and our Excellence," Octavius formally intoned, dipping his head in a bow, "may I present a new candidate for induction, Sam_K. Though not a Noble or a native of our lands, he has shown himself to be a rather rare *Aeolus Sorcerer,* a natural Mage, and will undoubtedly be a boon to our most prestigious order. It was I who found him and I who convinced him to join our ranks—not merely as a Licensed Mage but as a full member."

The man in the grandiose chair stood with a groan, his girth making the process precarious, and raised a hand, shushing the quiet chattering from the stands. "Well met, Peak Student Octavius Igenitor. Once more, you bring honor to your house and to the College. If you continue as you have, soon you will be ready to advance once more and join the ranks of our Journeymen. As for you, boy..."

The man pinned Sam in place with beady, cold eyes. "If you work hard and follow the will of your *betters*, you too may find your way into our exalted ranks, but the road is an arduous, costly one and requires the utmost obedience."

"The first step on that journey, a step of humility and trust in the College, is to sign The Accords." He turned and waved a plump hand toward the book suspended in the huge columns of glass. "The Accords, you see, are the sacred pact of our people. Magic is a powerful and potentially destructive force, and allowing it into the hands of the *uncouth*—those wholly unfit and lacking moral authority—is unacceptable."

"Those who do not bend to our way of thinking must never have access to the deep secrets of our ways. It is by signing these Accords that we all acknowledge that fundamental truth. It is by *signing* that you, Neophyte, submit yourself to the tutelage, tradition, and authority of this College. By signing, you recognize that *your* wild will must be supplemented by the wisdom of ours. Do you, Sam_K, agree to sign The Accords?"

The question hung heavy in the air; every eye was fixed on Sam now, and the whole room seemed to have stopped breathing as they waited on his answer. Every word the Archmage had said set Sam on edge, but he was probably just overreacting. Besides, this was just a game, Sam reminded himself. It *felt* like more than a game because of the graphics and how immersive the experience was, but in reality, this was *just* a game.

He wasn't *really* signing away his life or his rights. In all likelihood, Sam was going through some preprogrammed cutscene that all magic users were probably going to have to endure. He was making a mountain out of a molehill, which was just silly. He shook away his unease and nodded.

"Of course, I'm ready to sign," he croaked, his throat oddly dry. "I already paid the fee, right? Time to learn some cool magic. Let's do this thing."

"Excellent," the Archmage breathed, rubbing his flabby hands together greedily. "Then I declare you are no longer a Neophyte but a *Novice* of our exalted Order. Approach, Novice Sam_K, and sign The Accords as is our tradition!"

The whole room let out an odd, collective, *palpable* sigh of relief, then promptly burst into a round of wild applause. Octavius grabbed Sam by the shoulder and steered him up the marble stairs, stopping on a platform directly in front of the glowing book. The floating tome sprang open at once, the pages fluttering like mad before finally coming to a stop on a blank section with a line running across the bottom—ready and waiting for Sam to put his name on something he didn't fully understand.

His lawyer parents would be having *fits* right now. Although it was probably a dumb thought, Sam couldn't help but feel the book was actually *alive* somehow; its open pages strangely reminded him of a predatory animal ready to snap its mouth closed on some unsuspecting animal.

Sam licked his lips, sweat beading on his forehead, and extended a trembling hand. A beautiful quill of shining, blue light—a construct of pure Mana—materialized above the book, just mere inches from his outstretched fingers. Before Sam could overthink the situation and harpoon his chances of success with the College, he grasped the quill.

Energy surged through his hand, and he quickly jotted his name across the line. A small arc of power leaped from The Accords the second Sam finished writing, racing up his arm and blasting into the core of his being like a jolt of raw lightning. As that power washed through him like a wave, sweet relief and sharp-minded clarity followed.

"Why was I so worried about this?" Sam muttered, genuinely confused about how he could have had any possible reservations. Maybe he didn't fully understand what the Accords were, but it was now as crystal clear that they were *good*. Maybe Sam had a few issues with the College itself... but all that had to do with the snobby *people*. People like Octavius. Certainly, it had nothing to do with The Accords, which were the pillars that kept the institution from collapsing down on top of everyone. In fact, the Accords, *the rule of law*, were the only thing that kept people like Octavius in check.

A message appeared while those thoughts churned inside his skull:

Quest alert: The Arcane Path I. You have joined the Mage's College and signed The Accords, stepping onto the Arcane Path! Exp: 500.

For being one of the first 100 Travelers to sign The Accords, Reputation gain has been doubled! (Note: this is uncommon in a harsh, uncaring world such as Eternium, but so is being one of the first to do something!) Reputation with the Mage's College has been increased by 2000 points, from 'Neutral' directly to 'Friendly' (bypassing 'Reluctantly friendly'). 1000 reputation points remain to reach 'Friend of the Mage's College' status.

Since this is your first reputation gain, please note that there are many distinct levels of reputation. From lowest to highest: Blood Feud, Loathed, Hated, Hostile, Cautious, Neutral, Reluctantly Friendly, Friendly, Friend, Ally, and Extended Family. There are one thousand points between each level.

As he read, Sam felt a new surge of power; golden light swirled around him in a cloud, lifting him into the air. He'd never felt anything even *remotely* like the sheer euphoria zipping through his veins and blazing along his nerve endings. It was the bliss of a good night's sleep, the exhilaration of winning a marathon or acing a midterm, the intoxication of power, and a sense that *nothing* was impossible. Putting two and two together, Sam quickly realized that he must've leveled up. If this was what leveling up felt like... Sam needed to revise his earlier thoughts.

Eternium would *never* go out of business. No matter how hard the gameplay was or how much it cost, people would give up their left arm just to experience this brief flash of ecstasy over and over again. Then just like that, Sam was back on the ground, the light fading and dying while the onlookers hooted, hollered, and cheered, a legion of fists pumping in the air. Sam wanted to check out his character sheet, but he didn't have a chance.

Octavius led him out of the room, then twirled around and stood in front of him, arms crossed and a wicked grin on his otherwise smug face. "Congratulations on leveling up, *Novice*. Now, let me welcome you to our exalted ranks by giving you your first *formal* College assignment."

He paused, his smile deepening in a supremely unfriendly way. "Sewer Detail."

Quest alert: The Arcane Path II (Ongoing). As a Licensed Mage and Novice of the Mage's College, you are required to complete daily chores or officially sanctioned assignments on behalf of the College! Report daily to Peak Student Octavius Igenitor for details—failing to do so will earn you fines or other punitive measures and can result in loss of reputation with the Mage's College!

Oh joy, Sam's stomach started sinking. Sewer Detail; that was going to be fun. He wondered if it was as crappy a job as it sounded.

CHAPTER TEN

Sam found himself wading knee-deep through a slow-moving river of sewage beneath the city of Ardania. As the kid of an upper-crust family with massive real-estate holdings, their own private estate, and pretty much the best of anything that money could buy, Sam had never been in a place *remotely* like this before. He'd watched enough movies and played enough online games for the setting to feel familiar, but the reality was far worse than he ever could've imagined. For the first time, he was *very* happy about his terrible perception.

The tunnels were old, gray brick, covered with patches of black mold and green slime. There were cloth-wrapped torches along the walls at even intervals, orange firelight illuminating the passageway and casting deep pools of dancing shadow. Sadly, even the torches did nothing to eliminate the unnatural cool, damp air in the sewers, which cut through his simple robes all the way to the bone. The fact that Sam was standing in frigid sludge also didn't help things, but he supposed cold sludge was probably preferable to warm, *fresh* sludge. As a small silver lining, with his ungodly low perception he hardly even noticed the smell.

So, there was that, at least. Plus, Octavius was nowhere to be seen. So, a win overall? The 'Peak Student' had shoved him down here into this dank pit but apparently had better things to do than babysit 'riffraff' on such a common mission. Sam was glad. Sure, it would've been mildly cathartic to see the prissy jerk wading through the muck and mud like him with *unspeakable* things squelching between his toes, but then he'd also have to listen to him rant about dim-witted commoners. Sam wasn't completely alone; there was another pair of low-level Novices present, along with two warriors.

The first warrior was a tanky Fighter, named Geffrey the Red, who was broad as a barn and wearing heavy, silver-edged plate mail. Warrior number two, Karren the Blade, was lean, covered in chainmail, and carried a finger-slim rapier. The two of them were local guards—both NPCs as far as Sam could tell—and the guides for this particular mission.

The small party was waiting for one more latecomer, so Sam decided to use the time to check out his character stats now that he'd leveled up. As an Aeolus Sorcerer, he automatically gained one point of intelligence and wisdom on every even level, but he wouldn't get any points to manually distribute until he hit his next level. Still, he couldn't help glancing at the changes even though he knew they were going to be minimal at this point.

"Delta Status," he mumbled under his breath—a quick access command which allowed him to review only the portions of his character sheet that had changed.

Name: Sam_K 'High Five, I Tried!'

Class: Aeolus Sorcerer

Profession: Locked

Level: 2 Exp: 1,000 Exp to next level: 2,000

Hit Points: 70/70 (60+(10)*)

Mana: 190/190 (12.5 per point of intelligence-20% (Mana manipulation))

Mana regen: 5.23/sec (.25 per point of wisdom+20% (Coalescence))

Stamina: 65/65 (50+(10)**+(5)***)

*10 points for each point in Constitution, once it has increased above 10.

**5 points for each point in Strength, once it has increased above 10.

***5 points for each point in Constitution, once it has increased above 10.

Characteristic: Raw score (Modifier)

Strength: 12 (1.12)
Dexterity: 14 (1.14)
Constitution: 11 (1.11)
Intelligence: 19 (1.19)
Wisdom: 19 (1.19)
Charisma: 13 (1.13)
Perception: 7 (0.07)
Luck: 15 (1.15)
Karmic Luck: +2

Looking over his stats, Sam was starting to get frustrated. He hadn't done a ton in the game yet, but this was his second full day, and his numbers seemed like they'd barely budged at all! His intelligence and wisdom had both increased by two points apiece, and his Mana regeneration rate was up a good little bit, but the rest of his stats were the same, and his total Mana reserve was *down* significantly. After doing a little mental math, Sam realized that without the *Mana manipulation* skill zapping twenty percent of his overall pool, he'd be up closer to two hundred fifty Mana.

Yep, definitely a downer, so no point in dwelling on that. Besides, he needed to think about the long game, and skills like Mana manipulation would definitely pay out *big time* further down the road. "I'll be amazing soon enough, yup. I got this. Go Team Sam!"

The sudden splash of feet through rancid water caught Sam's ear, and he promptly dismissed his character sheet as the last member of the party arrived. He was a willowy young man—probably a year or two younger than Sam—with a shock of corn-silk hair, a set of glasses perched on a hawkish nose, and a wiry frame draped with robes that seemed far too big for him.

His robes, though oversized, looked expensive compared to Sam's plain brown version. Not to mention, the ornately worked staff he carried in one hand probably ran his parents a small fortune. This kid, or more likely his family, had some *seriously* deep pockets. That meant he was either another wealthy Traveler or some kind of Eternium Noble. But why in the world would a wealthy Eternium Noble be tromping around in the sewers?

"Good, now that we're all *here*," Karren the Blade jumped into conversation before Sam had a chance to introduce himself to the newcomer, "we can get started. I see a couple of new faces, so let me explain what we'll be about today. These sewers are full of all kinds of nasty things, though most are of the rather mundane variety—rats, spiders, the occasional fox that's managed to breach the city perimeters. Those beasties avoid parties like ours, so I wouldn't expect to see them, but there are also some nastier things. Most notably among them are the Jellies. Unnatural little buggers that grow as a result of Mana coalescing over time."

"These Jellies," she spat into the flowing muck, "most of 'em aren't all that dangerous, but they *are* magic. Their abilities depend on what type of Mana clumped together to make them; which means they can have powers that range from fire to ice to acid. Most are dumb as a bucket full of rocks. They just sort of wander about, eating whatever they can find, growing more powerful over time as they gain experience. At the early stages, they aren't much bigger than a house cat, but you leave 'em to their own devices for too long and they can grow into quite a nuisance. So, we come down here a couple times a week and do a sweep, make sure none of them get too big. Cull the herd as it were."

Sam tentatively stuck his hand into the air, forehead furrowed in confusion. The tanky male guard, Geffrey the Red, grunted and nodded his head. "*What*, boy?"

"This sounds like you guys know what're you're doing, and you both look quite a bit higher level than the rest of us." Sam paused, lips pursed into a thin line as he eyed their expensive-looking gear. *Yeah, definitely higher level.* "So, I guess my question is, why would you need a group of newbies like us on a mission like this?"

Geffrey grunted again, smacked his lips, and rolled his eyes. "Ya daft, lad? Were ya born yesterday, then?"

A blush crept into Sam's cheeks. He had, in fact, been born yesterday—at least so far as Eternium was concerned—but he didn't particularly want to admit it.

"It's the nature of the Jellies," the newcomer offered, his voice rather high pitched. "The City Guard currently has a contract to provide us with guides for the job, but since the Jellies themselves are formed from coalesced Mana, they can only be killed by magic. They do these patrols regularly, so the Jellies are pretty harmless. As a result, the new recruits and everyone at the bottom of the totem pole ends up running these missions. Especially if you've gotten on *someone's* bad side, but listen to me chattering away as though you don't know any of this!"

"Aye. What he said," the taciturn Guard, Geffrey, grunted.

"Now," Karren interjected, eyeing the smattering of young Mages, "we've deemed the threat to be minimal; these creatures are of a comparable difficulty with the foxes that roam the countryside with one exceptional difference—they are nearly invulnerable to normal weapons but are *extremely* susceptible to magic. So, to save time and cover more ground, we'll be splitting up into two parties."

"You two," she jabbed a finger at the pair of Mages lingering not far off, "will be with me. While you two," this time, she pointed at Sam and the helpful newcomer, "will be accompanying Geffrey. The requirement for today, for each group, is to finish off a total of fifty Jellies and retrieve any monster Cores that appear for the College. Word to the wise, don't even *think* about trying to pocket those monster Cores; the College *always* finds out. Always."

She paused, one hand resting on the pommel of her rapier, and speared each of them in turn with a withering glare. "Now, if there are no more questions, let's get moving, people. We're burning daylight, and I, for one, don't want to wade around down here for a second longer than I need to."

Quest alert: The Arcane Path II (Ongoing). As a Licensed Mage and Novice of the Mage College, you are required to complete daily chores or officially sanctioned assignments on behalf of the College! Today, you must clear the sewers beneath Ardania of living Jellies! 0/50 complete.

Super minor achievement: Joined a party! At least you're doing something—have some experience. Exp: 5.

Without further instruction, the group split; a decision that instantly sent off warning bells inside Sam's head—*never split the party*—but this wasn't up to him, so he kept his mouth shut and followed his guide down a branching tunnel with his new friend trailing along just behind.

"Thanks for the info back there." Sam smiled at the man as they made their way deeper into the warren of twisted passageways and disgusting muck. "This is my first time, and I'm new around here."

"You're a Traveler, then?" the kid in the glasses questioned, his eyes alive with excitement. Sam nodded, keeping his gaze fixed firmly on the waters for any sign of the creatures they were hunting. "I'd heard there were some new people making waves, but I didn't think they'd stick you on a detail like this."

"Yeah, me either," Sam grumbled as he stepped on something that squished like a rotten tomato beneath his boot.

"Let me guess, you met Octavius first?"

Sam grinned and nodded again. "You too?"

"Quite," the kid said, pushing his glasses up higher onto the bridge of his nose. "Octavius and I have something of... a *history*, so he goes out of his way to punish me pretty much any chance he gets. I'm Finn, by the way. Well, technically Lord Finneas Laustsen, but my friends call me Finn. At least, I imagine they *would* if I had friends, which I don't. Mine is a family of traitors, so we have business acquaintances at best."

"Sam." He offered Finn his hand which the boy reluctantly took, giving it one weak pump, then quickly pulling away.

"It's a pleasure," Finn spoke a little too seriously for Sam's comfort.

"What exactly do you mean 'family of traitors'?" Sam quizzed him, feeling a flash of worry. Finn seemed nice enough, but he was already on the outs with the Mage's College, so throwing in with someone who was deeply disliked might not be such a good idea.

"Old, old history, I'm afraid. History which puts me at odds with Octavius and his kin. House Laustsen and House Igenitor have had a blood feud for over two-hundred years, since before the centralization of power in the form of the Tyrants, King Henry and Queen Marie." Finn stole a long look at the guard, busy trudging ahead through the waters, a torch in one hand, a curved axe in the other.

Finn dropped his voice, keeping a conspiratorial eye on Geffrey. "Few citizens of Ardania talk about the old history, of course, but there was something of a war before the line of King Henry took power. House Igenitor was one of the most vocal supporters of the current regime, while my house supported the losing faction, the Sect leader of Charibert. Naturally, most of the opposing Houses were scrubbed from existence, but my Household was seen as too valuable to simply *remove* from existence."

"The decimation of House Laustsen would've thrown Ardania's economy into a death spiral, so we were pardoned by the Throne after having *seen the error of our ways.* House Igenitor, however, has never forgiven us. Octavius seems to somehow hold me personally responsible for the centuries-old 'insult' of..." Finn faltered and shrugged, "well, I'm not sure exactly of what, but apparently, it's bad. So, here I am, trudging through the sewers."

Great, of course, the first decent person I've met inside the College would turn out to be Octavius' mortal enemy. But, after thinking about it for a moment, Sam decided that actually made Finn even cooler. Anyone that Octavius hated was probably good to know, and Sam wasn't about to let some petty bully ruin a potentially good friendship.

"Well, you know what they say, any enemy of Octavius is a friend of mine." Sam held out a hand with a grin.

"Hey, Magelings," Geffrey barked over one shoulder, cutting off their conversation, "get ready. We got Jellies."

The man broke into a lumbering run, darting out of the hallway and into a hub-like chamber with tunnels forking off in every direction. Sam picked up the pace, water splashing as he charged after Geffrey with his hands raised, ready to deal out some magical damage.

The room beyond was *crawling* with critters in a host of different shapes, sizes, and colors. All were gelatinous blobs of neon-bright goo, which reminded Sam of miniature versions of the colossal creature that had chased him through the jungle; though, admittedly, none of these were filled with bones. Some edged through the waters toward them, while others dotted the walls and ceilings like cancerous, multi-colored growths. Sam skidded to a halt, taking up a position behind Geffrey, who now had a shield out and strapped to his left arm.

Sam scanned the room, counting as he went. There were sixteen of the creatures, and though they didn't appear to be particularly dangerous on the surface, he could vividly recall the sensation of being dissolved inside the belly of the monster from the jungle. With this many Jellies, if they all converged as one, it could prove to be problematic.

"Alright, you two," Geffrey bellowed, "I'll draw their ire, while you two dish out some damage, but make sure to keep your distance—even a touch might well send a young Mage like you off to an early grave. Now, who wants some, huh!" he shouted, wading forward and slamming axe against buckler, *clang-clang-clang*. The noise started drawing Jellies to him like a moth to a flame.

The first wave of creatures converged on the guard, swarming around him in a half-circle. Goopy tentacles lashed out like sentient whips. Those questing, gelatinous limbs slapped harmlessly against Geffrey's armor, but the man let out muffled grunts whenever they connected against exposed flesh. Sam heard skin sizzle as plumes of greasy smoke wafted up into the air, carrying the stench of burnt hair. *Super gross.* If Sam was smelling it with *his* pitiful perception, to someone like Finn, the scent probably would've been unbearable, but a glance at his new friend showed just the opposite.

Finn seemed to be the bookish type, probably cozier in a library than a party, but here in the heat of battle, he looked like he was finally in his comfort zone. He slammed his staff down in the muck, and a dome of shifting, blue light erupted around him in a circle, radiating unfathomable cold. Finn thrust his right hand straight out, palm up, and conjured a spike of pale-blue ice a foot in length. The ice spear zipped through the air like an arrow, blasting through an oozing, purple Jelly with a glimmer of red at its center. The creature didn't stand a chance and fell apart, disappearing into the muck.

Finn didn't celebrate the kill but moved on, coldly and methodically targeting an encroaching Jelly on the left that was making its way toward them along the wall. Dead ahead, Geffrey was bellowing while his body smoked and his health lurched and dropped in steady increments. He absorbed a fair number of attacks on his shield and armor, but there were just so *many* of the creatures. The man was laying into them with his axe, splitting the Jellies in two to slow them down, but the damage never seemed to take.

The creatures quickly reformed, no worse for the wear but as angry as brainless lumps could be. There was a *whoosh* as a churning fireball erupted, exploding against Geffrey's shield and rocking the big man back on his heels. The Jellies closed in even faster, more of the creatures working to flank him from the left and the right.

Sam felt a twinge of panic; Geffrey was going to die if he didn't do something. But what could he do? He hadn't even taken his Basics of Offensive Spell Casters course yet! He wasn't *prepared* for this! Suddenly, he was wishing he'd taken the cleric class. After all, that tutorial was probably *way* more fun and gentle.

But this was no time for doubt. A word from his Trial floated up to the top of his mind: *Decide.* He could run away, or he could confront these monsters just as he'd confronted those Trollish bullies in the bathroom. The choice was a no brainer. "Finn, watch my back and make sure those things don't get behind me!"

"What? I'm better at this than you are." Finn scoffed as he readied his next spell.

Sam waded into a gap just behind Geffrey, keeping a safe distance from the nearest Jelly. He didn't have a weapon, but he had finally remembered that he *was* a weapon. Acting on instinct—perhaps the single greatest tool in the Sorcerer's arsenal—Sam stuck both arms out at an angle, so they made a 'V', and began spamming Wind Blade, firing compressed air blasts from each hand. Although Sam knew the spell would be invisible to the naked eye, the results were obvious to anyone who could see. Jellies staggered away, goo cartwheeling through the air as they fell, sliced cleanly apart.

Using both hands was slower than casting it with just one hand, and he had a misfire every third attack or so, but it hardly mattered. Sam was still casting a spell every two and a half seconds. Since he could alternate hands, he was firing continuously, blasting away Jellies to either side of his tanky guard. Wind Blade wasn't powerful enough to kill the monsters straight out, but two or three shots seemed to do the trick in most cases.

Mana manipulation had reduced his overall reserve pool, true, but he still *felt* like he could do this all day. A surge of exhilaration sprinted through him. Now, this was what he'd come for! Action. Adventure. Monsters and battle! *Magic!*

"On your right!" Finn called out from behind him. "*Above!*"

Sam swiveled his head and caught sight of a basketball-sized Jelly clinging to the ceiling just above him. It dropped like a penny tossed from the Empire State building.

Frantic, Sam leaped to the right, throwing himself into a roll just as he'd done a hundred times in judo. Except, in judo, he hadn't been wearing Mage robes and he hadn't been in knee-deep sewage. Sam avoided the falling creature by inches but got a face full of rancid filth for his effort, and his health took a beating as well, costing him eight of his seventy HP.

He quickly gained his feet, gasping as he tried not to throw up all over himself. The blob was encroaching on his personal space, but an Ice Spike ripped through the air, parting the blob and killing it in an instant. Sam swiped a hand across his face, clearing the gunk from his eyes, then spun, searching for any other threats. There were none.

The fighting had happened so fast... and just like that, it was all over. Sixteen dead in a matter of a few seconds of desperate struggle. From the look of things, Finn had done the bulk of the heavy lifting. But a win was a win, and Sam felt inordinately excited, especially when he received an onslaught of notices, one right after the other:

Experience increased due to low average party level!
Exp: 240 (Sentient Jelly x 16) (10 per Jelly * 1.5 difficulty).

Quest updated: The Arcane Path II (Ongoing). As a Licensed Mage and Novice of the Mage College, you are required to complete daily chores or officially sanctioned

assignments on behalf of the College! Today you must clear the
sewers beneath Ardania of Sentient Jellies! 16/50 complete.

Skill gained: Dual casting (Novice I). Not having a
weapon in one hand may make it harder to fend off attacks, but
you have found a way to make yourself deadly without needing
to hold a stick or pointy chunk of metal! Whether casting the
same spell or a different one, as long as you only need a single
hand for each spell, you are able to cast two at once! Effect: Cast
two spells at the same time. Increase casting time by 51-1n%
where 'n' is skill level. 33% chance of failing due to faltering spell
stability, +1n% spell stability per skill level.

Sam grinned like a maniac as he read over the messages.
Was the College *kind* of the worst? Yes. Was Octavius the
human equivalent of rotten milk? Sure. Was Sam covered in
grime and sewage? Obviously. But boy oh *boy* was he having a
blast right now.

"Alright, then." Geffrey pulled a vial with red liquid
from a pouch at his side. "You lot better get rooting around for
the monster Cores, and then we're off. We have thirty-four more
of these things to kill before we're done for the day. Best to be
quick about it."

Sam didn't relish the idea of clawing through raw
sewage barehanded for monster Cores, but if this was the worst
thing that he had to do with the college, maybe this wouldn't be
so bad after all.

CHAPTER ELEVEN

Clawing through raw sewage barehanded was *not* the worst thing Sam had to do. Not by a long shot. The next four days passed in a blur of too little sleep, too little food—all of it bad—too little fun, and too *much* of everything else.

In fact, Sam's occasional trips into the sewers were actually the *highlight* of his time at the College because those were the few rare times where he got to adventure, earn combat experience, and do something that felt *useful.* The rest of the time felt like being a pledge at a frat—something Sam had rejected early on in his college days because he wasn't a fan of merciless hazing. Octavius, on the other hand, seemed like he'd been raised from the crib in a frat house designed to break the spirit.

Every day, the Peak Student had Sam and the others up before sunrise doing chores—more sewer patrols, cleaning toilets, scrubbing floors with the Eternium equivalent of toothbrushes, serving in the mess hall, and endless cataloging of books that he wasn't even allowed to open. Then it was a quick bath, a bite to eat if Sam was lucky, and off to classes for the rest of the day.

When he was finally done with classes? Party time! *Ha*! Just kidding. More chores. Grounds maintenance was common, followed by a short and tasteless dinner and a stint in the restricted library where he helped Octavius with some sort of research. Though *Sam's* part of the 'research' amounted to running books, balancing candles for hours at a time, fetching quills or fresh parchment, or holding down vellum maps of the surrounding countryside.

Though, if there was a bright side to all this, it was that his chore and class grind had earned Sam four thousand six hundred twenty experience. That meant that he had gained another two levels, bringing him up to level four. Nearly *five thousand* experience gained in the *most* demeaning way possible. Sam tried not to sigh too loudly. The Jellies in the sewers offered decent experience, and the classes—though boring for the most part—helped him increase his primary skills, which also contributed to level gain.

Moreover, his classes had garnered him five additional points in both intelligence and wisdom, and thanks to some rather rigorous training in the *Basics of Offensive Spell Casters* class, he'd even picked up a point apiece in strength, constitution, and dexterity. Sam's innate class abilities had given him four characteristic points to distribute at level three and one point in both intelligence and wisdom at level four.

But deciding how to spend his limited point allotment had been no easy choice. Sam bristled at how *slow* he was and how tired even relatively simple actions made him. Still, he couldn't justify dropping points into either strength or constitution. Instead, he added two points into intelligence—his primary class attribute—one into wisdom, and the last into perception. He *hated* using points for non-class stats, but at the same time, his low perception was starting to cost him.

Already, he'd been late for class once and chores twice because he simply lost track of time. He'd poisoned himself to boot by mistakenly eating a lump of sewer mold when thinking that it was some kind of new-fangled dessert. The stomach pains had lasted for *hours,* and he was lucky he'd survived at all. When he thought back on the incident, there was nothing that could explain *why* he would do that. It must have been some odd game mechanic.

His perception deficit *needed* to go away as soon as possible. So, until he hit 'normal' levels, he'd be dumping in at least one point at every third level. Sure, Sam wasn't exactly breaking records or making waves, but at least his progress wasn't *completely* stagnated, and at this stage in the game, he needed to take his victories where he could get them.

Name: Sam_K 'High Five, I Tried!'
Class: Aeolus Sorcerer
Profession: Locked
Level: 4 Exp: 6,003 Exp to next level: 3,997
Hit Points: 70/70
Mana: 270/270
Mana regen: 7.8/sec
Stamina: 75/75

Characteristic: Raw score (Modifier)

Strength: 13 (1.13)
Dexterity: 15 (1.15)
Constitution: 12 (1.2)
Intelligence: 27 (1.27)
Wisdom: 26 (1.26)
Charisma: 13 (1.13)
Perception: 8 (0.08)
Luck: 15 (1.15)
Karmic Luck: 2

He'd also learned a new spell automatically at level three; just another perk to being an Aeolus Sorcerer. Unfortunately, Sam hadn't been able to pick the spell, but it turned out to be a mightily effective defensive aura called *Mage Armor*. Thanks to his *Mage Shields and You: The Art of Defensive Magic* Class, he'd managed to push the technique all the way up to Beginner II, which seemed respectable, if *just* shy of extraordinary.

Mage Armor (Beginner II). Mages are basically made of paper and glass—even the slightest bump is liable to shuffle them right off the mortal coil, but thankfully, Mage Armor exists! With this in place, the typical Mage will be slightly more durable than a Styrofoam coffee cup! I mean, it's not much, but at least a strong wind won't kill you anymore. Well... medium strength wind. Effect: For every point of Mana devoted to this spell, negate one point of damage from primary sources of magic and half a point from primary sources of physical damage. Increase conversion by 0.025n where 'n' equals skill level.

Sam pushed the thoughts to the back of his head as he dropped onto a long, wooden bench positioned across a polished, wooden table in the College's rather expansive cafeteria. Finn was already seated on the other side, picking his way through a plateful of rice and mystery meat covered in a gooey, gray sauce that reminded Sam of his time in the sewers. The flavor was almost the same as well, at least to Sam's tongue.

They had this same meal at least once a day, and it never got any better. Just tasteless, bland, mush, with chewy bits of meat of questionable origin. The higher-ups got the good stuff, of course—steak, lobster, foie gras, and creme brulee. Basically, dishes fit for a King. Not so much for the Novices.

Sam was starving though, so he steeled his resolve, picked up a spoon, and ladled a heaping bite into his mouth, grimacing at the taste and texture. While he worked the goop in his jaws, he eyed Finn, who looked almost as tired as Sam felt. The Noble's normally pale complexion was even waxier than usual, and he had deep purple bags loitering beneath his eyes.

"Long night?" Sam dived back in with his spoon for another bite as soon as the question was out.

"Celestial *above*, don't even get me started," Finn groaned and stabbed his food with a spoon. "I was on library duty last night, and I *swear* that Octavius was up until a quarter to three. Don't think I got into bed until close to *five*. Then I had grounds duty at six-fifteen! *Then* Advance Combat Magics until eleven-thirty. I'm working on maybe an hour of sleep, and this afternoon, I have a test in Advanced Potions and Transmutative Substances. I'm fairly sure Octavius *knew* that and spent extra time in the library just to spite me. Kept mumbling about a potential breakthrough, but I saw a dirty glint in his eyes. He's out to *get* me, I tell you! I suppose that shouldn't be a shock to me, but it is *irksome*."

Sam grunted noncommittally and lifted another bite to his mouth, chewing purposefully to grind the meat, tough as shoe-leather, down to something digestible. When he finally was able to swallow, he asked, "Any idea what he's working on?"

"Actually, *yes!*" Finn's face visibly brightened. "I've been trying to work it out, and a bit of text from last night was the final clue. Peak Students—those on the verge of advancement to Journeyman status with the College—usually have to perform some great feat or work on behalf of the College."

Finn slurped down another mouthful with a grimace and continued, "Octavius is an Earth Mage class, and I think he's constructing a massive, earth-based spell construct. Hard to say exactly what the spell will do, but based on what I've gleaned, it's offensive in nature and potentially *devastating*. Much like Octavius' personality really, *offensive* and *devastating*. If I had to wager, I'd say it's likely some kind of preemptive strike against the Wolfmen. The spell at least. His personality is a strike against *women* for sure."

The Wolfmen... now *that*, at least, was one topic of study Sam had been enjoying. Speaking of, Sam needed to move his butt, or he was going to be late. *Again.* If that happened, Octavius would likely have him scrubbing toilets until it was time to log out of the game and get back to the real world. Hard pass on that front. Jamming the last bit of food into his mouth, he shot to his feet and clambered off of the bench.

"Sorry, Finn," he was choking down that last mouthful, "but I gotta get over to the annex for my dungeoneering class. Catch you later."

Sam offered the Noble a wave and hustled out of the cafeteria, trying not to lose his way through the warren of nonsensically twisting passageways and corridors, navigating via the runic system that he was still *ages* away from mastering. Sam picked up the pace, taking left after right, left after right. True, he didn't want to be late because he wanted to avoid Octavius' wrath, but he also wanted to make it because this was hands down his favorite class so far. The other classes—though practical—were dull as sin. dungeoneering, though, that was a whole different ball game.

Sam rounded a bend, and the world seemed to tilt on end. A sick sense of vertigo washed through him, leaving him reeling uncertainly for a moment before everything righted itself and his balance restored. *Gah.* Going into the Annex was the *worst.* Although the whole College was one giant Rubik's Cube, the Annex was by far the most troublesome section of the enormous complex.

The rest of the building, though confusing, joined seamlessly. There was never any significant physical or time distortion. Then there was the Annex. According to College historians, the Annex had been the first area of the College created using spatial magics—and it had come about when that particular field of study had still been largely untested and experimental.

The results screamed amateur. Time pockets. Gravity wells. Spatial anomalies and axis inversions. The College Annex, like almost all annexes, was where they stuck the people the College loathed, which included the professors who taught the 'adventuring' courses. These classes were universally looked down on by all the top Mages. After all, why would any self-respecting Mage take a class of field survival, medical aid *without the use of magic*, or dungeoneering?

Exploring dungeons and grinding low-level Mobs was for the unenlightened and was not the affair of a proper Mage. The professors that taught those courses weren't Mages at all but seasoned adventures who'd worked in partnership with the College for ages. Thankfully, Sam had no desire whatsoever to be a 'proper' Mage; otherwise, he would've missed out on this gem of a class.

Sam shot a look at a handful of the other students already at their seats—warriors, archers, and clerics, not another Mage in sight—and took a desk at the very front. Not a second too soon.

A door swung open, and in strutted an ancient man, his back slightly bent, his head balding save for a ring of sparse hair clinging to the sides of his skull, his skin like weathered saddle leather. Sir Tomas was an old-timey adventurer-turned-anthropologist who had to be creeping up on a hundred. Despite that, the man moved with a spry step and always seemed to have a grin on his face which showcased the many gaps where teeth should've been but weren't.

He wore dusky leathers and a suit of finely wrought scale mail over the top; the outfit was cinched tight at the center with a leather belt which housed a mace that looked impossibly large and heavy for such a small, otherwise frail man. Sam had seen Sir Tomas wield the weapon in a handful of brief demonstrations, and though he *looked* to have the strength and constitution of an anemic toddler, Sir Tomas used the weapon with ease and grace.

"I have quite the surprise for you, class!" Sir Tomas cackled, rubbing wrinkled hands together. "Our past three sessions have been about language, culture, and general customs of the Wolfmen, but today we're going to learn about Wolfman anatomy. Then... well, *then* you'll get to see one of the creatures in the flesh! Or rather, in the *fur,* I suppose. I caught this particular specimen not three days ago. A Wolfman Scout. He was loitering around the edges of the city, and all by his lonesome no less; which is quite rare, believe you me. Generally, these fellas like to fight in packs, and they almost always have regular wolf familiars along with 'em for the action.

"That's one lesson you always need to keep in your head! When you find these creatures in the wild, always be on the lookout for backup. Not our guy, though. He was probably trying to probe the city defenses, find weak points in our system, and that's pretty much the only reason I was able to bag 'im alive. If there had been others of his ilk around, I reckon I never would've had a chance at catching 'im." He *tsked* and shook his head. "Bugger still fought like a bearcat, lemme tell you what. I've interrogated 'im at length, but he hasn't betrayed 'is people or 'is purpose."

"Not that I really expected him to sell them out, mind you. See, that's one of the curious things about the Wolfmen—it's Abyss-near impossible to torture them properly, on account of the fact that every interaction they have even with their own kind *has to* produce pain. It's the way of their kind. They believe pampering the flesh is weakness and that only through strength and pain can purity of purpose and mind follow."

"We know that what they are doing just builds up their constitution and strength, but how do you convince an *animal* to think rationally? So, you put the screws to these fellas, and they'll just grin and thank you for helping them along their path. They take that old adage *'anything that doesn't kill you makes you stronger'* extraordinarily serious. Makes 'em daunting foes on the battlefield."

"So far, the best luck I've had was with this thing." Sir Tomas drew a long feather free from a leather pouch at his belt. "I've been tickling the beastman for *hours* at a time, but somehow, he's held strong. Which is a good segue to our first lesson of the day—Wolfmen Anatomy."

He walked over to a freestanding chalkboard and turned it around, revealing a diagram of a Wolfman carefully sketched out in his neat hand.

"Now, the Beastmen, they don't have the same physiology as you or me. Sure, they might look humanoid, but they have joints and muscle groups we don't. So, a lot of the things that might cripple us will only minorly hinder 'em. On the flip side, that also gives 'em unique vulnerabilities. If, for example, you can take out the hock," he jabbed a gnarled finger at a lower leg on the diagram, "which is rarely protected since doing so restricts movement, you can cripple them something fierce."

For the next thirty minutes, Sir Tomas went through Wolfman anatomy, which was as dry and dusty as the Sahara in summer, but it did earn Sam a new skill and a +1 to intelligence, which was always appreciated.

Skill increased: Wolfman Physiology (Beginner III). The foot bone's connected to the leg bone, the leg bone's connected to the knee bone, the knee bone's connected to the thigh bone, now you're doin' that Wolfman skeleton dance! If knowing thy

enemy is the key to victory, then you are closer than almost
anyone. Increase damage or healing by 1n% where n=skill level.
Use your knowledge wisely. Intelligence +1!

"Alright," Sir Tomas finally slapped his hands on his legs once he was done with the lecture, "guess it's time for the *real* show. Now, like I said earlier, I doubt we'll get much out of 'im, but the way I figure it, you'll be able to see the furry scoundrel here in the safety of a classroom and maybe even try out a little bit of your budding language skills. Stay on your toes, and make sure to keep a safe distance; these fellas are notorious as master escape artists. They're smart buggers and will take any possible advantage you give 'em. There's a damned good reason why they're the biggest threat currently facing humanity. Without further ado..."

Sir Tomas slipped from the room, propped the heavy wooden door open, then carefully wheeled a massive cage into the room. The class had been going over Wolfmen, but seeing one alive was a sobering experience. The beast was a little taller than an average man but looked far closer to a wolf than to a human.

This one had a rather lean frame; his body was covered in coarse, gray fur and crude, leather armor adorned its shoulders and legs. The creature had wicked claws, vicious fangs, and amber eyes that seemed to take in every student, every angle, every detail all at once. So far, the deadliest threat Sam had faced was sewer Jellies, but this thing was terror on a whole new level.

Sam could hardly believe that people were expected to fight something this daunting and obviously deadly. Sir Tomas shuffled over to one side and waved at the creature with a liver-spotted hand. "As you can see, this fella doesn't have a weapon on him, yet he is a *living* weapon. Wolfmen prefer to fight with blades, axes, and arrows—all of them liberally coated in poison—but if push comes to shove, they are just as deadly in hand-to-hand combat as most of our Kingdom's best warriors are with a weapon."

"I've never met one that wasn't stronger or faster than a human of the same level. The real benefit *we* have is that the Wolfmen tend to favor light armors made of linen, leather, and hides, which means *if* you can land a solid blow, you'll hurt 'em right and proper. They seem to think that mining, crafting, and forging are only respectable jobs at high levels when impressive things can be done, so most of their population *heavily* favors combat roles."

"Well, we're not getting any younger here—especially not me! *Ha!* Form a line and try out some of the basic language skills we've been going over. Don't be surprised if you earn a new skill here—often times, these language skills won't take properly until you try them out on a native. If he doesn't reply... Well, don't think too much on it. He hates all of you and wants to see every one of us dead. So, nothing personal." Sir Tomas paused and canted his head, a hazy look in his eyes. "Or *completely* personal, depending on how you look at it, I suppose. Anywho, let's get this show on the road."

The class quickly lined up to get their shot at the Wolfman, but Sam lingered back. All of a sudden, he kind of didn't want to be here anymore. This class was fun and all—the best of the bunch really—but at the same time, this all felt subtly... *wrong.* The Wolfman in the cage with his feet chained to the floor was just code in a computer game; Sam *knew* that intellectually, but it didn't *feel* like code in a computer game.

This thing wasn't some mindless Jelly crawling around down in a rancid sewer. It was a thinking creature with a culture and a society. Fighting something like this out in the wild as part of the broader game was one thing, but this just seemed a little cruel.

Finally, though, Sam pushed his doubt to the back of his mind and got to the end of the line. He mentally went through the rudimentary language training they'd gone over, and in no time flat, it was his turn. The Wolfman was before him, amber eyes burning like hot coals, fangs bared in obvious hostility. Sam licked his lips nervously but refrained from smiling, knowing the creature would take it as a sign of threat, not reassurance. Instead, Sam raised his hands, palms out, fingers open, then lifted his chin, revealing his throat—a sign of trust. The Wolfman was still snarling at him, but there was something new in his eyes, something that might almost have been interest.

That... or *hope*? Sam hoped not, as there was nothing he could do that would help this beast. He lowered his chin and hunched forward, making sure he was lower than the captured creature, then began working through the harsh, guttural words they'd been taught, *"Greetings, fur brother. I am called Sam."*

The creature considered him for a long moment before speaking a deluge of words. Sam had no hope of understanding everything, only catching one word in three. *"We are not brothers, vragnik. Only the cruelest enemy would treat another in this way."* His ears twitched—something akin to a shrug. *"My people have a saying, 'Ruazhi noare vragnik, ibois najstarkei vragnu prinosit velichayshuyu silzha.' It is from the eldest tongue, from before the world shattered."*

"It means 'render honor to the enemy, for the truest enemy forces the greatest strength'. Yet your kind treats me with contempt—like an animal to parade around before the young. If our situations were reversed, at least you would be given the honor of a quick, clean death. Remember my name. I am

Velkan of the Redmane Tribe. I will be free yet, and you and your kind will pay."

With that, he bared his fangs and fell silent. A system message immediately followed:

Skill gained: Wolfman Language (Spoken/body) (3/10). You have learned the basics of the Wolfman language and can now speak enough common phrases to have your intentions understood! For the most part. As this is a basic racial language skill, there are only ten levels available, unlike the typical ranking. Skill points cannot be devoted to this skill; it must be increased through study and practice.

Title gained: Budding Anthropologist. By taking the time to study the culture and language of a foreign race—and an enemy race at that—you have taken the first step on the path of the anthropologist. Continue to explore cultures, languages, and races other than your own to earn the chance to unlock the Anthropologist Profession! +20% speed in learning all spoken or body language, +500 Reputation among hostile races, +1 Wisdom.

Abyss yeah! That was pretty good, though Sam still had a vaguely uneasy feeling about this whole thing as Sir Tomas rolled away the silver-furred creature. It didn't help that the Wolfman's golden gaze never left Sam; his stare practically seemed to radiate death and dismemberment in the not too distant future.

Unfortunately, there was little time to dwell on the uncomfortable feeling taking root inside his chest. Class was over, and he had evening chores to get to, but thankfully, tomorrow would be his first official 'day off'. Sam would still have morning chores to do, but then the rest of the day belonged to him, and truthfully, he *couldn't wait* to get away from the College and mix with some of the other players. He grinned like a loon at the thought as he slipped from the room, through the Annex, and headed for Mage Greentouched, a plant-based Master Mage responsible for maintaining the College grounds. Just a few hours there, a quick bite to eat, and then onto his evening shift with Octavius in the library.

Sigh. Tomorrow couldn't come soon enough.

Chapter Twelve

Sam sprinted down the twisting hallways of the College, sweating like mad. The small nicks, cuts, and bruises covering his face and arms burned like hellfire. His stamina dropped while he pumped his arms and legs, his lungs burned almost as badly as the army of small wounds, but he was *so* close to the library now. He skidded blindly around a corner and wheeled left, narrowly avoiding a senior Mage with silvered hair and golden robes—his nose buried in some dusty volume or another—then crossed the threshold into the massive library which held the College's collective knowledge.

He doubled over, panting and wheezing, hands on his knees. Mage Greentouched had kept him until the *last* conceivable second, even though the man knew that meant *one*: Sam wouldn't get dinner, and *two*: he would likely be late for his duties with Octavius. Did Mage Greentouched care?

Nope. He was a little less gleeful in the suffering of new initiates than Octavius, but only a *little*. When Sam had reported for duty and told him his work schedule, the man had insisted that the carnivorous roses—a *vital* ingredient in many alchemic mixtures, Mage Greentouched assured him—needed tending.

Unfortunately, the garden proper where the alchemic ingredients were grown was about as far from the library as possible. When you accounted for the spatial magic that governed the building, that ended up being *miles*. When Sam politely pointed that out, the old man had offered him some sage advice, which basically amounted to 'go suck eggs'. *You must be as supple as the willow yet as sturdy as the oak, only then will you have the fortitude a Mage needs to thrive.* Pretentious old bag.

"Are you *quite* alright, young man?" Came a creaky voice from just ahead. Sam righted himself, hands planted on hips, his breathing still ragged though slightly better than it had been a handful of moments before.

Dead ahead was a bent old soul, Mage Solis, the night librarian and guardian of the stacks. He was rail-thin, his back bent from countless nights spent hunched over books, glasses as thick as bottle caps perched on his crooked nose. Unlike many of the Mages, he wore plain, brown robes and seemed to perpetually have ink smudges on his wrinkled cheeks. He regarded Sam, squinting and adjusting his glasses.

"Ah, young master Sam," he wheezed, and Sam could have *sworn* that dust filtered out with the air. A health potion appeared in his hand from under his desk, and he took a long drink. He shuddered, then spoke with greater vigor, "I suppose you're looking for Peak Student Octavius then, hmm?"

"Yes, sir," Sam bobbed his head in reply. "Is... is he already in?"

"No, no," Mage Solis replied in his grandfatherly voice, waving away Sam's obvious concern with one scrawny hand, "but you, my boy, look to be at your very wits' end. Covered in cuts, green stains, and dirt... I assume that is Greentouched's doing, then?"

Sam nodded again.

"He always was a mean spirited one, young Greentouched. For someone so close to the restorative and balancing properties of the earth, he is an oddly cantankerous fellow. I think that one inherited the empathy of a boulder... which is to say he has none." The old man chuffed dryly at his own joke. "A trait he and young Master Octavius share in common."

He lifted a hand and twisted at the tip of a wispy handle-bar mustache which dropped down from his sagging cheeks. "I suppose ol' Greentouched worked you long enough to miss the mess hall, hmmm?"

Sam shifted uncomfortably from foot to foot—suffering in stoic silence was a principal tenet of the Mage's College—but his stomach chose that exact moment to growl like an angry bobcat. The old man chuckled again and turned back toward his desk, waving Sam over as he shuffled away on tired feet. Mage Solis resumed his seat with a groan and pulled out a small linen napkin. He unwrapped the small package, revealing a heel of poppyseed bread slathered in thick, golden butter.

Solis wrinkled his brow and shoved the morsel toward Sam. "Was saving this for later—a little midnight snack. But these old bones don't need any food, and I think you might enjoy it more. Then maybe the next time you come around, you can pick up my order of health potions from the alchemy department? I tend to go through them pretty fast these days."

"It'd be my pleasure." Sam stared at the bread, his mouth salivating at just the thought of eating. So far, his experience had taught him that if someone in the College seemed to be showing even the slightest bit of concern, it was so they could violently pull the rug out from underneath him. But... Mage Solis *had* always seemed different. Kinder. Patient. Generous and gracious. Before Sam could reconsider, he took the bread and scarfed it down. Even with his low perception, the bread tasted like divine Mana from heaven above, proving that the food served to him *was* just terrible.

"Now there's a good, lad." Mage Solis nodded sagely. "You just hang in there. They can only break your spirit if you let them, and eventually, it'll get better."

"Not ever *great* but better." He paused and coughed *hard*, eyes misting and widening as though he wanted to say more.

The clicking of boots on tile drew Sam's ear. He shoved the last bite of bread into his mouth, gulped it down, brushed his palms off on his pants, and turned to find Octavius strolling casually toward him, seemingly without a care in the world. Octavius was late, but the rules that governed Sam and the other newly-minted Mages didn't apply to people like *Octavius*.

"There you are," Octavius sneered with casual contempt. "That's too bad, really. The chef in the cafeteria over-braised the short ribs, and I was really hoping you'd be late so I could beat you properly to work out my frustration."

He sighed and threw up his hands; *such is life*, the gesture seemed to say. "Well, I'm sure you'll mess something *else* up soon enough, and then I'll have all the cause I need. Now, if you're done lounging about and slacking in the presence of your betters, attend me. I'm close to a breakthrough, and I think tonight just *might* be the night!"

Without another word, Octavius headed into the towering stacks, hands folded behind his back, the edges of his robes swishing around his ankles as he moved. Octavius didn't even bother to glance back to see if Sam was following... because, *of course,* Sam would be following close behind.

For an *inferior* Mage to do anything different was simply unthinkable, and such overt insubordination would be met with swift and terrible punishment. The sheer arrogance drove Sam nuts, but he bit his tongue and tried to push the growing anger away by focusing on the towering bookcases filled to the brim with arcane volumes of the rarest knowledge.

The College was a rather plain affair overall, but the Exalted Library Arcana was a different issue entirely. The floors were covered in planks of dark wood but fitted so perfectly together that they never let out a squeak or a groan. In fact, just the opposite—those floors swallowed sound like a ravenous lion.

The whole area was a twisting, turning labyrinth of interconnected bookcases, interrupted by the occasional open area where there were tables and chairs for studying or small nooks and alcoves with ancient artifacts and powerful relics prominently displayed but obviously protected. Ghostly candles and impossible oil lamps floated in the air, perpetually burning with pale purple witchlight, though giving off no discernible heat.

Pretty cool, if Sam was being honest. Coolest of all were the walkways that hung in the air overhead, completely unsupported, flanked by ever-more bookcases and ever-more books. Staring up was a little like looking at a painting of oddly jointed stairs and hallways, all rising up without any sort of ceiling in sight. This place was the ultimate in spatial magic, and despite all the time Sam had spent here so far, he couldn't make heads or tails of *how* this place existed.

Still, it sure was fun to look at.

After wandering the stacks for nearly ten minutes, Octavius headed into a small study nook which the Peak Student had reserved for himself and his research. The alcove was a roomy space, twenty feet by twenty feet, with a colossal mahogany desk at the center accompanied by a plush leather chair. There was only a single chair, naturally, because Octavius was the only one who would be sitting tonight. On the desk was a brass oil lamp, enchanted to shine with yellow light that never flickered or failed. Often times, however, Octavius would turn *off* the enchanted lamp, forcing his assistants to hold candles. He claimed the weak, watery light was easier on his eyes.

The rest of the desk was taken up by piles of vellum and enchanted parchment, quills and ink pots, teetering stacks of books, geographical maps of the city and surrounding countryside, and blueprints for something that looked vaguely like a portable siege tower. Printed in a neat script across the top of the blueprints was a single word: *LAW*.

Octavius promptly flopped into his seat, crossing his ankles primly, then pulled over a thick volume entitled *Magical Theory of Sympathetic Magic: Mastering the Arcane Forces of Spell Twining*. Of all the volumes Octavius fussed over, that was the one Sam had seen him studying the most often and most diligently. Obviously, it was the key to his research.

From what Sam had gathered so far—with a few helpful tidbits from Finn—it appeared as though Octavius wasn't just trying to perform some big complicated spell; he was attempting to create something new. A weapon of some sort, from the looks of the blueprints Octavius was constantly tweaking. Octavius' notes were far too complicated for Sam to understand the specifics of the spell—*or was it a machine? Both maybe?*—but chances were high that whatever he was building would be seriously deadly once the Mage worked out the finer mechanics.

For the next half hour, Sam stood to the side of the desk, hands folded behind him, back perfectly straight, not moving, not talking, not doing anything. Well, not *officially* doing anything, at any rate. He *did* study the bits of text he could get a glimpse at, and he carefully surveyed one of the large maps, noting the variety of red 'X's which denoted Wolfman troop movements and possible camp locations. Just when Sam thought he'd fall over from sheer boredom, Octavius cleared his throat and pulled a set of keys from his belt. With a flick of his wrist, the Peak Student tossed the keys at Sam.

"I need a text from the restricted section." Octavius restlessly drummed his fingers on the table. "It'll be in a new section of the restricted library you haven't been in before—the

Sage's Vault. When you get into the Prime Chamber, enter into the purple portal, take your first right until you reach an area labeled *Advanced Displacement Mechanics*. Oh, and just so you know, there's a talking book in that section. It's locked behind some rather formidable bars, but you should still ignore whatever it says or suffer unending despair."

"Or listen to it. That might make things more fun for me," Octavius offered the instruction with the unwavering scorn he was so well-known for, then dismissed Sam with shooing gesture. "*Do* be quick. I don't want to be up until an unreasonable hour."

Sam grit his teeth, turned on his heel, and carefully navigated his way back to the library's entrance. Stupid Octavius. *He* didn't want to be up until an unreasonable hour? Now *that* was funny.

Mage Solis was still at his desk, drinking something that smelled suspiciously like coffee from a large porcelain mug while he flipped through a thick, leather-bound volume. Sam caught a look at the title, which decorated the top of each page. He was more than a little bit surprised to see it read, *The Riveting Adventures of D.K. Esquire: Dungeon Delver*. What? He wasn't studying the deep mysteries of the universe; he was reading a pulpy *adventure* novel? The old man glanced up with a guilty grin before offering Sam a wink and a shrug.

"There's more to life than just *studying*, young man." His watery gaze fell on the thick brass keyring in Sam's hand. "Ah, off to the restricted section, I suppose. That young Octavius is certainly hungry for power. Hopefully, he knows just what he's about."

The old man grumbled, "Working with titanic forces such as he is *trying* to do can have *devastating* consequences if even the slightest calculation goes amiss. Why, an errant *breeze* can often be the end of a Noble line. But listen to me ramble, you run along, young one. Wouldn't want Octavius scolding you for my flapping lips."

Mage Solis waved toward a set of looming double doors off to the left. The rest of the library was open to all students ranked Apprentice or higher, but that section was meant only for the most established Mages—generally those ranked Journeymen or higher. Octavius, Sam had learned, was something of an exception to the rules; both because he was *almost* a Journeymen and because he was considered something of an Earth Mage prodigy.

Moreover, House Igenitor was thick as thieves with the current monarch and a long-time supporter of the College Archmage. Such renown and support carried more than a little weight in these vaulted halls of learning—enough weight for Octavius to have access to just about every section of the College, including areas meant only for the most powerful Mages alive. Which proved one thing to Sam—the greatest power in Eternium was not magic but money and nepotism. Those two could open any door far better even than the most potent spells.

Not so different from the real world, unfortunately. The doors guarding the restricted section were built with dull black steel and covered in glyphs and runes of power. They had large handles protruding outward, but wrapped around them was a chain as thick as Sam's forearm. Securing the chain was a lock the size of Sam's skull. Assuming a thief ever made it this far into the College—*doubtful* as even people that were used to this place got lost—that lock would stop them cold.

Sam lifted the bronze keyring, flipping through a number of different keys—he had no idea what they all did or where they lead—until he got to a golden key with a diamond the size of a robin's egg inset into the key head. The lock gave way under the onslaught of the key's jagged teeth and popped open without the slightest resistance. On the other side of the colossal doors was a rectangular hallway, twenty feet long, five feet wide.

Running along either side of the hallway were doors; though *portals* was probably a better term since there wasn't truly a proper door to be seen. Just seven shimmering, *door-shaped* gateways, each in a different hue. Three portals on the left side of the hall, three on the right, and one at the very end of the hall burning with ethereal purple light that called to Sam like a flame to a moth. Each gateway represented one of the *elevated* ranks: Apprentice, Student, Journeyman, Expert, Master, Grandmaster, and Sage.

So far in his time serving as Octavius' research assistant, Sam had only ever gone through two doors, the crimson Apprentice gate and the tangerine-colored Student gate. Not this time, though.

This time, Sam marched straight toward the end of the hall, pressing his eyes shut tight as he passed through the purple gate. Icy power washed over his skin like a waterfall as he stepped through the wall of light, but the sensation passed quickly; in the span of a heartbeat, he'd left the Prime Chamber behind. Instantly, he found himself on a hallway much like the ones in the lower library. Although there was one *notable* and very important difference: the floors below him were not dark, seamless wood but bricks of semi-translucent purple glass. Sam had never had a problem with heights, but he was now on the highest level of the floating library, and he could see all the other walkways and floors stretching out beneath him like an ant farm.

Sam gulped and licked suddenly parched lips. He must've been three hundred feet up, maybe more. As far as he could tell, nothing whatsoever supported the floor he was currently standing on. *This is a game*, he reminded himself—not for the first or even one-hundred and first time. The rules of physics don't have to make sense. *Code* is holding me up, and in a video game, code is as solid as steel. With the thought firmly in mind, Sam took a tentative step forward. When the purple glass didn't immediately crack and send him to his certain doom, he took a few more.

Not wanting to spend a second more than strictly necessary in the Sage's area, Sam hustled until he was jogging along the crystalline floors, working hard not to focus overlong on the various books filling the shelves. These were strange tomes that glittered with magic; he could almost hear the whisper of a ghostly voice fluttering in the air as he passed. Up ahead was the aisle Octavius had told him to turn down; a wooden placard reading *Advanced Displacement Mechanics* had been carefully hung from a peg at the intersection. Sam's feet faltered as he slipped by a nook, not much bigger than a broom closet, closed away with heavy steel bars.

Truthfully, it looked like a jail cell, and behind the bars was a simple stone pedestal with a burgundy volume propped up on top. There was no title on the cover of the book, though incomprehensible, golden runes sparkled along the spine. There was, however, a humanoid face jutting up from the leather, made in patchwork-fashion from various strips of hide all crudely stitched together. The book would never win any beauty contests, that was for sure, but Sam felt a strange tingle... almost an itching sensation telling him to reach out and *take* the book into his hands. Hesitantly, he glanced down at the keyring in his hand.

Sure enough, hanging there was a purple crystal key that looked to perfectly match the lock. But no. Octavius' warning— even more so, the chuckling smirk that told him to *do it*— lingered over him like an anvil. Sam shoved the keys firmly into a pouch at his belt, turned his back on the strange book, and headed for the *Advanced Displacement Mechanics* section.

He already had enough trouble with the Mage's College, and he wasn't about to jeopardize things now—the night before his first day off, no less—to go poking around some book that would probably incinerate him into fine ash the second he laid a finger on it. There was obviously a reason the book was up on the highest floor in the restricted library and then *further* secured behind a locked gate.

He turned the corner and found Octavius' book without much trouble, but on the way back out... he could've sworn he heard the pages of the strange book rustling as he shuffled past.

Chapter Thirteen

Sam slept like the dead, woke up early, and worked through his morning shift in the kitchen like a zombie, his mind entirely fixated on what awesome things he would do when he got out of the College. He planned on leaving the city; that was for sure. Smiting Jellies with his wind-based powers was fun, but tromping around in sewage was *not*. Besides, he was looking forward to seeing some of the other challenging creatures the game had to offer. He doubted he'd come face to face against the Wolfmen—considering he was only a level four—but any change of pace would be nice.

Rabbits? Foxes? Wolves? Bring 'em on! Truthfully, all he really wanted to do was grind Mobs until his muscles felt like Jell-O and rack up as much experience as humanly possible. To do that would take a little planning.

Sam had picked up several health and Mana potions from the College the day before—along with a leather bandolier for potion storage—even though the magical concoctions were *prohibitively* expensive. But since Clerics and other magic users were so rare, it was unlikely he would manage to party up with a group that had a proper healer. Sam was the frailest of glass cannons, and that meant he needed potions. Beyond that, the Mage's College *did* have the best prices on potions. The *only* prices, actually, as they owned the means of production and chose who they would sell to, but according to Finn, the rest of their gear was *wildly* overpriced. Finn said he knew a place in town where Sam could get some smoking good deals without losing an arm or a leg.

For being a Noble with loads of gold, Finn was surprisingly frugal. Which was good, because Sam needed to stock up. His *Neophyte's Robe* were hardly more than serviceable, he didn't have any sort of backup weapon—a must in case his Mana pool ever ran dry—and he needed at *least* a backpack if he expected to collect any loot at all.

Unlike many of the games he'd played previously, there was no bottomless inventory to stash items; though word on the street was that could be fixed if you had enough money to throw around or had the good luck and fortune to vanquish a rare boss. Spatial storage items *were* apparently a thing and functioned much like the College did—by creating a personal pocket dimension where gear could be stored.

Sam would be on the lookout for one of those. He was going to be here for six months straight. There was no reason he should have to lug around everything in a bulky backpack that would probably weigh on his already terrible stamina. So, he and Finn would stop to get properly geared up, then they would make their way into town and find a group to party with.

Truthfully, that was the part Sam was least worried about. Although Sam had spent precious little time so far in the wider Ardania, his brief encounter with Kathleen—the woman who'd directed him to the College—and the handful of melee-class Fighters he'd encountered on the College grounds all pointed to the fact that he wouldn't have any problem finding a group. Chances were, he and Finn would have to *fight* off the swarm of offers.

When Sam finally finished the last round of dishes, he stripped out of his kitchen apron then slipped through the hallways, making his way to the courtyard. Only eight-thirty in the morning. Not too shabby at all. If they moved quickly, Sam would have almost the whole day to grind!

He found Finn lounging on a bench in the courtyard. The young Noble sat by himself, conjuring and banishing little orbs of frozen power over and over again—no doubt working to level up his Frost Orb spell. The boy looked rather lonely and withdrawn, his face sunken, his eyes hollow, but he lit up like a candle when he saw Sam carving his way across the courtyard toward him.

"Excellent! I was almost starting to think you'd gotten *cold feet* cast on you," he waggled his eyebrows at Sam, obviously smug about his ice-based pun, "and decided to cling to the College grounds like the rest of these spell-sniffing jerks."

"Yeah right," Sam snorted as he rolled his eyes. "I would've been here sooner, but I got stuck with breakfast duty."

"Ah, that explains it then. I was fortunate enough to get a stint with the Enchanter Claifax. She didn't have anything for me to do, so she shooed me off almost as soon as I got there. But enough of that! There's adventuring to be done, and I finally have someone to do it with! This is a treat, you know. I've never actually been on a proper adventure before. Strictly speaking, we Nobles aren't supposed to go out and 'fraternize' with the lower castes. It's not precisely a formal law, understand, but sort of an unspoken rule. As a Mage, it's even worse—gallivanting around with non-initiates is heavily frowned upon."

"Wait, are we not supposed to do this?" Sam paused even as Finn slung an arm around his shoulders and pulled him toward the portcullis.

Finn shrugged, and a mischievous smile broke across his face. "Another one of those unspoken rules. I think if you want to get into the weeds about *technicalities,* then yes, we're not supposed to party up randomly—the College likes to control which parties and groups are sanctioned and which ones aren't. But..."

He paused and shot Sam a wink. "That only matters if we get caught, and we *won't*. Now, do you want to get some adventuring in or not?"

The College was *obsessed* with control—controlling magic, controlling who could practice it and how, even going so far as to control who their members could associate with? Well, Sam was getting supremely tired of not having any control over his in-game life. So *what* if they were breaking some minor rule? He'd come to Eternium to play the game, meet new friends, and embark on some awesome quests! He wasn't going to let some buzz-killington jerk like Octavius strip this world of every ounce of fun available.

Instead, Sam smiled, nodded, and kept right on walking, leaving the school behind, at least for a few hours. They worked their way through the town, enjoying the color, life, and vitality blooming everywhere outside the quiet, hallowed halls of magical academia. Things had already changed significantly since Sam had come this way a few days before.

The buildings were all the same, but the streets were packed with bodies now. He saw far more Travelers weaving through traffic, munching food on the side of the street, or trickling out of the myriad of different shops, inns, and taverns dotting the cityscape. The Travelers stuck out like sore thumbs due to the ratty noob armor and rusty weapons most of them carried.

It made sense that people didn't have amazing gear yet. Although time was wonky here, he'd been in Eternium for approximately six days. That meant the game had been live for *three* days, real-world time. That was just long enough for the first wave of players to get their feet wet but hardly enough time for anyone to make real strides in the game. Leveling was too difficult, and the nature of the quests were too open-ended for anyone to power their way through the early game content. Heck, Sam wasn't even sure there was 'early game content'—at least not in the traditional sense of the phrase.

Finn eventually led him to a second-hand gear store called *Nick's Knacks: Secondhand Goods at Thirdhand Prices! Just watch out for the Razor Blades!*

Of all of the places Sam had visited so far, this one was the sketchiest by far. The shop was surprisingly *thin*, the whole storefront not much wider than a standard hallway, with a wooden door which had been painted a bright green at one point. Now, most of the paint was dull and chipped, showing the rough wood beneath.

The sign overhead was likewise in a terrible state of repair, and the awning jutting from the front of the building had more holes than a standard slice of swiss cheese. Sam hadn't even noticed the place before Finn took the liberty to point it out; it was almost like his eyes slipped around the innocuous little shop. Probably just another casualty of his low perception... or was it another sign of shenanigans afoot?

"Really?" Sam faltered as Finn headed for the door. "*This* is the place we should get our gear from? Unless I'm totally mistaken, aren't you a *Noble*? Why would someone like you *ever* shop in a place like this? This is the kind of place you cross the street to *avoid*. Have you ever heard of tetanus? Because going in there," Sam hooked a thumb toward the door, "is how you get tetanus, and that's coming from a guy who's spent the last few days wading through actual sewage."

Finn raised his hands, a wry smile on his lips. "I know how it looks, but this place is the best, Sam. Truly. This is one time where it's best not to judge a book by its cover. Trust me on this."

Suspicion roamed through Sam, but Finn hadn't led him wrong yet, so he reluctantly followed the Noble into the interior of the ratty shop. "If I get stabbed or a serious debuff, I'm holding you responsible."

Except, the inside was anything *but* ratty. Somehow, it defied the laws of physics just as the Mage's College did. The interior was spacious, the hardwood floorboards underfoot gleamed with a dull glow from diligent polishing, and well-crafted tables littered the room displaying goods of all varieties: armor, weapons, backpacks, and satchels. Lining the walls were bookcases filled with old, leather-bound tomes and shelves packed with crafting ingredients of one sort or another. Sam thought he felt his jaw hit the floor, and he checked his health bar, expecting to have taken damage.

At the back of the well-appointed shop was a sales counter, behind which stood a too-thin man in a tweed suit. He looked like a Victorian-era nobleman, what with his pencil-thin mustache and the air of smug satisfaction that hung around him like a velvet cloak.

"Lord *Laustsen*," the man practically beamed while folding his hands on the counter. "It's so good to see you, young sir. You've brought a little friend along this time. Lovely!"

Frosty blue eyes as sharp, cold, and calculating as a hawk surveyed Sam. "How *very* lovely, indeed. Is there anything I can help the two young masters with today?"

"We're preparing to do a little adventuring, Mister Nicolas, but for the moment, I think we'll just look around. Assuming, you don't mind?"

"Of *course* not, Lord Laustsen," the man replied as slick and greasy as an oil spill.

"Your household has always been one of our greatest supporters. I'll be in the back. Just let out a little ring," he tapped on a small brass bell sitting on the counter, "and I'll be right out to assist with whatever you might need."

With that, Mister Nicolas of Nick's Knacks gave his tweed coat a tug, then promptly disappeared through a bat-winged door. Sam was fairly certain that connected to a storage room behind the counter; either way, just like that... they were alone.

"Isn't he worried about *thieves*?" Sam dropped his voice to a low whisper.

"Hardly," Finn planted a hand on Sam's shoulder and guided him over to a table piled high with robes and various scholarly garments. "This place is... special. It really *is* a second-hand store, but one for the Noble houses. The finances of Noble houses, you see, are a tricky thing. Specifically, they're a topic that isn't discussed in polite society, but just like all people, Noble houses *occasionally* fall on hard times and have to sell off valuable items for a variety of reasons. As a Noble, you can't very well just walk into a high-end store over in the North Waterside and sell off priceless family heirlooms. Not unless you want to set every tongue in the Kingdom waggling."

Finn fell quiet, examining a set of icy blue robes that seemed to be made out of silk. "To sell such valuable items would be tremendously *tacky* and reflect terribly on the house in question. We *buy* lavishly. We don't sell, we don't haggle, and we certainly don't pinch coppers. So, Nick's Knacks was opened as another one of those unspoken social niceties so prevalent in high society. This place is in one of the worst parts of town and is warded by powerful illusion magic to keep the wrong sort from finding it. When Nobles need to sell or buy on a budget—and don't want to be seen doing so—they send a servant here to pick up necessary items."

"This is the best the city has to offer and at comparably cut-rate prices. Unfortunately, my household fell on *particularly* hard times after losing the war. Needless to say, we do most of our business here, and *everyone* knows it." Finn gave Sam a sidelong smile though there was hurt hiding just behind his eyes. "Yet one more reason for every other house to loathe our existence. We Laustsens are high born, true, but only in the strictest sense of the word—too rich to slum around with the lower castes, too poor to properly fit in with our peers—but such is life in Ardania. Now, let's raid this place, make out like bandits, and find some real adventure, shall we?"

Finn's words resonated with Sam, and though this gawky, awkward kid was just a simulated bit of code, Sam connected with him deeply. He was happy to have a friend, even if he wasn't exactly... real. Sam couldn't just *say* that, so instead he nodded and dove into the piles of epic gear, rooting around with absolute glee.

The young man hadn't been wrong about this place; it had just about everything. A lot of it still seemed overpriced to Sam, but he could afford to spend more than the average player, and Finn assured him he wasn't likely to find better prices anywhere else in town. At least not on gear of this quality. They spent the next half hour outfitting themselves for whatever perils might await them in the wide and wild world outside the city gates.

Sam picked up a pair of standard leather boots edged with silver that offered a benefit to constitution, movement speed, and the acrobatics skill; though it also dropped his luck by two points, which was an unfortunate trade-off.

Boots of the City Slicker. These fanciful boots are a custom item, crafted by a minor Noble who fancied himself an adventurer even though he'd never stepped foot into the wilds of

Eternium. Needless to say, he died a horrible and painful death the very first time he ventured out into the great unknown. Be wiser than he was! +2 Constitution, +2% movement speed, damage from falling has been reduced 2%, -2 Luck.

Sam also sold his old Neophyte robes for forty silvers then upgraded to an outfit crafted from light cloth and leather called the *Arcana's Finery*. He regarded himself in a full-length mirror near the clothing tables, noting that he now looked a sixteen-century cosplayer spoiling for a fight. Like one of the three musketeers, maybe, though he was missing their signature, wide-brimmed cavalier hat.

Everything else was perfect—fancy pants, form-fitting vest, an ornate outer jacket that resembled a trench coat, though with a high, stiff collar. The odd outfit came with a plus one charisma bonus and lowered prices on items by five percent, which Sam knew could add up to some serious money over time. It also looked as sharp as a dagger's edge, and the overall armor rating was excellent. Best of all, he wasn't wearing robes, could move normally again, and the 'armor' didn't inhibit any of his spell-casting abilities.

Win-win-win as far as Sam was concerned. He did spend some time glancing at an assortment of backpacks but finally decided on a spatial container called the *Unending Flask of the Drunkard*. On the surface, it was just a worn silver flask, except this thing would allow the owner of the flask to store either a virtually unlimited amount of wine or an extra two hundred pounds worth of goods and items.

According to Finn, spatial trinkets such as the flask were *technically* restricted, since smugglers had once used them to import copious quantities of drugs into the Noble districts... but there was one set of rules for the vast majority of the Ardania citizenry and *another* set of rules entirely for people who know about Nick's Knacks. Pay to play at its ugliest, but in this case, he didn't mind being on the winning end. Sam needed the container, and refusing to buy wasn't going to fix the problem anytime soon. He also picked up an enchanted dagger that could be used by spellcasters. It came with some nice bonuses for those embarking on the path of the arcane.

Dagger of the Mystic Path. So, you've decided to become a spellcaster, eh? Well, good for you, but it's always nice to have a little backup when you run out of magic to sling around all willy-nilly. Never forget that a bit of metal with a pointy end can be just as deadly as a flying Ice Spike in the right hands. +1 strength, +1 to any Bladed Weapons skill (Sword, dagger, saber, ect.) (Locked). Can be used in off-hand.

After some strenuous haggling with the shopkeeper, Sam walked away loaded down and ready to get to killin'. He also walked away forty gold lighter, though after paying for all his classes at the Mage's College, that felt like a steal. He tried not to think of how much actual money he had thrown away to get everything and started to sweat. No, come on, it was time for fun!

All that was left to do was party up and kick some *serious* butt.

CHAPTER FOURTEEN

After leaving Nick's Knacks in the dust, Sam and Finn found themselves shouldering their way into a dimly lit inn on the outskirts of the city, not far from the perimeter gate which let out onto the rolling field lands. The inn itself was a three-story ramshackle of a building; the floorboards were creaky, the tables rough-hewn wood, and the patrons just as gruff and dirty as the rest of the interior. Servers wearing linen shirts and green, woolen garments circulated around the floor, delivering platters of steaming food or steins full of amber beer. Sam's eyes followed the food and drink hungrily, to the point that he needed to remind himself why he was here.

On a raised stage was a broad-shouldered bard—sporting a *kilt* of all things—belting out an overly loud rendition of what *could* have been 'Danny Boy' on what Sam guessed was a set of make-shift bagpipes. *There* was definitely something you didn't see every day. But the bar-goers were enjoying the tunes, eating, talking, joking good-naturedly over their steaming plates. A handful of customers even swayed happily on a cleared space in front of the stage.

Despite the grime and the sickly-sweet aroma of unwashed bodies and dried blood, the atmosphere was friendly. Inviting. On the surface, the Mage's College was classier, cleaner, more refined, but this place had one thing the College didn't—and this place had it in *spades*—fun.

Most of the folks in this tavern were players, and as Sam surveyed their faces, he could tell every single one of them was glad to be here. They were *happy* with their gaming experience. Suddenly, he was rethinking *all* of his Eternium choices. As a former gamer, Sam assumed that having a more powerful class would make gameplay more interesting and therefore more fun in the long run, but... but maybe he'd been *wrong*. If he were honest with himself, he hadn't had as much fun in this game as these people were clearly having. Not *ever*. Had he really chosen so poorly?

He didn't know, but he was here *now,* and he intended to soak up as much of the atmosphere as he could. Sam leaned over and spoke into Finn's ear to be heard over the crowd, "Come on, dude. This looks absolutely amazing. How about a drink before we party up?"

"You read my mind! That's a *totally* illegal spell!" Finn replied with an easy, lopsided grin, even he looked more alive than Sam had ever seen him on the College campus.

Sam lead the way, weaving through the patrons, narrowly avoiding servers, customers, and drunken dancers. He felt like a wrecking ball as he moved through the tight quarters. His dexterity score didn't help things much, and his ungodly low perception was almost entirely responsible for what happened next. Sam swerved to avoid a server holding a wooden tray piled high with dirty dishes, missing her by inches... only to plow face-first into another woman, this one with a shock of red hair and a round of full mugs clasped in her hands. Her light green eyes flared wide, lips pulling back from perfectly straight teeth as she and Sam collided.

Hitting her was like careening into a brick wall. She was all hard steel and tight muscle, without an ounce of give in her body. Sam bounced back, his health dropping by a few points from the collision. She didn't seem hurt in the least, but the four mugs she was carrying didn't handle the impact quite so well. Beer exploded like a geyser of gold, drenching Sam and spraying her directly in the face. She, at least, had the wherewithal to hang onto the mugs so they didn't shatter on the floor.

Sam reeled, arms pinwheeling to keep his balance, his face almost as red as the woman's hair. He thought he might die from sheer embarrassment. Finn leaned in from behind and steadied him with one hand, clearly struggling to maintain his composure. "Smooth move, my friend. Slick as ice. This is *exactly* the way I expected things to go."

"Oh, I am *so* sorry!" Sam blurted out once he finally got his balance. "I was trying to avoid someone else, and... I didn't even see you there."

He looked around frantically, trying to find some napkins to help clean the mess up, but *of course,* there were no napkins. This was a fantasy world, not a burger joint back in Anaheim. That made him want to die even more. Thankfully, the woman didn't look furious. She actually grinned and just shook her head before depositing the now empty mugs on a nearby table.

"It's okay." She pulled a tan handkerchief from a pouch at her belt, quickly mopping the suds from her face and hands. "It could've happened to anyone. Really. How about you just buy another round of drinks for me and my friends to make up for it?"

Sam froze as he listened to her. That *voice.* He *knew* that voice! He'd never met this person in real life, but he'd heard her run a hundred guild raids and talk to him through a thousand hours of gameplay. Sam stood stock still, mouth open, studying her. She was a few inches shorter than him but looked twice as wide, thanks to the heavy, silver plate mail weighing down her frame. She wore a ragged cloak of scarlet, a dagger riding on one hip, a massive maul on the other, and had an enormous shield attached to her back. With the shield, she looked a bit like a medieval version of a Ninja Turtle.

This woman had to be a Barbarian class or maybe even some sort of Paladin; assuming this game had a Paladin equivalent. That fit what he knew. This *had* to be her.

"Hello?" She snapped her fingers in his face. "You okay? Did I lose you? Laggy set-up maybe? That or getting hit must've knocked something loose in your head."

Sam felt at a complete loss for words, so instead of actually answering her questions like a normal human being, he blurted out the only thing on his mind. "Rachel? Rachel Poulson? Is... is that you?"

"Yes." This time, it was her turn to stand stock still and thunderstruck. She finally answered after a long, *tense* beat, one hand dropping down to the hilt of her dagger. "How did you know that? Who are you?"

Her eyes narrowed in suspicion, and her previously friendly demeanor vanished, replaced by a snarl and the cold look of warning.

"It's me," Sam ignored all the blatant 'back off' signs, "Sam King! I mean, I know it's been a while, but it hasn't been *that* long. You ran the Bannergarde Guild in Masterwind Chronicles and were the squad leader for the Shivercrawlers in Celestial Conquest Online! We must've played a *gajillion* times online together."

The snarl turned into a grimace before slowly disappearing, though she still looked skeptical. As though testing the words, she finally asked, "Sam King from Anaheim?"

"Yeah. I used to run under the gamertag BadKraken. Decided to go with something closer to my real name this time around, since my parents got me a DIVE pod and I'll be in-game full time for the next three months."

She grabbed his arm—her fingers felt like steel bands digging into his flesh—and pulled him close. She glanced furtively around, looking for anyone who might've heard him. When it was clear no one had heard—or at least didn't care—she let out a ragged sigh and eased up a bit on his arm. "I'd keep that pod stuff to yourself, if I were you," she hissed.

"These are early days, but there are already some bad apples roaming around Eternium. Groups of PKers that specifically go out of their way to target divers. That's not the only thing; don't go throwing *real* names around in here, okay? I know you didn't mean anything by it, but seriously, there are some people I don't want knowing who I am. My gamertag's the same as it always was, DizzySparrow, but I'm just going by Dizzy for now. Trying to stay on the down-low."

She hesitated like she wanted to say more but then clammed up at the last second. Finn slid up next to Sam. The Noble was blushing furiously, an overwide smile on his pinched face. "Well, are you going to introduce me to your... acquaintance?"

"I'm Finn of the House Laustsen. Sam and I are in the same cohort over at the Mage's College," he crowed proudly, puffing out his chest like a preening peacock.

"No way. You're both Mages?" Dizzy's eyes flared. She glanced around again, this time like a greedy thief who'd just spotted an epic pile of loot. "Like legit Mages who can do *magic*?"

She whispered the last word. In response, Finn lifted a hand and effortlessly conjured a globe of slowly spinning ice which hung suspended above his palm.

"I'm an Ice Guard, and Sam here is an Aeolus Sorcerer—basically a Wind Mage, though it's a little more complicated than that. Pretty *cool*, right?"

She smiled and slung an arm around both of them. "Know what? Forget about getting us drinks. The next round is on me and my friends, who, by the way, I would *love* to introduce you guys to."

Before they could protest—not that Sam wanted to protest exactly; he'd come to find a party after all—she ushered them through the press of bodies and over to a rectangular table where three other players waited—two men and another woman. Based on gear, Sam guessed they were probably new to the game. Rachel, that is, *Dizzy,* definitely looked like the ranking member of the party, which was pretty standard. She was a natural leader, so much so that she always ended up taking charge in every guild or squad Sam had ever been in. She was a great all-purpose player, but she also understood meta strategy and kept a cool head even when things got heated and tense.

She pushed both Sam and Finn into a pair of empty stools, then plopped down on one of her own. She shot a look at a brown-haired man in shoddy leathers with a recurve-bow strapped to his back. "Arrow, go get us all a round of drinks, would ya? Make sure to get enough for our new friends, too."

"But *Dizzy*—" he began to protest.

She cut him short with a glower that plainly said, 'Now is not the time or place. *Go* get the *drinks.'* Sam wondered if that was some sort of intimidation technique. If so, he wanted it. Arrow cleared his throat and stood, rubbing at the back of his neck. "*Sure.* I'll be right back. You fellas drinking anything special?"

Sam just shrugged and shook his head.

"Yes, I'll take the finest Flower Brandy they have available, or barring that, I'll deign to take whatever the house brew is, I suppose." Finn offered with a white-toothed smile. His words earned him a rather long set of stares from everyone present, but Finn didn't seem to notice.

"So, Sam, your friend was saying you two are both Mages with the College," Dizzy jumped in before things could get awkward. "We haven't run into anyone else from the College yet. I've heard rumors there are a few priests running around, but you're the first actual magic users I've seen. What's it like? How did you manage to unlock a Mage class? Do you have some other primary class?"

She rattled the questions off like machine-gun fire, *boom-boom-boom*. Sam wasn't even sure where to begin. "Well, I don't think Finn unlocked the class."

He continued slowly, not sure how to explain Finn, "He's from *here*. He's from one of the Ardania Noble houses. As for me, I underwent the trials during the early game phase, and it was just one of the options available for me. I honestly didn't know it would be so rare when I picked it."

Sam shrugged apologetically. "Honestly, though, it hasn't been as much fun as I thought it would be. I've been here in Eternium for six days so far, and I've spent virtually the whole time at the College doing chores, running errands, and going to classes on magical theory and application. Not exactly the exciting summer vacation I had in mind."

"Well, *all* of that is about to change," Dizzy promised him, she waved confidently at the assembled members. "Now that you found us, that is. There aren't really any player clans or guilds yet, but we're working to establish one. It's kind of the Wild West out here right now. Everyone's fresh, fully noobs, and no one knows what to do. On top of that, the wikis are useless at this point. No one's gotten very far, and we're not even sure what the requirements *are* to form a guild. But with *you two* in our squad, we'd stand a real chance of pulling ahead once that info *does* come out."

She leaned in on her elbows and dropped her voice, glancing furtively to the left and right. "I'm telling you, Sam, there are like *no* magic users out there. What if that's one of the requirements for forming a Guild? I mean, I'm not saying it *is*, but it *could* be, right? Even if it's not, having a squad with two verified Mages can only help us. We'll draw attention, be able to grind higher level mobs, recruit better players, and complete missions no one else can, which will only grow our renown. If you come on board with us, I'll make you both officers, give you a huge cut of the loot... whatever you want."

The brown-haired Ranger, Arrow, returned with a round of drinks balanced impossibly high on his hands. The guy had six tankards all stacked up like a house of cards, but they didn't so much as *wobble* when the man moved. As a Ranger—or whatever the Eternium equivalent was—he probably had a ridiculously high dexterity stat, and it showed. Sam tried to hold back the jealousy. With a smile, Arrow quickly distributed drinks to everyone. The distraction gave Sam a moment to mull over Dizzy's proposition, and he kicked her words around inside his skull.

Sam couldn't speak for Finn—though he *strongly* suspected the Noble would go with whatever course of action Sam decided on—but he was pretty keen on the idea. Sam liked Dizzy. He'd worked with her on more occasions than he could remember. He trusted her to do right by him and to put a good squad together, a squad that had a chance of being a serious contender in late-game play. To join up this early? It was an *amazing* opportunity. Plus, he wanted to quest, and this would give him the perfect chance to accomplish what he'd come into the game to do.

He picked up his tankard, swirled the amber liquid, and finally took a long pull of honeyed beer. "Finn will have to make up his own mind, but I think I'd be interested. Being an officer is a definite bonus, but I don't need a bigger cut of the loot than anyone else. I want things to be equal; otherwise, everyone else will just end up resenting me. But there are a couple of things. One, the Mage's College is demanding, and I think it will continue to be that way for a while yet. That means I'll have to work you guys in *around* my course load and responsibilities with the College. Two, I need experience. Right now, I only get one day a week off for myself, so I need to make it count."

"Not a problem at all." Dizzy rubbed her hands together. "Those both seem like perfectly responsible requests. What about you. It's Finn, right?"

"Yes. Finn." The Noble bobbed his head rather energetically. "As to your most *gracious* offer, if Sam vouches for you, I'll throw my lot in with you as well. If you can grant me a deal with the same benefits, then I see no reason not to join our collective might together. I *highly* doubt any of my fellow Nobles will be likely to join such a group any time soon, so there are a number of potential upsides for my house. Perhaps I might even be able to help grease the wheels, so to speak, in your quest to form a Guild. My connections to the court might well be enough to open the right doors."

Dizzy and the others shared a quick look. "Would you guys mind just giving us a minute alone to make sure everyone is cool with this? As a team, it's important for us to make decisions together."

"Absolutely." Sam was glad to hear that. It meant if they did accept, Dizzy wouldn't steamroll over his opinion or thoughts. Sam got to his feet, wobbling a little bit from his drink. That was his low constitution at work, no doubt. Thankfully, he'd only had a few sips. He'd have to remember how easy it was to get tipsy in the future. Good to know that Mages and alcohol didn't mix. He tapped Finn on the shoulder and jerked his head toward the exit. "We'll be waiting outside."

"Well, that went particularly well. Don't you think?" Finn beamed, quite pleased with himself, and he rocked back and forth on his heels as they stepped out into the crisp morning air. "I must confess I've never actually gone out with a *common* raiding party, but this sounds positively brilliant."

He paused and stole a sidelong glance at Sam. "What... *exactly* is the story behind the knight, Dizzy? She is quite..."

Finn faltered, clearly struggling for the right word. "*Interesting*. So confident and *bold*. Quite straight forward and unpretentious. It's rather... *refreshing*, really. So unlike the Nobles of the court, scheming your downfall and ruination all while hiding it behind crocodile smiles. The unrepentant beauty she holds does not hurt my interest either."

"Dizzy and I go back a long time," Sam replied with half his mind on other things. "We've worked together before, and she's good people. Not sure about the rest of her crew, but if she trusts them, I'd say they're probably a solid bunch."

The wooden door squeaked open on rusty hinges, spilling Dizzy and her teammates out on to the cobblestone street. She had a grin as wide as the Grand Canyon on her face and a twinkle in her eyes.

"Alright," she spoke with a nod. "You're both in. We'll have to wait to officially found a Guild before I can draft up a contract for you two, but you have my word. Once we get this thing rolling, you'll both be officers and *founders* with a full share of whatever loot we take. But all of that can wait; you guys said you wanted to grind some experience, so let's go get you some experience. It's time to power level."

Sam bumped knuckles with Finn. "*Sweet.*"

CHAPTER FIFTEEN

The newly-formed party was heading through the eastern gates—enormous things, easily large enough to accommodate a swarm of T-rexes—when they found their way barred by a group of swaggering, armor-clad adventurers. The second Sam laid eyes on their leader, he knew this guy was trouble. He decided it would be best to avoid him if at all possible.

There was something about the way he stood—shoulders back, a contemptuous sneer gracing his lips, eyes squinted, one hand resting on the hilt of a sword at his hip. This guy wasn't an ostentatious overblown jerk like Octavius or even Barron Calloway... no. Something worse by far. This guy gave off the vibe of a sociopath, the kind of person who liked to pull off spider legs for the sheer pleasure. Even worse, he was walking toward them.

"*Dizzy.*" The obvious sociopath leaned over and spit onto the street while his team fanned out around him in a semi-circle. "You give any thought to my *offer?* Time's running out, but there's still room for you and your... *playmates* in the Hardcores."

"Not a chance, *Headshot.*" Her voice was dripping venom. Dizzy rolled her eyes and dropped a hand to her massive maul, mirroring the man's posture. "Especially not after that crap you pulled a few days ago. I'm *done* with you. Let me say this clearly enough that someone with even a walnut-sized brain like you can understand. *You. Are. Toxic.* Anyone with even a *shred* of common sense will stay as far away from you as they can get."

"I always love it when you talk pretty to me." Headshot's gaze was bouncing to each member of Dizzy's party in turn. It came to rest on Sam and Finn. "Ooh, *fancy* boys! What do we have here, huh? Robes, staff, potions. Why, if I didn't know any better, Dizz, I'd think you'd found a couple *magic* users and were holding out on me."

Dizzy repositioned herself in front of the man and extended an arm, planting her palm on his chest so he couldn't take another step forward. "I'm not holding out on you because I don't owe you *anything. Anything.* You stay away from them, Headshot, and you stay away from my guys, or I'll make it my personal mission to burn *you* and everything *around* you to the ground. You hear me?"

"Oh, I *hear* you, but how's about you open up those pretty little ears of yours for a second. You'll regret this." His voice was as sharp and as cutting as a live blade. Sam's mouth was dry. How did someone get that freaky in just a few days? It had to be a skill, intimidation, maybe? Sounded right.

"Yeah, good luck with that." Her lips were pulled back in a snarling grin. "You'll *never* be strong enough to take me out if you keep losing experience from player killing. Now, if you're done, how about you stop harassing *real* gamers and get lost, loser. You and your whole brain-dead crew. Who should *all* abandon you before you do something too stupid and get caught in your mess."

Before Headshot could reply, she moved, shoulder checking him and subsequently punching a hole right through their ranks. Sam followed behind her, offering the big talker a frosty stare of his own.

"Should we be worried about him?" Sam quietly asked once they were finally clear of the gates, leaving Headshot and the rest of the Hardcores behind.

"Guy's a total punk," she scoffed, the epitome of confidence. "Don't sweat him or the Hardcores. They talk a mean game, but they can only really target the newest of newbs. The only thing you have to worry about is staying alive long enough to take out all the mobs we're about to pull for you guys."

Avoiding bad company is the key to long term success, everyone knows that! Well, except all the people who constantly get it wrong. Not you, though! Even with your abysmal perception, you know a truly bad apple when you see it. Good work! Wisdom +1, Perception +1. Seriously, though, those guys are the worst!

"Wow. The *game* is rewarding me for staying away from them." Sam told his group. The glares turned onto him for a long moment, before snapping back to Dizzy.

"Alright, everyone," Dizzy boomed, projecting her voice so the whole crew could hear her. "Now, I know your blood is hot right now, but don't let those guys get into your heads. We can't afford to play sloppy. Instead, use that anger to be absolute murder-machines out there! Today is all about our two new teammates. We're gonna pull mobs and push them to level like no one's ever leveled!"

"To that end," Dizzy continued her speech, "I think it's best if we split up for the time being. Bigger parties mean fewer challenging encounters, which means less overall experience. So, we'll chop it down the center. Me and Arrow," she nodded to the gangly Ranger who'd gotten them drinks earlier, "will take Finn due east, bypassing rabbit territory and making for the fox zone. Since Finn is a native and can't respawn like the rest of us, we'll be playing it safe and conservatively."

Finn looked pleased as punch that he'd been paired with Dizzy.

"Sam, Finn, this is Cobra_Kai_Guy." She waved a hand at a stocky man with flowing hair tied up in a top-knot, beef-slab arms, and a heavy linen garment that looked like a judogi, though one without sleeves. "Everyone just calls him Kai or Guy. Sam, for the time being, he's gonna be your group's squad leader. Kai, I want you and Sphinx to take Sam out to the northwest. Rumor in the bar is that there's a Direwolf or maybe even a pack of Wolfmen lurking around that area.

"Intel isn't close to accurate since all we have is gossip, but the high number of player deaths over that way tells me there's something going on. Since Sam is looking to grind and grind fast, your crew can play things a little closer to the edge. Take some risks. True, you might all get wiped out, but the chances of pulling down big experience are *way~y~y* better if you're all willing to roll the dice a little. He's still low level, so I say it's worth the gamble. Anyone have any questions or comments about that?"

Nothing but crickets in reply. Everyone knew to hold their tongues when it came to grinding hard. "Good. Then let's get out there and make it happen. Remember, everyone! Play smart. Play your roles. We don't need heroes; we have *plans*, and good plans are better than heroes any day of the week. Stick to it, and we'll rendezvous inside the gates before dark."

She paused and look at each of them in turn. "This last bit is important. If, for some reason you get separated, you get back here. Make *sure* you get back before dark."

"What happens at dark?" Sam felt naive, but it was better to ask than to get in trouble.

"They close the gates, which is the next best thing to a guaranteed death sentence. So far, not a single soul that's been trapped outside the gates after dark has survived." Plan made, the two teams split. Dizzy, Finn, and Arrow taking off in one direction, while Sam and his two new teammates started trekking in another, cutting through the tall grasses and low-clinging scrub brush outside the city walls.

Game trails covered the area, which made finding the mobs closest to the city walls ridiculously easy.

"Bro, we've *totally* got incoming," Kai called, his light voice mellow like some of the SoCal surfer kids Sam had gone to Berkeley with. Up ahead, Sam caught his first glimpse of the Mobs that called this little chunk of land home. Bunnies. Although, to be fair, these weren't precisely your average, run-of-the-mill rabbits. They were the size of large bobcats, and each had a small, blunt horn protruding from their skulls. They were also quick, territorial, and *mean* little things.

"Sam. See that little hill?" Kai waved toward a small rise, positioned at the end of a grassy valley. "Just post up there, and I'll funnel these little dudes your way. Hopefully, they'll come at you one at a time. Sphinx, there's another burrow about thirty feet up, go pull 'em back this way."

Sam followed instructions as the surfer-turned-Monk slipped among the small swarm of incoming bunnies, moving like a serpent as he evaded bashing techniques and narrowly avoided chomping, square teeth. It almost looked like he was performing some sort of complicated, pre-rehearsed kata. Twirling, ducking, diving, moving from one stance to another, many of the stances Sam recognized on sight from long nights in his dojo. Back Stance. Cat Stance. Half Moon Stance. Open Leg Stance. There were about twenty other stances that Sam couldn't even *begin* to guess at.

Despite the absurd number of bunnies closing in around Kai, he never took a hit and never delivered one either. Definitely a Monk class. Kai continued to dance and weave, drawing the vicious rabbits into the narrow valley between the two hills, luring them closer and closer... ten feet out, then nine, eight.

Finally, when he was just a few mere feet from Sam, the Monk leaped into the air, flipping and twirling as he sailed *over* Sam, landing as gently as a kitten on the grass. Which, of course, left Sam open and completely exposed to the horde of furry death. The rabbits faltered for a moment, apparently bewildered and mystified by the Monk's sudden disappearance, but they quickly located a new target to focus their furry fury on—the poor little Mage just a handful of feet away. As one, they let out a cacophony of squeaky roars and charged en masse, moving more quickly than the sewer Jellies ever had.

Sam was ready and responded on sheer instinct. He lifted his hands. The voluminous sleeves of his new coat fell away. Sam began pumping his arms, spamming *Wind Blade* like there was no tomorrow. His time down in the sewers had bumped the skill up to *Novice III*, which hadn't increased the damage, though it *had* added a tint of blue light to each attack. As a result, a flurry of blue slashes filled the air, chewing through the rabbits with pitiful ease. The first blow landed straight on and cut the lead rabbit clean in two, while his next sheared off a bunny leg, crippling the creature before a third finished the task for good.

The fearless rabbits kept right on coming, leaping over their downed brethren in a mad scramble to exact vengeance. The problem for them was that the valley forced them to come at Sam in a single file line. It was a perfect chokepoint of sorts, which turned the depression into a killing field. Obliterating the whole lot of them was the work of seconds and felt almost... *unfair.* Seriously, it was like shooting fish in a barrel—or in this case, rabbits in a funnel. Thanks to the almost *absurd* amount of Mana he could bring to bear and the relatively low cost of his

Wind Blade spell, it didn't even sap all that much of Sam's Mana pool.

But before he could get settled, Sphinx materialized out of thin air, her legs a virtual blur as she sprinted toward him, shooting up trails of dirt in her wake. Following behind her was another fifteen or twenty rabbits, though the precise number was hard to count. "*Ope*, get ready, sweetheart! This little group of misters is *very* angry. Oopsie!"

This was the first time Sam had heard the mysterious-looking Sphinx speak, and he was completely blindsided by what he heard. She sounded like a Wisconsin native! Who in the world were these people, and *where* had Dizzy recruited them from?

Sam shook his head—there would be time to answer questions like that later. For now, he was in bunny slayer mode. He planted his feet wide, took a few deep breaths, and unleashed the next round of Wind Blades. The spell took one and a half seconds to cast, a tiny bit more when he was casting it with each hand, but currently did nine damage on hit. As far as he could tell, that was nearly triple the health these things had. If the Wind Blade wasn't stopped by something, it continued for the entire ten-meter range.

This translated into *slaughtering* the incoming wave of bunnies, who followed the exact same route as the previous group, despite the fact that the way was littered with bodies and bunny gore. This group of rabbits, though far more numerous than the last, didn't fare any better. Sam cut them down like a farmer taking a sharpened scythe to a grain harvest. Once the last long-eared head toppled from furry shoulders, Sam just stopped and stared at the corpses. "Yikes. I guess I needed to have *sharp* words with them, but still. It was *knife* to know them. *Shanks* for your time."

Wow. This whole time he'd been thinking his training at the College was worthless, but if this encounter was any indication, then he'd been woefully wrong. He was *awesome!* So was magic! Really a *cut* above the rest!

Angry Horned Rabbit x23 defeated. Bonus: Unassisted Victory, Flawless Victory. Exp: 138 (4xp * 23 rabbits * 1.5 for Bonus Content). For fighting smarter not harder, Wisdom +1.

Skill increase: Wind Blade (Novice VI). Killing makes you better at killing again. Yay you!

Title unlocked: Bunny Reaper. When this title is actively displayed, you strike fear into the hearts of Rabbits, making them take 11% bonus damage! Good job striking terror into rabbits. You must be really proud of yourself.

Bunny Reaper! Oh, heck yeah, that was a *way* better title than *High Five, I Tried!* Plus, his previous titles would still work even when not actively equipped, while this new one required him to display it for the bonus. That was a no-brainer considering the circumstances. He quickly pulled up his character sheet and swapped titles with a thought. A glance at his Wind Blade spell made him pause. The damage had jumped to eighteen per hit, but the cost had also jumped to twenty-four per cast after spell efficiency reduced the Mana cost. He could only send off twelve or so blades at a *maximum* now!

"Whoa. Dang, dude," Kai the Monk guy slapped him roughly on his shoulder. The friendly gesture sapped Sam's health by five points, doing more damage than the entire group of rabbits had. The Monk hardly even seemed to notice. "Cool attacks, but you really need to work on your kill-quips."

"They died from natural causes. A blade of wind cutting them apart would *naturally* kill anyone." Sam got a nod for this attempt at humor.

"That was some seriously impressive grindage, bro. Like, I don't think I've ever seen anyone kill the rabbits like that. No wonder Dizz was so gung-ho to recruit you and your buddy."

"You can say that again, Kai!" Sphinx appeared on Sam's other side. "That was some gosh darn impressive work, buddy! I like my class, but maybe I should rethink it all and go back ta try again! I took the tests too, but maybe I just didn't push far enough to get a class like that."

"Dudette, that's not the way to think about it, ya know?" Kai headed over to the slaughtered bunnies and dropped down onto a knee, pulling a simple stone knife from a thick silken sash wrapped around his midsection. His hands moved with practiced ease as he parted skin and muscle, parceling up the meat and pelts. "Like, if you're always measuring yourself against other players, you're constantly gonna be rerolling. And here's the thing—every class has its own, like, advantages and stuff, ya know? Besides, your class is *totally* cool. Gonna be super powerful in the late game."

"Oh gosh, you really think so?" Sphinx responded, a hint of red creeping into her cheeks.

"Totes, sister. Totes."

"What is your class, if you don't mind me asking?" Sam asked as he watched the pelts practically fall off the rabbits.

"Oh, of course, I don't mind sharing, sweetheart. I'm an *Infiltrator*, which is a sub-class of Rogue with a bent toward killing and sabotage. I've been talking with a few Master Rogues, and apparently, it's the best sub-class for those who will later go on to specialize as Assassins."

"Specialize?" Sam quirked an eyebrow. "I haven't heard that term before."

"Whadda ya mean, ya big goof? You mean to tell me that no one at that fancy College of yours has explained the way specialization works?" She pursed her lips into a thin line and shook her head. "Okay. Let me see if I can explain it for you. Everyone starts off with a base class—some rare, some basic, and just about everything in between, know—but they don't keep their base class forever, now do they?"

"No, no. When a person reaches level ten, they get to specialize, and there are an awful lot of different specializations. Even some *hidden* ones that no one knows about, if ya believe the gossip out there. Having a rare base class almost guarantees you'll get a rare specialization, but even the most common base classes can unlock some gosh darn intriguing playable options under the right set of circumstances."

"As an Infiltrator, chances are I'll end up as some sorta specialized Assassin. If I keep progressing, I'll find a proper class trainer to initiate me into the Assassins, at which point my class will officially turn from Infiltrator to Assassin. From there, I'll keep working, training, completing assignments until I specialize even further—probably end up as a Death Adept, Free Blade, or a Temple Assassin. Going that route will mean I can't pickpocket or steal like a typical Rogue, but I'll be stealthier than a shadow and deadlier than a mama moose protecting her calf."

"You *want* to be an Assassin?" Sam was more than a little shocked. It just didn't seem to fit. Why in the world would this sweet, midwestern mom want to go online and murder people?

"Sure do. It's a nice change of pace, I suppose," she offered Sam a smile and a shrug. "Quite different from what I do normally. I'm a middle school teacher, but since school's out, I thought spending some time in here would do me good. Get back to my gaming roots, dontcha know. At first, I was a little worried about the Assassin path, since this whole game is just so gosh-darn real, but I talked to my therapist about it and she seems to think it'll be cathartic for me. Just sort of purge all the simmering, pent-up rage building inside my chest like a hurricane of blood and fire. Use it up in a game, yah?"

Wow, that had gotten really dark, really quick.

"Okay then. So, where do we go next?" Sam edged a few steps away from Sphinx, eager to change the topic to *literally* anything else.

"Well, bro, if you want the big experience gains, we gotta head into Wolfman territory. No way you're gonna put up big numbers taking out these guys." He nudged the corpse of a bunny with the toe of his canvas shoe. "For now, we'll work our way into fox territory and see how you do against those little, furry dudes. They're tougher than the bun-buns, but I think you'll be okay. After that, the *real* grindage starts."

CHAPTER SIXTEEN

For the next several hours, they murdered their way through rabbit and fox territory while the sun slowly traced an arc through the sky. They finally paused when the blazing orb stood directly overhead like the watchful eye of some great, golden god. Since it was noon, they decided on a quick bite to eat—grilled rabbit meat and bread provided by Sphinx. After all her talk of death, killing, and assassinations, Sam was understandably wary about eating anything she'd touched, but the food ended up being excellent. He was sure the taste was helped by the fact that he didn't immediately die. Strange how that can change how you perceive a meal.

Then, bellies full, they packed up and set off again, heading farther and farther north and west. The landscape hadn't changed much so far, although there were pine trees not far off on the horizon. According to Kai, that was the hallmark of wolf territory. Where there were wolves, there was also a high likelihood of finding Wolf*men.*

"I'm seeing some movement up ahead," Sphinx called in a low tone that carried only to the edge of the group. She raised a closed fist. *Halt.* "Gray fur, and more than one. Definitely wolves, but I don't think we've entered the aggro trigger zone yet."

Sam squinted, brow furrowed, trying to spot whatever she'd seen. To him, everything just looked like a blob of green and brown marring the horizon. She must've had *crazy* good perception to see anything from this distance, but then he supposed that made perfect sense. A would-be Assassin probably needed a healthy dose of perception to blend in seamlessly with a crowd and trail potential marks without attracting notice. Kai just grunted and nodded in agreement, rubbing thoughtfully at his chin.

"Okay, you handled yourself against the bun-buns and the fox-bros," he stole a sidelong glance at Sam, "but these wolves are a different story, my dude. We've squared off against them a few times, and these hombres are serious business. The terrain doesn't favor us here, and the wolves won't come at you one at a time. They fight in a pack. First, they totally surround you, and then they'll harry you from every side—wear you down and bleed you dry one bite at a time."

"So far, you've done well because you've been able to kill at range, but these things have high health. There's no way you'll be able to one or even *two* shot these bad boys, and they're fast enough to get all up in your grill. Which means you're gonna take hits. Do you have any sort of defensive abilities?"

"Mage Armor," Sam replied with a nod. "I have a dagger too, for close combat; though... hopefully, it won't come to that. Never used it before."

"It'll come to that," Sphinx promised with crossed arms, eyes trained on the tree line.

"Probably best if we don't let you solo these guys." Kai nodded as though finally coming to a firm decision. "If they get close, they'll shred your health before we ever have a chance to intervene. That happens, and the AI will *totes* punish you for dying a stupid death."

"So, we'll play it safe." Kai turned in a slow circle, surveying the landscape. "There."

About fifty feet off was craggy boulder jutting up from the swaying sea of grass like a broken tooth. The boulder wasn't large, maybe six feet high and five wide, but it did offer a certain vantage over the battlefield.

"We can make that work for us. Dude," Kai lightly thumped Sam with the back of his hand, "I'm gonna have you post up on top of that thing. You'll be skylined, which will make you the target, but since we're dealing with wolves, we should be able to handle it like a boss."

"I'll tank about eight feet out, and you're just gonna rain down your air slash thingy. Sphinx," Kai shot her a look, "you're gonna pull the fur bros while we set up, but then you'll get over directly in front of the rock. Sam's gonna be laying down *hardcore* suppressive spellfire, so you'll be our mobile defender. I want you moving left and right, playing a wide range so the wolves can't flank us from the sides."

"Okie-dokie, artichokie!" Sphinx nodded in agreement, extracting a gleaming knife from a sheath and spinning it nimble in one hand. "That sounds like a good plan, but there's a good chance this still goes wrong. I'm counting at least four wolves. If we don't play this *just* right, these fellas are gonna chew us up. We sure we want to try this?"

Interestingly, she turned a questioning gaze to Sam, not to Kai. Sam didn't even have to think about it. "Go big or go home, right? I haven't earned enough experience yet to go home, and home is the Mage's College. Bleh. Let's do this."

"My dude." Kai nodded in appreciation, then offered a fist for Sam to bump. The two of them immediately set out for the boulder, slipping through the tall grasses and around the occasional, low-lying scrub bush. Kai got into position in seconds, but scaling the rock proved to be far tougher than it should've been for Sam.

The lip of the boulder was a little higher than his shoulder, but the rock face itself was almost perfectly smooth, so there were no good finger or toe holds to boost himself up with. Although he wasn't much of a sports enthusiast, he and his dad had done some rock-climbing classes on and off throughout his high school years. This should've been *nothing*, but his mediocre strength and remedial constitution increased the difficulty a hundred-fold. He could've just asked Kai for a hand up, but he didn't think his ego could take the blow, so he stuck it out. A rock bit into his hand, and he realized he should probably get his defenses in place.

With a thought, he conjured Mage Armor. A semi-translucent blue barrier shimmered to life around him before vanishing from view, leaving only a faint glow in its wake. He devoted two hundred fifty Mana to his spell, nearly draining himself. Ten percent of the allocated cost wouldn't regen while it was active, but twenty-five Mana locked away to prevent something like a hundred twenty-five physical damage was well worth the cost. He looked forward to increasing the spell rank so that it would have a better conversion.

A wave of fatigue almost made him miss his next handhold, but that cleared up as his Mana started to regenerate. He might not need the protection, but in a fight like this, it was better to be safe than sorry. As his dad often said, *Semper Prepared,* the *real* motto of the field Marine. It took a solid three minutes—which let his Mana regenerate to normal levels—but at long last, he crested the summit of the boulder and even managed to earn a notice for his trouble and persistence.

I'll give you one thing; you don't like to quit. For reaching the top of the highest peak, here's some experience. 100 experience. But maybe next time just try to keep a little dignity? Because, Sam, this is only the highest peak for you.

With a grumble, Sam dismissed the overly judgmental message and prepared himself for the battle, which was already roaring toward him. Sphinx was nowhere to be seen, probably cloaked in stealth, but the gray blurs blazing through the grass like low-flying fur missiles were obvious even with his terrible perception. He counted four quick-moving shapes.

Each one was the size of a small horse; wiry muscle curled and flexed beneath silver pelts; lips pulled away from great fangs custom-built for ripping flesh and tearing muscle. They were crossing ground at an *absurd* rate, and for the first time since leaving the city's fortified walls, Sam was starting to think he'd made a mistake. The bunnies and foxes were one thing, but these creatures were on a different level entirely.

"Get ready, dude!" Kai called as he dropped into a horse stance, one hand extended outward, palm open, the other curled up and ready to block. Fear gnawed at Sam, but he pushed it away—not so much for himself but for Kai and Sphinx. Sam was a killing *machine*, and though they were outnumbered, he could level the playing field with his sorcerous arts but only if he remained as focused as a laser beam.

If he slipped up, even for an instant, the wolves would outmaneuver Sphinx and overwhelm Kai with their sheer numbers, killing the party in one fell swoop. That he wasn't going to *let* happen. Sam hadn't known these two for long, but they were his team; he wasn't going to fail them against their first real opponent.

Sam planted his feet and raised his arms just as the first two wolves arrived. The first, a big male with a scar running down its muzzle, leaped high, jaws snapping as he went for Kai's throat. The Monk blurred with an unnatural speed of his own, sidestepping the lunge and lashing out with a closed fist, his hand thudding into the wolf's throat and knocking the creature to one side.

The second wolf—a smaller female with a lean frame—bolted in low and from the left, tearing into Kai's unprotected side. Teeth sank into vulnerable flesh—or tried to, at least.

Instead, the she-wolf's attack failed to find purchase, as though Kai's skin were covered with hardened steel instead of simple cloth and silk. Not wasting a moment, the Monk struck with a thunderous side kick that hurled the she-wolf back half a dozen feet, clearly sapping a good chunk of the creature's health in the process.

Sam's time to shine had arrived. He started casting Wind Blade, sending deadly arcs of sharpened air at the female still reeling from the Monk's blow. The razor blades of compressed air sliced through fur and skin, leaving deep furrows in the flesh beneath. Unfortunately, Sam's attacks just weren't doing enough damage to take the wolf out of the fight for good. The she-wolf quickly recovered and broke into a series of nimble, evasive maneuvers, bolting left and right with ungodly speed.

Sam tried desperately to follow—hurling wave after wave of magical attacks—but she was too fast, and his dexterity and perception were just too *low* for him to aim with the kind of precision he needed. His spells plowed harmlessly into the dirt and grass, shearing stalks of green and kicking up bursts of brown earth but not yet shedding another drop of blood.

Meanwhile, the big alpha male was circling Kai, playing things a bit more cautiously this time while the two remaining wolves closed in. They'd taken longer to enter the fray, and the reason *why* quickly became apparent; they'd circled out and around to the flanks so they could come in hard from either side.

Sphinx appeared like a puff of sooty smoke, her legs cartwheeling through the air with uncanny grace as she hurled slim, night-black daggers at the incoming wolf on the left. Her blades scored a direct hit, one digging into the creature's chest, the other slicing one of the wolf's triangle-shaped ears clean off. The injured beast faltered and let out a yelp of panicked pain. Sphinx capitalized on the moment of hesitation, closing the distance in an eyeblink and pulling a fighting knife from the sheath on her belt.

That left the other encroaching wolf flanking them from the right. Sam simply couldn't allow that to happen. If the wolf managed to get behind Kai, it could hamstring the Monk, and then it would be game over for the front-line fighter. That, or it would throw itself at Sam, which would be just as devastating—at least to Sam.

He had kept up his barrage of Wind Blades on the rangy female. Though he hadn't hit her again since his first wave of attacks, the onslaught had driven her back, buying him a little breathing room. Not enough breathing room to take the pressure off *completely*, but still... maybe enough to get creative.

Since he could dual cast, it was at least *possible* for him to put pressure on both the lean she-wolf and the incoming canine menace. His accuracy would be garbage, and the chances of actually landing a hit—especially with the increased spell failure rate while Dual casting—were low. That was *fine* with him. Sam didn't need to put both wolves down by himself; all he had to do was lay down enough suppressive firepower to give Kai and Sphinx the time they needed to dispatch the first two wolves. Sam let out a primal yell while he jackhammered his arms back and forth, aiming in the general vicinity of the two wolves.

The encroaching wolf on the right flank wasn't prepared for Sam's fury, and he managed to land a lucky blow across one leg, slowing the furry critter down, though failing to hobble the creature. The she-wolf, however, was as quick as ever, almost effortlessly dodging Sam's attacks as she maneuvered closer and closer to his boulder-turned-perch. She hadn't been able to gain ground before, but then Sam hadn't been dividing his attention before either. She was slowly gaining on him, and there was nothing Sam could do about it except hope that Kai and Sphinx were winning their respective battles.

A sharp *squeal* raked at Sam's ears, the sound like nails on a chalkboard, and he chanced a look toward Sphinx. *Yes!* The Infiltrator had taken down the wolf down, its furry body covered in blood and lying in a heap in the tall grasses. One down, three to go. Sam tore his eyes away from the scene of victory... oh no.

He'd lost track of the she-wolf. He'd taken his eyes off her for two seconds at most, and somehow, she'd exploited his minor slip in focus. The wolf angling in from the right was less than ten feet out. He knew it was a risk, but he brought both hands to bear on the creature, concentrating all of his magical prowess on the single beast. He needed to take it down before she mauled Sam like a rabid... wolf. Right. The consecutive blasts tore through the air. His poorly-aimed wind rent the ground and various landscape features, but thankfully, the wolf took the brunt of the assault.

It was simply too close to avoid the attacks completely, and unlike the lean wolf who'd managed to slip Sam's notice, this creature had yet to experience Sam's full attention. His Wind Blades *devastated* the creature at this range, and after several consecutive hits, the beast toppled, a pool of blood turning the churned earth into crimson mud. A few more puffs of air tore up the corpse before he was certain that it wasn't moving anymore. "*Howl* you guys doing?"

Sam looked away, which is when something hit him from the side like a sack full of furry bricks. His Mage Armor flared to life with a brilliant explosion of blue, absorbing most of the damage, though swiftly running through the Mana that had been used to power it. Sam toppled from the rock, flipping ass over tea kettle, the world spinning in flashes of blue sky and green earth. A lance of pain did a fun, little jig along his ribcage; *abyss*, that had hurt. Then he hit the ground like an asteroid, a dust cloud mushrooming up around him as the air filling his lungs **whooshed** out. He struggled to breathe—every inhale felt like sucking through a wet towel—and his mind frantically worked through what had just happened.

The answer came quickly; the she-wolf had made her play. With a grunt, Sam pushed himself up on to his palms, his head still spinning from the tumble, and immediately spotted the furry adversary. "I'm gonna call you Mozart 'cause you're hanging out in a wolf gang."

Skill increase: Mage Armor (Beginner III). Getting hit makes you better at getting hit without getting hurt!

She was crouched low on her haunches, her hackles raised, her fangs exposed. Something told Sam that the only way she would appreciate his wit was if she was enjoying it as a snack. She was less than four feet away, well within striking distance, but she was waiting... almost as though she were trying to decide if he had any more nasty tricks up his sleeves.

Unfortunately, he didn't. Not really. The Mage Armor had kept him alive and more or less intact, but he'd still lost a solid quarter of his minuscule health pool from the fall. Terrain 'true damage'? Sam's mind buzzed; he had more than enough Mana to dual cast Wind Blade, but at this range, his spell would do next to nothing.

He could hit the she-wolf but probably only *once*. Then she would be on him, tearing into his throat and face. The Mage Armor was a helpful skill, but if there was one thing his *Art of Defensive Magic* Professor had taught him, it was that Mage Armor could *not* stand up to sustained melee damage—not for long, at any rate. It was built to protect the user from the occasional stray arrow, dagger strike to the back, but apparently not a tumble off a large rock. It was not Mystic Plate Mail, capable of keeping someone alive through a full-on animal mauling.

Sam did have his blade though, and if he was going to die... he planned to do it on his feet and swinging with everything he had. Sam snarled—knowing from his Wolfman course that the creature would take it as the threat it was—and regained his feet. He drew the dagger from the sheath at his belt and waved it around. He had no idea how to *use* it, but the wolf didn't know that. Maybe he would be able to bluff his way out of this situation. He dropped into a back stance and raised the knife in his right hand, his left hand out with his palm open.

"Come on, then," he spit, simultaneously launching a Wind Blade with his free hand. The she-wolf charged, taking the spell on the chin like a prizefighter and running even though her face had been gouged by the compressed air. Welp. So much for bluffing.

Sam screamed, striking with the knife, a clumsy blow that wouldn't hurt a wet paper bag. As the short blade cut a path through the air, Sam instinctively channeled Wind Blade through his right arm, directing it *into* the dagger and out through the blade. Sam was completely taken aback as a ghostly blue curve extended from the end of the dagger, turning the simple weapon into a cleaving saber. The trick caught the wolf *completely* off guard, and as a result, the creature *zigged* left when it should've *zagged* right. The conjured blade sunk into the wolf's skull with a meaty **thunk**, a stroke of pure luck rather than any skill. The game confirmed this for him in the next instant.

Luck +1! That was terrible. Wow. You had a six percent chance of pulling that off. Just wow.

Skill increase: Wind Blade (Novice IX). Getting pretty good at this, aren't you?

The wolf's eyes glazed over as the last of her health disappeared in a blink. A raging inferno of golden light exploded all around Sam, gently lifting him into the air, caressing him with golden fingers, obliterating the dirt and blood splattered across his clothing and skin.

It seemed that while he was tumbling and fending off a wolf, the fighting had finished. He only knew this because golden light started flooding out of him. What was...? He gained a *level!* Sam reveled in the moment, basking in the glorious, euphoric feelings, not caring at all about what he had needed to do in order to get to this point. Still, the feeling fled far too quickly. He heard hoots and whoops coming from both Kai and Sphinx, who had apparently joined him after their fight completed. They were currently crowded around him, clearly enjoying the area effect of the leveling up process.

Sam didn't blame them in the least. While his new teammates celebrated the kills and set about looting the corpses— Kai insisted that both the meat and non-ruined pelts would go for a decent price back in town—Sam took a minute to glance at his stats and the new skill he'd unlocked during his final showdown with the deadly she-wolf.

Name: Sam_K 'Bunny Reaper'
Class: Aeolus Sorcerer
Profession: Unlocked
Level: 5 Exp: 10,043 Exp to next level: 4,957
Hit Points: 67/90
Mana: 280/280
Mana regen: 8.1/sec
Stamina: 90/90

Characteristic: Raw score (Modifier)

Strength: 14 (1.14)
Dexterity: 15 (1.15)
Constitution: 14 (1.14)
Intelligence: 28 (1.28)
Wisdom: 27 (1.27)
Charisma: 13 (1.13)
Perception: 9 (0.09)
Luck: 16 (1.16)
Karmic Luck: 2

Level five was kind of the worst in some ways because it was hard-earned but came with no tangible skill point increases for his class. He earned a point of intelligence and wisdom on even levels and his customary four characteristic points every third level. So, a big, fat nothing-burger this time around—though level six was going to be epic since all the points would hit at the same time, giving him a healthy boost to his overall scores. On the plus side, he was that much closer to level six, and now that he was level five, he'd be able to unlock a profession, assuming he ran across one that seemed both appropriate and interesting.

The icing on the cake was the new skill to consider:

Congratulations! By using your skills and arcane arts in some unconventional ways, you've learned a variant of the 'Wind Blade' spell: Aeolus Sword (Novice I). Effect: Channel your Wind Blade spell into a conventional weapon, transforming a simple object such as a dagger into a deadly short sword made of hardened air. Aeolus Sword is treated as a sword and deals $5n + 5x$ damage per hit where 'n' is skill level and 'x' is the Sword Mastery skill. (Wind Aligned magic) Cost $10n$ Mana to cast, $+2n$ per second to maintain.

Skill gained: Sword Mastery (Novice I). You have taken a step on the path of the Sword Master. You can now stick a pointy bit of metal into your opponent, though hopefully, you don't cut yourself in the process! Increases base weapon damage with swords by 1n%, where n = skill level. Dexterity +1!

Happy with his gains, Sam dismissed the notifications and found his team waiting for him. Kai and Sphinx had made short work of the wolf corpses, carefully carving them up with practiced finesse, making sure there was nothing left to go to waste.

"I would love to push on more, my bro," Kai wiped a trace of blood off his face when he saw that Sam was finally back with them, "but that was a close one for sure, and based on how late it is... I think the best thing to do would be to head back."

"Yep, I agree." Sphinx planted her hands on her hips. "This was a darn good first outing, but we got ourselves a late start there. Definitely don't want to miss the curfew and get stuck out here after dark. No, siree Bob. Plus, we'll rack up a little more experience on the way back in."

"Hey, this is my first time out the gate," Sam shrugged at their obvious persuasion attempts, "so I'll take your word for it." His stomach let out a long, low rumble. "Besides, I could go for a bite of something good to celebrate. Let's head back."

CHAPTER SEVENTEEN

The trek back to the city was, for the most part, uneventful. The party walked at a leisurely pace, getting to know each other better with every step. Sphinx hailed from Carson City, Michigan. She was thirty-five, divorced with no kids, despite the fact that she *loved* kids—obvious from her career choice as an educator—and wanted a brood of her own someday, but so far, it just hadn't come together. Although she was older than Sam by a far margin and not at all what Sam expected, she had some serious gamer cred. She'd played all of the greats—Masterwind, World of Alphastorm, Celestial Conquest—and had even dabbled in a few pen and paper offline campaigns.

Kai, by contrast, was only a few years older than Sam and lived in a small studio flat in San Diego. In many ways, his background was similar to Sam—the third son of wealthy financiers and *vulture* capitalists. Heh. Except, he'd done something Sam never would've dreamed of; Kai had bucked the system. He was a high school grad who'd vehemently *refused* to go to college, instead applying to a trade school. He planned on being a welder. He refused to follow the plan, to go with the flow, or head into the family business. Sam didn't regret his choices, though he had a strange mix of envy and pity for the surfer kid who'd had the courage to defy his carefully laid out 'destiny'.

As for how the surfer-turned-welder-turned-Monk ended up inside Eternium—what with its steep price tag—that was an interesting story too. Like Sam, the Monk was pod bound, but his trip into the game wasn't a graduation present; it was a means to help him disappear from the public eye.

His father was preparing to launch a run for political office, and the man thought it would be best if his 'failure of a son' was tucked away in some dusty corner of the internet where reporters couldn't find him—where Kai couldn't 'make a scene' or 'embarrass his family further'. Kai told the story casually, almost nonchalantly, but Sam could sense the hurt lurking just beneath the surface of the Monk's shiny, easy-going façade.

While the three talked, they killed their way through any foxes or rabbits that were unfortunate enough to stumble into their path. After contending against the wolf pack, taking out the uncoordinated groups of animals felt like child's play. Instead of obliterating the critters with his ranged Wind Blade spell, he used his new *Aeolus Sword* spell; calling forth the mystic short sword in a flash of cerulean light. Thanks to his rather low constitution and strength, going toe-to-toe with the furry beasts was *far* more challenging than he expected, but they seemed like perfect targets to practice the basics on.

At first, his sword work was simply awful. He'd never held a real sword before, and he had exactly *zero* idea how to use it effectively. His swings were wild and sloppy, and he missed *far* more often than he landed a blow. Even when he did manage to score a hit, he was as likely to connect with the flat of the conjured blade as its edge.

Sam really had gotten tremendously lucky in his bout against the she-wolf. Maybe having an elevated luck stat only paid off when push came to shove; it was the only thing that made sense. Eventually, Sphinx had mercy on him and took some time to walk him through the essentials of sword fighting one on one.

True, she used daggers, not swords, but she was excellent with a blade and the most important tricks she had to impart had more to do with dynamic movement than anything else. Her lessons were far from extensive—taught casually in between bouts of conversation or mob grinding—but by the time they finished, Sam was feeling a hundred times better off than when he'd set out in the morning.

Sphinx drilled him on the correct way to hold the sword—gripped in the dominant hand, blade edge down—and showed him a variety of stances, combined with some rudimentary footwork exercises he could practice during his downtime. If he ever got downtime. When he practiced now, his feet were shoulder-width apart, hips slightly cocked, his weight evenly distributed on the balls of his feet, allowing him to dart in any direction. He would never overwhelm an opponent with brute force—that wasn't in the cards as a spellcaster—but he could potentially outmaneuver an underprepared enemy if he got his dexterity up high enough.

Once he had stances more or less down, she ran him through a variety of offensive and defensive maneuvers. He wasn't going to win a duel any time in the near future, but he could execute a basic lunge and thrust. He also understood the fundamentals behind a feint, parry, flick, and riposte. Then she—combined with a few helpful tidbits from Kai—taught him about 'combat mindset' before going over the various *non-physical* factors he needed to think on.

For instance, falling into a predictable pattern was an easy habit to form and one that would get you killed sooner or later. How to control the tempo of the fight by using distance. Techniques for maintaining situational awareness even in the heat of battle.

He only earned a handful of skill experience from the impromptu tutorial, but he managed to nudge his *Sword Mastery* up to Novice V—VI when he included his bonus from *Dagger of the Mystic Path*—and he earned another point of dexterity and constitution for his efforts. He was thinking he might just have to make these sessions with Sphinx and Kai a more regular part of his schedule. He didn't want to go the multi-class route, but no one would expect a Mage to have *any* skill in a melee bout. That meant he could potentially catch a foe completely off-guard at some crucial juncture. An edge like that was *well* worth developing.

They were maybe two miles out from the city walls when they spotted the second half of their party, trudging across the grassy plains. Good timing, since the sun was already sinking into the ground, beams of late daylight painting the skyline with brilliant fingers of pink and gold, wispy, purple clouds the color of fresh plums scattered through the sky.

"Imagine running into you hooligans," Finn called as they got closer, waving one hand in the air, his robes flapping and flailing from the motion. "I can't even begin to tell you how *fantastic* today was! Perhaps the single greatest day of my *life*. I pushed up to level six, which is no small feat, let me tell you, and got some *excellent* combat advice from the magnificent Dizzy."

The Mage turned a thousand-watt grin on the armored warrior. "She was simply fantastic. Truly."

Dizzy just shrugged away the compliment, but Sam noticed she also glanced away, a faint trace of red creeping into her cheeks. Despite being gangly and rather awkward, Finn could be charming when he wanted to be. Clearly, he'd turned that charisma on Dizzy.

"You hit level six?" Sam idly thought through his own day. "That can't be right. You're *from* Ardania. *Surely*, you've got to be higher level than that... right?"

Finn grimaced and shook his head. "I can certainly see why you might think so, but you're an outsider. You've come here for adventure and action, but most locals just want to get by. More importantly, you lot respawn should you meet an unfortunate and untimely fate. Not me and my kin. Most of the fine citizens of Ardania pursue commercial jobs that are far less risky. You'll find the majority of higher-level citizens in Ardania tend to be merchants and craftsmen. Venturing out beyond the gates is a death sentence for most people, and the results are rarely worth the effort. There are mercenaries of course—like the warriors who escort us on our sewer missions—but they are actually quite rare.

"Of course, there are the guards to consider, but as a rule of thumb, they avoid venturing out just as much as the rest of us. Mages are an exception to that rule. We can level up in the relative safety of the College and—if your experience today was anything like mine—I'm sure you've seen that our kind can be quite powerful. But I have no formal martial training as a Noble, and since I've only *just* been admitted into the College, my level is still rather low. I think if we can keep doing missions like this, however, that will all change." His smile spread. "Why, even if we can only quest like this once a *week*, I think you and I, Sam, have the potential to be the most powerful Mages in a century."

"That's *if* you survive," came a familiar and *very* unwelcome voice. Headshot.

The PKer and his crew slipped out from behind a copse of oaks and pines not far from the road, their weapons drawn. They'd been waiting to launch an ambush? How long had they just... *sat* there?

Possible scenarios raced through Sam's head in the few seconds of tense silence that followed. They were only half a mile at most from the gate, easily within view of the portcullis and the formidable gates, but there was no way they could make a run for it. Headshot had three archers with him, all of them carrying sleek bows and wearing full quivers bristling with arrows. Even if the archers were complete noobs, they'd pincushion Sam and his friends before they made it more than a hundred feet, and that was assuming they could get past Headshot and his heavy hitters in the first place.

Which they couldn't. At least, not without a fight. Headshot and half a dozen warriors in plate or chainmail were arrayed before them, making sure there would be no easy escape. Sam supposed they could pull a tactical retreat, slowly backing away until they could turn and flee into the wilderness, but that too was a fruitless option. It might work short-term, but the sun would set in half an hour or so, which meant they would survive the Hardcores only to die at the hands of whatever horrors prowled the wilds after dark.

No, if they wanted to get back into the city, there were only two options: *one*, call Headshot's bluff just as Dizzy had done earlier, or *two*, let this turn into a brawl and hope for the best. They were outnumbered nine to six, but Sam *knew* they could take these clowns if things got rough. He and Finn had both leveled up, and with their arcane powers, they could call down some serious devastation.

"What do you want?" Dizzy barked, stepping forward until she was in striking range of Headshot. Headshot pulled out a long, curved sword, the single blade edge catching the light of the fading sun, glimmering with a bloody glow.

"That's *easy*, Dizz." He popped one finger into the air. "One, I want money. Ten gold apiece for me to let *some* of your crew go."

"You want to know who's in the *hospital?*" Sam tried to intimidate the group. No one answered, but all eyes were on him. "*Sick* people! You want to join them?"

Another finger lifted into the air alongside Headshot's first. "Two, I want these Mages with the Hardcores, so either they agree to join, or I gut them where they stand. If we can't have them, then *no one* will. Period."

A third finger got added to the mix. "Three, I'm going to kill *you* on principle because no one disrespects *me*."

He lunged forward, blade flashing out as he tried to drive the tip into Dizzy's belly. She was prepared for the cheap shot, leaping back and turning his strike with her gauntleted forearm. The action narrowly avoided a critical and probably *fatal* hit, but she was too close to draw her heavy maul. Without a weapon in hand, Headshot had a significant advantage. At least, he *had* an advantage until Finn lurched into motion, thrusting his staff forward with a primal war cry, unleashing a wrist-thick javelin of ice that slammed into Headshot's shoulder. The frozen lance of magic punched through Headshot's plate armor like a nail through the side of an aluminum can, spinning the dirty PKer in a circle.

With that, the tenuous truce was broken, and *everyone* lurched into action, a bevy of chaotic and often contradictory commands filling the air. No one had been ready for things to go this way; as a result, no one really seemed to know what in the abyss they were supposed to *do*.

Sam just had to hope that everyone on his side of the equation would play solid fundamentals and stick to their given roles. Instead of jumping into the fray and laying about with his sword, Sam backpedaled, gaining some much-needed distance to work his magic. Arrow, the Ranger, did the same, posting about ten feet away from the battle line as he fired arrows, meticulously targeting the ranged support on the Hardcores' team. Feathered shafts sank into leather armor or found vulnerable flesh. There were too many of the enemy Rangers, so Sam thought it was high time he evened the odds.

Sam had recast Mage Armor when he was fighting rabbits, so he was able to focus his offensive efforts on a slim Ranger clad in lightweight, black brigandine armor studded with brass rivets. Sam thrust his hands forward, loosing a wide Wind Blade. The blue arc of light slammed into the Ranger, cutting through his health with devastating effectiveness. At Novice IX, the spell hit for twenty-seven damage. Sam didn't think that someone who likely put all his points in dexterity and perception would have much more than the base of fifty health, and he decided to test his theory.

The Ranger let out a gurgle, blood bubbling from his mouth as he scurried left, trying to gain some distance and time. After battling the lightning-fast wolves, this guy seemed as slow as frozen molasses. Sam sent another Wind Blade, chopping through the remainder of the Ranger's health in an instant. Theory proven. Without missing a beat, Sam scanned the field, searching for where he was most needed.

Two of the three Rangers were down—one by his hand—and Arrow was currently engaged with the third, strafing the blonde-haired woman with shaft after shaft. Headshot was somehow still alive, but Dizzy was coming at him like an enraged rhino, hammering away with her enormous maul, which she'd finally managed to draw. This was the first time Sam had seen her in action, and *wow,* could she hit. She moved more sluggishly than Kai, Sphinx, or Arrow, but she was an unstoppable juggernaut constantly closing with her enemy. She swung around that maul of hers as though it weighed no more than a plastic wiffleball bat, but when it *did* hit... there was proof positive that it deserved its classification of a *heavy* weapon.

Finn was throwing his metaphysical might against the leader of the Hardcores as well, using freeze spells to sap Headshot's movement rate while also hurling an Ice Lance at every available opportunity.

Meanwhile, Kai had taken up a position on the right, battling two chainmail-clad warriors wielding pitted broadswords. Though he was outnumbered, the Monk flowed between the two opponents like smoke, bobbing, weaving, and ultimately diverting their clumsy attacks. Simultaneously, he was delivering a bombardment of blazing-fast palm strikes that chipped away at their health.

Sphinx, on the other hand, was on the verge of being overwhelmed as three Hardcores closed in around her. They had obviously fought Assassins before and steadily hemmed her in so she couldn't slip into a pool of shadow. Two of the three Hardcores looked to be run-of-the-mill Fighters, but a third was dressed in garb similar to Sphinx—dark, soft leathers, a bandolier of throwing knives running across his chest, a cowl covering the bottom half of his face. Some sort of thief or would-be-Assassin, and he was giving the intrepid Infiltrator a run for her money. She needed help, and she needed it *now.* Unfortunately, their battle was a tangle of limbs, a whirlwind of flashing blades, and twirling bodies.

Sphinx and her trio of assailants were moving so quickly that Sam was just as likely to hit Sphinx as the Hardcores. He wasn't sure whether or not his spells could deal friendly fire, but now was most definitely *not* the time to find out. He could repay her lessons in sword fighting by putting the knowledge she'd taught him to use right now, though he'd have to play it safe considering his stamina would run out quickly. Still, it was his best option. After all, who would expect a glass-cannon *Mage* to charge into battle with a sword?

Silent as a screaming toddler, Sam shot forward, pulling the dagger from his belt and muttering the words to call forth his *Aeolus Sword*. The magical blade extended to full size—cool blue and deadly—moments before he launched himself at the enemy Rogue, who *conveniently* had his back turned to Sam. The ironic justice of backstabbing a thief as a Mage was not lost on Sam. He lunged forward, executing a textbook—though rather simple—thrust. Sometimes the simple things were the most effective because the blade punched into the Rogue's lower back and knocked off sixteen points of health.

Not even *close* to killing the thief, but more than enough damage to get his attention. The Rogue let out a guttural howl and rounded on Sam, a black dagger in each hand. "You are gonna regret that, you little turd."

"Turds are brown, not stained a bloody red like my clothes... unless you are having *other* issues?" Sam taunted the killer. Perhaps not his brightest move.

The Rogue broke away from Sphinx, dancing toward Sam with liquid grace; the guy's obviously high dexterity was on full display. He came at Sam like a constipated cobra, creating a constant combo of coordinated thrusts and slashes. Sam retreated backward, drawing the Rogue away, but it took everything he had to fend off the assault.

Sam was *far* too slow to respond with a proper counter-attack of his own. The Rogue launched into a series of broad, slashing sweeps, then flipped into the air, hurling a pair of throwing knives with his off-hand. Both struck dead on, piercing Sam's Mage Armor. One punched into his right shoulder, while the other penetrated his gut. The pain was worse than anything Sam had ever felt before, and that was with his *miserable* perception stat lowering it.

Back in the sixth grade, Sam had dislocated his shoulder. He could remember the day in exquisite detail; the sun high above him, the hot steel of a half-pipe dropping off below the lip of his skateboard, the *clang* and *clatter* of metal on metal. He'd teetered precariously on the edge of the pipe, his heart thumping as he worked up the nerve to drop in for the first time. This was the small half-pipe, only a six-foot drop, but to sixth grade Sammy, that descent looked *unimaginably* high—like taking a flying leap off the edge of the Grand Canyon. Yet, despite the fear, he leaned forward and plunged straight down.

He began fishtailing almost instantly, dislocating his shoulder in the process. This felt like that, though the pain was somehow more *jagged* and stomach-turning. The *Aeolus Sword* guttered and died as he fumbled the blade, unable to hold on to the hilt through the waves of agony. He stumbled, drunk from shock and trauma, and fell on to his back, his good hand scrambling at the dagger protruding from his belly.

His Mage Armor had saved him from certain death, but his health was down to less than half, and he was hemorrhaging points every second the knives remained planted in his body. With a wheeze and a grimace, he pulled the dagger in his belly free, then went to work at the blade jutting from his shoulder.

That one was stuck more solidly—at a guess, it had probably hit bone—so he had to wiggle it free, which was about a hundred times more painful than getting stabbed in the first place. Finally, the blades were gone, discarded in a patch of grass nearby, but he wasn't out of hot water yet. The Rogue was stalking forward with the lethal movements of a hunting panther, ready to end its prey... though this predator killed with cold iron instead of rending jaws.

"Shoulda joined us when you had the chance, dweeb," the Rogue growled, his voice scratchy and slightly distorted from the interference of a microphone. This guy wasn't in a pod, that much was for certain.

"I'd rather die," Sam spat, his spittle tinged red with blood.

"Good," the Rogue replied, twirling his daggers with a flourish. "Allow me to help y–"

He never finished the sentence. An Ice Lance slammed into the side of his throat, driving all the way through and leaving a ragged hole behind. The Rogue gulped, working his jaws like a fish out of water, then keeled over, gravity taking hold as his legs gave out. Just like that, Sam and company actually had a chance here.

Filled with a new surge of adrenaline, Sam sprang to his feet, bringing his hands to the ready, but... there was no one left to fight, no one left to kill. Every single member of the Hardcores lay dead in the grass, pools of sludgy blood surrounding their corpses like ghastly halos. Somehow, miraculously, they'd done it!

They'd beaten the unlikely odds, and even more impressive, *every single member* of their crew had survived the encounter. They'd just taken on an aggressive ambushing force without taking a single casualty! Glancing around, Sam saw that Finn had done the bulk of the heavy lifting since four out of nine bodies were liberally peppered with blue-white Ice Spikes.

The message was clear—Mages were *not* to be trifled with. The folks at the College might be a bunch of pompous know-it-alls, but there was a reason for their feelings of superiority.

"Get wrecked!" Dizzy hollered, thrusting her maul into the air. She threw back her head and cackled. "You boys are a *game* changer!"

Her mad laughter slowly subsided. "With you two on our team, *no one* is gonna be able to stop us! Let's get into town before they shut the gates and have a little celebration. Drinks are on me!"

CHAPTER EIGHTEEN

They made it back through the gates fifteen minutes before full dark set in. Cutting it close, considering the potential repercussions, but everyone was far too elated to care. The group was high off their gains of the day, and taking out the Hardcores was just the cherry on top of it all. Sure, they didn't *earn* anything for taking out Headshot and his goons—Eternium dissuaded PKers by ensuring they earned no experience and couldn't loot corpses—but they also didn't get in any *trouble*. On top of there being no tangible *benefit* for PKing, the game actively *punished* Pkers by docking experience, reputation, giving you a player-killer aura that let people kill *you* for rewards or collect bounties from the local guards.

Of course, if you killed another player in an act of *self-defense*, there was no negative downside. In this case, there was at least one upside—they got to teach the Hardcores a well-deserved lesson. To celebrate the victory, they made their way to the Square Dog Inn, which was nearly packed to the rafters with adventurers fresh from a long day grinding out experience and killing the local fauna with reckless abandon. By the greenery some were covered in, Sam surmised that there was a significant amount of *flora* destroyed as well.

The bagpipe-playing bard was gone, replaced by a troupe of scantily clad brunette triplets, each playing a different instrument. One sat on a low stool, plucking the many strings of a zither, while another beat out an upbeat tempo on a leather-topped instrument that looked like a mix between a snare drum and a modern tambourine. The racket sounded like... racket. Everyone *else* seemed to like it, so Sam simply sighed and added another reason to get his perception up. As he was grumbling, the third triplet stood front and center, swaying and sashaying across the stage as she crooned a tune that left Sam's cheeks burning red when he took the time to actually *listen* to the lyrics. It seemed this tavern only allowed those who were eighteen and older.

The pub-goers, however, didn't seem upset at the lyrics, just the opposite. They stomped along, waving full flagons of beer while more than a few sang along like a round of ye olde karaoke. Most of the singers couldn't carry a tune if they had a bucket to hold it in, but that didn't matter; everyone in the tavern was having the absolute time of their lives. Splashes of colored lights whisked across a dance floor filled with grooving bodies. Sam glanced up and saw that some enterprising soul had attached bits of colored glass to the massive wrought iron chandelier overhead, turning the whole apparatus into a makeshift disco ball. The sheer ingenuity of humans never ceased to amaze Sam.

"Come on," Dizzy called over her shoulder as she jostled her way into the press of bodies, clearing a path with her physical prowess. They fought their way all the way to the back of the inn, where Dizzy proceeded to order meals and drinks for everyone on the team. Not that Sam had any idea where exactly they were going to sit; abyss, even finding *standing* room was going to be a challenge considering how stuffed this place was. Dizzy leaned forward and exchanged a few quiet words with the bartender. After a few moments, a small leather bag left her palm and found its way into his pocket.

"Follow me," Dizzy called, cupping one hand around her mouth to be heard over the clamor and racket of the room. "I managed to get us a private room in the back for a little extra coin."

Beside the bar was a door, which Sam had just assumed led back into the kitchen. False. The door led into a long hallway with a couple of private rooms off to the left and the right. The spaces weren't huge, but they were recessed into the walls and far more secluded than the seating in the common area. The tables and chairs were also of a much finer quality than what was available for the masses. Instead of creaky wooden floorboards, the private rooms had colorful carpets laid out, candelabras poking out from the walls, and elegant trestle tables made of polished walnut.

Dizzy had just bought them access to the VIP section of the Square Dog Inn. Nice. Sam thought that he could get used to this kind of treatment. Most of the private rooms were already occupied with parties of finely dressed heroes, but the last room on the right was open and waiting for them.

Mugs and dinner were already set out on the table. Sam hadn't seen any servers bustling through, but somehow, they'd managed to get the food and drinks out in the short span of time it had taken the party to walk back here. Now, *that* was service! Or the food had been sitting there for a while... he chose to believe in good service. The party crowded around the table and dropped into padded leather chairs—chairs a *thousand* times more comfortable than the wooden benches in the front. Sam let out an involuntary groan as he settled in; this felt *celestial* to his aching feet and adventure-sore legs.

Then the aroma from the food hit him in the nose, and all thoughts of exhaustion fled as Sam recalled just how hungry he was... and how long it had been since lunch. He hunched forward, forearms resting on the polished tabletop, and inhaled the steam wafting from the wooden bowl in front of him.

Sam picked up a spoon and ladled a bite into his mouth, burning his tongue in the process. In his mind, he circled 'good service' and scratched out 'food had been sitting'; then he turned back to the food. It was a stew with chunks of tender lamb, sliced carrots, and cubes of potato all covered in a thick, brown gravy that tried to sing on his tongue. Rich, salty, with just a little bit of spice to balance out the lamb. The only downside was that after the initial burst of flavor, his perception ensured that all he tasted was the *texture* of the food. At that point, it may as well have been sewer special surprise.

At least he wasn't the only one eating, or he may have just given up. As it was, he was sure he would get some kind of 'quality food' bonus, so he kept going. The table was silent except for the scrape of spoons against bowls and the soft smacking of lips as everyone ate.

About halfway through the meal, a serving girl in a wool outfit brought out several fresh loaves of bread, along with small wooden bowls filled to overflowing with creamy whipped butter. Sam was slogging his way through a second bowl of stew when Dizzy raised her mug and rapped against the side with a silver spoon, the *ting-ting-ting* drawing everyone's attention.

"Everyone who knows me knows that I'm not really one for making big speeches, but after a day like today... I figured someone should say *something*." She shrugged apologetically. "Anyway, I just wanted to say *thank* you all for putting everything you had on the line today. We pushed hard, took some serious risks, and won a battle that we probably shouldn't have walked away from.

"But we *did* because we held our ground, worked together as a team, and trusted each other. I couldn't be prouder. I think with the addition of these two spell-slingers... we are going to be *unstoppable*. I can feel it in my bones. Although we still don't know how to form a proper Guild yet, I think it's high time we come up with a name for ourselves. Folks like the

Hardcores should know who to cuss out after we kick their teeth in." She paused, glancing at each face in turn, her eyes curiously lingering on Finn. "So. Ideas?"

A contemplative silence fell over the gathering like a thick blanket.

"How about the Wolf Pack?" Sphinx offered after enough time had passed for things to move into awkward territory.

"But... the wolves are our *enemies*," Finn politely pointed out, one eyebrow cocked as he swirled his mug.

"That sure is true, ya know," Sphinx bobbed her head in acknowledgment, "but I think that makes it even *better*. It lets everyone know they'd better not cross us unless they want more trouble than you can shake a stick at. Plus, we saw a pack fight today. They almost killed us and probably *would* have under any other circumstances. They worked as a team, and they weren't afraid to protect what was theirs. They weren't gonna let anyone push 'em around, right? It reminded me a lot of us, today, taking out the Hardcores. Those fur boys fought fierce, and they fought smart, but they're still just overgrown dogs. Imagine us, having that coordination, but with the smarts and leadership to back it up."

"Dude," Kai intoned solemnly, as though the single word were some great proclamation. "That's like... super deep or whatever. I totally agree with you. There are a thousand worse examples for a team to, like, model themselves after. You've got my vote, pack sister."

"The Wolf Pack," Dizzy slowly tested how the words felt on the tip of her tongue. "Wolf Pack. Yeah, I like it. Sam, Finn, Arrow? Any thoughts?"

"I, for one, am just happy to be here," Finn deflected with a wide grin. "I'll add that I'm also in favor of the name;

though full disclosure, I'm more than a little bit biased since the crest of House Laustsen is a lunging wolf on a field of gold and black."

"Well, that has to be a sign, right?" Sam added. "For what it's worth, I think it's cool too."

He thrust his hand into the center of the table. "So, can I get a 'Wolf Pack' on three?"

They all piled their hands into the center, one on top of the other—Finn looked utterly lost but added his palm to the pile without comment—then broke after a brief three count, followed by a 'Go~o~o Wolf Pack!'

"Now," Sam stood from the table, "if no one has anything else, there's a party out there! Since this is my only day off for a week, I *fully* intend to take advantage of it! Who's with me?"

Bellies full and alcohol working through their systems, they ambled back out into the common room. Sam was more than a little surprised to see Dizzy grab Finn by the hand and pull him over to the dance floor, a grin on her face and a blush in her checks. Sam just stood there letting the intoxicating atmosphere wash over him like the incoming tide, taking in the shrill cry of the stringed instrument, the pounding of the drum, and the sultry voice of the lead singer. Trying to enjoy the scent of pipe smoke and roasted lamb in the air the instant before it all switched to smelling like... body odor. At least he could enjoy the good-natured laughter, the clinking of glasses, and the tinkle of silver coins as they changed hands or were shuffled across tabletops.

This... *this* is what Sam had been missing since coming into Eternium. Right then and there, he decided that he was done playing by other people's rules. He loved his class and wanted to see it through, but he wasn't going to let those goobers at the College walk all over him anymore. He needed to perform his chores and attend his classes, but the second he got some free time tomorrow, he was going to pack up his meager belongs and find somewhere else to hunker down. Staying at the College was *convenient*—especially considering the hours he worked—but he refused to let Octavius suck the fun out of this awesome world.

Arrow slipped up beside him and clapped him on the shoulder. "It's really something, isn't it? Hard to believe that this is all just part of some massive video game. I've only been here a few days, but I'm already starting to think that maybe it wouldn't be so bad to stay here forever."

Sam choked. "Wait, is that possible?"

"Not *officially*," the man replied, thumping the side of his nose conspiratorially. "Word on the street, though, is there are a handful of people who are going *perma*. Mostly folks that are terminally ill but have heaps and heaps of moolah to throw around, but enough of that; leave it to me to rain on your good time."

Arrow fell silent as though unsure how to proceed. After a moment, he asked, "Hey, don't suppose you play cards, do you?"

The only cards Sam had ever played was Enchanted Gathering, but he doubted *that* was the card game the Ranger meant. Still, he was in great spirits and was more than happy to lose a little silver if it meant more time with his new friends.

"Nope," Sam replied, "but I'd love to learn! Lead the way..."

The rest of the night passed in a blur of too loud music, free-flowing booze, and one hand of cards after another. Sam had never played Texas Hold 'Em before, and he lost twenty silver and forty copper as a result, but he hadn't had that much fun in *ages*. It seemed that there was a secondary benefit to playing games of chance as well.

Characteristic point training completed! +1 to luck! This stat cannot be increased further by any means other than system rewards or lucky encounters for twenty-four hours game time.

Eventually, Sphinx pulled him out onto the dance floor, where he cut a rug for nearly half an hour. He'd honestly never had more fun in his adult life. Sam was genuinely sad when a mostly sober Finn wrapped an arm around his shoulders and practically dragged him into the street.

The time was well past midnight—therefore technically the next day—and both Sam and Finn had to be up by six to prepare for their round of morning chores. It was going to be an *awfully* early day, that was for sure, and considering just *how* much liquor he'd downed, Sam figured it was going to be an awfully *painful* morning at that. He hadn't been hung-over since freshman year, when he 'accidentally' downed an entire blender of margaritas at his first Berkeley party. First *and* last, as it turned out.

Sam clearly recalled the following morning, when he'd woken up wrapped in a shower curtain and missing his left eyebrow—some generous soul had shaved it clean off in the night. He'd had to pencil on a fake brow, which didn't look even *remotely* natural, for almost a month. He felt that drunk tonight and silently prayed that come first light, things would be a little less messy this time around. Together, Sam and Finn headed back for the College, sticking to the well-lit portions of the city since they were both snookered and Sam doubted very much whether their magic would even work.

The pair of them earned some curious or even outright disapproving looks from the night patrol, but no one stopped them on their way back to the College. The fact that Finn was dressed like a Noble and kept summoning a flurry of snow around him as a cloak *may* have had something to do with that. Sam didn't know everything about this city, but it seemed unlikely that the guards would willingly pick a fight with a scion of even a *minor* house since the political consequences could be devastating. That probably went *double* for Apprentices with the College proper.

The Mages of Ardania wielded an unhealthy amount of power and influence over the city, and no one, it seemed, wanted that power turned against them. Just a little after one in the morning, Sam and Finn stumbled through the portcullis and into the eastern courtyard. Sam didn't particularly care for the College, but he was certainly looking forward to faceplanting on his uncomfortable little cot and stealing whatever shuteye he could before the new day officially started with its litany of chores, classes, and responsibilities.

"Uhhhh, Sam," came Finn's voice, his words slurred and jumbled, "I think we may have a problem."

Sam blinked lazily and focused on the present... How in the world had he failed to notice there was a small crowd of people milling about in the courtyard at this ungodly hour? Oh right. Lousy, no good, low perception. That and the alcohol.

Upon closer inspection, Sam saw it was a group of Mages, ten strong, along with a pair of College thugs wearing heavy armor and carrying enchanted halberds that glimmered with opalescent light like pent-up moonbeams. A cold feeling of dread filled Sam, sobering him in an instant as a Mage stepped forth from the assembled group and lowered his cowl, revealing none other than Octavius Ignitor, Earth Mage and Peak Student in charge of making their lives absolutely miserable.

Sam had no idea what these assembled Mages wanted, but it obviously had to do with him and Finn, and considering the circumstances... Well, these guys probably weren't here to congratulate them on their victory over the Hardcores.

"If it isn't our two wayward children, come home after a long day of breaking *every* rule that governs proper Mage society. Drunk, no less, which is a further indictment against you. Public slovenliness is unbefitting of a member of our illustrious order. Guards," Octavius looked at the two armor-clad guards waiting in the wings to swoop in, "please take them into custody now."

Finn pushed away from Sam, swaying slightly, blinking heavy-lidded eyes as he lifted his hands and conjured a slowly spinning ball of frost. The surrounding Mages acted at once, magic springing forth in bursts of color. Blue Mage Armor shimmered to life here, a cloud of emerald light formed in the air there... as they prepared to put Finn down by force if necessary.

"I *wouldn't* do that if I were you," Octavius was growing more smug by the second. "We intend to bring both of you in *alive*, but I'm sure the Archmage will forgive us if an *accident* were to happen while we were trying to detain you two *gentlemen*."

Somehow, Octavius imbued *so* much scorn into the word 'gentlemen' that he made it sound like a curse word.

"Like bloody hells you're going to take us into custody you sadistic, sanctimonious bellend." The confrontation had, apparently, not sobered Finn up at all. "Me and my friend Sam," the ice Mage gestured in the wrong direction with his free hand, "haven't done *anything* wrong. Under *what* charge are you arresting us, then, Lord Fancy Pants? Hmm? Perhaps the high crimes of having *fun*? I *can* see how you lot of morose, self-important losers might be against anything resembling entertainment."

Octavius glanced at a balding Mage in purple robes and issued a terse nod. The man moved at once, uttering a slick chant as violet light built in his palms like a dying star. The spell rocketed from his hands, slamming into Finn like a torpedo, but it didn't seem to do any tangible harm. For a long beat, Sam wasn't sure what purpose the spell was. Then Finn opened his mouth, no doubt to unleash another vicious and drunken tirade, but nothing came out. Not a word. Finn's eyes bulged as he grabbed at his throat. Silence reigned.

"Ah, now *that's* what I like to hear out of you, Novice Laustsen." Octavius wasn't bothering to hide his smile this time. "As for your crimes, why... I wouldn't even know where to begin!"

Octavius folded his hands behind his back and began pacing slowly, boots *clicking* and robes swishing. "So, I *won't* bother. Besides, I imagine you both are too intoxicated to properly comprehend the charges anyway. But never fear, all will be explained tomorrow and by none other than the Archmage himself! I hope you have a *lovely* night. We'll be seeing each other again very, *very* soon."

CHAPTER NINETEEN

"Novice Mages Sam_K and Finneas Laustsen," the Archmage intoned, his greasy voice sending shivers racing along Sam's spine, "stand before the Council and prepare to receive our verdict."

"Verdict!" Sam shouted in shock and jumping to his feet. "We don't even know what we've done *wrong*... your excellency."

He tried to keep a lid on his simmering anger, but it was no easy thing. The guards had tossed Sam and Finn into a frigid cell that was so cramped they'd barely been able to sit, and laying down was absolutely out of the question. They hadn't received anything—no blankets, no water, no food, no information. Despite the cramped, terrible, and inhumane conditions of the cell, Finn had somehow managed to pass out for a few hours... Not so much for Sam.

He's spent the remainder of the night sitting in a tepid puddle, his back pressed against cold, gray stone, his knees pulled in tight against his chest. He hadn't slept a wink. Then bright and early, the guards returned, hauling them from the cell and parading them before the Council, who stared on with pitiless gazes, their brows furrowed in disappointment and judgment.

Worse, the same balding, purple-robed Mage from the night before had slapped another Silence spell on Finn so he couldn't even defend himself against this kangaroo court. Sam had asked for a lawyer—because *due process*. The guards had openly laughed in his face as though he'd just asked whether the moon was made out of blue cheese. Which meant that it was up to Sam to handle things. He'd never *wanted* to be a lawyer, but he'd go to the abyss before he was going to roll over without a fight.

"I refuse to accept any verdict rendered by this body until I know *exactly* which laws we've violated," Sam growled, hands curling into tight fists.

"The charges should be *obvious*, even to one as new you, but I suppose for the sake of the other Mages present, I can edify you, *child*. You two formed an unauthorized party with heroes, a group *unapproved* by the Mage's College. Moreover, you engaged in unsanctioned questing outside of the city proper without first receiving a writ of approval from the Mage's Hunting and Wildlife Division. Further, while doing so, you engaged in the willful killing of *ten* Travelers without *our* express permission! To top it all off, the pair of you engaged in debauchery and revelry in a *common* tavern, which is conduct unbecoming of this august body."

Each new charge felt like a slap to the face. *That was it? Questing with a party in a game designed to go questing? Killing the Hardcores in self-defense? Having a few beers to celebrate?*

"Seriously?" Sam's features were contorting in bewilderment. "Those are the charges? This is a joke, right? Like... some kind of hazing ritual designed to mess with our heads?"

"How *dare* you take these proceedings so lightly," the Archmage growled, leaning forward like an attack dog ready to pounce. Another sucker punch to the face came swiftly. "Mage Suetonius, make a note of this one's insolence. He will receive an additional week's punishment for Contempt against the Council."

"*What?* I'm *not* trying to be insolent. Seriously, I'm not! I just genuinely don't understand. We didn't do anything wrong!"

"Octavius," the Archmage's jowls flapped like leather handbags in a hurricane as he spoke, "I am not going to waste my breath explaining what should be *plain*. Inform this fool, if you will."

"Gladly, Archmage," Octavius replied, swooshing forward in a swirl of fabric. "This party that you joined yourself with, were they *pre*approved by the Mage's College?"

"No," Sam replied slowly, "but what does that matt–"

"If they were not *preapproved*," Octavius cut him off, "then how do you know for certain they weren't engaged in behavior that might be in opposition to the will of the College, hmmm? What of these other warriors you killed? Even though your actions were in 'alleged' self-defense, you could well have attacked a group that had ties to our College, causing a potential diplomatic *incident* with your foolishness."

"*Were* they a group with ties to the College?" Sam shot back.

"No," Octavius replied flatly, "but that is immaterial to the matter at hand. The important point is that they *could* have been, and you didn't *know* they weren't, yet you acted in your *own* self-interest... instead of the interest of the College. Even your unauthorized questing seriously jeopardized the College and even the human Kingdom of Ardania itself! We Mages serve the *Crown*, and if there had been a Wolfman assault, our members would have needed to mobilize for battle. Generally, Novices man the College's defense, freeing up our more senior members to neutralize the threat, but with you and Lord Laustsen off *gallivanting* in the countryside, a more senior member of the College would be forced to remain behind to pick up your slack."

"But none of that *happened*," Sam sputtered, though he already knew he wasn't going to win this argument.

"No," Octavius said again, "but it *could* have. When you signed The Accords, you agreed to humble yourself, exchanging your own worldly wisdom for the wisdom of your betters. For the wisdom of this body."

He spread his hands out and turned in a slow circle. "But you and Lord Laustsen have failed spectacularly, bringing disgrace upon yourself, your houses, and this College. For that, you must learn your lesson."

"Well said, Octavius," the Archmage nodded his bulbous head. His many chins wobbled at the motion like a bowl of fleshy Jell-O. "Since this is your first offense, and we *do* believe it was a violation made in *ignorance* and not malice, the sentence will be light. You each shall be fined fifty gold, and your off-campus liberty shall be revoked for a month."

"No leaving these premises for *any* reason unless explicitly instructed by Peak Student Octavius or any Mage ranked Expert or above. To ensure the lesson is one that sticks, you shall each spend an hour a day—in *addition* to your regular duties and classes—devoting your Mana to The Accords. This will last no less than a month, and the first session shall commence at this very moment."

There was a round of quiet gasps, followed by the soft murmuring of voices from the viewing stands. Sam wasn't sure what 'devoting your Mana to The Accords' meant, but based on the reactions around the room, it was bad. *Really* bad.

You have been offered a quest. Punishment for your crimes! Serve your sentence with the Mage's College by paying fifty gold, forfeiting liberty rights for one month and one week, and fueling the Mana of The Accords for one hour a day for one month and one week (Additional penalty for Contempt against the Council)! This quest is mandatory if you have signed The

Accords, as it has been offered by the Archmage. Rewards: You will not be hunted by the College. Accept? Yes / Yes

Sam couldn't believe what he was reading right now—a mandatory quest he couldn't turn down? This was absolutely *ridiculous*. Punished for questing with friends and killing someone who'd tried to shake them down? Absurd and not even *remotely* what he'd signed up for. This was *garbage*, and he wasn't going to spend a month and change locked up in this boring prison. *Nope*.

Sam flat-out *refused* to spend a month slaving away for people like Octavius and the Archmage. Hard pass. He'd put up with *a lot* of crap since entering Eternium and making his way to the Mage's College. He'd scrubbed dishes, mucked stables, waded through sewers, and waited on Octavius hand and foot instead of venturing out into the wider world and playing the game like *every other* sane and rational person out in the big, wide world. This was it. He wasn't putting up with *any* more of this. For a moment, he considered ignoring the quest, spitting in the Archmage's face, punching Octavius in his, then going out in a blaze of glory as he hurled magic until someone laid him out cold.

But as tempting as that route was—and it *was*—now wasn't the time or place. For one, if he did ignore the quest and start an impromptu revolt, there was every chance that Finn would get caught up in the mayhem and killed. Sam would respawn, Finn would not, and that wasn't okay. At this point, the idea of being a Rogue Mage didn't even sound all that bad; if things *really* veered wildly out of control, he could always quit and reroll a new character. Not Finn, though. This was Finn's *life*, and if Sam self-destructed, there was a solid chance the young ice Mage would never recover.

There was also another ulterior motive to consider...
Yes, he could punch Octavius in the face, which would be
deeply rewarding, but his victory would be short-lived. But there
was a way that Sam could hurt the Peak Student far worse; he
could get him in trouble with the Mage's College. He knew
exactly how to do it, though it would mean following through
with the Archmage's stupid punishment quest. Sam was sure that
whatever they had in store for him was going to be horrifying,
but getting even with Octavius would be totally worth it in the
end. So, reluctantly, he pressed 'Yes' and steeled himself for a
world of hurt.

"Excellent," the Archmage boomed. "This esteemed
Council has much work to be about today, so let us conclude
our business, shall we? Octavius, prepare our wayward Initiates
for their punishment."

The Peak Student nodded, a deadly gleam in his eyes as
he grabbed Finn with one hand and Sam with the other.
Octavius marched the pair of them up the marble stairs and on
to the same dais where Sam had signed the strange book only a
few short days ago. Without a word of warning, Octavius pushed
Finn away, then took Sam's wrists and rudely shoved his hands
against the glowing glass tube containing The Accords. The
instant Sam's hands made contact, fire and ice rocketed up his
arms and zipped through his body; his muscles locked tight as he
seized from the shock of raw power blasting through him.

Once, when Sam had been six, he'd decided to
experiment with the electrical sockets by using a small
screwdriver he'd pilfered from his dad's toolbox. His parents had
warned him a thousand times not to mess around with the
sockets, but Sam—using the infinite wisdom that only six-year-
olds possess—decided they must be hiding something *fun*. After
all, most fun things had to do with the electrical sockets. They

made the TV come alive, made his game console work, and charged the stereo system, which brought music to the house during the evenings. What awesome things, young Sam wondered, would the light socket do for him?

Very nearly gave him a *heart attack* was the answer. An answer and a lesson Sam had never forgotten. Now this? This was almost *exactly* like that—the power surging through his body, frying his nerve endings, searing his mind and scorching his lungs—making it nearly impossible to breathe. After a few brief seconds, the pain intensified even more as the biting power flowed into his Mana channels and worked its way into the blue-white core churning at his Center. Mana poured out of him like a tsunami, threatening to overwhelm him with its ferocity. It was so hard to think through the pain, but he heard Mage Akora's lecture in the back of his mind.

This vast reservoir of power can be dangerous to those who do not understand its proper use. If one of you were to cast a spell without directing that rush of power through the appropriate channels, it could cause great damage—everything from exhaustion to pain to fits of severe nausea. In some ways, it would be like the reservoir flooding its banks, all of that water rushing around without anywhere to go, destroying anything in its path indiscriminately. You must master your Mana, you must guide the power along the appropriate pathways, or you will be mastered by it.

The pain was intense, far worse even than getting stabbed in the guts with a blade. If Sam was going to survive, he needed to master the process, not be controlled by it. So, letting Mage Akora's words run through his head over and over again like a record on repeat, Sam pushed through the pain and forced the massive exodus of power to flow out through his Mana channels, just as he'd been taught. The pain didn't lessen in the least, but Sam's *awareness* of the sensation faded, turning into ambient background noise inside his head. Every time his Mana ran out, the pain flipped off only to jolt him as his Mana regen replaced a drop of power.

Still, he couldn't *afford* to acknowledge the pain because he needed complete and total concentration to keep the raging tides of power confined to his Mana channels. Directing that mad rush of arcane energy felt like trying to wrangle a hungry anaconda barehanded, but as he finally got things under control, the rate of his Mana depletion began to rapidly slow. As an Aeolus Sorcerer, he had a hefty Mana pool, and his wisdom meant that he had a naturally high Mana regeneration rate. Not enough to allow him to keep up with the Mana *loss*, but it kept him on his feet a lot longer than Finn.

The ice Mage convulsed violently the whole time, his body shaking like a leaf in a strong breeze, his head flopping, his teeth chattering uncontrollably. His friend lasted ten minutes or less before his knees buckled and gave out, dropping Finn to the floor. He was unconscious, but his hands never left the glass tubing. Instead of rushing to Finn's aid, Octavius just watched, arms crossed, an amused smile on his face.

This was brutal beyond belief, and he and Finn had been sentenced to an hour of this every single day for a *month*. If Sam had any second thoughts about betraying the College, they vanished the instant his hands were finally pried away from the glass. He grimaced as he regarded his palms. The skin was as raw and red as if he'd just had them pressed against a hot stovetop for the past hour. A notification icon flickered in the corner of his eye, and he brought it up on instinct.

Skill increased: Mana manipulation (Beginner III). Your training under Mage Akora has paid off in spades, and thanks to an iron will and a hard head, you've thrived where few others could endure. Great work!

Skill Gained: Channeling (Novice I). Congratulations! Through focus and use, you have learned to effectively channel your Mana! At seventy-five percent spell cost per second, you can maintain a connection to a spell that would otherwise use up the Mana allotted to it, increasing its effect over time. -.2% Mana cost and +1% spell damage per second per skill level.

"That will be enough for today, I suppose," the Archmage *magnanimously* declared, his voice sounding like a gong in the otherwise quiet chamber. "Octavius, get these miscreants out of my presence this instant. Oh, and Octavius, I shouldn't *need* to say this... but I will. These two are *your* responsibility as Peak Student, which means their failures are partly your own as well. Ensure they cause no further trouble of any sort, or it is *you* who will be up here replenishing The Accords with your Mana. That is abundantly clear, I hope."

"Yes, Archmage," Octavius replied, his voice as frigid as an arctic blizzard. "I will guarantee they never put one *toe* out of line again."

The Earth Mage glowered at them. "Now, both of you. Up. Your presence in this hall is a stain, and I shall see it removed."

Finn gained his feet with a groan, his legs wobbling, face slick with sweat. Sam followed a moment later but couldn't quite seem to get his balance. His legs felt as limp and useless as wet noodles. He took one tentative step and reeled to the side, nearly falling off the raised dais, which would've been a fitting end to this terrible evening. Octavius caught him by the arm, his fingers digging into Sam's flesh as he dragged him away from the edge.

"You won't get away from me that easily, Novice. Now *march*," Octavius growled in a low tone. He gave Sam a rough shove, spurring him into motion. "You'll be cleaning toilets until you fall asleep in the porcelain bowl."

As Sam headed down the stairs, trailing after Finn, he had to suppress a wicked smile. Clutched in his hand were a set of keys, carefully lifted off Octavius' belt as the Peak Student manhandled him. If *he* was going down, he was going to burn as much of this place down as he could in the process—especially Octavius' budding career. As Sam's dad often said, '*Play stupid games, win stupid prizes*'. These Mages had played a *very* stupid game, and now they were about to get the most fitting prize of all.

Chapter Twenty

The rest of the day passed in a whirl of chores and classes, interspersed by the briefest moments of rest where Sam was allowed to scramble for a bite of hard bread or a sip of water. He had his regular classes to attend for the day, of course. Today it was a session at *Mana Manipulation and Mana Coalescence,* which was pure murder after the session with The Accords earlier. Then there was dungeoneering, but every other second was chores or 'working parties'.

Not that there was anything even remotely *fun* about those parties. Octavius shuffled him from one miserable activity to the next. Toilets and bathroom patrol, followed by grounds maintenance, followed by kitchen detail... on and on and on. Octavius seemed to have transformed into a being fueled entirely by spite and vindictiveness.

But all of that is about to change, Sam thought darkly. He had missed breakfast and lunch but *had* managed to grab a meager dinner while working the kitchen line, shoving food into his face while the senior Kitchen Mage, Nesren Misrokovy, was busy elsewhere. He'd just finished his shift and—mercy of mercies—he had no other chores for the day. It was late, creeping up on nine at night, and he was supposed to be up bright and early at five in the morning for *another* turn at draining his Mana into The Accords.

That wasn't going to happen. Not ever again. Instead of heading to his room, Sam patted at his pocket, feeling the bulge of the brass keyring he'd lifted off Octavius. It was only a matter of time before the Peak Student noticed the keys were missing—if he hadn't already—so now was the time to act before anyone inside the College could prepare.

Sam worked his way through the dimly lit hallways, heading for the library just as he had so many times before. The hallways were mostly empty at this hour—though a few Scribes and Apprentices scuttled about—but still, he walked quickly, head down, trying not to draw any unwanted attention. The whole while his heart beat like a jackhammer inside his chest, and white-hot adrenaline coursed through his veins. He felt as though everyone was stealing sidelong glances at him, and he couldn't help but wonder if they somehow *knew* about the caper he was going to pull off.

It was paranoia, he knew, but as another wise wizard once said, *'Just because you're paranoid, that doesn't mean there isn't a monster about to eat your face'*.

There was one potential pitfall to his scheme that Sam couldn't completely discount—Octavius. Sam had absolutely no idea *where* the Peak Student was at the moment; if Octavius found him in the library, it would without a doubt spell disaster. Sam licked his lips and picked up his pace; that was just another reason to move quickly. He rounded a familiar bend, and a wave of vertigo slammed into him like a shield bash. The whole world wobbled, and his legs quivered frantically as the gravitational distortion marking the transition to the Annex washed over him.

That unfortunate feeling was one thing, among many, that Sam wouldn't miss about this place. He *hated* going through the Annex, but there was a little-known corridor that connected to a secondary entrance to the *Infinity Athenaeum* and chances were slim Octavius would ever go this way. The Peak Student was too 'good' to trek through the Annex if it could be helped. Sam followed the runic markers on the archways until he eventually slipped into a hallway that dead-ended at a simple doorway, far less grand than the proper entrance to the library.

With bated breath and sweat-slick hands, Sam pulled the door open and popped his head into the library.

He half expected to see Octavius waiting for him in the foyer, surrounded by a squad of sword-wielding guards waiting to clap Sam in irons and haul him off to the prison. But no. The entryway was empty, save for wizened Mage Solis sitting behind the librarian's desk, his bearded chin resting on his chest and his eyes closed. He was snoring loudly, the sound like a whirling buzzsaw; on the desk in front of him was his copy of *The Riveting Adventures of D.K. Esquire: Dungeon Delver.* He'd fallen asleep while captivated by a good book, a plight Sam could sympathize with from lots of personal experience.

Of every Mage in the College, gentle, kind-hearted Solis was the only one Sam would even remotely miss—not accounting for Finn, who was just as much an outsider as Sam himself. Honestly, Sam felt a little bad for what he was going to do since there was a slim chance that Mage Solis might take some of the heat for it. Hopefully, the responsibility—and therefore the punishment—would fall squarely on Octavius, but there was no way to be certain of that. Mage Solis was the Chief Librarian on night shift, after all, but Mage Solis was a Master, so if there *was* any fallout at all for the elderly book lover, Sam was fairly sure it would be minimal at most.

Steeling his nerves, Sam stole into the library, padding across the mosaic floors toward the hulking, black steel doors covered in glyphs and runes of power, guarding the restricted floors—a section that contained the most coveted treasures of the College, a section Sam just so *happened* to have the keys for, thanks to Octavius.

That was one of the College's major shortcomings—one among many—when it came to the College's Novices. They treated the neophytes like garbage while *simultaneously* entrusting them with unprecedented power and untold secrets. They never even thought twice about doing so because the Senior Mages were so arrogant that they couldn't ever *conceive* of the notion of a Novice bucking the system in any significant way.

Sam was about to teach them a painful and costly lesson for their short-sightedness. Octavius' keys let him into the Prime Chamber with its colorful portals, all in different hues. Mage Solis never even stirred, to Sam's relief.

Sam now had access to every level of the library, but he wasn't sure where to go. He couldn't tarry too long here; he'd managed to get in clean, but the longer he stayed, the better his chances of running into another Mage. The *obvious* choice was to head into the Sage's section—that was where the most valuable tomes and treasures were—and he *would* head there... eventually. The problem was, most of those books were far and away too complicated for Sam. They were more powerful and rare, but he wouldn't be able to understand or use them for *ages*.

There was a good chance this whole thing would go sideways, and he would have to reroll his character, but he wanted to at least make an honest go of it as a Rogue Mage. Would it be easy? No. But it couldn't be much harder than being a Novice. He wouldn't have access to the College and its myriad of classes or class trainers, so he needed to think about his short-term future, and that meant grabbing a few texts that were a little more *immediately* practical. So, the first stop was the tangerine-colored Student gate.

Sam opted to skip past the lower-level Apprentice gate since he figured he would learn some of the more basic skills and spells naturally, thanks to his class and his Instinctual Casting, but the Apprentice level spells were far more complicated. He'd also spent the most time on the Apprentice floor during his time as a research assistant to Octavius, so he knew exactly where he needed to go. He took a deep breath and slipped through the orange portal and into a section of the library that looked like something out of a medieval castle.

This section of the restricted library was all weather-beaten, gray stone—the floors, walls, and ceilings—accented by the occasional rug or tapestry, which showcased some of the more illustrious scenes from the Mage's College history. One tapestry depicted a Mage with locks of flowing, black hair standing tall and proud on a spit of rock, his battle staff raised high in the air as a sea of deformed, pale faces flooded toward him. *Brenward the Bold's Last Stand against the Goblin Scourge.* Another showed the current Archmage—although a *far* slimmer, younger, and more dashing version of the man—with a stately man wearing a crown, both standing in reverence before The Accords.

Sam broke into a slow jog, which put a strain on his stamina, but he didn't have far to go. He hooked left then took a hard right, entering into a section of basic spells and Mage-form applications. The books were legion, but Sam had already mentally cataloged the list of titles he wanted to pilfer before moving on. His gaze skipped over dusty tome after dusty tome. Moving quickly, he plucked the appropriate books from the shelves, shoving each one into the handy-dandy *Unending Flask of the Drunkard*—the spatial container he'd picked up from Nick's Knacks.

But the container only allowed him to carry an extra two-hundred pounds, and as anyone who has ever moved a box of books can confirm, they are *heavy.* These monstrosities even more so, since most of the volumes were thicker than phone books and bound in leather.

In went *Fundamentals of Core Cultivation* followed in short order by *Brilliant Blossoms: A field guide to basic herbology; The Book of Lost Incantations, Rediscovered!; A Compendium of Magical Omens;* and finally *Compact Fundamentals of Elemental Magic, Aeolus Edition.* There were so many more books that he wanted to take, but already he was feeling his skin crawl and itch as though there were eyes in every shadow watching him at his task.

"No need to be greedy," he muttered to himself. Besides, he wanted to save room for anything particularly interesting he might discover up in the Sage's section. Task complete, he backtracked to the Prime Chamber and made for his final destination—the burning, purple door at the end of the hallway.

As before, cold power rushed over Sam's skin like arctic fire, but the sensation passed in a blink as he stepped out onto the semi-translucent floor constructed of violet glass. Since he'd only been on this floor a single time—and briefly at that—he wasn't nearly as confident about where he should go or what he should grab in his grand escape. Well, that wasn't *entirely* true.

He did have *one* item firmly in mind—the real treasure that would make this all worthwhile and hopefully sink Octavius' good reputation for ages to come, the book locked away behind the crystalline bars. Sam had absolutely no idea what the book was—what spells or forbidden knowledge it contained—but anything locked up *that* tightly had to be valuable beyond belief.

Adding in the fact that Octavius had threatened him with unending doom for trifling with the volume lent some serious weight to its likely value. So, Sam set off at a sprint—or what passed for a sprint as a Mage—down the hall, boots rapping softly on the floors with every footfall. While he ran, he scanned the towering bookcases, looking for anything that popped out at him. Most of the titles—when there were titles at all—were far too complicated for him to make heads or tails of—*Unabridged Advice of Transfigurations and Metamorphing, Analytic Calibrations on Arcanum Amplatures, Essential Data for Vital Medimagic Sages.*

Sam was sure the information in those arcane tomes was valuable, but he had no idea if the info was valuable to *him*. He did falter, however, as his eyes flitted over a volume that screamed *Quest* to the inner gamer inside him. *Compendium on Protected and Dangerous Locations.* Without properly perusing the pages, Sam couldn't be sure what was inside the book, but if the title was even *remotely* similar to the content between the covers, then it had the potential to be a treasure trove. *Literally.* So, he popped that sucker into the flask after a brief pause then continued on his way.

Before Sam knew it, he was standing in front of a nook not much bigger than a broom closet, locked away from the world by formidable steel bars, which were *further* secured by a hefty, purple lock. Loitering on the stone pedestal beyond the prison bars was the burgundy book, crafted from strips of rough leather, all crudely stitched together so they formed a twisted, humanoid face. What were the chances, Sam idly wondered, that this thing was the Eternium equivalent of the Necronomicon? A book that would unleash some grand, unspeakable evil upon the world?

Based on looks alone, the chances were pretty high, Sam decided. *But so what?* As long as said unspeakable evil laid into the Mage's College first, Sam would be fine with the outcome. Hey, maybe it wasn't evil at all, and this was just one of those cases of never judge a book by its cover? Either way, this was the grand prize, and Sam was going to have it. Once more, he pulled Octavius' stolen keyring from his pocket, quickly flipping through keys until he pulled up the purple crystal key that appeared—at least on the surface—to match the lock. A tremor raced up Sam's arm, the hair standing up along his neck. This was it. The moment of truth.

Sam took a few deep breaths to calm his frazzled nerves, *in, out, in, out,* then slowly slid the key into the lock, accompanied by the soft rasp of stone scraping against stone. With a gulp, he twisted the key. *Click*.

Instead of opening, the lock simply dissolved in a shimmer of prismatic light, and as it did, the bars standing sentry over the nook began to glow with an amber light, which grew in brilliance by the second. The light intensified until Sam had to shield his eyes or go blind. After a few moments, which seemed to stretch on and on into eternity, the golden light gave one last dazzling flare, tattooing a purple after image across Sam's vision—and he'd had his eyes pressed tightly closed. When he cracked his eyelids a moment later, the bars were gone, vanished just as the lock had.

As for the book on the pedestal... it was moving on its *own*. Sam hesitated only a second before darting into the alcove and pulling the leather book from its resting place. The moment he did, the world erupted into chaos, and an alarm blared, ringing out like a thousand gongs struck as one.

Chapter Twenty-One

The sound filling the air was as loud as a thunderstorm, the boom of warning bells echoing up and down the hallways and bouncing off the high ceilings of the library. Welp, that probably wasn't a good thing. Sam temporarily ignored the deafening racket of the alarms as he turned his attention to a prompt which had appeared in the corner of his eye:

Would you like to bond with the Bibliomancer's Sacred Tome? Doing so will form a permanent soul bond and might annul previous contractual obligations. As you have found the book, you have obviously studied the possibilities and repercussions of this action. Yes / No?

What was this now, Sam wondered? He could *bind* with this strange thing? He wasn't entirely sure what binding with an object entailed, nor what the long-term ramifications would be, but there was one thing he did know from endless campaigns as a gamer—when an ancient magic presented you with a chance to do something, you *did* it. Because *obviously*, you just *do* it. Here was a sacred book, secreted away in the Sage's section and *further* locked down behind a set of mystical bars that required a special key to unlock. If that didn't earn him some kind of secret, ultra-rare questline... then nothing ever would.

Every instinct he had screamed in frantic joy, so he only thought about for less than a heartbeat before pressing 'Yes'.

Contract formed with The Bibliomancer's Sacred Tome! Bonding with this artifact has nullified your signature in The Accords of the Mage's College; you have become an enemy of the Mage's College and are now a Rogue Wizard! Your reputation with the College has decreased by -6,000. Current reputation: Loathed. Wow, that escalated quickly! You don't do things in half measures, do you? I guess congratulations are in order? So... congratulations, you rapscallion! Way to stick it to the man! Might want to run.

Sam staggered drunkenly as a wave of golden light and unbridled energy washed out of the book, rushing into him like water soaking into a bone-dry sponge. The light lifted him from the ground, which before now meant he was leveling up. This didn't *feel* at all like the other times he'd leveled up before. It *hurt*. This time around, the golden power *burned*, almost as if there was magma coursing through his veins and slivers of powdered glass had been injected directly into his muscles. His breathing came in short, sporadic bursts, and his head throbbed as though his brain was swelling up and ramming up against the inside of his skull... except, it didn't have the room it needed to grow adequately.

As Sam hung there in the air, rotating slowly, knowledge bloomed inside his head while he was inundated with a host of new notifications.

Warning! Forced Class Change! You have lost the Class 'Aeolus Sorcerer', and all the following class-specific spells are <u>*locked*</u>: *Wind Blade, Aeolus Sword, Mage Armor! You have assumed the Class 'Bibliomantic Sorcerer'! You have retained the ability: Instinctual Casting. You have formed a permanently binding Mana contract with the Bibliomancer's Sacred Tome, known as Bill, more formally known as Sir William the Bravi.*

You have completed a Hidden Unique quest: Symbiotic Knowledge! Experience gained: 10,000.

You have gained a Character level! Current level: 6.

You have earned a New Title: Stick it to the Man! When hitting a male with a stick, there is a 1% chance that he will explode into meaty chunks! Careful not to strike yourself!

Bibliomantic Sorcerer (Artifact). Unlike other Sorcerer Classes, this extremely rare subclass derives their powers and spells not from the arcane forces of nature but from the Ancient Artifact to which they have bound themselves. In this way, they are actually closer to Summoners than Sorcerers. Additionally, though Bibliomantic Sorcerers have a large potential pool of spells to call on, they must often prepare materials in advance and can only cast a limited number of spells based on how many Orbital Spell Tomes they have available at any given time.

The Bibliomantic Sorcerer intuitively understands the magic of their given class—it is a part of him that is as natural as breathing. Those choosing this class have naturally large Mana pools and regenerate Mana at a faster rate than their more generalized brethren. Overall, their spells are less powerful than those of a basic Mage at the same level, but the spells can cost less than half the Mana. They also naturally learn new class-compatible spells every third level without any training from an outside source, though in this case, the Bound Artifact can act as a Class Trainer, allowing them to unlock new abilities and spells at a far faster rate than most Mages.

Because of their wide potential spell pool, Bibliomantic Sorcerers can operate in a number of different party capacities depending on how they build out their available spell slots. Everything from combat Mage to party support caster is possible with enough training and plenty of prior preparation. The Bibliomantic Sorcerer gains four characteristic points to spend per three levels and +2 Intelligence, +2 Wisdom, and +1 Dexterity on every even level (Artifact Bonus). They gain three free skill points to spend per level. They also gain a small boost to their overall characteristic points as they merge more closely with their chosen Artifact!

Because of their affinity for spellcraft, the suggested characteristics for this class are intelligence, wisdom, and dexterity.

That was only the start of the notices, however, a flood of information followed in a raging torrent.

By binding with the Bibliomancer's Sacred Tome, you have unlocked the Title Soul-Bound Level 1 (Upgradeable). Effect: Receive a one-time character bonus as a result of absorbing a portion of the Bibliomancer's Sacred Tome's Characteristic Points. +1 Strength, +3 Dexterity, +1 Constitution, +5 Intelligence, +4 Wisdom, +2 Charisma, +2 Perception, -5 Luck, -5 Karmic Luck (Artificially Artifact bonus). As you bind more closely with the Bibliomancer's Sacred Tome, you can upgrade this title to a maximum of Soul-Bound Level 4, unlocking a new, one-time character bonus with each successive upgrade! Until the maximum rank, this title cannot be combined with any other title nor removed for any reason.

Name: Sam_K 'Bunny Reaper'
Class: ~~Aeolus Sorcerer~~ -> Bibliomantic Sorcerer
Profession: Unlocked
Level: 6 Exp: 20,043 Exp to next level: 957
Hit Points: 110/110
Mana: 373/373
Mana regen: 12.24/sec (.25 -> .3 per point of wisdom)
Stamina: 105/105

Characteristic: Raw score (Modifier)

Strength: 15 (1.15)
Dexterity: 21 (1.21)
Constitution: 16 (1.16)

Intelligence: 36 (1.36)

Wisdom: 34 (1.34)

Charisma: 15 (1.15)

Perception: 11 (1.11)

Luck: 11 (1.11)

Karmic Luck: -3

You have unlocked the following Spells:

Orbital Tome Casting (Novice I): This is the primary mechanism by which Bibliomantic Sorcerers cast spells. You can bind up to (6) tomes, which circle around you. Each tome can contain $1x/2$ rounded up prepared spells, where x=skill level; spells can be swapped out at will, but this is time-consuming and not recommended during combat, so choose wisely. Furthermore, the quality—trash, damaged, common, uncommon, rare, special, unique, artifact—of the book paper, ink, and page count within will affect the strength and number of available spell slots.

Magical Origami (Novice I): Using prepared paper and optional inks, create a set of instructions that automatically fold and create a paper weapon. Quality and potential damage of the created weapon are based upon skill level. $10n$ potential damage where n=skill level, damage increased based upon materials used. Cost: 5 Mana per second until completed or attempt is failed. Caution! Not all materials can contain high amounts of Mana!

Origami Activation (Novice I): Select an enemy target to attack with a prepared spell, inflicting $2n$ damage + damage equal to the prepared spell. $20\text{-}n\%$ chance of activation failure, where n=skill level (Paper-aligned magic) Range: Ten meters. Cost: $2n$ Mana. Limited by number of prepared spells in Bound

Orbital Tomes. Cooldown: 1.5 seconds; hand gestures must be completed to cast.

You have learned the most basic variant form of 'Magical Origami' spell: Paper Shuriken (Novice I). Effect: Assign Paper Origami to one of your bound Orbital Tomes, allowing you to automatically hurl a folded Paper Shuriken at your enemies for magical slashing damage. Damage, cost, and range are derived from the base skills, Magical Origami and Origami Activation. Paper Shuriken does an additional 0.5 damage against earth-aligned beings but suffers a 0.5 penalty against fire-aligned beings.

Alert! Mage Armor has been absorbed and transformed into Papier-Mache Mage!

Papier-Mache Mage (Beginner III): Cocoon yourself in a layer of flexible and versatile papier-mache, which acts as Mage Armor! Sure, people will laugh, but you'll have the last laugh by not dying horrifically! Effect: For every point of Mana devoted to this spell, negate two points of damage from primary sources of physical damage and half a point from primary sources of magical damage. Negate an additional 0.75 damage from the element effects wind and earth, but suffer an additional 0.75 damage against the elemental effects fire and water. Increase conversion by $0.025n$ where 'n' equals skill level.

Alert! Aeolus Sword has been absorbed and transformed into Quill Blade!

Quill Blade (Novice I): Call upon the Bibliomancer Artifact, Bill's Quill. Quill Blade acts as a one-handed sword and deals a maximum of $2n$ damage per hit where 'n' is skill level + $2x$ damage per hit where 'x' is the Sword Mastery skill. (Paper Aligned magic) Cost: $10n$ Mana to cast, $+2n$ per second to maintain. Why settle for having a pen that is mightier than the sword when you can have a pen that is a sword?

Warning! Minimum threshold for normalcy achieved for characteristic: Perception! Body modification in process in three... two... one...

The golden glow surrounding Sam in a cloud disappeared, and he dropped from the air, collapsing into a heap as he struggled to breathe and think. For a long moment, *everything* cut off. As though he were in a sensory deprivation chamber, he lost contact with the world around him. This could have lasted an instant or an eternity, but then everything came rushing back to him.

With a groan, he pushed up on to his palms, then winced from the cacophony of sound assaulting his ears. Wow, but everything *hurt*. His muscles felt sorer than he could ever remember, and the most minor sensation was amplified tenfold like he had the world's worst migraine. The area around him was far more *solid* and real than it had been just seconds before. The blur in his vision was gone, banished without a trace; every sound was sharper, *clearer*, and even his nose seemed to be working overtime... Dang, did he stink.

He had some kind of black slime coating his skin, and it reeked like a porta-potty that had been left too long in the sun. Eww. More than anything, Sam wanted to strip down and take a long hot shower both to rid himself of the sore muscles and the lingering odor. No! What he *really* needed was to level up again; that would solve all his stench problems. Unfortunately, he needed another nine hundred and fifty-seven experience points to advance to the next level, which likely wasn't going to happen anytime soon.

<Hey, you! We gotta get moving.> The voice came out of nowhere, and Sam sprang to his feet in a panic, whirling about as he searched for the source of the voice. Had the guards *already* managed to find him? If so, there was a chance that he

wasn't going to walk out of here alive. Walking out dead would be even more impressive but also unlikely. Sam scanned the stretching hallways running off in either direction and saw no one. There were no pounding footsteps, no guards charging toward him with upraised weapons and bloodthirsty intent.

"Hello?" Sam called softly, the hairs at the back of his neck standing stiff. "Is someone there?"

He raised his hands, ready to cast Wind Blade, which is when he remembered that he *couldn't*. Not anymore. He'd closed that door, it seemed, and now, he had a new set of skills to master if he hoped to survive for any length of time.

<Down here. Come on, you can't tell me this is outside your realm of possibilities,> the voice came again. There was a flutter of movement by Sam's feet. There, lying on the floor, was the book.

It was *moving*. Pages were flapping and rustling against each other like the legs of some enormous cricket. Even more disconcerting, however, was that the face protruding from the cover like a cancerous growth had opened its eyes and was now frowning at him in stern disapproval.

"I'm sorry," Sam managed to speak while the world was spinning topsy-turvy around him. "Is... are you the book? The person talking to me, I mean?"

<Ding, ding, ding, give the kid a cookie,> the book replied, even though its pouty, leathery lips never moved. <Yeah. I'm 'the book'. Though, if I'm being honest—and I really feel like we should start our relationship off right with complete honesty—the term *book* feels a little dismissive... I'm just messing around with you. 'Book' is fine, though mostly, I go by Bill. That was my human name before I got all bookafied by the Mage's College."

"So... you were a person before? You're a talking book?" Sam was still reeling from the interaction.

The great, leather-bound volume rolled its emerald eyes. <That's a long story, and now probably isn't the best time to have it. Also, *talking* is a bit subjective since I'm actually speaking to you with my *mind*—just one of the many benefits of sharing a soul, but like I said, we can sort out all the details once we get outta here.>

Still, Sam hesitated. "Before I pick you up and tote you around, tell me why you were locked up. If you're some sort of *prime evil*, I'm not sure I want to help."

<*Phft.* Evil. What? No, not even a little bit. I'm not even really all that dangerous; more like dangerously *annoying*, if you ask the stuffy, old fuddy-duddies hanging around the College. All I did was challenge The Accords—because *they* are evil—and instigate one *smallish* rebellion. Boom. Long story short, I wind up as a book. They would've destroyed me—these Mage types don't like that I'm a free thinker, ya know?—but turns out I'm indestructible. They hurt me and managed to whittle me down to level one, but they couldn't get *rid* of me. So, magic coma. Pretty standard as these things go.>

<Besides, all of that is behind me. Ancient history. Right now, we should really focus on the present because, like it or not, we're partners in crime. You didn't just open my prison, you bound me to your soul. Speaking of crimes, there are a *whole* bunch of Mages coming our way, and if I had to make an educated guess, they are going to be awfully grumpy when they see what you did. So, unless you want to get Dewey-decimated, maybe we... book it?>

"Yeah, that's... I can see why you were locked up," Sam mumbled. The gongs were still clanging overhead, and it was only a matter of time before the other Mages found him. If the punishment for joining an 'unauthorized group' for a basic grind session was a month of fueling The Accords with his Mana, Sam couldn't even begin to *imagine* what they'd do to him for this little transgression. So, probably best to beat feet before he became mincemeat.

Sam bent over and scooped the book up from the floor. The second the hefty volume was in hand, a ghostly, silver chain erupted from the book's spine, snaking down and digging into Sam's hip with a sharp pinch. Sam fumbled the book in shock, but instead of falling to the ground, the tome just hung suspended in the air before him. It was floating. Sam glanced down at the odd chain and noticed there was a gentle ebb of blue light flowing from him to the book.

<Just pretend I'm a book about anti-gravity. I'm impossible to put down. C'mon, don't look so surprised!> Bill demanded his attention. <We share a soul—a Core—which means we also share a Mana bond. That's the chain thingy. We're *literally* stuck together now, so I hope you're not an introvert because I'll be with you wherever you go. Forever! Muhu-ha-ha!>

Sam felt his stomach lurch at the idea of being stuck with this thing for the rest of his time in Eternium. He didn't exactly *relish* the notion. There would be time to worry about that later, though. Over the top of the clanging gongs, Sam could now hear the distant call of voices and the heavy pounding of footfalls. Footfalls which were slowly drawing closer to his position.

"Okay, how in the abyss are we supposed to get out of here?" Sam whispered, gaze skipping along the hallway. "We're trapped in the most secure section of the most secure library in Ardania."

<Just so happens that we're in luck because *I* can check *you* out of here. I know just about everything there is to know

about the College. I was around when the first Rituarchitect, Sage Cognitionis, *built* this place. Guy was kind of a stick in the mud, but we were still buddies. That was before they murdered him for trying to expand his Coven, of course. The administration here really doesn't like people trying new things. Anywho... all of that is to say, I know ways in and out of this place that *no one* else does, but, uh... sounds like they're getting close. Might have to throw a few punches to clear the way. Here, take this.>

There was a brilliant shimmer of opalescent light, and a wide-brimmed cavalier hat made from fine felt appeared in Sam's hands. A red velvet band encircled the hat, and protruding from it was an enormous, cobalt-colored ostrich feather.

"Where in the abyss did *this* thing come from?" Sam sputtered, turning the hat over in his hands.

<Soul Space,> Bill explained dryly. <I can store one item inside me, sort of like a spatial container. Except books. I can store all the books that your skill allows to orbit you. That's where we'll stash the other books when we're not using them to cast. Unfortunately, I only have the hat at the moment.>

<Why a hat? Also, why *this* hat?>

<Hey, no judgment now. That was my *favorite* hat, for the record. You should really be less sassy and more thankful! Where do you think your quill blade comes from, some *random* quill?> The book pointedly blinked toward the huge feather poking up from the brim. Sam quickly pulled up the item description.

Bill's Foppish Hat. Well, don't you just look ridiculous. With the rest of the outfit, you could pass as a Three Musketeers reenactor. Now, to give credit where credit is due, the hat is a really potent magical artifact. While wearing this hat: Strength +5,

Dexterity +5, Charisma +5, +10% Resistance against Fire, +2 Skill Level to Bladed Weapons. In addition to being an interesting fashion statement, Bill's Foppish Hat acts as a sheath for the Bibliomancer Artifact, Bill's Quill. This item cannot be sold, stolen, or destroyed as it is Soul-Bound to the Bibliomancer's Sacred Tome.

<Hey, looking better already! We *really* need to hurry. How's about you grab a couple of those books there.> The book motioned toward a nearby shelf with his eyes. <They're all magical, so we should be good to go. Just get a couple of big, ol', fat volumes—the more pages the better—doesn't really matter which ones, but we'll need them to cast spells. You better move your butt because the bad guys are closing in on us, and once they're in range, you won't be able to quick slot spells. You'll learn pretty soon how awesome this class is, but it has a few... limitations. Prior preparation is one of 'em.>

Moving in a daze, Sam slipped over to the bookcase and pulled out the two thickest doorstoppers he could find—*Fantastic Fallacies and Where to Find Them*, bound in blue leather, and the *Dangers of Arithmancy*, bound in crimson. Instinctual information bloomed inside Sam's head—just as it had when he was an Aeolus Sorcerer—and with a thought and a brief effort of will, Sam started assigning *Magical Origami* to one tome.

Mana flooded out of him, taking three-point-seven-five Mana a second. It seemed that his spell stability *and* his channeling reduction bonuses were taken into account here, thank goodness. Ten... fifteen seconds passed, and fifty-six Mana was out of his system and contained in the book. Thirty seconds later, Papier-Mache Mage was assigned to the other tome.

Moving with effortless ease, Sam tossed both books into the air without a second thought, as though he'd done this very thing a thousand times before. Instead of plummeting to the ground with a dull *thud*, the books floated in the air, breaking into a slow orbit around him like a pair of tiny planets circling a Sam-shaped sun. Not a moment too soon. A trio of Mages in brightly colored robes skidded around the end of the hallway.

"There he is!" one of them shouted, a finger outthrust and quivering. "We can't let him get away, or the Archmage will have all our heads! Silence him, tear off his limbs, and cauterize the holes so we can take him alive!"

CHAPTER TWENTY-TWO

<Well, don't just *bookstand* there!> Bill thundered inside his head. <Run! And I mean *move* it, or this becomes a book*end!*>

Sam didn't have to think twice; he turned away from the Mages at the end of the hall and took off in the opposite direction, a surge of adrenaline propelling him onward, faster and faster. Air rushed past his face, and his lungs worked in overdrive as bookcases whipped by him on either side, the titles blending together in a blur of glimmering magic and colored leather. Interestingly, his floating trio of books—Bill in front, linked by the silver soul chain, the other two twirling around him—kept pace without missing a beat or interfering with his movements in the slightest.

That was a nice perk. While he sprinted, Bill called out directions to him, <Left! Right! Oh no, new group incoming, double back!>

After only a few minutes of running all out, his stamina was flagging, and Sam was seriously beginning to worry how long he'd be able to keep the escape up. The worst that could happen was a quick death at the hands of an angry Mage followed by a respawn back in the Ardania town square. Or... was that the *best* option? He thought back to Bill, imprisoned behind magical bars... what if they didn't kill him but managed to take him alive? If *that* happened, they'd toss him in that cramped dungeon and throw away the key.

Even *if*—and it was a big *if*—Sam managed to force them to kill him, there was no guarantee they wouldn't simply be waiting for him at the fountain when he respawned. From there, it would be a simple thing to apprehend him. Once he got into that cycle, he'd almost certainly be forced to quit this character and start over; something he now wanted to avoid if at all possible. True, he didn't know exactly what the Bibliomancer class had in store for him long term, but he was guessing this class was just about as rare as they came, which meant huge potential down the road.

Sam just needed to survive and escape. That thought kept him going, even when it felt like his legs would give out and his lungs would explode from the strain. He skittered around a corner and found himself at a four-way juncture with vaulted arches; dead ahead was a contingent of Mages, four deep, and at their head was none other than Octavius Igenitor. Boy. Oh. *Boy*. Did he look *mad*.

"You," Octavius snarled, his face twisted up in a grimace of absolute hatred. "*You* did this. You stole my keys and thought to *rob* this esteemed institution of one of its most *valuable* prizes. You have *embarrassed* me for the *last*–"

Sam didn't wait for the Peak Student to finish flapping his gums. A trickle of Mana flowed out of him, and the red-covered 'Dangers of Arithmancy' shot front and center, the book springing open as Sam instinctually spammed his Wind Blade replacement spell–*Paper Shuriken*. A four-bladed paper ninja star no larger than Sam's palm exploded from the book, screaming toward the Earth Mage like an enraged harpy.

"Don't you *ever* shut up?" Sam spat as the paper blade slammed into the Peak Student's shoulder. Some part of Sam fully expected the silly origami star to bounce away fruitlessly–it was just a bit of paper, after all–but surprisingly, the Shuriken bit deep, slicing effortlessly through Octavius' robes and lodging in flesh. The rock Mage let out a startled squawk and backpaddled a step; he hadn't even bothered to cast Mage Armor. Thanks to

Sam's time in judo, he knew a weakness when he saw one and fully intended to exploit it.

But he also refused to make the same mistake that Octavius had. He was outnumbered and significantly outgunned. Abyss, really the only thing he had going for him was the element of surprise; chances were good that no one at the College knew precisely *what* tricks a Bibliomantic Sorcerer had up their sleeves. The other advantage was Bill's knowledge of the College's layout. With a thought and a small pulse of Mana, he cast Papier-Mache Mage. The blue-bound volume, *Fantastic Fallacies and Where to Find Them,* popped open just as the first book had and vomited out a torrent of paper.

The pages swirled around Sam for the briefest instant before latching on to his form, molding themselves around his body. In less than an eyeblink, the pages settled, and Sam found himself encased in what appeared to be Spanish conquistador armor with its rounded breastplate, flared pauldrons, tapered waist, and bulbous, balloon-like pants. The outfit was completed by boots, gauntlets, and even a short, fluttering half-cape which trailed down his back... except all of it—every single piece—was constructed from overlapping sheets of papier-mache. As a result, the 'armor' weighed next to nothing and didn't impede his movements in the least. It *did* look absolutely ridiculous.

Better alive and ridiculous than dead and sensible. The Mages at the end of the hall stared, clearly flabbergasted by his sudden transformation. Sam rewarded them for their quick thinking and prompt action by sending another Paper Shuriken spinning toward the dumbstruck Mages.

<Good work, but don't stand around gloating!> Bill roared in his head. <The left-hand path! Go now! We have another party of casters coming up behind us.>

Not wasting a second, Sam took off, but he didn't stop casting Paper Shuriken each time it came off cooldown. Wonder of wonders, the crimson-leather book swung *behind* him, and though Sam couldn't see what he was doing, he felt the rush of Mana flowing from his core. This told him he was still hurling folded ninja stars at anyone who might be trying to follow him from behind.

Skill gained: Sightless casting (Novice I). As a Bibliomantic Sorcerer you don't need to look where you're casting! By relying on your Soul-Bound connection to Bill, the Bibliomancer's Sacred Tome, you can sense the rough location of your enemies and deploy your Orbital Tomes to launch spells at enemies in any direction, even if that direction is behind you! Here's a firm reminder that sometimes the best offense is a good defense, and sometimes, the best defense is to run away as fast as you can! Effect: Cast any spell hot-keyed to an active Orbital Tome in any direction. 15+n% accuracy while using Sightless casting where n =skill level.

Wicked cool. Maybe Sightless casting wasn't terribly accurate—yet—but being able to hurl spells even while you retreated seemed like a nasty surprise for people chasing him. A quick glance over one shoulder confirmed his suspicions. The Paper Shurikens weren't really *hitting* anyone, but it *was* buying him just enough time to slowly widen the gap between him and his pursuers.

There was *one* other thing that he could do which would assuredly slow Octavius down even further. Sam swerved to the right, grabbed a bunch of books—most of them glimmering with mystic energy—and rudely pulled them from the shelves. Books *thudded* on the floor, eliciting a high-pitched shriek from Octavius and his fellow magical lackeys. Sam could understand. As a book lover, the idea of hurling perfectly good books onto the floor was abhorrent, but if he had to choose between his neck and a random book? He'd do what needed doing.

<Quick thinking, kid!> Bill crowed inside his head. <You just gave me an idea! Take the next four rights, then an immediate switchback with four lefts.>

Sam's flagging stamina was going to be an issue before long, but that was a problem for future Sam. Present Sam needed to move, and he needed to move *fast*. So, despite his pounding heart, burning lungs, and the sweat rolling down his face in a sheet, he kicked on another burst of speed, following Bill's instructions even though they seemed extremely counterintuitive. He flew around each turn, but no matter how fast he ran, the sounds of the chase grew louder and louder.

Octavius—or maybe some other group of Mages—was gaining on him, and he really couldn't keep this going forever. Sam wheeled around the final turn then immediately skidded to a halt as an ominous straightaway appeared. This section of the Sage's library was... *different* than the others he'd been to so far. Semi-translucent purple stones still lined the floor, but the bookcases here were all a black obsidian that gleamed with a cancerous green light. There were no candles or lights in the hallway, but there was no need since churning clouds of jade energy swirled through the air, painting everything with spectral illumination.

A placard was affixed to the aisle endcap which read: *Arcanum of Eldritch Taboo! Proceed with EXTREME Caution!*

"You *want* me to go this way?" Sam hollered, eyes wide, mouth suddenly dusty and dry.

<Phft! You worry too much. This is *perfectly* safe as long as you do *exactly* what I say and *only* touch things I tell you to touch. Seriously, though, don't touch *anything* else, or we'll

totally get pulled into an Eldritch Nightmare from which we may or may *not* ever escape. Good talk. Now move.>

"*There he is!*" someone thundered from behind.

Sam stole a look back. Not Octavius and his crew but another group of Mages five strong. He didn't recognize any of them on sight, but that didn't really mean much; they would be just as effective mopping the floor with him. Their sudden appearance decided Sam, and he padded forward, moving at a much slower pace than he wanted. His stamina was running low, so he didn't really have much choice in the matter.

"No, you fool!" the Mages shouted from behind him. "Don't go *any* farther if you value life and sanity!"

Sam ignored them completely and continued deeper into the aisleway. Before long, the clouds of green witchlight were twirling and dancing around Sam as he moved, caressing his skin and whispering odd words into his ears. Those words didn't seem to be in any language Sam had ever heard before, yet he somehow seemed to grasp them regardless.

"*Come, Disciple. This way,*" they whispered gently. "*Know the madness. Embrace the darkness. Breathe in the Chaos. Speak the words. Deskhidati porta sik aduketi al-berk patrulea ororile adankului adenci.*"

As the words flowed through his mind, Sam could've *sworn* he saw faces manifest in the green light; though it was always *just* out of the corner of his eye. A flash of saggy skin studded by spikes, here. The curved edges of protruding horns there. Glimmers of serrated teeth and tearing claws. Several titles tugged at his mind, urging him in closer and closer, *begging* with him, *pleading* with him, *commanding* him to crack the covers and just take a little look-see at the wonders contained within.

<This guy is *mine!*> Bill shouted, though Sam got the distinct impression that he wasn't speaking to Sam. <I was here

first. I called dibs, and I know even Eldritch Horrors respect the ye olde compact of dibs! Let's not be barbaric here.>

That's legit, one of the scraping voices whispered in return. *All hail the dibs and the binding laws of the great compact. Inklinatie-va inainte ve compaktual sacruk et Dibs.*

<These guys aren't nearly as benevolent as me, but I've always said they get a bad rep. I mean, sure, they'll destroy your mind and melt the eyes from your head if you glance at their content, but hey... everyone has their issues, am I right?>

"Steel yourselves, Mages! Brace your minds, and touch *nothing*—no matter what is promised. Only death and madness lie that way. For the love of The Accords, no one fire off a spell; we can't afford to accidentally hit one of these books."

Sam didn't look back. They were almost to the end of the strange aisleway when Bill piped up again, <Yes! I was hoping it would still be here. See that book over there on the right? The one covered in what looks like snakeskin?>

Sam did. It was hard to not to see the book since the snakeskin leather twisted and slithered as though it were a living thing. Worse, this book *hated* him, *hated* the world, and every living thing in it. There was also another feeling thrumming beneath those other sensations, something deeper and far more primal like a powerful ocean current. *Hunger.* That book, whatever it was and whatever it contained, wanted to *eat.*

"Yep," Sam responded with a terse nod, subconsciously taking a step *away* from the tome. "Hard to ignore the book that is eyeing us like a bag of Cheetos."

<Yeah, don't worry about that. We totally go way back, and he owes me one. Just, uh... pull down the book, *gently* set it on the floor, then open the pages, and run like something enormous wants to eat you. Also, I *cannot* stress strongly enough that I am not making a metaphor.>

Everything about that sentence sent up red flags for Sam. One, he was now sharing a soul with an artifact–person–who went back a long way with an *Eldritch horror* who *owed* him a *favor*. In retrospect, that was probably a bad thing. Also, it occurred to Sam that all of these extremely powerful tomes were *not* locked up, while Bill *had* been, which begged the question– just what in the abyss was the Bibliomancer's Sacred Tome? Exactly *how* dangerous was Bill? Those were questions Sam had no answer for, but he was already *way~y~y* too committed to turn back now.

So, though he didn't really *want* to do so, Sam followed Bill's instructions. The Mages pursuing him were gaining quickly, but Sam didn't rush the process. He gingerly lifted the book from the shelf–a sharp lance of fear exploded inside his gut the minute he touched the tome–and placed it on the floor, right in the middle of the hallway. His survival instinct was gibbering like a panicked monkey in the back of his head, just screeching over and over and over again what a *terrible* idea this was. He ignored the fear gibbon... and flung the pages wide.

Constitution +1! Wisdom -1!

The cover landed with a thump and hiss, like two drums and a snake falling down a hill. *Ba-dum, hiss!* Sam was already moving, and he did *not* look back. His stamina had recovered just enough for him to make a break for it, and by golly, he was breaking for it like no one had ever broken for it before. By the time he made it to the end of the aisle, screaming had started in earnest. Although he didn't *want* to, he felt compelled to look and see what terror he and his new pal Bill had unleashed upon the world.

"Shouldn't have looked back." Sam gagged, unable to tear his eyes away. Enormous, purple tentacles studded with neon-pink suckers–each the size of a teacup–and onyx-black spikes bigger than Sam's thumb, were flailing about in the air. One rubbery limb, easily as thick as Sam's thigh, pulled a Mage from her feet, while another tentacle constricted around her middle like a python. A second Mage lobbed a brilliant ball of orange-gold fire, which splashed against the forest of whipping appendages. The attack didn't seem to hurt the otherworld horror even a *little* but *did* get the creature's attention.

A smaller tentacle, no thicker than Sam's wrist, snaked toward the fire-thrower's head. One quick squeeze later and the Mage crumpled to the floor, everything above his shoulder simply *missing*.

"You *know* that thing?" Sam was deeply disturbed.

<Yeah. Vh'uzathel the Hundred-Armed, Ninth Principality of the Depths, Consul of Mysteries, and Unholy Divine of the East. An all-around great guy who throws an *abyss* of a cookout, believe me.> There was a long pause, as though Bill was thinking. <He does have a tiny mean streak when he gets hangry. But hey, that's *their* problem. Furthermore, look who they are *not* paying attention to, huh? *Huh?* It worked!>

On that, at least, the book wasn't wrong. The Mages were so preoccupied with trying not to die—while simultaneously attempting to force the creature back into the pages—that no one had a second glance to spare for Sam. So, a win... Sam supposed? He shook his head, turned his back on the scene of carnage, and hoofed it into a connecting hallway. Bill continued to guide him, and before long, they found themselves in a dusty, dead-end passageway that looked like it hadn't seen a human visitor in the past hundred years. The floors and shelves were coated in a thick layer of undisturbed dust, and even a few cobwebs decorated the shelves; though Sam didn't see any spiders.

Chances were they were regular, ordinary spiders, but after meeting Bill's 'friend' and fellow book-dweller Vh'uzathel the Hundred-Armed, Sam had absolutely *zero* desire to see what other things might call this place home.

Wisdom +1!

"Where to now?" Sam questioned in a low whisper.

They hadn't seen any new groups of Mages since unleashing the Eldritch Horror, but that didn't mean they hadn't *heard* the pounding feet of frantic Mages and the shouts of search parties. Somehow, Bill had allowed them to fly just under the radar, but the Sage's section wasn't infinitely large. As far as Sam knew, there was only one way out—through the Prime Chamber with its many-colored doors. Which meant it was only a matter of time before they ran into another group. Unless the Bibliomancer's Sacred Tome had some other nifty tricks, they'd be out of luck.

<You think this is my first escape, Legs? Also, do you mind if I call you Legs? Since, you know, you're the legs of the operation?>

"Yes, I *mind*," Sam snapped.

<*Jeesh*. A real sensitive type. Fine, I'll keep trying for a good nickname. As for getting out of this place, don't worry your pretty little head. I've got this covered! Or, more specifically, that tapestry at the end of the hallway does. You see it?>

Yep. A faded, threadbare thing that covered the entire stone face of the wall. Truthfully, it wasn't much to look at—a rather plain item embroidered with a variety of complex geometric shapes in muted tones of gray and brown. Sam concentrated on the fabric and found he had a *particularly* hard time focusing. His gaze sort of... *slid* around the tapestry, and he had the strangest urge to simply turn around and walk away. *Mind your own business. There is nothing for you to see here.* It reminded him of the first time he'd seen Nick's Knacks, though the sensation to *look* but *not see* was about a thousand percent stronger.

<You feel *that*, Legs? That's a mystic ward designed to force those with low perception to ignore its existence, bu~u~t the guy who made *this* one kinda overcharged it, which is why this aisle looks abandoned. No one's been here in years. Magic is so cool sometimes. Anywho, this right here is our way out. Now here's what you gotta do...>

Sam crept to the end of the hallway and perfectly followed Bill's instructions, pressing and probing the bricks surrounding the tapestry, then tracing his fingers over the various geometric shapes and patterns worked into the fabric. At first, it seemed like nothing was happening, but after thirty seconds or so, the intricate shapes and lines on the faded fabric began to glow, fed by a trickle of ghostly blue Mana which seeped from Sam's fingertips. After another few passes, there was an audible *click*, and the bottom of the tapestry fluttered in some unfelt breeze. Feeling a rush of exhilaration, Sam lifted the tapestry and found a yawning hallway gouged into the wall.

Perception +1!

<See! I *told* you I had this covered. We won't have long now. With the passageway open, the Perception Ward will be down, and all of the Mana you just used to unlock the way will be like a bonfire to the other Mages. Thankfully, the passageway is filled with some *incredibly* deadly traps that will almost *certainly* murder anyone who follows us through!>

"Wait, what's that now?" Sam faltered on the verge of the threshold. "Incredibly deadly traps?"

<Yep. Chock full of 'em! This place was made by Arch-Magnus Zigrun the Paranoid. Guy was way~y~y into traps, but I was around, so we should be fine; like I already mentioned!

Probably. Now get running! Err... run only fast enough that you can stop on a dime though.>

Sam didn't like any of this, but what other choice did he have? With a reluctant sigh, he ducked into the passageway, bracing himself for whatever fresh horror the Mage's College was going to toss at him.

CHAPTER TWENTY-THREE

Sam spent the next hour *carefully* navigating the secret passageway, even though the path itself was as straight as an arrow. Various traps were scattered throughout, some as deadly as the hungry snake book. Apparently, Arch-Magnus Zigrun the Paranoid had earned his moniker for good reason because there were enough traps to take out a not-so-small army, and each was more deadly and inventive than the last.

Pressure plates which triggered gouts of magical fire that burned like falling stars, scorching anything in a ten-foot radius. Dead drop darts coated with rancid poison that erupted from the walls. Enormous, magically-glowing, axe-bladed pendulums. False floors littered with everything from spikes to acid.

The hallway was an absolute death trap, but Bill proved to be *uncanny* at spotting the trouble. Sam asked the book *why* he was so good at it. Had Bill been some sort of Rogue? Or was trap detection part and parcel of the Bibliomancer class? Bill *insisted* it had nothing to do with either of those options. According to him, he and Zigrun the Paranoid had actually been friends prior to the *current* Archmage's ascension to prominence on the back of The Accords.

If Bill was to be believed, he helped Zigrun *set* most of the traps in this place, but neither of them had ever gotten to *use* the escape tunnel. Zigrun's paranoia had proved to be entirely justified since the current Archmage had staged a coup and removed him by force.

"So, is that why the Archmage locked you up?" Sam quizzed as the pair of them crept through the tunnel, ears straining for the distant sounds of angry guards. Nothing so far. "Because you were buddies with the guy he overthrew?"

<Well, that was certainly a big part of it,> Bill replied easily, <but mostly, it was because I knew what he was *really* up to with those Accords of his. See, in principle, the contract you formed with *me* is nearly identical with the one you formed with The Accords. As a Bibliomancer, I was *intimately* familiar with contract law. So, when the Archmage started pushing for other Mages to sign The Accords as a way to 'hold ourselves accountable', I knew what he was up to.>

<That monster we unleashed? Vh'uzathel the Hundred-Armed? The Accords are *no different* than that creature. They are a living, not-exactly-breathing-but-close-enough being. The Accords are a creature empowered by magic which has enslaved the minds and hearts of the Mages at the College, but instead of feeding off torn flesh, it feeds off the vast Mana reservoirs of those forced to sign. The kind of bond you now have with me? That's the *same* kind of bond the current Archmage has with The Accords. That jerk sold out his people for personal power. I knew it, and I tried to *tell* people, which is why he tried to destroy me. When he couldn't, he settled for locking me down so his dirty little secret would never get out.>

"That's awful," Sam whispered, although it also made so much sense. "We've got to *do* something."

<*Do* we?> Bill offered cheerily. <Not sure if you were following my story, but knowing too much and trying to help, is how I got turned into a book and imprisoned for the last three hundred years. Besides, we're not in any kind of position to help *anyone*. We'll be lucky if we can help *ourselves*. Let's face it; *I'm* awesome, but you're the equivalent of a half-trained monkey. No offense.>

"That was super offensive."

<No, see. I said '*no offense*', so it's fine. Anyway. All of that is to say, let's focus on getting through the next twenty-four hours. Then we can reevaluate. Mkay, pumpkin? Speaking of surviving, we've reached the end of the escape tunnel! Teamwork makes the dream work!>

Up ahead was another dead-end capped with a tapestry exactly like the one that had allowed them into this place. Once more, Bill walked Sam through the elaborate and carefully rehearsed movements required to open the exit. A *click* soon followed, and this time, the tapestry disappeared entirely, letting in a bitterly cold gust of wind that cut through his paper armor like a flaming dagger. The breath caught in Sam's throat as he glanced down. What in the heck? They were easily twenty feet up, and straight down were rolling fields of grass and gentle hillocks covered in an assortment of long grass and small bushes.

Not far off were the dark shapes of trees, standing tall and gaunt against the night-dark horizon. This was impossible. Had to be.

Somehow, they were *inside* the exterior wall that surrounded Ardania, but that couldn't be. The Mage's College was about as far from the exterior wall as you could get—rivaled only by the Royal Palace. True, they'd been walking for an hour, but they hadn't been moving *quickly*, not with all the deadly traps to navigate.

If Sam had to guess, he'd say they'd covered *maybe* a little more than a mile, but that wasn't near far enough to get them to the edge of the city. Based on the countryside and the location of the tree line, this wasn't anywhere near the gate he'd ventured through before with the Wolf Pack, but that didn't really change anything. He finally sputtered, "But *how?*"

<See, this is why I called you a half-trained monkey. No offense. There's still a lot you don't know about this world. The Spatial Magic that works inside the College doesn't work *just* inside the College. It's *easiest* to fold space there because the

building is *designed* as a conduit to make Mana manipulation easier and more efficient, but the same principle can be used elsewhere; assuming you have the Mana pool and the skills required to do so... which almost no one does. Not these days. But there was a time when such extraordinary feats were *far* more commonplace.>

<I will admit that I also don't have the skill to make something like this, but I understand the theory behind it. You make two anchor points. In this case, an anchor point in the College and a connecting anchor point wherever you want the exit to be, and then you simply punch a hole through space! Details are a little fuzzy, but I'm pretty sure you have to construct an ethereal Mana bridge between the two points, which hardens into a temporal hallway like this one. More or less.> The book couldn't shrug because it had no shoulders, but Sam could certainly *hear* the shrug in Bill's voice.

"I think you might need to reevaluate your definition of *simple*." Sam started rubbing at the bridge of his nose. He felt a headache coming on; though whether it was from stress, lack of sleep, or dehydration, he couldn't rightly say. It might even have been from the terrible smell emanating off the black goop covering his body and clothes. "The bigger problem, though, is what the heck are we supposed to do now?"

<Eh, I mean, I'm not the one with the legs in this relationship—don't want to tell you how to do your job or anything—but it seems like jumping might be a good idea.>

"It's like... twenty feet down!"

<Okay, so... tuck and roll? Doesn't seem that complicated. Also, you have Papier-Mache Armor, which will definitely help with the impact. At least enough for us to survive.>

"You're missing a bigger issue," Sam flatly informed the condescending book, "It's midnight. If we jump now, there's no way for us to get back into the city until morning, and from all accounts, getting stuck outside the city gates after dark is an absolute death sentence."

<Huh. Guess things have changed a tiny bit since the last time I was awake. *Hmmm.* I mean... I suppose we could just sort of camp here and hope that those idjits up at the College somehow miss the tapestry and the emergency exit? Or get blasted by all the traps? We can just wait for the sun to come up, hop on down, then slip back into the city unnoticed.>

Sam broke into restless pacing, running through his options. Waiting wasn't a great plan, and it left a lot to chance, but it wasn't like he had a huge number of options. They couldn't go back the way they'd come—that much was certain—and he didn't want to risk the sprawling wilderness. If he died, he would respawn, sure, but he would respawn in the Ardania town square just like everyone else. What was to stop the Mages from deploying a squad of bounty hunters who would just camp the town square until he reappeared? Absolutely nothing. In fact, Sam had to admit that's what he would do if their roles were reversed.

So, finally, he dropped down on to the floor and pressed his back against the wall, feeling more than a little defeated. He was exhausted to his core—quite literally—thanks to the incredibly long day he'd had—a day that felt like it was never going to quit. While he'd been fighting for his life, he hadn't noticed just how tired he was, not with all that adrenaline flowing through his veins. But the white-hot surge of adrenaline was gone now, and it left him feeling hollow and weak by its absence. Now, here he was stranded in a dusty hallway at the end of a murder corridor, silently praying that he wouldn't have to jump to his doom.

Sam propped his knees up and rubbed at his eyes, grinding his palms into his eye-sockets, but it was no use. He groaned softly, sprawled his legs out, and took a few deep breaths before closing his eyes. Which was exactly when the sound of approaching footsteps caught his ear. The noise was soft—just a distant crunch of accumulated dust and grime on a stone floor—but it was distinct enough to immediately catch his attention. Sam was on his feet in an instant, eyes shut, ears straining toward the sound. Was someone really there... or was his exhaustion-addled brain just inventing things?

<I heard it too,> Bill's voice came a second later, <but it's hard to feel any kind of magical signatures here. There's too much Mana in the air thanks to all the traps and spatial distort->

There was a loud *click-thump* and flare of light as someone set off a trap. "Gah! It set my bloody arm on fire! Put it out!"

That was a voice Sam could never forget. Octavius. That one of the traps had just set the Peak Student on fire offered Sam a small burst of smug satisfaction, but the fact that Octavius had managed to survive at *all* was deeply disappointing. Worse, the noise was close—*so very close now*—and it still wasn't anywhere near dawn—five or six hours away, at least. There was a flash of movement and Octavius appeared from the darkness of the tunnel, materializing like an angry poltergeist come to exact its revenge. A trio of Mages accompanied the Earth Mage; somehow all lower-ranked Mages. Two were at the Student level, just like Octavius.

Tullus Adventus was a thick-shouldered brute, while Elsia Derumaux was a blade-thin woman. He recognized them by sight, and the only thing Sam really *knew* about them was that they followed Octavius around like faithful bloodhounds and would do anything he said at the drop of a hat. The third

Mage present, however, was a knife to the guts—Finn. The ice Mage stood apart from the others, and the bruises lining his arms and ringing his eyes told Sam everything he needed to know.

His friend hadn't sold him out, but it was clear Finn was going to suffer terribly for Sam's actions. Octavius would be punished too, but there was an old saying that Sam's dad liked to use, *feces inevitably rolls downhill*. It seemed that Finn was going to receive more than his fair share of it.

"Looks like there's nowhere left for you to run." Octavius' sneer was as deep and wide as a chasm. "You've caused me more shame than you can ever imagine, but I can assure you I will get my recompense out of your flesh, you commoner piece of *filth*. If you give up *now*, it's possible I'll be able to persuade the Archmage to show some level of leniency... not that you *deserve* it. Still, I can be both magnanimous and gracious, but if you resist even in the slightest..."

Octavius faltered, his sneer transforming into a vicious, feral smile that promised pain. "Well, you will regret it until your dying day... however far off that may be."

He turned his cold, calculating gaze on Finn. "You. Failure. Talk some sense into him. That's what we brought you along for, after all. Mayhap if you can convince him to capitulate without further resistance, it will lessen *your* sentence as well."

The words were spoken casually, cruelly, and Sam suspected they were as much for his ears as for Finn. Sam hesitated, *not* because he really thought Octavius would show *any* measure of leniency, but because he was worried about what might happen to Finn if he made a run for it. For Sam, this was a game, one he could quit and restart at any time, but for the young Lordling, this was life. There was no respawn. No quick log out and new character creation. Finn would be stuck with whatever decision Sam made... He would be the one to *really* pay the price.

But before Sam could make up his mind one way or another, Finn acted. The ice Mage moved quickly, throwing himself against the square-jawed Tullus Adventus while simultaneously launching an ice-bolt into Elsia Derumaux's neck. Neither attack would seriously hurt the Mage Armor-clad students, but it made for one heck of a distraction, and that— more than anything else—decided Sam.

With a thought, he conjured his Origami tome and brought it to bear, tossing a Paper Shuriken at Octavius, who looked *completely* stunned by this current turn of events. The paper stars hit true, slamming Octavius back and into the far wall while arcs of bright blue Mana sprayed off his armor and into the air.

"Run, Sam!" Finn shouted, launching a wave of Ice Spikes at Octavius and his sidekicks. In a heartbeat, the scholarly boy was racing toward the yawning hole at the end of the passageway. Finn grabbed Sam's sleeve in passing and pulled him into motion. "Don't just stand there! We're only going to get one shot at this thing!"

Before Sam could think about it, Finn shoved him with both hands. The next instant, he was plummeting from the side of the wall, his arms pinwheeling like mad as butterflies swooped and dove in his gut. Sam hit the ground like a sack of potatoes, the shock of the impact jolting up his legs.

Thankfully, his judo training kicked in. If there was *one* thing you learned in judo, it was how to take a fall. Working on pure muscle memory, Sam angled himself forward, tucking into a tight forward roll that dispersed the majority of the impact and quickly brought him back to his feet, more or less uninjured.

Sure, he'd burned through the entirety of his armor and ten health from the tumble, but he hadn't broken a leg or otherwise seriously damaged himself. The numbers spun in his head, and he realized that even with the excellent landing, he still burned through the equivalent of two hundred health from that fall.

He spun in a circle, searching for any sign of Finn, but a commotion high in the wall drew his eye instead. Octavius' hulking thug, Tullus, had the smaller ice Mage wrapped up from behind in a tight bear hug. Finn was kicking wildly, jerking this way and that as he tried to free himself, but the older Student looked entirely unaffected. He held Finn like a father restraining a grumpy toddler throwing a temper tantrum.

<Hate to tell you this, but we haven't been fully checked out yet!> Bill spoke an instant before a Fireball the size of Sam's skull slammed into the earth not three feet away. The ground erupted in a geyser of light, heat, and rocky shrapnel. Elsia pushed her way to the front edge of the tunnel; she'd apparently recovered from Finn's attack. Even from here, her expression looked like a thunderhead, her face illuminated by a cloak of flame surrounding her like a halo. Clearly, she was a fire Mage, and now, she had a personal vendetta against Sam.

Perfect. It wasn't like Bibliomantic Sorcerers were *especially* weak again flame attacks or anything. Sam needed to run, but he couldn't just leave Finn to the mercy of these magical bullies. He used his Origami tome to launch a Shuriken, but a cone of flame burst from thin air and incinerated his folded star. Ash rained down in plumes of gray and black. Yep. That had been *exactly* as effective as he imagined it would be.

<I'm sorry, kid,> Bill whispered in the back of Sam's head. <There's nothing you can do for him. Not now. The only thing we can do here is go.>

If Sam didn't know any better, he'd say the book sounded genuinely apologetic. Octavius thrust one hand forward, and the earth rumbled beneath Sam's feet. A lance of hardened rock exploded upward, the spear of stone slashing the outside of Sam's arm, biting through a full quarter of Sam's health and leaving a white-hot line of pain in its wake. Celestial *Feces*! A few inches to the left, and that thing would've spit him like a roast pig!

With a yelp, Sam spun on a heel and bolted for the tree line before Octavius or one of his buddies got another clean shot. While Sam ran—weaving left and right so it would be harder to target his fleeing back—he sent his tome zipping around to the rear, unleashing a folded star at the Mages still standing at the mouth of the secret tunnel every time the spell was off cooldown.

<Yeah, really sorry to have to remind you of this, but the range on those bad boys is only ten meters. You're wasting Mana, stop.> Bill's words cut through Sam's fugue, and he simply focused on running.

He didn't look back and didn't stop as he got past the low-lying brush and into the cover of the tree line, which would shelter him from any of the deadly spells the trio might hurl his way. Sam quickly ducked behind a broad oak, then fished a health potion from the leather bandolier slung across his chest. He popped the cork with his thumb, then forced the concoction down, gagging a little from the syrupy consistency and the sickly-sweet taste of over-ripe fruit.

The grossness was well worth the result; energy and a sense of well-being rippled through him, instantly knitting torn flesh back together. His whole body itched and tingled as the magical brew took full effect, but the odd sensation was gone almost as quickly as it had come. In an instant, he was back in fighting form.

Sam slipped the empty glass vial into his Unending Flask—waste not and all that—then popped his head around the trunk of the tree, scanning the wall. There was no sign of Tullus or Finn, but Elsia held an orb of flickering fire in each upraised hand, marking out her and Octavius even in the dark. The pair of them were scanning the landscape, but Sam knew that was a useless endeavor thanks to the darkness lying over the countryside like a thick winter quilt.

"It doesn't matter!" Octavius shouted into the night, his voice ringing crystal clear in the still area. "You won't survive an *hour* out there! You're out of the city walls at night, and the spells and shouting are going to bring *everything* to this area! You've only prolonged the inevitable, trading in one death for another. When you respawn, I'll be *waiting* for you! You hear me, you *traitor*? I'll be *waiting*!"

As much as Sam hated to admit it, Octavius wasn't wrong. A branch cracked not far off, and in the distance, a ghostly howl pierced the air. It was going to be a very, *very* long night... or a very short one.

CHAPTER TWENTY-FOUR

Sam bolted left and unleashed a Paper Shuriken at a lunging, rust-colored fox the size of a pony. The folded ninja star embedded itself in the creature's neck and chin, finally eating away at the last of its health. It dropped with a meaty *thud*, kicking up a small plume of dusty earth. Sam didn't have a moment to breathe, though, because a second fox was closing in on his right, fur bristling, black lips pulled back from fangs that gleamed silver in the moonlight. Sam considered launching Shurikens at the ferocious beast but immediately decided against it.

Contrary to Octavius' assertion, he *had* survived for more than an hour. The monsters were thick as flies on a fresh carcass, and they were *way* more powerful and bloodthirsty than when he'd ventured out with Dizzy and the rest of the Wolf Pack crew. They were *bigger.* They moved faster, hit harder, and worked more efficiently. Most importantly, they *didn't* quit. His time stumbling through the wilderness had been a near-constant onslaught of attacks from bear-sized bunnies, pony-sized foxes... Only Bill being able to tell where the enemies were around them was keeping Sam alive.

The darkness was *not* his friend, and if he had needed to rely on his eyes, he would have been dead a dozen times over. On a positive note, his Paper Shuriken attack was deadly effective against these unarmored foes, but he was quickly learning that his new class had one *significant* limitation that might just end up getting him killed—paper.

Although casting the spells via Origami Activation cost next to nothing, actually sitting at... one-point-five-four Mana per use, he was *severely* limited by the amount of paper he had on hand. Run out of magical paper, and you were out of spells. He could assign spells to tomes while enemies were in range, but it cost about four Mana a second until the process was complete. Bill said that interrupting the process would be a bad idea, and it seemed there were *always* enemies in range and ready to interrupt him out here. All of this meant that he couldn't risk using any of the extra books he had stashed away in his flask.

Sam did have one trick left. With a snarl, he summoned his new Quill Blade. Twenty-three Mana vanished from his Core, and the oversized ostrich feather jutting from his cavalier hat took to the air, shimmering and morphing as it leaped into his outstretched hand.

In an instant, the cobalt feather was coated in gleaming silver, ghostly blue runes running down the length of the blade. The quill-portion of the oversized feather was wrapped in supple, black leather and acted as a sword hilt, and instead of a proper pommel, there was a spiked, silver nib that, according to Bill, actually wrote quite nicely.

Bill claimed that at higher levels, a well-trained Bibliomancer could actually inscribe some spells on the air itself—no paper required—creating near-impenetrable wards and mystic barriers. The feathery plumage acted as the weapon's cutting edge, while the tip was more than sharp enough to impale any creature unlucky enough to get in range. Once again, it seemed that his channeling skill was reducing the Mana cost to maintain the blade, as his Mana only slipped away at just over four and a half points a second.

The fox in front of Sam snarled and darted in low, slathering jaws spread wide, but Sam was ready for the attack. The foxes were fast, true, but they were rather predictable and seemed to follow a relatively small number of scripted attack combinations. That meant that, after a while, it was easy enough to predict what they would do and where they would go. The feint right and lunge in low was almost always followed by a ferocious leap. Sam sidestepped right as the fox launched into the air. He brought the Quill Blade screaming down like a woodcutter's axe, catching the furry critter mid-flight.

The jagged, razor-sharp feathers bit deeply into the fox's shoulder, chomping through twenty points of its health. On a fox during the day, that would have been enough to end the fight. Not here, not now. The fox let out a yelp as it tumbled to the ground but quickly gained its feet. At least Sam's counterassault had crippled one of its front legs, severely slowing its movement rate. Another blazing-fast slash across the distorted neck ended the fox before it had a chance to evade and recuperate.

Experience gained: 420 (240 Dartmoor Fox x4 + 180 Bunny-Bear x 6 (Mystically altered creatures)).

Skill increase: Paper Shuriken (Novice IV). Big gains for having this spell for only a couple hours! Murder spree or something else going on?

Skill increase: Magical Origami (Novice IV). Hard for a derivative skill to outrank the skill it comes from, know what I mean?

Skill increase: Origami Activation (Novice II). Activate lots and bunches of various abilities to rank this up faster! Repetition makes for slow learning.

Breathing hard, his stamina ridiculously low and his health at just over sixty percent, Sam banished the Quill Blade from his hand before it could consume any more of his Mana. The feather shimmered and darted back to the brim of his hat, just a gaudy plume once more. He was once again thankful for his training with Sphinx. If it wasn't for the Rogue's instruction in bladed weapons, he'd already be long dead.

<That was some pretty fancy footwork, Legs.> Bill chuckled as Sam rolled his eyes at the moniker. <Most Mages avoid learning even the basics when it comes to physical combat, as if killing someone with magic is somehow more impressive than stabbing someone in the eye with a dagger. Good to see you have the fundamentals down. Knowing how to use that blade saved my neck more times than I can count on two hands, not that I have hands at all, mind you. Or a neck. Not anymore.>

"You have a *spine*, don't you?" Sam grinned at the groan he got in reply. Maybe the 'Legs' thing would vanish if he kept this up. "Problem is, I don't think I'm good enough to keep us alive until dawn. These attacks are getting worse, and any noise we make brings more of them to us. Plus, sooner or later, I'm going to run out of spells. Once that happens, it's only a matter of time before my stamina gives out and these things overwhelm me. We need a plan, Bill."

<Well, you're not wrong about that,> the book agreed. <You know, what we could *really* use is an easily defensible position to hole up in until morning. We could scale a tree, maybe? Just hunker down on a branch and try to wait it out? How far off can morning be?>

It wasn't the worst idea Sam had ever heard, but he suspected it wouldn't be that easy. He could easily envision himself clambering to a high bough, falling asleep against the tree... only to wake up to find a pack of hungry wolves circling the trunk, but the book's words did give him an idea. Sam headed over to a monstrous fir tree that went up, up, and then up a little more, rising impossibly high above the canopy overhead. It was a bit of a gamble, but if Sam could get to a high enough vantage point, he might be able to find a spot which would act as a good defensible position.

So up he went, clambering hand over foot, slipping from one branch to another until he was fifty feet in the air. His stamina was draining each second that he was climbing, so he needed to take frequent breaks to stand on a branch. It didn't take Sam long to spot Ardania's outer wall, a sinuous serpent of gray stone snaking its way across the wild landscape. From the total darkness on the land, sunrise was still four or five hours off. Heading for the wall right now wouldn't do him any favors—just the opposite.

It would leave him out in the open with no cover, no place to run, and nowhere to make a stand if things got tough. He did, however, spot what he hoped was a cluster of rocks jutting up from a heavily wooded section a good distance off. Thank goodness for moonlight. He squinted, brow scrunching up as he studied the stone formation. He could be wrong, but it looked like there was a dark fissure in the rock face.

"Bill," he whispered, thrusting one finger toward the rocks, "you think that's a cave?"

<Yeah... could be,> the book agreed after a long beat. <Since we aren't exactly in a position to be picky, I say we go give it a little look-see.>

"What if something is... in there?" Sam's tired and paranoid mind was working through all the possible ways this plan could go horribly wrong.

<Eh. Truthfully? It probably *is* inhabited. Things have changed since I've been gone, but there *were* bears around this area. That looks *exactly* like the kind of place a bear would call home sweet home. If I was a gambling man... err... *book*, I'd say there's about an eighty percent chance we'll run up against a night-changed black bear.>

"That's not in *any* way happy-making," Sam replied, his addled mind losing track of proper word choices.

<Yeah. If there *is* a bear... you know what? Here's a little food for thought. If there's something nasty in there and we somehow manage to kill a bear, then we'll almost *certainly* make it until morning! See, the animal won't respawn for at least eight hours, and most lesser creatures tend to avoid the haunts of greater predators, which means the bunnies, foxes, and even wolves would give that place space since they don't want to be eaten either.>

Bill waited but got no reply. <Do we have great odds of killing whatever lives there? No. Do I think we have a fair shot at it? Also no! But it's either that or blundering around in the wilderness for the next five hours. Basically, it boils down to trying to kill *one* big thing or a *hundred* small things.>

"If it's not a bear's den? If it's something worse, like a secret dungeon?"

<Well, at least we'll be warm when we perish horrifically. Go big or die trying, am I right?> As crazy as it sounded, Sam had to admit there *was* a certain logic to Bill's argument. <Are we going or what? You know what, while we have a few seconds, how about you just go ahead and assign a spell?>

Eighteen seconds later, a second book was filled with the magical requirements for Paper Shuriken. "Did that take longer to activate? Hey... why is it called Paper *Shuriken* if I keep throwing out ninja stars? They *are* different things."

<How about you just get moving instead of analyzing incongruencies?> Bill shot back. <You increased the rank of your Origami, right? That means you can pack more Mana into the pages, and *that* is what is really doing damage. That's why it takes longer, as well.>

Sam sighed and began to descend the tree. They set off through the thick press of trees, moving at little more than a snail's pace since they had to navigate the forest under the cover of darkness. Sam's perception had reached the minimal level, so at least he was no longer working in a deficit, but it was *still* nearly impossible to see anything. The thick canopy overhead blocked out most of the watery, silver moonlight, and the tangle of small shrubs and jutting roots lining the forest floor threatened to trip him up at every possible turn.

One hour of hard trekking and another fox ambush later, Sam shouldered his way through a copse of pines and emerged in a starlit clearing with rocks protruding from the ground like a spiked crown.

Experience gained: 60 (60 Dartmoor Fox x1 (Mystically altered)).

This close up, it was clear the fissure he'd seen in the rockface was, in fact, the entrance to some sort of cave system. How deep the cave went, he couldn't say—not without going in and exploring more thoroughly. Sam dropped into a crouch and watched the entrance for a few minutes, staying utterly silent. There was no discernible movement, and he didn't hear any monstrous roars echoing up from the cave depths. Still, this now seemed like a *terrible* idea.

Staying in the open was a worse idea, and deep down, he knew it. Decided, he stole from the tree line and noiselessly padded across the meadow. He decided *not* to summon his orbiting tomes just yet since a trio of glowing and whirling magic books would almost certainly get him spotted, but he was ready to summon his Quill Blade at the first hint of trouble.

The fissure was rather narrow, and he had to turn sideways to make it through the passage. After a few feet, the rocky crevice expanded dramatically, opening up into a large chamber with rough walls. The stink of musky fur and the metallic tang of old blood hit him in the nose like a roundhouse kick to the face. Pungent. Overpowering. *Bestial.* He took a step, and something crunched then snapped beneath the sole of his boot, the sound like the report of a rifle in the enclosed space. Lining the sandy floor was a myriad of yellowing bones. Most of them were from bunnies or foxes, but a few suspiciously long femurs could've easily come from a human.

Yep, this cave *definitely* belonged to some sort of animal. If whatever lived here happened to be home at the moment, it would know there was an intruder thanks to the shotgun blast of snapping bone. Suddenly, Sam was deeply regretting that he hadn't let Sphinx show him some of the fundamentals of stealth. But that was why parties existed—because a game like this wasn't *meant* to be soloed. No one could do *everything.* He was just in the unenviable position of having no other choice, no options, and no friends to rely on. If he made it out of this alive, he planned to rectify that.

A shaft of moonlight illuminated another tunnel at the far side of the small cavern. It snaked out of sight, presumably leading deeper into the earth. Sam *absolutely* didn't want to delve any further—knowing that certain death likely awaited him below—but he couldn't stay here with a potentially deadly enemy at his exposed back. Running had served him well so far, but this time around, Sam knew the best course of action was... well... *action.* If he was going to survive until morning, he needed to clear the cave system.

He cracked Bill's pages and summoned his bound books from their holding reservoir in Bill's Soul Space. The tomes appeared around him in a flash of light and began their slow rotation around him. Sam wanted to conserve as much of his magic as he could, so instead of summoning his Quill Blade, he pulled his dagger from the sheath at his belt, his knuckles white as he clenched the hilt. With that done, he summoned Papier-

Mache Armor once more; a whirlwind of pages swirled out from one of his books, encasing him once more in flexible, ink-covered conquistador armor. He winced as he saw how *thin* that book was getting.

He was as ready as he was going to get, and stalling was a bad idea. The passageway at the end of the chamber hooked sharply left, then curved back on itself for ten feet or so. The moonlight from the entrance didn't reach this deep into the cave system, and he shouldn't have been able to see a thing... yet there was a faint orange glow emanating from just up ahead.

<I don't like this, Le– *Sam*. Could be wrong, but that looks a lot like fire.> Sam didn't disagree with Bill, but he didn't dare speak and risk further alerting any potential enemies that he was here. Despite the fact that everything about this situation was sending up red flags, Sam pushed on. They'd already worked through this plan, and this was still their best option of surviving the night. The passageway curled away, ending at a carved staircase with torch-lined walls.

<I have no idea what this is, but I know what it's not—a bear den. Could be a bandit's camp or maybe even something worse. We won't survive it, whatever it is. I'll be the first to admit when I'm wrong, and I was wrong. We need to turn around and beat feet. Now.>

Sam faltered, knowing that Bill was probably right. Yet, his gamer sense was tingling; this right here was quest fodder. Turning back was the *smart* thing to do, but whatever mystery lay at the bottom of this staircase was probably game-changing. Yeah, if he ventured any farther, he might die, but even if he turned back, he was probably going to die anyway. Dying in a night-dark forest, devoured by a bunch of hungry, overgrown rabbits was certainly *not* any better than getting run through by a bandit's blade.

Better to go out in a blaze of glory with the potential upside of a huge quest or a 'first to accomplish' reward." Feeling a heady rush of exhilaration, he whispered, "Nope. Get ready to fight. We're going in."

<I like your spunk, Legs. You're clearly dumber than a box of rocks—weird, considering your intelligence score—but you've got grit. Just be sure to let me know what being wrong tastes like after the thing that lives here gets done ripping us to pieces.>

Sam slipped down the staircase, moving like a shadow, holding his breath for fear of being heard. After dropping twenty feet, the staircase let out into an enormous chamber, but unlike the natural cavern above, this place was some sort of ancient temple sunken into the earth. Sam had never seen anything like it. Fluted columns ran along the natural stone walls, supporting an elaborate vaulted ceiling, which, in turn, supported a trio of huge chandeliers crafted from black wrought iron and pale bone. More black candelabras decorated the columns, all filled with yellow tallow candles which burned with sooty orange light.

At the far end of the chamber was a raised dais adorned by a looming statue of some great horned beast with a lupine face, standing upright on powerful legs, clawed hands raised in supplication toward the heavens. Positioned in front of the statue was a crude stone block, which Sam guessed was a sacrificial altar. The bloody body splayed out across the surface of the table went a *long* way to supporting his theory. Attending to the altar was a Wolfman wielding a ceremonial dagger of black glass and green emerald. The Shaman's fur was a pale silver, and brown woolen robes hung from his gaunt body like ill-fitting hand-me-downs.

This was bad but maybe not impossible. After all, there were no other Wolfmen present. It would be one on one; Sam had the element of surprise going for him, and since this guy was a spellcaster... Sam would probably only have to land a couple of solid hits to put him down for keeps. Plus, killing a Wolfman in the middle of a sacrificial ritual would undoubtedly win him some serious points.

Yep. He could do this. Feeling a sudden boost of confidence, he raised his hands, his Shuriken Tomes zipping to the front. The book covers spread, ready to unleash paper fury... which is precisely when an enormous, callus-covered palm closed around his throat, razor-sharp claws pressing against his tender flesh.

CHAPTER TWENTY-FIVE

"I wouldn't were I you, morsel," came a growling rasp, the words guttural. A pair of Wolfmen stepped into view on his left and right. One was a hulking male with tawny fur while the other was a lithe female with a jet-black coat. Both wore dark brown leather armor and carried wicked, single-edged blades that looked more than sharp enough to cut him in two. Clearly, Sam had vastly overestimated his abilities, and now, he was going to pay the price. He briefly considered attacking anyway but dismissed that idea since he would likely die before he ever even got a single spell off.

Reluctantly, he dismissed his floating books, which returned to Bill's Soul Space in a glimmer of magical light. The pressure eased up minutely around Sam's delicate throat, and his captor growled, "Wise choice."

Wisdom +1!

The tawny-furred guard produced a pair of heavy shackles from a leather satchel hanging at his side and quickly clamped the irons around Sam's wrists. That done, the Wolfman let go of Sam's throat entirely—a welcome relief—then roughly shoved him into motion. The silver-furred Shaman watched Sam through golden eyes as the guards marched him across the chamber and secured him to the wall with another set of heavy-duty chains.

<I *tried* to warn you,> Bill muttered inside his head, sounding rather smug. <I mean, I'm not *really* one to say I told you so, but I *absolutely* told you so. On the bright side, it looks like they're probably going to ritually sacrifice us.>

"Failing to see how ritual sacrifice is a good thing," Sam hissed as he watched the lead guard—the thug who'd nearly choked the life out of him—exchange harsh words with the Shaman.

<Well, I've seen a sacrificial ritual or two in my day, and from what I remember, they use a special knife that kills on touch. In *theory,* it shouldn't even hurt! At least I don't think so. I mean, I don't have nerve endings, so maybe I'm not the best one to ask.>

"That can't happen, Bill. We *need* to get out of here. Isn't there something you can do? Some Bibliomancer trick you haven't taught me yet?"

<Obviously, there are a *ton* of things I haven't taught you, but this class doesn't pair well with 'improvisation'. We're *not* on-the-fly evocation Mages. We can go toe-to-toe with any spell caster out there, but only if we are *ready* for it. Getting out of here in one piece is a total pipedream... but good on you for staying so optimistic!>

"Bring him," the Shaman Wolfman barked at the red-furred guard in the guttural Wolfman tongue before gesturing toward the altar with one claw-tipped hand.

"No, no, no!" Sam hissed, panic surging through him. "This is *not* how my story ends. I made it too far to die here. I *refuse* to let these things kill me, just to respawn right into Octavius' hands. But what could possibly...?"

Well, there was *one* thing he hadn't tried. As the guard approached, Sam hunched his shoulders, lowered his eyes, and raised his chin in submission, mimicking the body language that he'd learned in his dungeoneering class. Then he pressed his eyes shut—mind whirling like mad—as he attempted to conjure the strange phrase he'd heard the Wolfman from his class say. *"Greetings, fur brothers. Ruazhi noare vragnik, ibois najstarkei vragnu prinosit velichayshuyu silzha."*

The guard faltered, ears flicking back, confusion flashing across his muzzle then capering through his muddy-brown eyes. He glanced back at the Shaman over one shoulder. The Shaman looked equally skeptical, lips pulled back from gleaming fangs, golden eyes narrowed in suspicion. The Shaman waved the guard off, then approached, nose sniffing at the air as though he might be able to smell Sam's deception. *"How is it you speak our tongue, Mageling?"*

"Who is it that taught you those words?" the Shaman barked back in the Wolfman tongue. *"Choose your words wisely. If I sense any trickery, I will see you dead before you can blink twice."*

Check. No deception or trickery.

"The Mage's College," Sam blurted out. *"I took course on Wolfman word-speak. Class Alpha had captured one of your Scouts, a Wolfman name..."*

Sam faltered, mind straining for the name of the creature. *Velman?* No. *Veklek?* No, that wasn't quite right either, but it was close. He pressed his eyes closed, picturing the creature with his coarse, gray fur and amber eyes, not so different from the eyes of the Shaman. Unable to translate, he finished with, "Velkan of the Redmane Tribe."

*"*So, you are of College of magic,*"* the Shaman snarled in the human tongue. "An enemy to The People."

"No! Not!" Sam practically spat the words out while vigorously shaking his head.

<Smooth. You sound super convincing and not at *all* suspicious.>

"I speak truth!" Sam continued, ignoring Bill entirely. *"I'm enemy of Mage training group! I just like you. I train for while. Tonight I'm no friend of Mages no longer. That's why I'm*

out of after dark. I'm on runaway. Rogue Mage. I stole big meaning books and made unhappy kill-on-sight on way out."

The Wolfman Shaman rubbed at his chin with a clawed thumb, a dangerous gleam in his eye.

"Pups," he growled after a beat, "this one shall serve us in other ways. Prepare to move the Traveler. We will take him to The O'Baba and let her decide his fate."

Sam simply watched blankly as words were exchanged that he couldn't understand, not knowing how much they would change his future.

***

The steely gray pre-dawn light had invaded the sky by the time Sam finally saw the jagged teeth of the wooden outpost poking up through the canopy of the forest. The trip had been an uncomfortable one; the Wolfmen had tried to take Bill, but when they realized the chain connecting Sam to the book couldn't be severed, they settled for hog-tying Sam, gagging him, and carrying him like a sack of potatoes. Unlike the Hardcores, who had so badly underestimated him not long ago, the Wolfmen were taking no chances with a potential enemy Mage in their midst. They treated him like a cobra—powerful, deadly, and liable to strike at any moment.

The Wolfman outpost itself was the size of a small town and was entirely surrounded by a tribal-style wooden palisade at least twenty-five feet tall. The Wolfmen had cleared back every tree for a hundred feet from the wall, ensuring that no sly Rogue or daring adventurer would be able to sneak in under the tree cover and infiltrate the camp unseen. Curiously, though, the trees *inside* the palisade remained fully intact. Ancient ash trees and thick-trunked oaks lifted leafy branches skyward like saints in prayer, while the lower boughs supported a variety of wooden huts, all connected by a series of narrow walkways and precarious-looking rope bridges.

Those weren't the only oddities about this strange tree-village or perhaps... military outpost? The oddest thing of all was that there wasn't a gate in the palisade—no visible way that Sam could see for getting in and out of the settlement. That didn't seem to deter the Wolfmen in the least. Sam watched as one of the many guards patrolling the grounds scampered up the face of the palisade as effortlessly as a spider, using its long claws to reach the top of the battlements in seconds before simply leaping into the air, catching a dangling rope, then swinging over to a nearby platform.

It was like watching a Tarzan flick, except this time, the vine-swinging ape-man had contracted a bad case of lycanthropy. Sam's captors exchanged a few guttural phrases with the guards patrolling the perimeter and were then waved through for admittance to the camp.

The Wolfmen lowered a rope cradle which they used to haul Sam to the top, knowing that there was no way he was scaling the wall trussed like a Thanksgiving turkey. The others scrambled over the wooden wall without so much as breaking a sweat. Sam had to admit it was a pretty remarkable display of speed, strength, and agility.

Though a number of huts adorned the thick tree boughs, the larger communal buildings were built on the ground. Unlike the human capital, Ardania, which was laid out in a neat grid—a place for everything and everything in its place—the Wolfman village was a haphazard sprawl that didn't seem to have any real rhyme or reason behind the layout.

Rather, Sam reminded himself, there didn't *seem* to be a reason *he* could figure out. To the Wolfmen, it probably made perfect sense. Although a great many of the buildings were constructed from wood, several were meticulously constructed from stone. The thunderous *clang-clang-clang* of steel striking steel drifted from one such building—probably a smithy, though the building was not marked in any discernible way.

Sam and company wound their way through the village, earning curious glances from onlooking fur-faced residents, eventually finding themselves outside a hulking long-house that appeared to be some sort of central meeting hall.

<Woo *doggie*, this place has some *serious* stench.> Sam felt a shiver of anxiety race along his spine, but he couldn't ask for clarification. Thankfully, Bill continued without prompting, <Seriously, this place just *oozes* magic. To have that much juice emanating from the place, they must have enchantments baked into every stone and board.>

<Abyss, I can't even imagine how much power it would take to do something like that. Come to think of it, I'm not actually sure *what* the magic here is supposed to do. The workings and bindings are foreign to me, which is really saying something 'cause I've been around a *long* time. I'll tell you this; it's impressive as all get out.>

Finally, after what felt like *hours*, the Wolfmen unceremoniously dropped Sam into the dirt, plucked the gag from his mouth, then cut the bindings securing his feet and legs so that he'd be able to walk on his own. When he tried to stand, he nearly fell right back over; his legs had gone to sleep on him. Fuzzy pinpricks raced along his lower limbs, and his feet felt like a pair of lead weights tied to the end of each ankle.

"Wait here," the Shaman tersely instructed the other guards before grabbing Sam by the nape of the neck. His claws were pressing down hard enough to draw blood, and Sam was being steered through the wide doors and into the longhouse

proper. Every step felt like a perilous endeavor thanks to his uncooperative legs. Sam was expecting the inside of the hut to be crude but was surprised yet again.

The floor was covered in a lush carpet of flawless green grass, accented in spots by the colorful blooms of wildflowers. There were a number of low wooden tables spread throughout the hall, obviously meant for eating, though you would need to sit on the floor instead of using a chair. There were also colorful tapestries decorating the walls, woven from gossamer silk and decorated with intricate, Celtic-like knots and hard-edged geometric patterns. The Wolfmen weren't human, and their society was obviously vastly different from the human version... but these were no savages.

The Shaman forcefully guided Sam past the tables, then pushed him through yet *another* door that connected to a large kitchen area. The floors were polished cobblestone, the walls were wood, and a massive fireplace lurked against the far side of the room. Granite countertops lined the other walls, all covered with an assortment of pots and pans, knives and cleavers, racks of spices, and mounds of meat. There was a square, waist-high worktable positioned smack-dab in the middle of the room. Standing behind it was the kitchen's sole occupant—an ancient female Wolfman.

She stood at the counter, carving up a slab of blood-red meat with an enormous cleaver. She had to be the single oldest Wolfman Sam had ever seen. Her size was rather small, her back bent from age, fur a nearly metallic silver speckled with white. She wore a silk shawl draped across her back and shoulders and a long leather apron that covered her front.

"O'Baba," Sam's Shaman captor growled in the Wolfman tongue, hunching in on himself until he was smaller

than the bent she-wolf carving up the meat. *"This is the one of which I sent word."*

She surveyed Sam for a moment with eyes that were so gold they almost appeared to be a burnt orange, her nostrils flaring wide as she tasted the air. *"You have done well, BrightBlood. Honor to you and your house."*

She dipped her head just a fraction of an inch in respect. *"Now leave us."*

The Wolfman hesitated for a beat. *"Are you sure it is safe, O'Baba."*

Her eyes narrowed, and her fangs flashed. *"I can handle the whelp well enough on my own, pup. If you think otherwise, I would be more than happy to demonstrate my prowess as Alpha Female."*

The cleaver in her hand began to bleed a septic black light that looked like juiced death. The male Shaman's eyes widened visibly in shock, quickly turning to fear. He lowered himself even more until he was nearly bent in two.

"That will not be necessary, great O'Baba." He bowed himself back out of the room, never exposing his back to the crone and never taking his eyes from her face.

<Woof. She just put him in his place, hard! Stay sharp around this one, Sammy. She's a force to be reckoned with.>

"Whelps these days," The O'Baba muttered, this time in accented English. After a moment, she sighed and turned her fiery gaze squarely on Sam. "You. Mage-pup. Before you get any funny notions, know that I could kill you without batting an eye, *ya*? Now, if I understand correctly, you are an outsider. A Rogue Mage. One hunted by your own people. Is this true?"

Sam licked his lips, eyes fixed on the heavy cleaver in her hand. Considering the outright *terror* he'd seen in the Shaman's face, he had to assume this woman was the leader of this group of Wolfmen and was probably far deadlier than she appeared to be on the surface. Lying to her or trying to trick her in any way would probably end with him dead, his head adorning a spike somewhere as a warning to other would-be heroes. He would respawn, but he wanted to avoid that if he could. After all, they'd kept him alive for this long, which meant he had a real possibility of getting out of this mess in one piece.

"Yes," he finally said. "All of that is true."

"So. If we were to let you live, let you *run*," she waved her free hand as though shooing a bothersome fly, "what would you do, hmmm? Where would you go?"

Sam paused and frowned. Of all the questions he'd expected, that wasn't among them. His frown turned into a grimace as he ran a host of potential options through his head. "Honestly? I don't know. There's no life for me back at the College, but I have a cool new class, which I kinda want to keep. I'd rather avoid starting over if I can."

He seesawed his head back and forth. "I suppose Ardania is big enough for me to hide in? There's *got* to be a way for me to fly under the radar, so chances are I'll try to vanish. Keep out of sight of the guards. Maybe work to sabotage the Mage's College; they have it coming."

The she-wolf regarded him for a long, long time, her inhuman gaze cutting deep, flaying him all the way to his soul, exposing his every thought and motive. She was weighing him, measuring him... but for *what?*

"What if there was *another* option, young pup?" she finally allowed after what felt like an eternity. "You are an outsider now—you have said as much yourself."

She paused, licking her fangs, then returning to her work with the cleaver, chopping at the slab of bloody meat on the table. "You are no fan of your own people. You seek the destruction of the Mage's College, as do we. We could help you. Might be, you join with us instead of your own ilk. There would be *many* advantages."

"Wait. I'm sorry? Are you trying to *recruit* me?"

<She is *obviously* trying to recruit *me*! I think that you should let her know that if I go, you'll follow. Also, I like bribes. Have her find me a romance novel.>

"I thought the Wolfmen... *hated* humans?" Sam was doing his best to ignore Bill.

"Hate? No." She shook her shaggy head. "We *honor* our enemies. There is no hate in it. Rather, it is a matter of survival, young pup. Your kind or mine. Only one may survive, unbroken. It seems that you work against the best interest of your own people anyway, so why not help us? We need eyes and ears inside the walls of Ardania. We need saboteurs."

"The benefits of such an arrangement are many. Should we win the conflict to come, you will be a Lord of our people. You are also a Mage. We have many Shamans and books that even the College knows nothing of. Unlike the Mages, we will not gouge you with exorbitant fees or force you into 'Accords'. We offer *training*. We can give you a new soulbind location, here among our people. We even have assets inside the city to help as needed."

Sam thought about it. Honestly, this sounded *awesome*. In most games, he chose a race other than human, and this was his chance to do so again. He wouldn't actually become a Wolfman, but he would be working in tandem with them; which was cool as heck. The idea of betraying all of humanity left him feeling a little uncomfortable, but this was a *game*. Playing as a spy for the rebel faction sounded rad. Especially if it meant taking down the College and that jerk Octavius. Going this route also meant no reroll! This was *exactly* the answer he'd been looking for. Still, he didn't give in right away.

"I'd be lying if I said I wasn't intrigued. But I do have one question. What if I brought in a few other people? Others that I could vouch for? I'm part of a team that wants to be a Guild, except we don't even know how to begin with the human faction. If you guaranteed us a Guild Charter inside the Wolfman faction, I'm sure they'd be on board as well."

O'Baba pondered his request for only a second. "We will give refuge to your packmates, Mageling. If they defect of their own volition, I will personally grant them a Guild Charter. They shall be the first human guild of our people and exalted among our kind for it, but there is one thing. You... *specifically...* must prove yourself to us first. We have found that your kind is more than happy to spill an endless ocean of words but rarely are you willing to spill *blood.* If you and your packmates would be one with The People, you must prove your allegiance to our cause."

Sam nodded slowly. Of course, there would be some sort of test. "Okay. I can see how that makes sense. What exactly do you have in mind?"

"Two things, pup." Her nostrils flared, and she raised two gnarled fingers riddled with arthritis into the air. "First. My Scouts have discovered that the Mage's College is planning to send a Mage here to perform a powerful spell, possibly even capable of wiping this outpost off the map. The ancient magics of The People have protected us thus far, but this new spell will swallow our whole outpost into the heart of the earth itself. If you and your packmates would be one spirit with us, you must disrupt this. Sabotage any hope of making it happen. In this, you must not fail. Succeed, and you will be one of us.

"The second matter is of a personal nature, whelp. You mentioned to my Shaman that a certain Wolfman is being held captive by the College, Velkan of the Redmane Tribe. He is known to me." She snarled, white-hot anger flashing in her eyes. "He is my blood. My grand-whelp. If he still lives, I would see him freed. If he is dead, there is nothing to be done. As we say in the ancient tongue, *suntse ikzlazi kade na nas vsekh. The sun rises and falls on us all, in time.* If you can save him, I will be in your debt. This is no small thing."

She brought the meat cleaver down with a thud, cleaning hacking through a meaty joint. Sam solemnly stated, "I accept. You also mentioned that I would be able to fix my bind point here. Is..."

He faltered. He was on uncertain ground here, and asking for favors could cost him what little goodwill he'd somehow managed to earn so far. <Oh, just *ask* her already. What's the worst thing that can happen? She kills you? That's what we expected coming into this thing. She clearly needs us, so don't sweat it.>

Bill was right. "Is it possible for me to bind my respawn point here right now?"

"It is not only possible, it is *required*," The O'Baba growled in response. "We are not trusting. You must *prove* yourself to be one of us. As is our way, there are consequences for failure. Should you fail in your quest to stop the College, you will die and be reborn here; only to die again and again. *Many* times over to fuel our spells. If you should reject my offer right now, I will kill you once—but *only* once. A painless death, and we part ways, or you can risk everything and prove your worth to The People. It is your choice. What would you have?"

Quest alert! Trust of the Pack: The O'Baba has offered you and any teammates you recruit a chance to betray humanity in exchange for a permanent place among The People. In order to earn the trust of The People, you must uncover and thwart a deadly new spell that the Mage's College is planning to unleash, which will destroy the Wolfman Outpost known as Narvik. You have one week to accomplish this portion of the quest, or you will automatically die to the curse of the Shaman O'Baba.

Accomplishing this task will earn you the favor of the Wolfmen and change your racial alignment. As a reward, you have been promised a Guild Charter and a questline to grant you a Lordship. Warning! Changing racial alignments has serious consequences! You will be pitting yourself against all of humanity! Additional Rewards: +2,000 Reputation with The People. Exp: 10,000. Accept / Decline

Quest Alert! Blood Runs Deep: The O'Baba has additionally asked you to free her blood-kin, Velkan of the Redmane Tribe, who is being held captive at the Mage's College. There is no penalty for failing to accomplish this task! Accomplishing this task, however, will elevate your overall reputation with The People and your personal reputation with O'Baba. Reward: +1,000 Reputation with The People. Exp: 1,000. Blessing of The O'Baba. Accept / Decline

Sam read over both prompts, but he'd already made up his mind. This was *exactly* what he wanted. Even better, he already had a good idea about the nature of the spell he needed to thwart. *Octavius* was an Earth Mage. He had been working on a new spell which could be used to strike out at the Wolfmen. It didn't take a genius to work out that his job was to throw a monkey wrench into the Peak Student's plans.

Awesome! Not only would he get to join the underdogs—pun intended—but he'd get to royally screw over Octavius in the process. That was a win-win all around. Sam accepted both prompts. "Okay! I'm all in!"

"Excellent," The O'Baba allowed a wolfy smile to flash across her muzzle. "Then you have one week to accomplish this mission. I would wish you luck, but my People believe you make your own luck by the strength of your arm. So, let your arm be strong and your wits sharp. You will need both to succeed."

Chapter Twenty-Six

Sam loitered behind in a clump of bushes not far outside the western gate into Ardania. When he'd gone questing with Dizzy and the others, they'd exited through the northern gate, but apparently, the secret passage from the Sage's section of the library had dumped him *far* from that locale. Getting back to the city after finishing his business with The O'Baba had been relatively easy. After spending a night on the run, being assaulted by foxes, wolves, and Wolfmen... killing a few rabbits felt like a leisurely walk in the park. Speaking of surviving the night, his little feat had earned him a fancy new title and a boost of experience.

It seemed he was the first Traveler to survive a night alone outside the walls.

Ding-ding-ding! World's First! Title unlocked: Night Prowler. There are dark and deadly things that go bump in the night, but do you care? Nope! In fact, you might just be one of those things! When the rest of the world is tucked into warm beds and hunkered down behind the safety of high walls, you're out in the deepest darkness! For being the very first to survive a full night outside the city gates, you gain +2 skill points, +1 to Luck, and +75 personal fame with Ardania! Effect: Gain passive skill Darkvision.

Skill gained: Darkvision (Novice I). You are able to see in total darkness with no penalties. Range of vision is halved. Passive, no cost.

Of all the titles he'd earned so far, this one had the most practical effect. If everything went well over the next week, he'd officially be on team Wolfman, which meant he'd probably be doing a fair number of night ops. Having the ability to see perfectly in the dark, even if his range of vision was reduced, would be a *tremendous* help.

Sam bided his time for a few more minutes, watching the flow of traffic and keeping an eye out for anyone who might be from the College. Sam doubted very much that he would see Octavius or company skulking around here. Why would the Mages watch the gates, when no one survived a night outside the walls? Still, Sam hadn't come this far to lose everything due to recklessness. That was how he *got* here; now was the time to take things *carefully*.

So, he waited. Watching the players, yes, but mostly watching the pair of city guards in chainmail armor. Both guards were older, mid-forties or early fifties, and looked worn out from countless nights of too little sleep. They lazily waved folks through the gate with hardly a look; one stifled a tremendous yawn with his closed fist. The poor guy looked as if he might pass out where he stood any second.

Satisfied that this wasn't some elaborate trap designed to lure him into a false sense of security, Sam waited for a particularly big party of adventurers to slip *out* before breaking from his hiding spot and sneaking *in*. Still, Sam half expected to hear the clatter of weapons and the clang of warning bells, but none of that happened. He'd done it! He had escaped the College against all odds, weathered the night outdoors, and somehow made it back *into* the city without incident. Sam grinned like a loon and whistled softly as he strode into the warren of streets and alleys that comprised the city.

Despite his sudden good mood and fresh burst of optimism, there was still one thing he needed to check—the town square where players bound to Ardania respawned. If the Mages were out in force and searching for him, that was the most likely place for them to be camped out. Sam didn't want to get caught, but he also wanted to know just what kind of opposition he was up against. If the College had dispatched a single bounty hunter, it would be easy to avoid a single person in a city this size. If, on the other hand, they'd dispatched a platoon of bounty hunters and a squadron of Mages to wrangle him, Sam would have to step much more lightly in the days and weeks to come.

Plan set, Sam set off at a brisk walk—not strolling but not running either. He wanted to look like someone with a place to be but *not* someone who had something to hide.

<Wow, this place sure has changed since the last time I was free,> Bill marveled inside his head. <I never much liked the Archmage, but King Henry was always a good enough kiddo. I fought for him to take the crown during the early days, and he's definitely done right by the city.>

"Wait. What?" Sam whispered furiously. "You personally knew the King?"

<Hey, you know we can talk without *talking*, right?> Bill sounded a little exasperated. <We have a *telepathic* connection, so if you think real hard at me, we can chat mind to mind and no one will be the wiser. Maybe you could give that a shot, so it doesn't look like you're an insane hobo nattering to yourself. That will *definitely* draw some unwanted attention.>

Sam felt like someone had just slapped him in the face. He could talk to Bill telepathically? But how? Sam's steps faltered, and he stopped cold in the middle of the street, causing a minor human traffic-jam that earned him a few heated words from passing Travelers. His Instinctual Casting ability seemed to aid him here as well because, after only a handful of seconds, he was able to locate a clump of nerves *inside* him. Now *that* was interesting.

He shuffled off to the side of the road, leaning against a brick-sided building as he pressed his eyes closed tight. He pictured his Core, just as Mage Akora had taught him. His Center unfurled before him like a scroll. Sam instantly spotted the blue-white hurricane that was his own Core, but curiously, not far from his Core was a secondary ball of swirling, golden energy.

Bill's Core?

The two were connected by a thin tendril of energy no thicker than a few strands of hair. Sam pictured the golden ball that was Bill and sent a wave of intention out from his Core, shoving it through the tenuous tether of connective Mana.

<Can... you hear me?>

<Hey, wow. No need to scream,> Bill shot back smugly. <Maybe focus a little less, huh? Yeah, I can definitely hear you.>

<Sorry about that,> Sam sent, this time only allowing a trickle of 'intention' through the tether.

<Perfect. Right there is the sweet spot. Don't sweat it. That was actually pretty good considering this was your first time with the whole mind-talking thing. Now, why don't we get moving? People are already giving us some funny looks.>

<Right. Of course,> Sam ducked his head and coaxed his feet back into motion. <So back to you personally knowing the King. That seems like something you maybe should've mentioned before.>

<Hey, we've known each other for all of twelve hours. In case you didn't get the message, I'm over three *hundred* years old. It's hard to pass on a lifetime worth of stories during the lifespan of a typical mayfly. Also, it's worth mentioning that we were sorta preoccupied with not being murdered by Mages and Wolfmen. But, yes. I did know the King. Believe it or not, but I started off my career as a Bravi. *Sword Callers.* We could summon blades to ourselves no matter where we were, and

though the Bravi is a melee class, we could channel Mana through conjured steel.>

<We were the best, Legs,> he continued, sounding almost wistful. <The *very* best. My Order and I were sell-swords; we took contract work for the highest bidder. At the time, the highest bidder was a plucky young ex-Prince named Henry who hoped to consolidate the shards of shattered humanity and forge them into something new. Something better. He wanted to build the city you see here. He was a good kid. Smart. Powerful like you wouldn't believe, and most importantly, he had the coin to secure my Order's services. That's where the hat and the Quill Blade came from, you know. Those were hallmarks of the *Bravi*, though as far as I know, there are no more practitioners of my art.>

<So how did you go from being a mercenary, in the service of the future King, to a Bibliomancer, and then... well, you know. A book?>

<That's a story for a different time, Sam. Stay sharp. We're here.>

The street connected directly to the city's main square, dominated by the enormous fountain that acted as a bind point for the vast majority of the players aligned with the human race. Sam crept into a pool of deep shade cast by a colorful silk awning. He snatched the flamboyant hat from his head, pulling an Apprentice's cowl from his Flask of the Drunkard. The Bravi's hat was impressive, but it marked him out in the crowd like a road flare that screamed '*Look at me!*' That was attention he didn't want.

Sam surveyed the veritable sea of people milling about the square. It took less than thirty seconds to spot Octavius. The Peak Student stood out thanks to his colorful and stately robes, the scowl adorning his face like a thundercloud and, of course, the four College guards standing around him in a loose circle, all trying to look casual, all failing miserably.

<Boy, we really kicked the hornet's nest,> Bill remarked.

<Yeah, I see Octavius,> Sam replied silently.

<Ha. You're so cute. I'm not talking about the *obvious* Mage with the *obvious* guards all being extremely *obvious*. Look closer. Pay attention to the side streets, the upper house windows. Abyss, even the number of plain-looking 'citizens' just hanging around in clusters of two or three.>

Sam paused, pulling his eyes away from Octavius to *really* look at the square for the first time. What he saw this time around stole the breath from his lungs. Plainly dressed men and women, clutching at weapons far too impressive for this early in the game. City guards with shifty eyes. A disproportionate number of 'citizens' sporting plain brown robes—obviously 'new player' gear—simultaneously holding enchantment-covered staffs and sleek wands. Those magical weapons told the true story— high-powered Mages hiding in plain sight. These people were all just waiting for one pesky Rogue Mage to reappear so they could apprehend him without issue.

"Wow, I'm in *so* much trouble," Sam murmured. He knew he'd made some powerful enemies by raiding the library and freeing Bill, but there must've been a full twenty Mages here, and at least twice that number of College guards. He was going to have to step carefully, especially over the next several days. His living quarters at the College were clearly compromised, so he'd have to find a new place to stay while dodging the College's bounty hunters. To top it off, he'd have to figure out a way to free the captured Wolfman, make sure Finn was okay, derail Octavius' spell, all while trying to master a brand-new class.

"I'm going to have to do it all alone," he whispered under his breath as he watched the Mages.

<Alone?> Bill chipped in cheerfully, <You're *never* alone. Not anymore! Who needs healthy boundaries anyway?>

<I couldn't be more thrilled,> Sam replied flatly.

<I feel like maybe you're being sarcastic. Do they have sarcasm where you come from?> Sam scowled at the book in reply. <Okay. Then that was *definitely* sarcasm. But, here's the thing. You really *should* be excited to have me riding shotgun inside your head because I am a *vast* storehouse of knowledge. One, I know just about everything there is to know about the layout of the College, so if anyone can get us in *and back out,* it'll be me. Although, to do that, you're gonna need to seriously up your game, but *that* brings me to point two. I happen to be a Bibliomantic Skill and Class Trainer. The *only* one, in fact.>

<Wait,> Sam's eyebrows rose toward his hairline in utter shock, <you're a skill trainer? Are you telling me that *you* can teach me spells and passives?>

<Uh, yeah. Duh! I mean, as the inventor and founder of this particular path, I can teach you everything you need to know to be the baddest book-slinger around. As a former Bravi, I'm not half bad with a blade, which means I can teach you a thing or two about using your Quill Blade. Admittedly, there are some skills and abilities you won't be able to learn yet because you have the level of a common house cat, but we'll turn you into something special with a little time, persistence, and training. Because we're partners in crime, I wouldn't even charge you for my services... aside from the room and board of letting me live inside your head.>

<Gee. How very generous of you,> Sam sent back, but he couldn't stop himself from grinning.

<Ah, think nothing of it. Wait. No. I take that back. Please, think about how *generous* I am on a regular basis. Best if we get moving, though. We only have a week to work with, so we have some serious montaging to do. That starts with a trip to the store. Unfortunately, being a Bibliomaniac Sorcerer can be expensive, so I hope you have some extra coin lying around; either that or we're gonna have to get creative. Turn you into a *klepto-mancer.* First stop we need is a custom bookstore. Anywhere they might sell bulk parchment, custom inks, or infusion elements.>

Sam turned away, moving slowly yet purposefully so as not to draw unwanted notice, and backtracked away from the town square.

Once he was a few blocks away, he swapped the run-of-the-mill Apprentice's cowl for his flamboyant cavalier hat. Now that Sam knew the history of the hat—that it was a link to a three-hundred-year-old class, long-since dead; he felt a renewed wave of pride to have it on top of his head no matter how goofy it looked.

It took half an hour and a round of polite inquiries, but eventually, Sam found himself in front of a brownstone-style bookstore called *The Summoned Scroll.* According to the handful of folks he'd chatted with, this was the single best—and most *affordable*—book and paper wholesaler in the entire northern block of the city, which locals referred to as the Upper North Fulham, or UpNoHam.

The inside of The Summoned Scroll was almost exactly what Sam had envisioned a magical bookstore to be. The place was rather dimly lit and smelled of polished wood, old leather, the acrid stink of bottled ink, and the musty scent of reams upon reams of ancient paper. Massive bookcases took up most of the wall space, displaying a healthy number of leather-bound tomes.

After spending time in the *Infinity Athenaeum,* this place seemed positively... quaint. Leather club chairs dotted the otherwise open floor plan, all positioned in front of heavy desks which looked like workspaces for the studious. There were also several glass-fronted display cases holding particularly valuable books, pots of magical ink, and enchanted quills.

"Well, hello there, young man!" squawked a rather mousy woman tending to one of the display cases near the rear of the shop.

She was taller than Sam by a good five inches but almost skeletally gaunt with hawkish features and a rather pinched face. Her brown hair was pulled up into a tight knot at the back of her head, emphasizing her cheekbones, which looked sharp enough to cut glass. She wore a pair of thick-rimmed spectacles etched with odd runes directly across the lens. She folded her hands on top of the frosted glass case and smiled, which instantly transformed her face from severe to warm and open. "What can I help you with today?"

<Oh, this place will do *nicely*,> Bill crowed greedily. <Ooh... look at that *novel* section! I bet I could practice the Comma Sutra all *day* over there! Oh, ah... tell her this is what we need...>

CHAPTER TWENTY-SEVEN

"The room is right this way, young master. Right this way." The innkeeper hobbled in front of Sam, his knees oddly bowed as though he'd spent a lifetime on horseback. Which made sense, considering the name of the inn was *The Rugged Saddleback.* The boards creaked, squeaked, and moaned under the innkeeper's heavy footfalls, and the weak, orange flames dancing at the end of tallow candles flickered as Sam slipped by.

The innkeeper seemed perfectly nice, but The Rugged Saddleback? Not so much. It was situated firmly in a sliver of the city known as 'Cheapside', and Sam was beginning to suspect the name was well earned. Unlike the other areas of Ardania he'd visited so far, Cheapside was run down. The inn was no different. Everything was serviceable—at least in the most *technical* sense of the word—but worn, dirty, and held together with some good ol' fashion elbow grease. Sam had never actually *seen* elbow grease, but he was pretty sure the gobs of black ... *something* ... holding the staircase together was the real stuff.

But if there was one place he would likely be safe, it was Cheapside. The Mages were powerful, no doubt about that, but Cheapside was home to bad actors of every sort. After leaving *The Summoned Scroll* a full two *hundred* gold lighter and loaded down with enough quills, parchment, and ink to drown an elephant; Sam had learned that Cheapside belonged to the Brotherhood of Upright Men—the Thieves' Guild—just as surely as the College belonged to the Mages. The guard also avoided this area unless there were full-blown riots, and although the Mages could come here, in *theory*, they wouldn't.

For one thing, no Mage would willingly debase themselves by putting one 'Noble' foot anywhere near what amounted to a slum. For another, the Upright Men were in something of a silent war with the Mages, which made it a perilous prospect for any spellcaster to be down this way. It was a *perfect* place for Sam to hide out; though he'd have to keep an eye out for cutthroats looking to slit his throat and rob him blind. Not necessarily in that order.

The innkeeper finally stopped in front of a nondescript door on the third floor, fishing a set of dangling keys from his belt. His hands trembled slightly as he slipped off a thick brass key and opened the lock on the door with a hefty *clank*. The innkeeper glanced over one hunched shoulder and offered Sam a hearty, lopsided smile filled with gaps from missing teeth. He pushed the door open, offered Sam the key, made sure to mention that the continental breakfast ran between six and nine, then bowed himself away after a brief round of 'sleep tights'.

Sam's temporary lodgings were just as run-down as everything else in the inn, but the space itself was significantly *larger* than his room at the Mage's College had been. Honestly, it wasn't in worse shape, which said everything that needed to be said about how the College treated their acolytes. There was a narrow twin bed with a horrifically lumpy looking mattress and a small end table with a chipped porcelain bowl and a pitcher of water. In the corner was a hulking wardrobe that appeared to have survived being dropped off a third-story balcony. Maybe several times.

<This is *perfect!*> Bill boomed, flapping his cover. <Well, I mean it's all *terrible*—I'm actually sorta glad I no longer have a body... Sleeping on that mattress is probably a worse torment than anything the Mage's would've done to you—but the space *itself* will work fine for our purposes! We should have more than

adequate room for what we need to do. I mean, it's always possible we'll burn this whole flea-infested hovel down by accident, but we'll do our very best to avoid that! Now, I say we get to *work*!>

"Yeah, about that." Sam kicked off his boots. "Just one little thing."

<What's that?>

In response, Sam belly-flopped onto the bed, which was exactly as uncomfortable as it looked, his head finding the pillow in an instant. Despite both the bed—and Bill's nattering voice—droning on, Sam was asleep in less than an eyeblink.

He startled awake sometime later, though just how long he'd slept was hard to say. When he glanced through the wooden slats covering the room's only window, he saw the golden light of late afternoon washing over everything, making Cheapside look like some sort of idyllic tourist town, exactly the kind of place he would've expected to find in the European countryside. Looked like he was getting that vacation after all or at least bits and pieces of it. This vacation came with an added bonus—*magic*.

Sam grinned at the thought and pulled himself from the bed, feeling better than he had in *ages*.

Debuff removed: Sleep Deprivation III. Removed effect: -5 intelligence, -5 wisdom, -30% stamina.

Well... that explained things. He opened his status screen and decided to take a proper look around. Sam found and looked through an active effects tab and noted a 'Stinky IV' debuff that decreased his charisma by eight points and increased prices by four hundred percent. There was also a 'Starving II' and 'Dehydrated III' that reduced his Mana and stamina by twenty and thirty percent respectively. Then he noticed that he had fifteen unspent skill points.

"Should I spend them... or hold off until I can put them in something that matters?" Sam waffled back and forth, then decided that if he was going to wait this long, he could wait a little longer.

Name: Sam_K 'Bunny Reaper'
Class: Bibliomantic Sorcerer
Profession: Unlocked
Level: 6 Exp: 20,523 Exp to next level: 477
Hit Points: 120/120
Mana: 373.5/373.5
Mana regen: 12.6/sec
Stamina: 135/135

Characteristic: Raw score (Modifier)

Strength: 20 (15+5 gear bonus) (1.15)
Dexterity: 26 (21+5 gear bonus) (1.21)
Constitution: 17 (1.17)
Intelligence: 36 (1.36)
Wisdom: 35 (1.35)
Charisma: 20 (15+5 gear bonus) (1.15)
Perception: 12 (1.12)
Luck: 12 (1.12)
Karmic Luck: -6

Okay, things weren't *perfect*. He was a Rogue Mage on the run from the College and was about to betray all of humanity in favor of the Wolfmen. That was assuming he actually *managed* to stop Octavius in the first place, which was far from guaranteed. So... maybe everything wasn't coming up Sam, but he'd managed to escape the College and wasn't currently wrapped in chains. He'd gotten away with Bill, he had a new bind spot away from the city, and most importantly, he was going to dive into his new class with reckless abandon and hopefully learn some slick new tricks.

<I see you're finally done being annoyingly *human*,> Bill scoffed at him.

"What, you don't sleep?" Sam suppressed an enormous yawn while clambering to his feet.

<Phft. I wish. Sometimes I can meditate deeply enough to mimic sleep—sorta turn my mind off for a while—but books don't get the luxury of *true* sleep. Now, if you're done rubbing your fancy-pants ability to dream in my face, which I *do* have, let's get to the magic-making! If we're going to survive the week, you need to get *good*, and you need to do it *fast*. So... we really don't have any time to waste.>

"Maybe a little breakfast first?" Sam sheepishly suppressed the rumble in his stomach.

<Sleeping. Dreaming. Now eating? Let me guess, then you want a *bath*. You just want to see me suffer, don't you?> the book grumbled.

Sam slipped back into the room twenty minutes later, his belly full and satisfied after hoovering up a bowl of very questionable 'beef' stew that came courtesy of the inn. 'Continental breakfast' indeed. At least he wasn't a fan of coffee, or he would have been even more disappointed.

<Awesome. Now, if you're *actually* done, can we please, please, *please* get started?>

"Like a cornfield, I'm all ears," Sam agreed with a nod.

Bill was quiet for a long moment. <Was that a jab at me not having ears?>

"I could dog-ear your pages if you really want some?"

<I'm not even going to dignify that with a response. Let's just keep on track, huh? Now, first things first. We need to inventory our supply. Carefully lay out everything we bought yesterday... or was it this morning? Man, it's hard to keep track of time.>

"We're going to go over *why* you had me almost entirely empty my bank account for this stuff, right?" Sam tried not to think about spending over ten thousand real-world dollars on something he couldn't see the benefit of.

<You think that the College isn't going to start keeping an eye on the bank now that you've vanished? Consider the bank a level fifty hostile area now.> Bill's words rang true, so Sam could only grumble and kneel.

He opened his Unending Flask and carefully pulled each item out of the spatial compartment, arranging them in orderly columns and rows so it would be easier to catalog what they had. First came the paper, great stacks of finely pressed papyrus, high-grade parchment, and even more expensive vellum. Five hundred sheets worth of writing material all told. Next, he added the book-binder tool kit he'd picked up. Out came a wood-handled awl with a razor-sharp tip, a wolf-bone fold creaser, several spools of waxed thread in various colors, several long, curved needles, and a glue brush with an accompanying glass bottle of epoxy.

<A big part of being a Bibliomancer is supply and inventory management,> Bill explained as Sam worked, arranging the piles and sorting the equipment. <See, the thing is, we can perform some really cool spells—as you're about to find out—but everything we do is dependent on ingredients. Even though this is *technically* a Sorcerer class, which itself is a subclass of Mage, you are *functionally* a specialized Enchanter at this point. More on that in a second.>

With the parchment and bookbinding supplies all laid out and counted, Sam added quills of various sizes, types, and colors. Quills made of osprey feathers with fine metal nibs, others meticulously crafted from hawk feathers sporting bone tips. The feather variations were many—peacock, eagle, falcon, vulture—the nib types just as varied—iron, gold, silver, bronze, jade, bone... diamond.

To Sam, the differences seemed largely cosmetic, but Bill *insisted* that was only because he didn't know what he was doing, because he didn't yet have the true *eye* of a world-class Bibliomancer. According to Bill, the different varieties would allow Sam to write a wider variety of spells and make them far more powerful to boot.

Want to unleash a spell with decaying elements? Well, then you'll want an onyx vulture quill with a specialized basilisk-bone nib. An air spell? Hawk feather with a crystal tip. It all made an odd sort of sense as Bill explained it, but Sam couldn't even begin to figure out how anyone would *possibly* stumble across that kind of information without a guide.

After that came the inks, which were as unique, strange, and varied as the quills had been. There were several different types of black inks, which all looked the same at a glance. A little slip of paper affixed to each bottle with a bit of brown twine, however, painted quite a different picture for the inquisitive shopper. Yes, the ink *base* was the same, but each bottle was mixed with a variety of different alchemic ingredients— everything from wartsburrow and hawthorn bramble to plains hornet honey and rosemary.

Those alchemic mixtures *primed* the ink so that when it eventually became infused with Mana, it would naturally manifest various Mana aspects more easily. It was a devious little trick that would let a caster in the know supercharge spells;

causing increased damage, increase range, or increased effect duration to name a few possible benefits.

Sam pulled out the books he'd grabbed from his raid on the library. Feeling a surge of satisfaction at his haul, he laid out *Fundamentals of Core Cultivation*; *Brilliant Blossoms: A field guide to basic herbology*; *The Book of Lost Incantations, Rediscovered!*; *A Compendium of Magical Omens*; *Compact Fundamentals of Elemental Magic, Aeolus Edition*; and the final volume, which he'd picked up on the Sage's floor, *Compendium on Protected and Dangerous Locations*. With that done, he conjured the two bound tomes currently tucked away inside Bill's Soul Space, placing them just apart from the other books.

Bill whistled as he surveyed the treasure trove of items. <You done good, kid. Honest. This is going to go a *long* way to kicking some Mage College butt. Especially *those* books. That many books, of that quality? That's gonna be a game changer for us. See, the base spell we use for pretty much *everything* is Orbital Tome Casting. That's the foundation of the Bibliomancer class and the primary mechanic by which you and I sling magic, understand?>

Sam squinted, lips pursed, forehead creased. "Yeah, not entirely sure I do."

<Amateur. Fine, let me start out with the basics. As a Bibliomantic Sorcerer, which is a variation of the Bibliomancer class, you can learn a butt-ton of spells, but you can only have six *active* spells at any given time, and that is because you can only *bind* six books at any given time aside from me. The number is six because that's the max number of tomes *I* can bind to myself and store in my Soul Space for now. Does that make sense?>

Sam nodded. "Six books. Six spells. Following so far."

<Progress! Alright! Now, there are some exceptions to that rule, which we won't get into for now, but for *most* of your active spells, you'll bind a specific spell form to a specific book. One spell, one book. Then when you want to cast that spell, you summon the corresponding book which will orbit around you and launch spells at your enemies with a thought. One of the great things about that is the spells cost next to nothing to cast in the heat of battle. Meaning you'll *almost* never run out of Mana; especially since you already have a respectable pool of Mana to begin with and a *monster* regen rate.>

"Where's the *but?*" Sam narrowed his eyes. "From everything I've heard, most classes are pretty well balanced. That means if there's that big of an advantage, there is usually some sort of significant drawback."

<Someone gets a gold star,> Bill beamed at him. <The '*but*' is that your spell quantity is limited by two factors. The first is that it is *abyssally* hard to assign or swap spells during active combat, which means you need to be prepared going into a fight. You're going to learn more than six spells for sure, but you'll only have *access* to six at any given point. Second, the number of pages in any tome is the limiting factor for how many times you can cast a given spell. Some spells, like Paper Shuriken, have a one to one ratio. One sheet of magically infused paper per one Paper Shuriken cast.>

Chapter Twenty-Eight

<If you have three-hundred pages in a given book,> Bill continued teaching Sam, <you can spam that spell three-hundred times almost non-stop. But when you run dry? You're dry. Period. End of story. Other spells can have a *much* higher cost, depending on the complexity and damage output of the spell, meaning you can run dry a lot faster. Papier-Mache Mage costs twenty-five sheets per spell use since it takes proportionally more paper to cover a person than it does to fold a throwing star. Some spells are so potent and complex that they require an *entire* book's worth of pages, effectively making them one-off spells that can only be used a single time before needing to start over.>

"Not to mention that some of the higher end paper costs nearly a gold a pop. Okay," Sam sighed as he thought of his nearly drained bank account, "that all makes sense. I have a couple of questions; why was I able to cast Paper Shuriken and Papier-Mache Mage without first preparing books? What happens when the books run out of paper? Do I just shove a bunch of blank parchment in between the covers and keep on going?"

<Your questions are getting progressively better. You might just be sharp enough to make a proper Bibliomancer yet! So, to answer your first question, books of magic are *special.* Really, really, *really* special, which is why they are hoarded like dragon's gold. They are *impossibly* hard to get your hands on, extremely rare, and *crazy*-expensive, which is why we didn't see any at the Bookshop.>

Bill paused to make his next words really sink in. <Each one of those books you have in front of you costs at least five

thousand gold each, maybe more with the Mage's College suppressing the ability to buy them elsewhere. Which is why you should *totally* become a book klepto. You see a magic book that isn't nailed down to the table? You *steal* it.>

Sam just sat there for a moment, shocked to his core. Five *thousand* gold or more for a book? That was ludicrous. But if it was true... just how much wealth did the College have at their disposal? Sam sputtered after a second, "*Why* are they so valuable?"

<Well, the obvious reason is that they contain spells and other powerful information. Depending on the rarity of the book and the purity of its information, a magical volume can teach the reader a spell instantly or elevate a known spell as high as the Expert rank. Magical tomes also serve a *secondary* function for us Bibliomancers. Both the ink and parchment inside those books are *already* Mana-infused, which means you can cast spells with those books without ever preparing the materials. That's because some *other Mage* has already done the heavy lifting. Which means insta-cast for us when you *definitely steal them in the future*.>

"But the problem is, there aren't a lot of magical books just lying around all over the place," Sam spoke the issue out loud.

<Hit the nail right on the head.>

"So, what about non-magic books. Can we just use those instead?"

<Naw. Unfortunately, we can't cast spells from regular books. They won't take the commands, and they can't be bound. Try to bind a regular book, and it will absolutely just explode in your face. You're basically trying to force Mana through a vessel that isn't equipped to hold it. Very dangerous, and you'd probably kill yourself. Maybe some other people as well.>

<Which brings us to your second question,> Bill continued. <What happens when those fancy books of yours run out of Mana-infused paper? The short answer is, *you* have to refill them. Easy-peasy, lemon squeezy. That's what all these materials are for! We're gonna need to create page inserts. A *lot* of 'em. Then when a given book runs dry, you pop in the correctly paired insert and *boom*, you're good to go. That part you *can* do quickly during combat so long as you don't try and change the spell assignment on a book."

"Like replacing the magazine in a rifle..." Everything was starting to click into place in Sam's head. Although the magical books *looked like* books, they were basically six magical machine guns. Some fired fast and held a ton of rounds but were less powerful. Others were more powerful but had a lower capacity for ammunition, like a shotgun with big, deadly slugs. A few were uber-powerful, but single-use, like a rocket launcher. But Sam had to make his own bullets. The analogy wasn't perfect, but thinking about it that way helped Sam wrap his mind around the casting mechanics.

"Think I'm following." Sam absently sat down on the bed. "So, a couple more questions. If I have magically infused *paper*, could I use the outer cover of a regular book?"

<Nope. Magical books—outer binding *included*—are specially manufactured to contain Mana-infused paper. Without the proper cover, the Mana will slowly leak away and go bad over time. Sometimes fast, sometimes slow. Just like putting potions in special bottles or meat in an icebox. Also, magical books tend to be of a higher quality, and the better quality your materials are, the better quality your spells will be. They'll hit harder, be less likely to fail on casting, even offer additional damage or effect bonuses if you have *premium* materials.>

<Proper preparation goes a long way on that front. Though you can assign and cast spells from any properly infused magical text, those spells will be about thirty percent less effective than similar spells cast with material you've prepared yourself.>

"Wait. What? So all the spells I've been casting so far are *a third* less powerful than they could've been?"

<You got it,> Bill replied. <You've been operating with weak-sauce spells, which should tell you exactly how powerful we can become, given a little bit of time and money. See, the most *basic* element needed to cast your spells are magic books with magic paper. Now, if you prepare the materials yourself, you can scribe additional spells on to each page. Want a Paper Shuriken that explodes on contact? No problem, just inscribe a simple Fireball activation on to the page.>

Bill chuckled. <I say no problem, but that's an entire skillset on its own. Anyway. When it hits, the target takes the original damage but then takes *additional* damage as the spell scroll discharges. The problem is, the more complicated the spell, the more time and Mana it takes to create and the greater chance it will blow up in your face.>

Sam stood and paced, his mind whirling at all the possibilities. With this class, he might never be as purely powerful and instantly versatile as some of the other Mage classes. His spells were built on items, which he could run out of, but if he had the supplies, the money, the time, and the Mana reserve... it was possible he could essentially *change* his 'class' at will. If he wanted to focus entirely on combat, he could, *in theory,* bind six different versions of Paper Shuriken all with different elemental effects to six different books. He'd be able to hurl fire-based Shurikens or ice-based Shurikens with equal ease, making him a force to be reckoned with.

"This sounds amazing!" A wide grin broke out across Sam's face. Still pacing, he ran a hand through his short-cropped hair. "Where do we start?"

<Right at the beginning,> Bill replied somberly. <Contract Preparation one-oh-one and Fundamentals of Contract Magic.>

Sam felt the wind fade from his sails and a serpent of doubt rear its scared head inside his chest. Contract magic screamed 'The Accords', which left him deeply uneasy. Besides that, the term sounded suspiciously like some sort of magical law school jargon, and Sam didn't want *anything* to do with that; he'd left the real world behind in hopes of forgetting about things like contract law for a while. "I'm sorry, did you say... Contract Magic? How about starting with Fireballs? Or Ice Bolts? Can't we start with something *cool?*"

Bill sighed in his head, the sound like a wind blowing through tall grass in the summer. <Listen, Legs, I know it's not glamorous, but that's a lesson it's best for you to learn now. Being a Bibliomantic Sorcerer—and eventually a *Bibliomancer—* isn't glamorous. It's a lot of boring, tedious, unglamorous work *behind* the scenes in order for a few minutes of glory on the battlefield. Just because something *sounds* boring and tedious, doesn't mean that it isn't *powerful.* Take a stab at what class the Archmage of the College is?>

Before Sam could even hazard a guess, Bill answered for him, <An Arcana Contractualist—a specialist in contract magic. A Bibliomancer is actually not that much different from what he is. It's the other side of the same coin, really. Most Mages turn their noses up at contract magic because it's not flashy or stylish, and the Mages who practice it are *personally* weak. They might have huge Mana reserves, but they can't do hardly *anything* with all that power. Not on their own. More often than not,

Contractualists wind up with the short end of the stick; most of 'em get shuffled off to work in admin positions in dank rooms deep in the bowels of the College.>

<Except for me and the Archmage, that is. We both recognized the true power in contracts. Our formative work wasn't simply about handling paperwork, I can tell you that much. He and I both figured out that through the use of contract magic, we could bind the tremendous forces of magic to ourselves. True, we *personally* wouldn't be as powerful as other Mages, but we could *harness* the power of the most powerful and bend their magic to our will.>

<Me? I focused on creating contracts with the most powerful *items* I could think of—enchanted books. The Archmage, on the other hand... well, he realized he could use contract magic to enslave other Mages to his will, which is why he created The Accords. An invisible collar fitted around every other magic user's throat.>

<All of that is ancient history and doesn't much concern us at the moment, but there *is* an important lesson in there. *Real* power isn't always snazzy or flashy, and it rarely looks the way you think it should. Real power is not the sword blow of some soldier on the front line, it's the command of the general who can send a hundred thousand soldiers to the front. Real power, at its heart, relies on controlling forces *far* greater than the individual. To find a class like *that* in Eternium is rare. Contractualists, like that doofus the Archmage, Ritualists, and Bibliomancers to name only a few.>

"What's a Ritualist?" Sam asked, attention suddenly piqued.

<Ah. Nothing. Don't even think about it. The Archmage hunted down the last Ritualist two hundred years ago. I doubt we'll be seeing one of those again, but if we ever do, ick. They

can spread like a plague, and you never know what they have up their sleeve. They vanish for weeks at a time, then pop up with *one* just *ridiculous* spell before vanishing again. The point is, there are classes with real power out there, and *you* stumbled into one. Don't waste it because it requires actual *work*.>

Sam thought about the book's words, and as much as he wanted to argue, he knew just how right Bill was. He thought back to his real life, to the senators and CEOs who worked with his dad from time to time. Most of them were unassuming men and women. They weren't overtly famous, and at a glance, they didn't seem dangerous or powerful. Senator Lonstein was nearly seventy with a shock of silver hair and a double chin that wobbled like a bowl of Jell-O—reminded Sam of the Archmage, actually—but this unassuming man could pass or crush a bill in congress with a phone call. And Mrs. Robertson, CEO of BlackWater Trust, could bury someone with her army of lawyers or take them out in a more *physical* way with her platoons of black-suited, private 'security' guards.

Any one of those guards—most of them former military—could break Mrs. Robertson like a twig, yet *she* was the one who called the shots, not them. That was *real* power... and that was what Bill was offering Sam.

He had been running from power all his life, afraid that he wasn't 'worthy' or that he'd turn into someone like Barron Calloway. He couldn't run from power any longer, though. He'd be a fool to refuse Bill's instructions.

"Alright," Sam's voice was brimming with determination, "let's learn some contract magic."

CHAPTER TWENTY-NINE

Turned out that contract magic was as dull as it sounded. Thanks to Sam's background in prelaw, the class practically flew by. First, Bill walked him through the basics of material use—how to sharpen quills, choose proper paper, mix and maintain ink, and the basics of spell form calligraphy. All of this earned him four new skills in under an hour, and all of them started out at Beginner Level zero; an impressive feat that was only possible thanks to Bill's expertise in the area.

Being trained by a Master of a craft has greatly increased your speed of comprehension!

Skill gained: Quill preparation and maintenance. (Beginner 0). Sharp quills mean sharp and accurate writing or drawing! Each rank of this skill increases quill durability by 2%.

Skill gained: Ink preparation. (Beginner 0). Creating the correct color and consistency of ink is paramount to creating beautiful works of literature. Each rank of this skill increases ink purity by 2% and decreases time to create desired ink by 2%.

Skill gained: Papermaking and selection. (Beginner 0). Just because the paper is available doesn't mean it is worth using! Each rank of this skill increases paper durability by 2% when it is used or created by you.

Skill increased: Scribe (Beginner 0). Learning the basic skill set of this craft has resulted in a massive increase to the starting proficiency!

From there, Bill dove into the big picture complexities behind magical law and contract theory, which was actually quite a bit more fascinating—and *terrifying*—than Sam would've guessed. Truthfully, the principles of law here in Eternium were fundamentally the same as the principles of law back in the real world. It was a bevy of legalese, clauses, subordinate clauses, and other minutiae that any practicing lawyer would've recognized in an instant. The major difference, however, was in how contracts were *enforced.*

In real life, if a party signed a contract, they were *legally* obligated to fulfill the terms of the contract, but the only real recourse if one party failed to uphold their end of the bargain was legal proceedings and a judgment handed down by either a mediator or through a court. Contract *magic* worked a *little* bit differently, making the contracts of Eternium *far* more binding.

Not a matter of mere *legal* obligation but a matter of *enforced* magical obligation. Instead of simply swearing to abide by the terms of the bargain; when someone signed a contract here in the game, it was empowered by a Mana thread which connected the signer's *Core* to the contract. The Mana expended was so small it barely registered... right up until one of the parties *broke* the terms of the contract. Then the magical binding kicked into high gear, causing *terrible* consequences. Everything from excruciating pain to crippling Mana depletion to *compelled* behavior and personality changes.

Truly horrific penalties, which made Sam realize just how big of a bullet he dodged by *annulling* his contract with The Accords and not *breaking* his contract. If he hadn't bound himself to Bill—which created a forced class change, allowing him to escape the contract without major repercussions to his soul—he would have been enslaved heart and soul to the College for the rest of his days in the game.

<Alright,> Bill seemed almost impressed as Sam finished the lesson. <You done good, and we have a firm foundation to move on from. Now, it's time to get elbow deep into the nitty-gritty details of Magical Material Creation. Knowing the

metaphysical framework for how these contracts work isn't enough; you actually have to be able to *make* something.>

"Sounds like a blast!" Sam replied with a smirk, knuckling his back which was already aching from sitting for so long. "I'm *so* ready to start crafting."

<Glad to hear it, since you're going to have to learn Magical Material Creation *three* separate times back to back. Which *should* make things more fun. Nothing's better than endless repetition, am I right?>

"What was that now?" Sam was thinking he had *surely* just misheard the book. "It almost sounded like you said I was going to have to take Magical Material Creation three *separate* times? That's absurd. Why in the world would I possibly need to do that?"

<Nope. You heard right. Three times. In a row. Don't suppose you've learned about Soul Forging yet, huh?>

Sam grimaced and shook his head.

<Yeah. Figures. They *really* baby you at the College, and that's exactly the kind of information they'd want to keep under wraps until you were firmly in their pocket. Listen, the Soul Forge skill is as dangerous as it is powerful, and it's the primary way to forge a new and unique path. It's the mechanism I used to create the Bibliomancer class in the first place. Bibliomancer is basically a *synergization* between four different already-specialized classes: Contractualists, Enchanters, Sorcerers, and my original class, Bravi.>

<Some skills and abilities also have compatible *synergy*. That means that they work together in such a way that you can combine them together into a single, *new* skill. You can even combine more than one skill together, but that's where things get, well... a little *tricky*. Even the *order* you combine them matters, and if you do it wrong, you could end up with a single

rare-but-worthless skill instead of two or more mediocre-but-practical skills. Obviously, the College wants that kind of info kept secret because they don't want Initiates 'creating' unauthorized magic; unless, of course, said Initiate has the College's express 'blessing' in the endeavor.>

"But since you created this class," Sam now had a happy glint in his eye, "you know which skills to combine, in what order, to make the best Bibliomancer spells and abilities."

Not a question, but a statement of cold fact, and Bill knew it. <*Someone's* been paying attention. Since a big part of our class is an Enchanter base, by combining Magical Material Creation with some other important skills, we can open up a whole new world of opportunities.>

"Teach me," Sam half ordered, half asked, before lowering himself onto the floor in a meditation pose.

<Alright. Grab one of those ink bottles there.> Sam picked up a rather plain glass vial of black ink which had no specialized properties. He gave the ink a little swirl with his wrist, watching the goopy liquid slosh against the inside of the glass before settling. Just plain, ol' standard ink.

<Now, I'm gonna guide you through this part of the process since it can be a little tricky for first-timers. Though I imagine with your Instinctual Casting, you'll be alright. What you're gonna do here is *pack* that ink full of Mana. Imagine using a pair of bellows at the forge. The Mana is the air you push out from the bellows, feeding it into the fire to stoke the flames. You need to *slowly* force Mana from your Core into the ink. It'll try to escape, so you need to forge a shell of *will* and *Mana* around the ink as well. Think about that like the brick walls of a forge, which are designed to keep the heat in.>

Sam knew absolutely nothing about forges or bellows outside of what he'd seen in games and movies, but he thought he understood what Bill was getting at. He focused on the bottle in his hand, feeling the slickness of the glass, the weight of the ink in his palm. He opened his Core, forcing out a thin tendril of Mana and pushing it into the ink. In his mind, he envisioned himself blowing up a balloon, forcing air from his lungs, inflating the rubbery walls of the balloon which kept the air from escaping into the atmosphere. With a thought and an effort of sheer will, he forged a molecule-thin shell of Mana between the ink and the glass itself, isolating the goopy, black substance from the bottle.

But he left a thin hole no larger than a pinprick in that hardened shell—an opening for him to pump in more and more Mana. In the corner of his eye, his Mana dipped. First by fifty, then a hundred, then two hundred. Expending so much Mana so quickly left Sam reeling and light-headed, but he pressed on. To falter now was to fail completely. Sam saturated the concoction with energy until it felt as though the barrier he'd created around the ink was stretched so tight that even *one* more point of Mana would surely cause the whole thing to pop and explode right in his face.

<Good, good. That's perfect. Now, seal the hole and hold the tension. Just let the Mana *soak* into the ink. It's chicken marinating in a pot, absorbing all that good, magical flavor. Yum yum. Don't stir it.> Sam nodded slightly but didn't speak, too caught up in holding the Mana inside the shell to focus on anything else.

Minutes passed, and though he was no longer actively pumping Mana into the ink, Sam found sweat rolling down his forehead and dripping into his eyes. His arms shook from the invisible strain, and his lungs labored for air. It felt like he was trying to sprint a marathon while lugging a boulder above his head. Just when it seemed like he couldn't contain the energy for another second, he instinctively reopened the small breach in the shell, letting the excess Mana bleed off and into the air.

Thin wisps of ghostly blue light drifted up, dissipating into the atmosphere. After a few moments, the hiss of escaping Mana ebbed to a mere trickle, and something *clicked* in place within the ink, normalizing the pressure inside the bottle like the cabin of an airliner. Sam licked his lips, and ever so carefully released the sheath around the ink, wincing as he prepared for an explosion to rock his world. Instead, he received a pop up notifying him of a new skill:

Skill gained: Magical Material Creation (Beginner 0). Having a huge amount of raw Mana and no real use for it tends to lead to dangerous experiments. That's how this skill was originally created! Increase density of Mana matrix by 1n% per skill level.

<Hey, not too bad. I mean, you probably pumped five times the amount of Mana into that bottle as necessary. For a first try, I'd say you handled it like a champ. You'll be even better when you do it next time. Speaking of, let's get to the Soul Forging already! This first one is gonna be a bear, let me tell you, and it's gonna cost, but it'll be worth it in the end. What you're gonna do is toss your five shiny new skills into one giant cookpot and let 'em simmer for about the next sixty hours or so while we knock out some more skills.>

"Sixty hours!" Sam choked out.

<Eh. Part of the price we pay for knowledge. Gotta sit and wait for amazing things to simmer after you put in all the effort, but don't worry, you'll be so busy mixing ink and writing out spells you'll hardly notice the next sixty hours at all!>

Sam rolled his eyes and sighed but followed the book's instructions. Sam focused on the five new skills he'd gained, and a new prompt appeared:

Extreme skill synergy detected! Quill Preparation and Maintenance, Ink Preparation, Papermaking and selection, Scribe, and Magical Material Creation all share similar features and can be combined to form a new skill. By paying eight hundred gold, you can combine these five skills into one single skill.

The level of the new skill will be the average of the original skills, and any remaining skill points (rounded up) will be returned as free skill points! If you do not have the necessary gold on hand, you may combine these skills at a later date or choose to have the money taken from your bank account. As this is the first time you have found two or more skills with extreme synergy, you have been informed as a courtesy. You will receive no further information on skill synergy from the system.

New system menu available! Congratulations! You have unlocked the ability to use 'Soul Forging'! By meeting certain requirements, you can combine skills or even classes! Be careful, as combining skills with low synergy will lower the new skill's efficacy.

You are about to combine five skills: Quill Preparation and Maintenance, Ink Preparation, Papermaking and selection, Scribe, and Magical Material Creation. Are you sure? Yes / No.

Sam's eyes bulged at the price tag. *Eight hundred gold!* After his time spent at the College, his two supply runs—first to *Nick's Knacks* and then at *The Summoned Scroll*—he was down to two thousand gold. If he followed through with this course of action, he'd be down to twelve hundred gold, and he still had the better part of five in-game months to live through.

<Don't worry about the sticker shock,> Bill jumped in as though reading Sam's thoughts. <Once we get all your skills up and running, you're going to be a regular printing press of money. You'll be able to dash off scrolls in a *minute* that people

will pay through the *nose* for. That's another lesson about real power. When a skill is rare enough, it commands the ultimate premium because no one else can do it. Just trust me on this one, okay?>

Sam gulped, pressed his eyes shut, taking a few deep breaths to settle his nerves, and accepted before he could overthink the process and chicken out. In for a penny, in for a pound, right?

CHAPTER THIRTY

Ding-ding-ding! World's First! Sure, why not just mash five different skills together? Maybe it will turn out well, maybe not, but you aren't one to test the waters! No, you jump in with both feet. You're going places... probably to an early grave as a result of some catastrophic explosion of your own making... but definitely places! For being the very first player to use Soul Forge in Eternium, you gain a permanent +5 Intelligence, +5 Perception, -1 Wisdom, and +50 personal fame with Ardania! Title unlocked: Experimental Forger!

Experimental Forger: This title reduces the time necessary to use the Soul Forge by 15%! After creating ten skills or three classes, this title will turn into a skill which allows you to gauge skill synergy. (This is an advanced version of the title 'Never Satisfied')

Time until skills have combined: 60 hours. Notice! Title Experimental Forger has reduced the processing time by 15%. 51 hours until completion!

<Alright! We're rocking and rolling now! Next up is two more rounds of *Magical Material Creation*. See, thing is, when you combine a skill, spell, or ability... you *lose* that ability since it gets mashed up to form the new skill. Luckily, you can *relearn* the same skill over and over again—unless it is a Unique skill. Let's just knock these out back to back, and then we can move on to some of the flashier elements of our class.>

Sam picked up the next bottle of ink—this one a specialty blend that was filtered and distilled with various herbs—and went through the laborious process of learning to saturate the ink with Mana once more. This time around, he went even slower because Sam felt that he *should* have had an idea what he was doing. It frustrated him to no end to learn that he couldn't *remember* what he had done last time.

He *vastly* oversaturated the brew with his Mana. If he had wasted five times as much as was needed last time, this was enough to make his control almost slip time and again. When it was finally time to vent the brew, Mana hissed free like popping the vent on a pressure cooker. The ink had absorbed barely any of the Mana he'd invested, but all of a sudden, Sam realized what he was doing wrong as the skill information came into his head again.

Once more, Sam earned the *Magical Material Creation* skill, and in an interesting turn of events, the skill was once again Beginner-zero. Losing it meant *losing* it, apparently, but Sam found that he couldn't seem to stay upset about it. He had too much to do. <Alright, you get a short break here because we need *one* more skill for the next Soul Forge combination. Don't worry, this next skill will be a piece of cake. I want you to grab any sheet of paper there, that bottle of Mana-infused ink we just made, and one of our quills. Which one doesn't really matter for this bit of the lesson, so use a cheap one.>

Sam complied, arranging a sheet of parchment in front of him before grabbing ink and a fine nib quill crafted from a glossy blue-black raven's feather. <Boom. Perfect. Now, all I want you to do is write out the most basic spell form for Paper Shuriken. Nothing fancy. No flourishes. Just the single simple spell.>

That didn't seem so hard to Sam, but that might have been the Instinctual Casting talking. His brow furrowed as he hunched forward, dipped the quill, then carefully sketched out the simple lines and geometric shapes of his most basic spell. Mana had to turn *this* way, then rebound *here* to convert the paper from flat into *folded*. Then it went here for direction, velocity, range...

The moment he finished with the design, his *Magical Origami* skill activated, and he found Mana bleeding out of him in a trickle, filling the lines he'd scrawled onto the page with potent power. This process had seemed incredibly intuitive, so he was more than a little surprised when he earned a pop-up, and the sheet of paper in front of him exploded into a Fireball and threw him across the room.

Health: 92/120

Skill gained: Words of Power (Written) (Novice I). You have instinctually managed to distill a spell to its most basic design! By writing out the spellform on a scroll, anyone who reads the scroll will have a chance to learn the spell. Base probability of learning spell from scroll: 20%. Each rank in this skill increases the chance of learning the spell by 2%, but personal ability needs to be taken into account. Each scroll will have a minimum characteristic score needed in order to learn the spell. The spell must be in the basic spellform for the scroll to be valid.

<Oh. Right, that'll happen.> Bill paused as Sam got to his feet with a groan. <Let's put everything except what you are working with away, so we don't lose it in the next mishap.>

"The *next* one?" Sam demanded even as he swept everything into his flask.

<Well, yes. I suppose you can think of this as one of those 'drawbacks' you had asked about. To be fair, everyone gets hurt practicing their craft. Swordsmen get cut, archers get hit with bowstrings, Mages sometimes blow up. You get used to it. This time, infuse the paper before writing a spell on it. Also, infuse the quill. Oh. Whoops. Your ink bottle exploded. Forgot

to mention that we need to have you infuse the glass bottle before the ink, or you're going to lose a lot of material.>

Sam got to it, losing three glass ink bottles and two quills before getting the hang of it. His health had dropped to sixty-eight, and he had no easy way to heal up without using a healing potion; those were going to be *really* hard to get ahold of in the near future. Still, a few hours later, he had all of the basics ready and had even managed to get Magical Material Creation up to Beginner three.

<Hey, not too shabby. Plus, listen, knocking out Words of Power on your first try is as respectable as it comes. *Most* people blow themselves up on the first go, which is why chasing after Words of Power is so rare! Now that you have Words of Power: Written and all the basic gear, we can get to the most important skill combination of your young life! Though, word of warning... this next Soul Forge combination is gonna be *ridiculously* painful.>

Sam blanched, envisioning horrid scenes of his body being torn apart... that or an even steeper price tag than the last combination. Sam wasn't sure which would be the more painful experience. Apparently, some of those images seeped through the mental bond he had with the book because Bill immediately recoiled.

<Not *that* kinda pain, Legs! I meant it in the *figurative* sense. It's not actually gonna *hurt* you physically. This will be an *emotional* wound. I need you to combine Magical Material Creation and Words of Power: Written with the most valuable ability you have—Instinctual Casting.>

Sam froze at the words. Wat. But... but, Instinctual Casting was really the only thing left over from what he'd started the game with! Bill wasn't wrong; that ability was his single greatest strength. His *edge*. It had saved him time and time again, and if he combined it now with Magical Material Creation, it would be *gone*. Poof. Vanished. Since Instinctual Casting was an essential element to being a Sorcerer, it wasn't something that could be taught or relearned as far as he knew. Abyss, by Soul Forging that skill with another, he might cease to be a Sorcerer *entirely!*

Worse, he would no longer instinctively know how to use magic, nor learn a new spell at every third level.

<Look, I know it seems... drastic,> Bill spoke slowly inside his head, the way one might talk to a frightened animal or a car-crash victim. <It *is* a big loss. I know that better than most. You *don't* need it, okay? You have *me* to teach you spells and how to use 'em. It'll hurt, but I swear the skill you'll get on the other side will more than make up for any drawbacks to losing it.>

Sam hated this. Absolutely *hated* it. Making the choice felt like killing a part of himself... but he pulled the trigger anyway. He knew Bill wouldn't tell him to do it if the payout wasn't worth it. With only a little reluctance, Sam combined the three skills, which cost him two hundred gold. Combining a skill with another took twelve hours and added twelve hours per skill added. His title dropped the time by fifteen percent, and that meant...

Time until skills have combined: 20:24:00.

"Twenty hours, twenty-four minutes." Sam sighed as he thought of all of his spells. Right now, they looked like geometric garbage in his head, and he had no *idea* how to cast them. For the next day, he was absolutely defenseless.

CHAPTER THIRTY-ONE

<Okay, as they say around these parts, the thrice time is charmed. Let's knock out your final round of Magical Material Creation, and then we can get elbow deep in the really fun stuff.> Bill's voice knocked Sam out of his concerned reverie. Sam had thought that he would be unable to do anything magical, but in reality, he just needed to learn how to do it under the watchful eye of a professional, just like a... *shudder*... *normal* Mage.

A day of mixing inks, sharpening quills, and stacking paper passed slowly. At least relearning how to infuse things brought some light into the tunnel. How had people ever gotten through the day when they had nothing that needed to be done? Twenty-four hours of mindless waiting and infusing, all because neither of them had really considered how much Sam had been relying on his instincts.

Since he'd sacrificed his Instinctual Casting ability, his days of slinging magic unaided were gone. As soon as he'd lost the Instinctual Casting ability, he'd received a minor class change. No longer was he a Bibliomantic Sorcerer.

Now, for better or worse, he was a Bibliomancer.

Still, Bill had been right about getting rid of the Instinctual Casting or, rather, *combining* it with Magical Material Creation and Words of Power: Written. Thanks to that sacrifice, Sam had earned a new ability—Coreless Spell Infusion.

Skill gained: Coreless Spell Infusion (Novice V). Magic is a rare thing in this world, and the ability to effortlessly infuse magic into anything from scrolls and books to swords and shields is an even rarer talent. To do it without the need for monster Cores? Well, you might as well start walking toward Easy Street.

This is a powerful ability, so guard it with care. A wise *man might keep this particular skill to himself.*

Effect: Infuse any spell directly into a properly prepared item. The monster Core component required for most spell infusions is negated up to Uncommon-ranked Cores. Spells requiring Rare or above Cores are unaffected by the Coreless component of this ability. All other spell infusion effects and required components remain the same.

By infusing a spellform on a scroll, anyone who reads the scroll will have a chance to learn the spell at the tier below it was infused. i.e. if your understanding of the spell is at Beginner, the reader can learn the Novice version. Base probability of learning spell from an Infused scroll: 20%. Each rank in this skill increases the chance of learning the spell by 2%, but personal ability needs to be taken into account. Each scroll will have a minimum characteristic score needed in order to learn the spell. The spell must be in the <u>basic</u> spellform for the scroll to be valid. Variant spellforms cannot be learned by a reader.

Essentially, this class ability allowed him to infuse *any* spell effect he knew directly into a scroll, book, or item. For lower-tier spells, he didn't even have to use a monster Core, which would have some enormous benefits down the road since even minor Cores were rare and costly. There were some caveats to the ability.

Sam could, *in theory,* apply magical effects to items now... except for the fact that he had neither the knowledge of enchantments or blacksmithing to do so. With his ever-growing knowledge of scrolls, papers, inks, and books, he could *absolutely* infuse those spell effects into his books, allowing him to augment any of his Bibliomancer abilities with ease. Fireball Paper Shuriken? Check. Ninja stars that also paralyzed foes on contact? You *betcha*, as Sphinx would say. Thanks to Bill's nearly encyclopedic knowledge of the class, Sam's Bibliomancer spell arsenal had grown at an *astonishing* rate.

On top of Paper Shuriken, which was still his go-to combat spell, he'd also added a trio of new offensive spells to his roster. Then for the *fourth* new spell, he learned something classified as a *hypnotic* spell!

Skill gained: Bookmark (Novice V). Never lose your place again! This spell cannot be cast on its own but, rather, must be combined with any other offensive spell! Bookmark spell scripts must be inked onto appropriate materials prior to combat at an additional cost of 2 Mana per second until the spell is completed or the attempt fails.

Caster may activate a given bookmark during combat, fixing the spell on a specific location or target. Once a bookmark is activated, all subsequent bookmarked spells will automatically target the original bookmark, even if the target is on the move! Increases accuracy rate by 5n% and reduces spell failure rate by 5n%, where n = skill level. Activate a new bookmark at will to change location or target.

Skill gained: Ink Lance (Novice IV). The noble octopus isn't the only creature to randomly shoot ink at their opponents. You too have joined the vaunted peerage! Does that make you a spineless invertebrate? Hard to say! Launch a goopy blob of Mana-infused ink from the written page itself, entangling your enemies and drastically restricting their movement rate. Additionally, the ink is very hard to get out of fabric. So inconvenient!

Effects: Slows movement rate by 12+(n/2)% for 15 seconds; also deals 1n points of weak acid damage for the duration of the spell. Production Cost: 5 Mana per second until the spell script is completed or attempt is failed. Casting Cost: 1 sheet of ink-soaked paper per spell cast. As only the ink is used when this spell is cast, the paper can be re-inked at a later time!

Skill gained: Book Maker's Book Bomb (Novice VII). There is always an exception that proves the rule. This exception goes by the name of Book Maker's Book Bomb! As a Bibliomancer, most of your spells are delivered using the Orbital Tome Casting mechanic, but that won't stop you from weaponizing any book you can get your grubby, ink-stained fingers on! By inscribing a simple rune in the back of any book—mundane or magical—you can turn it into a deadly bomb!

There are three trigger rune variations; these trigger variations allow you to activate Book Bombs in three different ways: through voice command, pressure, or upon impact. Warning! Using Book Maker's Book Bomb permanently destroys the book in question! Production Cost: 1 book containing a minimum of 100 pages, 250 Mana. Casting Cost: None. 10n damage + damage equal to the prepared spell, where n = skill level.

Skill gained: Rorschach Test (Novice II). A giant scroll unfurls in the air 10 feet above the field of battle, showing a random inkblot. Any enemy in viewing distance of the inkblot (30 feet in a cone emanating from the summoned scroll) must make a saving throw against Intelligence, or the Rorschach will reveal their greatest fear, causing them to flee from battle for up to one minute.

Anyone failing a Constitution check will additionally suffer 1n psionic damage, where 'n' is equal to the skill level. Production Cost: 30 Mana per second until spell script is completed or the attempt has failed. Casting Cost: 150 sheets of paper per cast.

That last one was a potentially powerful area of effect—AoE—spell, though the Mana cost to create it was high, and the casting cost was equally formidable. At one hundred and fifty sheets of paper per cast, Sam would likely be able to cast the spell twice at *most* during any given battle. It would also cost him something like thirty real-world dollars per cast. That made him gag a little. So, there was no way it would be a go-to spell like Ink Lance or Paper Shuriken, but... as a backup spell to use in case things got *really* rough? Yeah, it was perfect for that.

The next three days passed in a sleepless blur, just rapid-fire reading of books and studying arcane points of law. All of this was offset by crafting item after item—infusing ink, preparing and inking scads of paper, binding book spines, and creating scrolls of power. Writing out spells took up the bulk of his time, and though the process was not precisely *complicated...* it *did* take an ungodly amount of time. Even a momentary lapse in concentration or judgment had devastating consequences. Each day, there was a little gray on his health bar that showed health that wouldn't naturally return until he was properly and magically healed.

Truthfully, it was a *grind* in the truest sense of the word. Sam only left his room for brief meals of cold porridge or day-old soup, but the results were worth the effort and *then* some. He learned more and leveled skills faster than he had during his entire stay at the College.

After they'd finished combining skills and what felt like endless iterations of Magical Materials Creation, Bill had Sam work through all the various spell books he'd snatched from the library. Those nearly priceless tomes contained magical ink on magical paper, which meant they were chock full of potential ammo. The downside was that once Sam used the original pages as cannon fodder, the knowledge and spells those books contained would be lost. Gone as irrevocably as his Instinctual Casting now was. That was a *terrible* waste.

So, Sam studied slavishly for most of each day when he wasn't working. *The Fundamentals of Core Cultivation* was a straightforward text that covered ground he'd already tread with Mage Akora, his *former* Mana Manipulation and Mana Coalescence teacher. Still, there were some new tidbits, including a strange deep breathing technique that would *allegedly* help him cycle Mana through his Core more effectively.

The proof of the claim was yet to be seen, but reading through the text *did* raise his Mana manipulation skill from Beginner three to Beginner five, which Bill said was amazing on its own. Not too shabby, considering the total time he'd spent in game so far. Though, when Sam thought about how *much* money he'd spent to get his stats, the achievement felt a little less impressive. Still, he took it all in stride. Pay to win was a valid strategy, right? Sure, people tended to frown on it, but what was done was done, and he needed to celebrate his victories where he could.

Brilliant Blossoms: A field guide to basic herbology was a rather simple manual that identified a number of common—as well as a few uncommon—plants located throughout Eternium. It also detailed their various uses in potions, tinctures, and enchantments. The guide was as dull as watching paint dry, but it did earn him a new skill called *Herbalism*.

New skill gained! Herbalism (Novice IV). Plant? What plant? All you see is ingredients! Whether they are for dinner or for creating potions is up to you! Usable raw plants are 1% easier to find, 1% easier to process, and have 1% greater effect per skill level!

Despite reading and even rereading *A Compendium of Magical Omens*, which was supposed to be an Apprentice-ranked text, Sam couldn't make heads or tails of the info inside.

The entire volume just made his brain ache and earned him a number of failed 'Perception and Knowledge checks', suggesting the book may have been inaccurately shelved. *Compendium on Protected and Dangerous Locations* had a similar effect, which told Sam that those books needed to be set aside for later inspection. Just because they were worthless *now* didn't mean they wouldn't provide some tangible value once he hit a higher level.

Thankfully, *The Book of Lost Incantations, Rediscovered!* and *Compact Fundamentals of Elemental Magic, Aeolus Edition,* proved to be invaluable finds. From those two volumes alone—and Bill talking him through what he needed to learn—he'd gained a bevy of basic spells: *Fireball (Novice I), Ice Orb (Novice I), Weak Acid Spray (Novice I), Weak Paralysis (Novice I),* and once more unlocked *Wind Blade (Novice I),* which seemed like a spell from a lifetime ago.

Unfortunately, he couldn't actually cast any of those spells, at least not outright like a Mage or Sorcerer could. Not anymore. Now, they were just spells on paper. Beyond all the success he was seeing, there had been a minor *setback* he'd had on the morning of his fourth day.

While inking out a page to use as a Paper Shuriken which was infused with both a Fireball spell and a Bookmark rune... Sam's attention wavered for just a moment—a minor, *tiny* lapse. The spell scripting was rather repetitive, so it was an easy mistake to make, especially since Sam was crafting not *one* but *hundreds* of pages. Still, it only took a second of absent-minded daydreaming for his Mana to slip out of control and activate the spell prematurely, which resulted in a rather nasty *kablooey.*

A *kablooey* that wiped his health in the span of an eyeblink and sent him for an eight hour respawn—just about the worst thing that could happen, given he was operating under a tight, *tight* deadline. So long, twelve hundred experience. Getting back into the city from the Wolfman outpost ate through another six hours he didn't have to spare. Not ideal, but Sam *had* used his boring respawn time to his advantage.

He hadn't touched base with his parents since entering the game. That was only a week in the real world, but it was great to talk with them. His mom and dad both jumped on to the call and understandably wanted to know everything there was to know. How's the game? What class had he picked? Had he made any friends yet? Was he having fun? Sam had to dodge and evade more than a few times, which made him feel guilty all the way down to his soul. He didn't want to lie to his parents, but he could only say so much without setting off red flags.

After that call, Sam took a few hours to hop online and pore over the various forums and wikis which had popped up about Eternium, seemingly overnight. Sadly, the info available at this point was absolutely *basic* and mostly revolved around graphics to the tune of '*OMG, are they so amazing or what?*', a few notes on attributes and leveling, and occasionally, some heated discussions about the pre-game 'Trials'. All interesting, but nothing that even remotely helped Sam. There wasn't *anything* about the Mage's College, other than it existed inside the game, almost as though there was some sort of information black hole in regards to the secretive organization.

Sam guessed the game developers were probably culling any information about the College because they wouldn't want the absurd 'pay-to-play' nature of the school to scare potential players away. A deeper search taught him that the reason any information at all was hard to find—any time information that was *actually* useful appeared, it was gone in under ten minutes. This was actually one of the *most* discussed aspects on the forums, as no one could figure out *how.*

The biggest thing Sam did was *relax*. All. By. Himself. Dying wasn't a pleasant experience by any stretch of the imagination, but if it did have one tangible upside; Bill's mental presence was nowhere to be found. Bill—for all his gruff and occasionally acrid personality—was growing on Sam like some kind of fungus, but to have a few minutes alone inside his own skull felt like heaven.

Just as quickly as his death had come, his life resumed. A step through the portal and it was right back into the grind, but this time with a walk of shame away from laughing Wolfmen. After that, Sam was *much* more careful about his work. Sure, he'd enjoyed the mini vacation, but he had too much to do and no time to spare.

Other than that one, minor slipup, everything went as well as possible. Dying had let his health come back fully, which was a positive that he didn't plan on taking advantage of again if he could help it. Aside from the spells and skill levels, he'd also earned a fistful of additional Characteristic points from some kind of 'characteristic training'. Intelligence, dexterity, and wisdom had gone up by four over the last four days, constitution and perception by two... and he'd managed to unlock his first profession—*Bookbinder*.

You may choose one profession at the fifth level and another at level ten. It is recommended that you choose a gathering profession first to gain the materials needed for the next profession you choose.

Bookbinder: Only those truly dedicated to books and literature ever find their way on to this humble path. The bookbinder is a specialized craftsman, one who knows the deep mysteries of Coptic binding, Ethiopian binding, long-stitch binding, and a thousand other methods besides. They can tell the difference between Vellum and Parchment at a thousand paces and are as familiar with various paper forms as they are with the backside of their own hand. With only a touch, they can repair even badly damaged texts or assess the rarity of a book in moments. These wandering craftsmen are a boon to any library, and their services are often sought by those with vast storehouses of knowledge.

Profession benefits at first level: Increases the speed of reading and writing by 50%. Reduces cost and production time for paper, ink, and book bindings by 25%.

The profession was much more involved than Sam had realized initially. He now knew the difference between the *recto* and *verso* side of a leaf face, could rattle off the definitions, explain distinctive features of spines, or teach someone how to employ a traditional binding while also adding a finish to any manuscript. Definitely a skillset Sam *never*–not in a million years–expected to have, but as a Bibliomancer, it was the *perfect* profession. Plus, it worked in harmony with his other newly combined skill.

Spellbinding (Beginner V). The creation of magical documents is arduous and difficult, oftentimes deadly. Mitigating the risks is the best you can hope for. Effect: Each rank of this skill increases magical quill durability by 3%, magical ink purity by 4%, infused paper durability by 3% when it is used or created by you and decreases time to create desired magical ink by 5%. +2% writing speed and accuracy. Increases possible written spell diagram complexity and stability by $2n\%$ per skill level, where n = skill level.

Skill increase: Coreless Spell Infusion (Novice IX). So close you can taste it, right? Looks like you might need a little inspiration to get past this bottleneck!

Name: Sam_K 'Experimental Forger'

Class: Bibliomancer
Profession: Bookbinder
Level: 6 Exp: 19,323 Exp to next level: 1,677
Hit Points: 140/140
Mana: 478/478
Mana regen: 13.68/sec
Stamina: 145/145

Characteristic: Raw score (Modifier)

Strength: 20 (15+5 gear bonus) (1.15)
Dexterity: 30 (25+5 gear bonus) (1.25)
Constitution: 19 (1.19)
Intelligence: 45 (1.45)
Wisdom: 38 (1.38)
Charisma: 20 (15+5 gear bonus) (1.15)
Perception: 19 (1.19)
Luck: 12 (1.12)
Karmic Luck: -11

Overall, Sam was incredibly happy with his progress, but the time for study—for skill grinding, spell scribing, and magical material creation—was at an end.

Skill increased: Channeling (Novice VIII). Interesting. Nearly all of your non-combat spell creation utilizes this skill, while nearly none of your in-combat spells do. What a nice deviation from the norm!

He'd already burned through most of his seven-day limit, and he was still no closer to putting an end to Octavius, stopping the Mages, saving the Wolfman outpost, or freeing Velkan of the Redmane Tribe. Assuming the Wolfman Scout was still alive. Sam had some time to think about just *how* to accomplish his daunting task during the long days and short, restless nights. There were still a lot of potential pitfalls to work out, but Sam was certain of two things.

One, he couldn't stop Octavius cooped up inside this little room. Two, he couldn't do it by himself. As much as he'd grown under Bill's watchful gaze, Sam knew he needed some serious help to pull this off. It was time to go recruiting. It was time to start the downfall of humanity.

Chapter Thirty-Two

<You *sure* they're here, Sam?> Bill sounded skeptical for a *talking book*. <I mean, not that I don't believe you. I'm sure you *have* real friends. Who are totally *real*, and not at all... *eh,* what's the phrase I'm looking for... ah, right—the lonely delusions of an isolated Mage. Even if they are real, we're wasting a *lot* of time just standing around and twiddling our collective thumbs. Well, your thumbs, since I am thumb-challenged.>

"I just spent the past four days inking the same eight spells five hundred times and burning through my health over and over," Sam replied flatly, crossing his arms for emphasis. "I think we can wait a *little* longer. Besides, there's no way we'll be able to do this mission without some help."

Sam skirted up to the edge of the alleyway, pressing his shoulder against the wall of a nearby building. He peered at the ramshackle structure—the Square Dog Inn. This was his rendezvous point with Dizzy and the rest of the Wolf Pack, and today was the day he and Finn were supposed to meet for their weekly grinding session. Sam was absolutely *positive* that Dizzy wouldn't stand him up. The problem was, he couldn't just waltz into the Square Dog all fancy-free, smiling, laughing, and pretending like nothing was wrong.

The Mage's College was still actively hunting him, and they *knew* the connection between him and Dizzy. It made sense that they'd stick a tail on the Wolf Pack just in *case* Sam popped up out of the blue looking for a little help. Even if the Mages *weren't* actively staking this place out, pitching rebellion against humanity inside a crowded bar full of human adventurers seemed like a pretty good way to get murdered by... well, pretty much everyone.

No, it wouldn't do to disclose his secrets anywhere inside fifty miles of another witness. That meant Sam's only option was to wait for Dizzy and her crew to leave the city, getting clear of any potential eavesdroppers, before cornering them with his offer of mutiny.

"They'll be here, Bill," Sam whispered, though a flutter of unease gave the lie to his words. *Hopefully* they'll be here, he silently amended.

<Let's say I believe you. What happens if this plan goes off flawlessly, but they turn you down? Have you even thought about that? Maybe they politely decline, or maybe they turn on you like rabid dogs. You think you can take down their whole party? Even if you *could,* do you actually have the stones to *do* it? To kill these 'friends' of yours?>

<Why are you so against this idea?> Sam sent back, choosing to speak wordlessly. They *were* going for inconspicuous. <You've been pretty grumpy ever since I mentioned bringing these guys on board. Almost as though you're defensive. Touchy about something? Have some kind of trust issues?>

<*Phft.* No. I'm not touchy about anything. If anything, *you're* the one being defensive. I think *you* just need to have more confidence in *us* as a team. We're good together, me and you. If I can just get you up past the first intelligence threshold, I can teach you some *epic* area of effect spells. After that? We won't *need* anyone else. Just you and me against the world.>

<See, that's the defensive thing I was talking about,> Sam replied, his mind going over the possibilities. Bill had been turned into a book; it wasn't a stretch to think that there was more to the story. <I can *literally* read you, so what gives?>

Bill was silent for a beat, almost as though his presence had withdrawn from Sam's skull. The feeling was eerie. It turned out that Bill was simply searching for the right words. <Fine. Look. *Maybe* I am being just a *little* defensive. The truth is, almost every friend I've ever had in my whole life burned me at some point. Even my brothers in the Order of the Bravi sold me down the river when it became more useful *not* to have me around.>

<There's a reason my best friends were *books*, not other people. Books don't stick a knife in your back when you're not looking. In my experience, depending on *anyone* for *anything* is a surefire way to end up in a magically induced coma for a couple hundred years.>

This was a side of Bill that Sam hadn't seen before. It was also a firm reminder that the non-player characters in this game were more than they seemed. On the surface, Bill appeared confident and so *sure* of himself... but underneath, he was an outsider just like Sam, a person who'd struggled with genuine friendships and wrestled with feelings of betrayal. In so many ways, Bill *was* Sam; the only difference was Bill had turned to library books while Sam had turned to gaming.

Another major difference—for the first time in his life, Sam realized going the lone wolf route wasn't an option. For better or worse, he *needed* other people. As much as he might like to—as convenient as it might have been—he simply couldn't do the group assignment by himself this time around.

<This will be different,> Sam promised, just as the front door of the Square Dog swung open, dumping Dizzy and the rest of the Wolf Pack on to the cobblestone street.

<I sure hope so, Sam. I sure hope so.> Bill didn't sound hopeful in the slightest.

"*Look*, Arrow," Dizzy threw her hands up in exasperation, "I don't *know* what to tell you. I thought they'd be here too, but obviously, Sam and Finn weren't as interested in teaming up with us as I thought, okay? Since they clearly aren't coming, there's no reason to wait around any longer. Let's just go kill some Mobs before this day is a complete waste."

Without another word, she turned and stormed off, her back ramrod straight, her fists curled into angry balls. Arrow grimaced, shrugged, and offered quiet words to the others. Sphinx nodded in reply to whatever Arrow had suggested, and together, the rest of the Wolf Pack set off after Dizzy's retreating back, the whole lot of them looking utterly dejected. Disheartened. Defeated.

<Hold up a sec,> Bill growled just as Sam was about to step from the shadows. Across the open area, another man slipped out from a pool of inky shade. His dark blue robes and gnarled staff marked him as a Mage. Probably a bounty hunter and not anyone Sam had seen before.

<Well this just got a whole lot more complicated,> Bill muttered wearily. <Could be nothing, but in the spirit of *healthy* paranoia... I say we give the whole lot of 'em some extra distance.> Bill wasn't wrong.

Sam waited for the blue-robed Mage to shoulder his way into the flow of human traffic, then ventured out himself. He followed behind, keeping a solid fifty paces back, though his gaze never left the bounty hunter nor the members of the Wolf Pack. This did complicate Sam's plans, but it didn't *necessarily* change them a whole lot.

He *needed* to talk to Dizzy and the others, and he needed to do it well away from nosy citizens who would report him to the authorities once he started yapping about allying with the Wolfmen. How *exactly* he would accomplish that with the Mage around, Sam wasn't sure, but he figured he'd cross that bridge once it was on fire and threatening to burn him alive.

Sam made it through the Northern Gates without a problem. That was a big relief; he had worried that the Mages might have someone posted at every entrance to the city. Luckily for him and unfortunately for humanity, the chainmail-wearing gate guards didn't have any interest whatsoever in people leaving the city. From the look of things, their job was to prevent unsavory folks or dangerous monsters from coming *into* Ardania, not to deter honest, monster-killing adventurers from *exiting* the city's enormous gates. Aside from the Mage in blue who stuck out like a sore thumb, there were no spell-slingers in sight.

For the next two hours, Sam followed the party and their unnoticed stalker, keeping a healthy distance as he stole from bushes to trees to rock outcroppings. One thing Sam learned almost immediately was that he was *terrible* at stealth. Every footfall sounded like thunder in his own ears, and he somehow managed to step on every twig that had ever fallen from a tree branch.

It was an absolute wonder that he wasn't caught in the first five minutes out the gate. His only real saving grace was that the Mage in blue was equally terrible at stealth. The guy, maybe in his late thirties with a mop of shaggy brown hair, made just as much noise as Sam. He was *so* focused on tracking Dizzy and the Wolf Pack that he didn't bother to look back even once.

As for Dizzy and the others, they were so preoccupied with slaying bunnies and foxes that they didn't seem to notice the blue-robed Mage stalking their trail. Honestly, why would they? They had no idea what had gone down at the College and therefore had no reason to suspect they were being tracked. Unfortunately, even after two hours, Sam still had no idea how to handle the situation on his hands.

He felt fairly certain he could get Dizzy's attention but not without also tipping off the magical bounty hunter. The second the enemy Mage spotted Sam, it would be royal rumble time. The problem was, Sam had no idea how strong this guy was. True, Sam had been hitting the books hard over the last few days, but he had no idea how effective his new spells would be. For all he knew, the not-so-sneaky Mage in front of him could've been a Master of battle magic. The chances of that were unlikely, as the College probably wouldn't waste a Master Mage on trailing a bunch of Travelers... but there was no way for Sam to be certain. Not without picking a fight.

But as Dizzy and the Wolf Pack crept up to the tree line, something happened which ripped the choice right out of Sam's hands. They'd barely entered into the shadowy canopy when an *actual* wolfpack, ten strong, leaped from nowhere. The entire pack seemed to materialize from thin air, fur bristling, muzzles snarling, drool hanging down in great strings as they closed in around Sam's friends on all sides. Worse, loitering in the trees overhead crouched down on a particularly thick bough was a different threat—a Wolfman Shaman. A Shaman that Sam recognized from his near brush with a sacrificial stone altar. Yurij BrightBlood.

A pack of wolves that large and guided by a Shaman with untold magical powers was as good as a death sentence for Dizzy and the others. Sam had no idea how much they had leveled since he'd seen them a week ago, but there was no way that it was enough to take out the *actual* wolfpack arrayed against them. Not without a little magical backup.

If Sam jumped into the fray, he might be able to turn the tide of battle, but he would sacrifice any element of surprise he had and would instantly alert the blue-robed Mage to his presence. It was a lose-lose situation. But what choice was there?

If he didn't help, he would live, but his friends would be dead, sent for a half-day wait for respawn. Then Sam would *still* need to go through this same rigmarole, and there was no guarantee that things would turn out any better next time around.

It was now or never. Steeling himself for battle, Sam reached to Bill and summoned his new spell books, instantly pulling them from Bill's Soul Space. Instead of two volumes springing to life around him, a full complement of *six* books took to the air. Spinning in a slow orbit, each volume glowed with soft blue witchlight. With a thought and a trickle of Mana, Sam activated Papier-Mache Mage, clothing himself with the odd but familiar conquistador-style armor.

He opted against conjuring his Quill Blade for the time being; ranged attacks were his best option in a fight like this. Then before he could second guess himself, he leaped into motion, breaking from cover as he charged the wolves already tearing into his friends.

"Not today, fur-faces!" Sam's voice was quiet but excited.

"Kai, I need you on the right flank!" Dizzy boomed even as she lashed out with her enormous maul, the blunt face connecting with a shaggy-furred head. She sent the creature scrambling with a yelp. "Sphinx, you're playing zone coverage. Arrow, we need suppressive cover fire! Make sure these things don't get behind us!"

It was too late for that. Three rangy wolves had already maneuvered behind the party, and try as Arrow might, he just wasn't quick enough nor accurate enough with his bow to pin down all three wolves at once.

Sam could fix that. Inside of a few heartbeats, he was in range. Instead of bringing just one book to the front, he brought two books forward, one at the ten-o-clock position, the other at two-o-clock. Since he had the Dual casting ability, he could launch two spells at the same time, though it would reduce the overall accuracy and increase the spell failure rate. That was a price Sam was willing to pay. Besides, with some of the upgrades he'd made over the past few days, he didn't even *need* to directly land a spell to break up the ambush.

With a war cry, Sam unleashed a double volley of Paper Shurikens. Two folded stars—one burning with soft orange light, the other radiating arctic-purple power—screamed from the pages of the volumes on his left and right. The first Shuriken landed with a bomb blast. It cut through fur with razor-sharp edges, embedding in flesh with ease, then exploded with eye-searing heat and force. A single clean hit and there were wolf pieces scattered across the densely vegetated forest floor.

Damage dealt: 39 (34 Paper Shuriken + 5 Fireball)

"*Rabblefrabble!*" Sam shouted in shock. He had added what he *thought* was a rather simple Fireball spell to each page in the red-leather volume. He'd expected a little extra fire-damage to each attack, maybe. Certainly not ninja-star hand grenades that he could launch at a rate of one-point-five per second. The Fireball added to the Shuriken made the *entire* damage pool have an area of effect, though it was only about three feet in diameter right now. Unsurprising, as this spell was starting at Novice one.

Meanwhile, the arctic-purple Shuriken had a more subtle effect but one that was equally brutal in its own special way. When the paper blades hit home, they unleashed a powerful burst of icy energy which clawed across a target's body like fingers of frostbite, inflicting extra cold damage over time.

Damage dealt: 25 (20 Paper Shuriken + 5 ice damage over three seconds). Target slowed 12% for three seconds!

Unfortunately, these new spells of his didn't discriminate between friend and foe, which meant he'd have to be very careful in just how he used them. Two of the three wolves were down in seconds—dead or dying—which freed up Arrow to take out the third wolf with a flurry of carefully aimed shots that punched through fur and muscle. It was a good start, but Dizzy and company were hardly out of the woods yet.

More wolves flooded in and converged on Dizzy. She was drawing aggro like the heavy-hitting tank she was. Kai and Sphinx both moved like greased lightning, the Monk delivering lightning-fast blows and blinding-quick kicks, while the Roguish Assassin hurled knives and slashed at vulnerable muzzles. There were just *so* many enemies.

In seconds, they were on the verge of being overwhelmed. Sam considered the situation only for a thin moment before toggling books, rotating his *Ice Orb* tome to the back and bringing a regular Paper Shuriken volume to the fore. With the press of bodies and the ebb and flow of battle, Sam couldn't reasonably expect to launch spell-laced folded stars without also inflicting friendly fire. Thankfully, he was far more accurate with his regular Shurikens... and he had another new trick to try out.

Five wolves were clustered before Dizzy like the fingers of a curled fist, fighting together in a unified front. It seemed to be a brutally effective tactic that forced Dizzy to play defense, constantly protecting herself from snapping teeth or tearing claws, without ever having the opportunity to strike an offensive blow in return.

Against Sam, staying clustered together like that was going to prove to be a terrible idea. He focused on the beefy wolf right in the center of the fist—his fur black as midnight, his eyes the color of molten copper—and unleashed a regular Shuriken, triggering the *Bookmark* effect as the spell took flight.

The folded paper screamed through the air like a buzz-saw, slicing past Dizzy's face by a bare inch before dropping and sinking into a hunched, wolfy shoulder. Dizzy glanced back over a shoulder, her eyes flaring wide in surprise at the sight of Sam. She gave him the merest nod, then threw herself back into the action. Curious to see just *how* Bookmark worked, Sam turned and fired a Shuriken *away* from the black-furred wolf. He felt a giddy sort of joy as the paper star shot out and curved like a boomerang, swinging around in a vicious arc before slamming into the wolf's side with deadly accuracy.

Then Sam watched in shock as the Shuriken zipped *back* toward him, rejoining the book. A pop up appeared in the corner of his vision.

Skill gained: Paperang (Novice I). Reduce, Reuse, Recycle! Being a Bibliomancer ain't cheap! But with Paperang, the costs can be marginally mitigated by responsibly reusing your weapons of death and destruction! Effect: Paper Shurikens and other items classified as Paper Origami have a 1n% chance, where n = skill level, to return to the caster for reuse unless the item is destroyed beyond the point of recovery on impact. Paper Shurikens and items classified as Paper Origami that do not hit their target or another object have a 2n% chance of returning to the caster.

Luck +1!

Sam dismissed the notice immediately and fired off a third Shuriken, this one from the red volume augmented with Fireball spellscript. An orange, glowing star burst forth, following the same trajectory as the last Shuriken. It curved sharply like a... *Paperang*, slamming into the wolf's rear. The spell roared, enveloping the wolf in a bonfire, burning it and the others around it for a total of thirty damage to each of them.

Things were still bad, but maybe they *could* win this. The last week had felt rather exhausting and more than a little hopeless, but for the first time since escaping the College... Sam found he was having *fun*! *This* was what he'd come here for! To fight the long odds with friends. To learn new skills. To adventure, quest, and *win*! This was what his life had been missing, and now that his goals were almost in reach... he needed to fight harder than ever. He was *not* about to let someone take this away from him.

"Sam, *behind you*!" Arrow jarred Sam from his moment of elated clarity. The archer looked positively frantic as he thrust a finger straight out, pointing at something just out of Sam's sight.

CHAPTER THIRTY-THREE

Sam wheeled around just in time to see the blue-robed Mage hurl a jagged lance of lightning. *Oh snap.* Sam scrambled left but *far* too slowly. The bolt of arcane energy slammed into him like a wrecking ball, lifting him from his feet and sending him cartwheeling through the air. Sam landed in a huff, head spinning, legs oddly heavy, bright starbursts of pain racing along both arms while his hair stood on end. Wow, the guy could throw a *mean* metaphysical punch. If not for Sam's Papier-Mache Mage, he would've been dead—no two ways about it.

Health -119 (449 damage taken. 330 damage absorbed by Papier-Mache Mage.)

Skill increase: Papier-Mache Mage (Beginner IV).
Taking damage grants you insight into how to not take damage the same way again! Yay!

He had invested four hundred Mana into that armor when he designed it, and it was gone in a *single* hit? As it stood, he was down to twenty-one health. A gust of wind or a tossed *rock* was liable to kill him at this point. Sam couldn't afford to take even a *glancing* blow from the lightning Mage.

A sharp *snap-crack* rent the air as another arc of lightning blazed toward Sam. He barrel-rolled to the right, narrowly avoiding the blast as it smacked into the space he'd occupied seconds before. Earth, grass, and stones kicked up as the blue-white arc carved out a meaty crater in the ground. Sam *forced* himself to his feet, calling forth a jet-black book. It had formerly been the *Fundamentals of Core Cultivation...* but it had a new purpose now.

The pages *snapped* open and vomited a javelin of black toward the enemy Mage. The lightning Mage conjured a dome of blue light, no doubt a Mage shield of one sort or another designed to absorb or deflect damage. Sam's Ink Lance landed like a hammer blow, but instead of shattering against the blue barrier, the black substance *splattered*, morphing into a blob of tar-like goop.

Ink Lance currently dealt three points of acid damage each second for fifteen seconds. Sadly, the blue shield merely *sizzled*, robbing the spell of its damage-dealing component. Luckily, that was only *one* portion of the spell effect. The ink began to writhe with a life all its own, tentacles of black questing along the conjured shield. Inky fingers dripped onto the Mage's upraised arms and promptly began to *climb*.

The Mage let out a squawk of shock, his shield dissipating as he fought off the strands of black inching across his body like a plague. The sheer *stickiness* of the creeping ink slowed the Mage, gumming up his fingers, wrapping around his wrists, making it harder for him to move—or cast spells... or evade. Suddenly, Sam had a little breathing room; he stole a look behind him at the desperate battle between the Wolf Pack and the actual wolves.

Things were going better, thanks in no small part to Sam's involvement, but his team still wasn't in the clear yet. Sam rotated his regular Shuriken Tome to the six-o-clock position and cast a fresh round of folded stars, targeting a shaggy-furred she-wolf busily assaulting Kai. The first paper star went wide, but the second hit true, and Sam capitalized by triggering Bookmark. Pairing his Dual casting and Sightless casting abilities, Sam began to spam Shurikens at the wolf while focusing his attention back on the blue-robed College Mage. The ink had finally stopped spreading and was drying on to the Mage's robes—how *inconvenient*—sadly taking the movement restriction debuff with it.

But the ink had done its job. Sam brought his Ice Orb tome to the fore, launching a glittering purple star at the Mage. The bounty hunter wasn't even *remotely* prepared to defend against an ice-based attack. The first star slammed into him, dropping the Mage to the ground as a rime of white ice spread across the Mage's ink-splattered robes. Sam hurled another round of stars, pulling his standard Shuriken around to join in the attack. The Mage, though busy crawling away, had the presence of mind to conjure his flickering blue barrier to life once more. Sam's stars bounced away harmlessly.

No, that was *unacceptable*. Sam couldn't give this man a chance to regroup. He needed to end this *now*. With a roar, Sam conjured his Quill Blade and charged. In seconds, he was on the Mage. He shot forward, thrusting the tip of his summoned sword into the magical barrier. The blade bounced away, but the shield flickered from the impact.

The shield was no doubt drawing from the Mage's Mana pool, and if it worked in a similar fashion as Mage Armor, then all Sam had to do was drain the shield of enough Mana, and it would dissolve on its own. *Poof.* Gone. So, with a fury born from the need to survive, Sam launched a series of attacks, thrusting, chopping, slicing—his blade carving away a chunk of the Mage's Mana pool with every blow he landed. Then it happened.

Sam brought his sword down in a powerful overhand strike, and the shield exploded in a dazzling display of golden bursts and lightning blue sparks. His swing carried straight through, the blade embedding itself in the Mage's neck with a wet **thump**.

Critical hit! 33 slashing damage dealt! Bleeding (Heavy): -10 health per second!

The Mage sputtered for a moment as though he simply couldn't *believe* what had just happened. A 'this shouldn't be possible,' look was plastered on his face. Sam planted a foot on the Mage's chest and kicked, dealing a single point of damage and pulling his blade free in the same instant. The Mage dropped, body limp, eyes glassy, mouth frozen in the shape of a shocked 'O'.

You have killed an active, tracked *agent of the Mage's College! I would say well done, but have you really thought this through? Whatever, you do you. Congratulations, you are no longer just a Rogue Mage! As you have broken the laws of the Kingdom, you've gained a new title! Your reputation with the College has decreased -1500! Current reputation: Blood Feud.*

Title gained: Warlock IV. You have broken the law of the Kingdom, and it shows! -10 charisma and prices increase by 50% when interacting with those loyal to the Kingdom of Ardania. If they will sell to you. Guards will look for any reason to detain or attack you. As you do not have an active warrant, they will not be able to do so without cause.

Skill increase: Dual casting (Novice VI). You have shown great strides in proficiency with Dual casting, and it is obviously starting to become second nature!

Skill increase: Quill Blade (Novice IV). Who said there was no reward for murder? Obviously, someone that can't see their quantified progression!

Skill increase: Orbital Tome Casting (Novice III). This is kind of a gimme. No way for you not to increase this if you are casting spells!

Magical Origami, Origami Activation, Paper Shuriken, Bookmark, Ink Lance, Fireball, and Ice Orb had also increased a rank, which was somewhat of a relief. The preparation for them hadn't made the spell increase at all, and it seemed that he needed to use them in combat for his understanding of them to increase. It did make sense in a way—how would he know what to focus on without seeing it in action? He looked down at the robe-clad body. Killing the enemy Mage was satisfying, as the College *had* put Sam through hell, but he couldn't relish in the victory for too long. There was still Dizzy and the others to consider.

He spun to find the battle had shifted dramatically in the handful of seconds he'd been occupied with the bounty-hunting Mage. Dizzy and the others had dispatched the rest of the wolves, but there was still one enemy left—the Wolfman Shaman, *Yurij BrightBlood.*

"No, no, *no!*" Sam couldn't let this happen. Not now. Dizzy and Yurij were both allies—or at least *potential* allies—and they were about to massacre each other. Sam needed a ceasefire, and there was one weapon in his arsenal that might do the trick, and though he *hated* using such a costly spell, there was nothing for it.

He brought a brown volume with a gold spine to the front and unleashed his only area of effect spell. Pages and ink burst forth in a whirlwind, spinning and distorting as they took to the sky, morphing into a single giant scroll. Because of his position, Sam couldn't see what was inked on the front side of the floating scroll, but from the spell description, he knew everyone else would be seeing a giant Rorschach Test—one designed to induce absolute terror.

The effects were immediate. *Yurij BrightBlood* howled in mad fear, his fur standing on end as he scrambled back... except there was nowhere for him to go since he was already on a tree branch high above the ground.

Dizzy, Kai, and Arrow all let out similar cries of panic, bolting in every direction, all thought of fighting completely forgotten for the time being. Their wild eyes, brimming with dread, told Sam that whatever they were seeing was far worse than any image he could've imagined on his own—a firm reminder that you were always your own worst enemy. Only Sphinx was unaffected, which meant she must've somehow been able to ignore the effects.

"Sam!" Sphinx turned with her weapons drawn, focusing him with killing intent. She practically growled at him, eyes narrowing to slits as she dropped into a crouch and circled left. "What's going *on* here? What have you done?"

<Could be I'm wrong,> Bill commented inside his head, <but I think your 'friend' is about to kill you with extreme prejudice.>

"Shut up," Sam hissed in reply, "you're not being even remotely helpful."

"*What* did you just say to me?" Sphinx shot back, now sounding positively venomous. "I thought you were a good kid, but gosh darn it, maybe I was wrong about you."

"What?" Sam's eyebrows climbed for his hairline. "No. No! Sphinx! I wasn't talking to you. I was talking to Bill."

He waved at the floating book attached to his hip by the ghostly silver chain. "Which *probably* doesn't make any sense. In fact, I know how this must look, but I *swear* I can explain everything. Just... not right now."

He shook his head, feeling so frustrated with himself. "Look, my spell is about to wear off any second. When it does, your crew is going to try to tear that Wolfman apart, but we *can't* let that happen. I know it's a lot to ask, but please, *please,* keep them away. I'll take care of the Shaman... and then I swear I'll explain it all. Okay?"

Sam studied her face, but her expression was largely unreadable. Finally, she sighed and nodded, though Sam noticed she didn't stow her weapons. "I'll help you, but please don't make me regret it, hon, or *you'll* regret it."

She offered him her back, a show of genuine trust, and hustled off to catch her teammates before they could regroup. Sam, in turn, used the moment of bedlam to position himself firmly between the heroes and the Wolfman Shaman. By the time he and Sphinx were both in position, the Rorschach-inspired terror had finally dissipated.

"Yurij BrightBlood," Sam called up to the Wolfman, exposing his neck while simultaneously hunching his shoulders. "It's me, Sam. You took me to The O'Baba several days ago."

"*I know your smell,*" the Shaman growled down to him in the guttural Wolfman tongue. He reached toward a bronze ceremonial dagger tucked into a leather belt wrapped around his waist. "*I knew The O'Baba was foolish to trust one of your kind. I should've killed you when I had the chance. An error I will fix now.*"

"No," Sam called up, raising his hands, palms in and angled toward his face to show he meant no harm. "It's *not* what you think. Just a terrible coincidence. These are my former teammates, and I'm working to recruit them to the Wolfman cause. I couldn't get in touch with them earlier because a Mage from the College has been tracking them."

He canted his shoulders and gestured at the corpse of the blue-robed Mage, lying dead not far off. "Your cunning ambush forced me to reveal myself prematurely. I can assure you, these humans are *not* your enemies. They are future allies, but you need to let me explain the situation."

The Shaman crouched, claws digging into the bark of the branch, and sniffed; his nostrils flaring wide. "I smell no deception in you, Mageling. If I find you have tricked me, I will declare you a blood enemy, and I will *not* stop until you are ruined by my claws. Understood?"

<Wow, and here I thought *I* was bad with people. *Everyone* wants to kill you! Honestly, I'm more impressed than anything.>

"Understood, esteemed Shaman," Sam barked, dipping his head so low it nearly touched the ground. "*I am entirely at your mercy.*"

When Sam looked up from the bow a moment later, the Shaman was gone. The claw marks, gouged into the rough bark of the tree, were the only sign Yurij had ever been there. Sam let out a sigh of deep relief. One potential crisis averted... only one left to handle. He pulled open his character sheet to look everything over while he waited for the team to regroup. It might be a little while.

Name: Sam_K 'Experimental Forger'
Class: Bibliomancer
Profession: Bookbinder
Level: 6 Exp: 19,646 Exp to next level: 1,354
Hit Points: 21/140
Mana: 478/478
Mana regen: 13.68/sec
Stamina: 145/145

Characteristic: Raw score (Modifier)

Strength: 20 (15+5 gear bonus) (1.15)
Dexterity: 30 (25+5 gear bonus) (1.25)
Constitution: 19 (1.19)
Intelligence: 45 (1.45)
Wisdom: 38 (1.38)
Charisma: 20 (15+5 gear bonus) (1.15)
Perception: 19 (1.19)

Luck: 14 (1.4)

Karmic Luck: -11

Huh... he had gained three hundred twenty-three experience killing wolves and such. When had that happened? Sam heard a snap, turned around, and froze. Behind him, arrayed in a loose semi-circle was his former team, the Wolf Pack. Dizzy stood front and center, her stance wide, her maul leaning against her shoulder. Kai stood on her left, his fists glowing with subtle orange light, his eyes blazing in wrathful anger. Sphinx waited off to the left, throwing daggers lined up and ready to hurl, while Arrow had somehow managed to position himself in a tree—just as Yurij had—an arrow nocked, the bowstring drawn taut.

Bill cackled madly. <This was *such* a great plan, Legs! I'm *so* glad I listened to you. See you tomorrow. Hope you enjoy your respawn.>

<We'll be fine,> Sam sent silently, calculating the odds of coming out of this situation alive. He didn't want to give Bill the satisfaction of being right, but if he couldn't convince the Wolf Pack to join his cause... Well, there was no way he was walking away. He was sure he could manage; they were here to play, to have fun, to finish some quests and earn some epic loot. This ploy? *This* was the best way to do all of those things.

"Sam," Dizzy's tone was icy, "I have no idea what's going on, but you have about five seconds to explain, or we're gonna drop you where you stand. Start talking."

"Happy to," Sam slowly lifted his arms and stored his orbiting tomes, "but I don't even know where to begin."

"Gee, *I* don't know. How about with the part where you stood us up, except you were actually *stalking* us? Or how about this? Last time I saw you—*just a week ago*—you were an air

Mage, but now you're," she glowered at him, pointedly staring at Bill, "some kind of magic librarian? And who is *that* guy?"

She nodded toward the enemy Mage, dead and sprawled across the ground. "Where is *Finn*? Why were you just talking to a Wolfman Shaman? *How?* More importantly, what could you have *possibly* said to get that monster to leave without a fight? Huh?"

Sam took a deep breath and blew out his cheeks as his mind raced. "What if I told you I had an... opportunity? That and a chance for us as a team to become the first Chartered Guild in the *entire* game?"

There was a moment of shocked stillness as Dizzy and the others traded guarded glances with one another. Dizzy's stance said she was as ready to pounce as ever. "We *might* be willing to listen."

"Good, then hear me out and promise not to kill me until I finish telling you everything. It all started last week when Finn and I went back to the College after our grinding session..." Sam spooled out the story bit by bit over the next half hour, talking them through the kangaroo court version of a trial he had and how Finn had been forced to endure under the oversight of the corrupt and power-hungry Archmage.

He explained about the library and the tricky sleight of hand which had resulted in him getting ahold of the keys to the most powerful repository of knowledge in all of Ardania. When he told them about unleashing Vh'uzathel the Hundred-Armed before escaping the library via a secret spatial tunnel that connected to the outer walls, Sphinx gasped while Dizzy howled with laughter.

Onward Sam forged, detailing his capture and subsequent deal with The O'Baba. His reentry into the city. His endless grinding over the past several days, followed by his plan to track them down. They listened intently, muttering darkly at all the right places and laughing at the sheer absurdity of it all. No one seemed interested in killing him by the time he trailed off into silence, the whole story finally told.

"*Dude,*" Kai's words were dripping with awe, lifting his hands to make a *mind-blown* gesture, "that's like. *Woah,* dude."

"So, the College really did all that *just* because you and Finn partied with us for a few hours?" Arrow sounded almost as shocked and impressed as Kai. "The thing with The Accords... I can't believe the game developers would allow something like that to just slip through the cracks. I mean, it's *so* predatory, you know?"

"Oh, believe me, I know," Sam replied with a firm nod, remembering just how painful it had been to 'replenish' The Accords with his Mana. "I think my experience is only the tip of the iceberg. When Mages advance, they have to sign The Accords again and again, and I think that gives the Archmage even more power over them."

"I betcha it's a quest chain." Sphinx started pacing restlessly behind the rest of the party, idly running one hand along the hilt of her dagger. "Probably some kinda hidden event with some huge rewards for anyone who figures out how to topple the Archmage."

"Yeah, probably," Dizzy agreed, stroking her chin thoughtfully.

"Which means that teaming up with Sam might be the best way to bring the whole system down," Arrow chipped in. The archer was now sitting in the grass cross-legged, absently spinning an arrow between his palms. "Plus, the benefits of joining with the Wolfmen are pretty significant. I mean, we could be Nobles. Think about that. *Nobles.* Every hour I'm not in-game, I'm on the forums, and I haven't heard of *anyone* unlocking an achievement like that yet. We could be *world-firsts*, guys."

"The guaranteed Guild Charter is a nice bonus, too," Dizzy added absently. "Everyone and their brother is trying to found a Noble Guild on the human side of the campaign. The competition is already crazy, and it's only going to get worse, but I bet things are wide open with the wolves. This could be our shot."

"Yeah, but like, we'll have to betray humanity." Kai didn't sound like he was *opposed* to the idea, just laying out the facts.

"So?" Dizzy shot back, arching an eyebrow. "It's just a *game.*"

She shrugged nonchalantly. "The fact that there *is* a viable route to join the Wolfmen—even if most people are unaware there's a Wolfman playable faction—means the developers meant for at least *some* of the player population to take that path. I think this is a golden opportunity. There's only one question I have..."

"What's that?" Sam was suddenly unsure of himself. So far, things were going well, but that could all change at any minute. One wrong answer and he could wind up with a sword rammed through his guts or an oversized maul cracking his head open.

"Finn," Dizzy's voice was as frigid as Sam's Ice Orb spell. "If what you're saying is true, then those Mages at the College are practically torturing him. We can't just *leave* him there. I'm in, but only if we can figure a way to break him out of the College."

"Actually, getting to Finn is an important part of the plan." Sam felt a flood of relief. "We can't really stop Octavius without him. He's signed The Accords but only one time. If we can force him away from the College, The O'Baba has a way to free him from the power of The Accords. He might fight us because The Accords will likely hurt him if he *doesn't*, but we can *make* it happen. As far as I can tell, officially joining the Wolfman faction automatically nullifies all previously held human bonds and allegiances. So, it's sorta perfect, actually."

"There is a hitch, though," Sam continued after a long pause. "See, I'm pretty sure Octavius' spell will take place outside the College walls. In fact, somewhere relatively close to the Wolfman outpost. The thing is, I'm not exactly sure *where* the location is, and I'm not exactly sure how to sabotage the spell, but I do know all of his research is inside the College Library. If we can bust in there, I think I can piece together what Octavius is planning, which should tell me how to stop him."

"Wait," Dizzy held one hand up. "You're saying we need to break *into* the College? A place which is full of the most powerful NPCs in the game, all of whom want you either dead or captured?"

"Well... when you say it like that, it sounds crazy," Sam muttered, shifting uncomfortably from foot to foot.

"I'm not saying you're crazy, and I'm not saying *no*. I just want to make sure I understand exactly what you're asking us to do."

"Yes," Sam replied bluntly with a dip of his chin. "That's what I'm asking you to do. I need to break into the College, help Finn escape, find a way to smuggle out a Wolfman, and figure out where Octavius is planning to cast this uber spell. All of this so that we can take him out before he turns the outpost into a smoking crater in the ground."

"No offense, dude," Kai folded his sleek arms, "but this sounds, like, totally impossible or whatever. I want to help, but

I'm not interested in a suicide mission. Like, how would we even get *into* the College?"

"We have a secret weapon." Sam nodded toward Bill with a grin. The book, hanging in the air beside him fluttered its pages, drawing every eye as its dusty leather lips creaked open for the first time.

"Hey, kids. I'm Bill," the book croaked, his voice drier and more papery than Sam remembered, but then again, Sam had never actually *heard* Bill speak before. Up until now, the book had only ever communicated with Sam telepathically. Honestly, Sam was a little surprised to find the book *could* speak out loud. "I've been around for about three hundred years and counting."

"For the record, I can get us into the sewers that run beneath the College. Because I'm awesome, I can also get us back *out* without anyone knowing we were ever there."

"I don't know," Dizzy scowled at the floating book as though she didn't entirely trust it.

Sphinx, however, let out a midwestern squee of delight. "If you can get us a way into the College and provide a way back out, I think we have a darn good chance to make this happen."

"Seriously?" Arrow's skepticism was almost as palpable as Dizzy's.

"Being an Infiltrator does have its perks," Sphinx sweetly offered the archer a dazzling grin. "If we're serious about this, I know just the people that can help us. I'm not saying we should agree to anything *yet*, but I *do* think it's time we went and had a conversation with some of my friends who joined a Thieves' Guild. The Upright Men will want to know all about this."

Chapter Thirty-four

Sphinx ushered the party through the narrow, dusty streets of Cheapside. Streets Sam had become not at all familiar with over the past few days, having been locked up in a small room. Eventually, they stopped in front of a two-story, white-plaster building that had seen its best days fifty years ago.

There was a light coat of paint which was badly worn, even chipped in places. Many of the windows dotting the building's face were boarded over. A pole jutted from above a single door painted a bright, vivid red; hanging from the pole on rust-covered chains was a badly weathered sign that read *The Pious Squires of Saint Saagar.*

Off to the right ran a narrow alley filled with shanty tents, lean-tos, and a wide swath of dirt-streaked faces and bodies which all reeked of BO even twenty feet out. A particularly gaunt man, buried beneath layers and layers and layers of unwashed clothing and gear, stood next to the door, staring out at the world with rheumy, milk-white eyes, which oddly reminded Sam of the boarded over windows above.

<Well, this couldn't look any more suspicious if they tried,> Bill grumbled. <Might as well just hang out a sign that says, *Criminals at Work.*>

"What is this place?" Sam hooked his thumbs into his belt as he regarded the front of the building, searching for any clues that might let on to its real purpose.

"Wouldn't'cha know, it's a homeless shelter and a soup kitchen for the downtrodden." Sphinx eyes crinkled as she offered them a wide smile.

"Why haven't you told us about any of this before?" Dizzy had no hint of amusement in her voice. "We're a team,

Sphinx. Seems like any dealings you might have with a 'homeless shelter' you might have shared with the rest of us."

Sphinx's cheeks flashed a subtle red. "This place is special, and we're not supposed to tell outsiders. One of the rules of the club, but if there was ever a time to break the rules, it seems like now's it."

<Oh, this one's a keeper, Legs. Anyone who can break the rules with *style* is good in my book.>

<You *are* a book,> Sam sent back silently.

<Then you know exactly how serious I take that compliment!>

"What's so special about it, dudette?" Kai dropped his voice low so the beggars wouldn't hear him.

"It's an entrance to the Brotherhood network. As a Novice, I'm only supposed to come here if I'm in serious trouble. I think this probably counts." She paused, tucking a loose strand of hair behind her ear. "Just give me a minute."

She headed over to the blind beggar stationed outside the brightly painted door. She fished a fat gold coin from her pocket, though even from a distance Sam could tell it wasn't a normal coin. It was too thin, the edges jagged and rough cut.

"Alms for the poor, miss?" the blind beggar asked breathlessly, flapping his lips and showing off a mouth mostly devoid of teeth. He extended one grimy hand, missing a finger, palm up.

"Of course, kind sir. Saint Saagar lives in my heart and in the hearts of all the truly pious and needy," Sphinx recited, pressing the coin into the center of his hand. "Who couldn't use a little help in a time of need?"

The beggar vanished the coin with a flash of fingers, bobbed his head, and resumed his post by the door. Sam noticed, however, that the beggar pressed his thumb against the outside of the building. The motion was quick, almost too quick to follow, but a soft flare of muted brown light–there and gone in a blink–caught his eye. Gouged into the face of the plaster was a tiny symbol, no bigger than a dime.

Sam wasn't sure what the symbol meant, but he'd seen a similar marking in the College corridors. He'd always assumed it was like the other marks, meant to help visitors and students navigate the sprawling hallways... but maybe it served some other function.

<It's a spatial containment rune,> Bill sent, likely picking up on Sam's stray thoughts. <Pretty advanced magic for a bunch of street thugs, if you ask me.>

<That's gotta be Mage work, right?> Sam asked in return. <How do you think a bunch of thieves would come by something like that?>

<Eh. Simple. The Mages are bound by The Accords, but that doesn't mean they can't get into trouble. I'm not familiar with the Upright Men, must've come along after my nap, but in my experience, thieves are a lot like mercenaries. They can make problems disappear if you have the money to pay. In a land where magic is rarer than gold, an IOU from a Mage is *far* more valuable than coin. All it would take is for one dumb Noble–of which there are hundreds, believe you me–with more magic than common sense to get in a bind and go to these folks for a favor. *Boom*, just like that, spatial safe house.>

Sphinx guided them inside, which–*shocker*–actually looked like a homeless soup kitchen. Down on their luck men and women huddled around rough tables, loudly slurping steaming soup from wooden bowls. That was just the front, as Sam and the others quickly learned when one of the 'Pious Squires' of Saint Saagar showed them to a closet in the back which positively *hummed* with potent magic.

"Seems pretty sleazy to hide a criminal organization behind a made-up charity," Dizzy groused as they stepped through the pantry door and into a midnight-black hallway that closely resembled a tear in the fabric of the universe. "Impersonating monks that help the needy seems low, even for thieves."

"Oh *gosh*." Sphinx broke out into a belly laugh. "The monks *aren't* fake, and neither is the shelter. The Pious Squires of Saint Saagar *is* a real holy order, one that takes care of the poor. The city and the Nobles rarely spend the time or money to help the disenfranchised, but the thieves do. Interesting tidbit, but the thieves didn't name themselves the Upright Men. The needy of Ardania bestowed that title on them. The Squires have shelters all over the city, most of which are completely legitimate, and the whole operation is bankrolled by the Brotherhood."

Her smile grew wider. "Not everything is as it seems, you know. Just because someone is a bad guy, doesn't mean they *are* a bad guy. Profession versus person."

Sphinx led them through the short tunnel and out into a room that couldn't possibly have existed inside the rundown shelter. It was an enormous, domed chamber that instantly reminded Sam of the subway stations in New York. He'd visited New York twice with his parents. Though neither trip had been for long, those memories stuck in Sam's head like a piece of gum lodged on the bottom of a tennis shoe. All the cars. The unending sea of humanity. Most of all, he remembered the sprawling subways, a whole underground world that seemed ancient somehow.

The walls were dark red brick, the floors covered with planks of polished wood; thirteen arched hallways broke away from the room like the spokes of some enormous bicycle. Metal candelabras flanked the entryway to each tunnel while an enormous chandelier—crafted from an armory-worth of daggers and short swords—hung from overhead. Men and women flowed through the chamber without offering the Wolf Pack a second glance. Why should they? If Sphinx was telling the truth, this place was the equivalent of Grand Central Station. Everyone, it seemed, had a place to be and no time to waste on a group of gawking tourists.

These were men and women who moved with both urgency and purpose. Although many of the folks in the chamber wore the dark leathers, soft boots, and long daggers that named them thieves, Rogues, or worse, there were just as many people sporting chef's attire or dressed as maids, innkeepers, or even city guards.

Perhaps the Upright Men weren't as overtly powerful as the Mages of the College, but if this little cross-section of humanity was any indication, they were *awfully* influential in their own way... and *far* more wide spread.

It took a handful of minutes and a few quick words to a lean gentleman milling behind a reception counter, but eventually, Sam and the others were ushered into richly appointed private quarters. They'd barely settled in when there was a knock on the door and a scullery maid in a black dress and tidy white apron pushed in a cart loaded down with a veritable feast. Mashed potatoes and thick brown gravy. Savory green beans cooked in some sort of garlic and basil sauce. For the main course, a thick roast ringed with tender carrots and bulbous onions.

As important as coming up with a plan was, Sam's mouth salivated. All he could think about was scarfing down as much food as humanly—or inhumanly—possible. Sure, he'd eaten during his days of relentless study and preparation, but he'd only eaten enough to survive and none of it had been what anyone other than a starving man would classify as *good*. Certainly nothing like this spread. Even better... his perception was high enough to *enjoy* this food!

<Dig in, kid,> Bill said without being prompted. <You're liable to chew out your own tongue if you don't eat, so let me handle this.>

<Thanks, Bill,> Sam immediately ladled a heaping portion of meat and vegetables onto a silver plate.

<Don't worry about it, kid,> Bill rose into the air until he was hovering above the table. <You got the map?>

<Yep. One sec.> Sam pulled open his spatial flask and withdrew an enormous, hand-drawn map of the College's first floor. Well, bits and pieces of it, anyway.

Since the entire College refused to conform to the laws of physics or nature, it was hard to render a truly accurate floor plan of the complex. With Bill's expert knowledge and insight, they'd done a respectable job. The hallways they needed were all carefully and painstakingly sketched out, along with the corresponding glyphs and runes that acted as road-signs for anyone who knew how to read them.

Bill had scoured his memories, searching not for the *fastest* ways to get from point A to point B but the most *convoluted* and least traveled ways. In theory, if the Wolf Pack followed the route he'd laid out, they would have almost no chance of running across the other College inhabitants. The biggest risks were right after leaving the sewers and right when entering the library. There was no way to get around those choke points, so they would just have to throw the dice and hope for the best.

"Okay," Bill's voice was gruff and unflappable. "The kid and I have already talked through this a hundred different times, and we think we have a solid plan for breaking into the College.

Like we said earlier, we're gonna need some help. The way in is relatively straightforward. Most people know there's a series of sewer tunnels that run beneath the College, but what most people *don't* know is that the Mage's College sends out a patrol four times a week to clear out those sewers."

"Thing is," Bill continued as the others ate, "the College produces *a lot* of magical waste, and all that Mana runoff coalesces into Sentient Jellies which, if left unchecked, can grow to enormous sizes. Those Jellies aren't really all that dangerous, but they are *magic*, which means run-of-the-mill violence won't kill them. Ergo, the College dispatches groups of Initiates to do the dirty work—wiping out the Jellies and farming monster Cores if they appear, which the College uses for spells and enchantments."

"The kid here," Bill rolled his unsettling emerald eyes toward Sam, "pulled that duty a couple of times, and Finn will almost certainly be stuck on sewer patrol since it's the detail *no one* wants. Also, he's on the College's naughty list. Me? I know the College better than the backside of my hand—figuratively speaking, obviously—and I can get us into the sewers without a problem. We infiltrate, ambush the patrol when they're busy dealing with Jellies, and just like that, we have a one-way ticket into the College."

"Sounds reasonable enough." Dizzy leaned back in her chair, hands folded across her belly. "What's the catch?"

"Who says there's a catch?" Sam asked innocently enough, talking around a mouthful of roast. *Celestial*, but the food was tasty—rich, hearty, savory, with just a dash of heat that lit up his taste-buds like a fireworks display.

"There's *always* a catch." Dizzy folded her arms. "Besides, you went through *a lot* of trouble to get to us, and you wouldn't have done that if this was all as easy as your floating book friend makes it sound."

"Fine," Sam piped in while dabbing the corner of his checks with a linen napkin. "Fine, so *maybe* there is a catch... Alright, a *couple* of catches. To start off, there are going to be at least two other Mages we'll have to incapacitate in the sewers. They'll be Novices, but even Novice Mages might be a threat in the right circumstances. Then there are the College guards to consider. Usually there's two of them, and both are high level. As good as Bill and I are, we can't take the whole crew out, especially since we can't kill them without earning massive bounties, which we absolutely don't want. That means we'll need to find a way to incapacitate them."

"Okay. I'll play along," Arrow interjected. "Let's say your book gets us in and somehow, we manage to take out the sewer cleaning crew, hopefully liberating Finn in the process. Then what? It's not like they're just going to let a bunch of outsiders caked in sewer muck tromp around the College unchallenged. Someone is going to notice us and start asking questions. Even if we get to the library, there's no way we get back out in one piece. No. Way."

"Eh. Agree to disagree," Bill matter-of-factly stated. "I'm telling you, me and Legs, we've worked it out. Basically, we're gonna pull the ol' '*dress as the enemy*' trick. We'll knock the sewer patrol out long enough for us to go back into the College in their place. A couple of you will dress as guards, everyone else will go as Novices decked out in run-of-the-mill, brown robes. From there, we'll split the group. Sam and I will head over to the Annex to rescue Velkan, assuming the mutt is still alive."

"Finn will need to be tied up as well unless he can resist the compulsion of The Accords long enough to take everyone else to the library. If he can't, the rest of you need to follow the map and grab what we need to take out Octavius and put the kibosh on this big bad spell. From there, Sam and I will circle back around with our Wolfman friend in tow, meet you guys in the library, then sneak out through another secret exit tucked away in the library's main floor. That exit will deposit us in the cellar of a cheese shop called *The Grater Good* over in North Waterside. "

"From there," Sam gave a lopsided shrug, "we simply regroup and set an ambush for Octavius and his spell-slinging buddies. It's simple, even if it won't be easy."

Everyone was quiet for a long moment. Which Sam took as a good sign... right up until Dizzy opened her mouth.

"Wow. I don't even know where to start with all the ways this plan could go wrong. First, splitting the party while *inside* the College? That's... that's *crazy.* Seriously, have you never played D&D before? You *never* split the party. It's a *thing.* Also, and I feel like I shouldn't *need* to say this, but how in the world do you think you're going to be able to sneak a *Wolfman* through the College without getting spotted? Huh?"

"Listen, I know how it sounds," Sam agreed, "but I've *been* inside the College, and Bill seriously knows that place better than anyone. Sneaking into the Annex by myself will be far easier than dragging the whole party along. As for getting *from* the Annex to the library, there's a back way that almost no one ever takes. The Mages *hate* using the Annex because of all the spatial distortions and time fluctuations, so I think there's at least a seventy percent chance I can make it through without anyone catching me. It's a calculated risk, and I'm *really* good at math."

Dizzy grunted noncommittally, crossing her arms as she glowered at the table, the cogs inside her head clearly working in overdrive as she tried to pick apart the plan.

"Seems to me that getting into the library itself is going to be tricky," Arrow chimed in. "I mean, I'll freely admit I *haven't* been inside the College before, but if it really is this giant repository for super rare books and other magical items... I doubt they'll just let a bunch of rando guards in."

"Except, it won't just be a bunch of 'rando' guards," Bill replied. "Trust me, if we can get to Finn, he'll be able to get you past the head librarian, no problem."

"Well, why don't we just go in *through* the library?" Kai demanded. He leaned forward, forearms resting against the edge of the table. "You dudes said there's, like, some kinda tunnel from the main floor of the library to that cheese shop, right? So why not just go through the cheese shop and pop out *inside* the library or whatever? That way we won't have to mess around with the sewer, the guards, or anything else."

"It's a good thought," Bill replied in begrudging admiration, "but this particular spatial tunnel only works in one direction. The doorway opens from the College side, not the cheese shop side. Once we're in the College, there are lots of ways to get out but very, *very* few ways to get *in*. Something like that would make it too easy for an enemy force to invade the College, so most of those escape tunnels are emergency exits only. No readmittance."

"So, the sewers are the only way in because of course they are," Dizzy noted absently, "but let's say that we do get in and take down the guards. There's still one big hitch. We can't just steal the guards' uniforms. Even if we kill them—which you already said we shouldn't do—there's no way to loot their corpses. So how do we pass ourselves off?"

Sphinx's hand shot up into the air, a smile breaking across her face. "Oh gosh, but this is perfect. This is what Infiltrators are *trained* to do. The Upright Men have tailors here at the facility who specialize in counterfeit uniforms and armor. It'll cost us a little money, but we should be able to get everything we need for the disguises. No problem at all."

She paused and squinted at him. "I can even help with Sam's Rogue Mage status. If you just hide your face under a cowl, you'll still glow red when anyone in the College looks at you, but Infiltrators can mask your class, your alignment, and *any* unwanted status effect. Heck, even your name on combat logs if you kill a player. It's one of the perks of the Infiltrator class. It won't last long—an hour or two at most—but if we can't pull this job off inside an hour, then we deserve to get caught."

"You think we really have a shot at this, Sphinx?" Dizzy didn't bother to mask her skepticism. The Infiltrator offered them a feral smile, so at odds with her sweet, school-teacher persona.

"This is what I was *made* for, Diz. It's going to be dangerous, but with Sam and Bill giving us the inside scoop, I think we have a real shot. For what it's worth, I think we should take it. Something I haven't told anyone, but I have an outstanding quest requirement. If I can infiltrate a building or organization with a difficulty rating of Rare or higher, I'll have a chance to advance in my specialization. The Mage's College is a *Unique* organization, so this is perfect for me. Plus, if we pull this off... we save Finn. Also, we get a chance to form the first Wolfman Guild in the game. There's a lot of risk, but the rewards are more than worth it."

"Fine. Alright." Dizzy sighed and rubbed at the bridge of her nose with one hand. She threw up her hands in clear exasperation. "Let's go rob the College, I *guess.*"

Chapter Thirty-Five

The soft splash of water and the chattering of voices echoed off the slime-coated tunnels deep in the bowels beneath the College. The voices were distorted by distance and the odd acoustics of the sewer, making it nearly impossible to tell what the speakers were saying, but they were drawing closer; that was the important part. Sam crouched in a foul-smelling nook, obscured by the shadows as he waited to trigger his carefully arranged traps which lay scattered through this section of tunnel.

<It's gonna be *fine*,> Bill whispered with complete confidence. The book didn't *need* to whisper, but it felt right given their current situation. Almost as though even an errant *thought* might give them away. <The spells are top-notch. Much as I hate admitting I was wrong, this crew of yours seems pretty sharp.>

Sam breathed the foul air in deeply—not to calm his nerves but rather to smooth out the jittery burst of excited adrenaline coursing through his veins. Bill thought Sam was scared, but just the opposite was true. He'd never been *more* excited. Were the stakes high? Sure. Was failure likely? Absolutely.

That made it all the better. This was the gameplay experience he'd come to Eternium for—sneaking through sewers—ambushing guards—raiding strongholds—fighting against the odds with friends at his back. He'd been unsure if breaking away from the College and joining with the Wolfmen had been the right call, but now he knew. This was where he *belonged.*

A flicker of dancing firelight bounced across the far wall, casting a long and ominous shadow across the wall adjacent to him. The shadowy form looked like some slender ghoul prowling through a graveyard, but Sam knew that was just his imagination at work.

"It's been oddly quiet," came the familiar and gruff voice of Geffery the Red—the beefy guard who was as broad as the side of a barn and decked out in silver-edged plate mail. "Haven't run across a single Jelly yet."

Sam peeked around the corner, trying to ignore the rancid, gray-green slime brushing up against his cheek. There were no Jellies because Sam and the rest of the Wolf Pack had already cleared the route, taking out the gelatinous creatures and collecting their five entire trash-tier Cores in the process. Since he'd unlocked *Coreless Spell Infusion,* he didn't strictly *need* the cores, but they would certainly fetch a fair price on the open market. Even *C*ores like these were coveted by Alchemists, Mages, and Enchanters.

The *splish-splash* of feet grew louder, and Geffery came into full view. Cowering behind him was a pair of brown-robed Mages that Sam hadn't seen before. Either new Novices or some old Apprentices that had gotten on someone's bad side. Neither looked particularly powerful, though Sam knew firsthand that it wasn't wise to underestimate anyone. Ever. *Especially* not Mages. Underestimating people was how you ended up with a Rogue Mage-turned-Bibliomancer on your hands. Plus, Sam *had* seen Geffery in a fight, and the guy was as tough and as ruthless as a spool of rust-covered razor-wire.

Unfortunately, there was no sign of Finn, but maybe that wasn't such a bad thing. The sewer party usually split into two groups—Geffery leading one team and his taciturn partner, Karren the Blade, leading the other. Of the two guards, Karren was the tougher—and arguably the *meaner*—so if Finn was in her party...

"There's something wrong in the air, here," Geffery's voice drew Sam from his thoughts. "Everyone stay sharp, eh? The Jellies aren't usually smart enough to lay a trap, but it's happened before. Once or twice, I reckon."

<Welp, we tried. Off to respawn,> Bill gave up instantly.

<Shut *up*,> Sam sent, licking his lips as he watched them creep closer. He crossed his fingers and muttered a silent prayer, hoping beyond hope that they didn't see the nasty surprise he'd left for them. Not until it was too late.

There was a soft *click* a moment later as Geffery pushed forward, and Sam felt a rush of exhilaration as the water erupted beneath the guard's feet with a thunderous roar. The geyser of water rippled in midair, sludgy, brown muck icing over in a flash of azure power. Geffery stumbled back, hollering incoherently as he fumbled for his weapon, searching for an enemy to attack... but there wasn't one. Not yet. He'd just been unfortunate enough to trigger one of the many Book Bombs Sam had painstakingly lined the bottom of the tunnel with.

Damage dealt: 75 (70 + 5 Ice Orb) Target slowed 12%!

Before Geffery could go more than a few steps, the arctic power creeping through the air brushed icy blue fingers along his armor. A layer of crystalline hoarfrost snaked across his steel cuirass, sending icy tendrils into the pauldrons, vambraces, and greaves, locking up Geffery's joints and imprisoning the Fighter in a cage made from his own armor. Geffery cursed and fought, raging fruitlessly against armor that now resisted any attempt at movement. One of the Novices accompanying Geffery let out a frantic squawk as he attempted to backpedal... only to step squarely on to a Book Bomb that had been infused with Weak Paralysis.

Damage dealt: 70. Target paralyzed for 0.5 seconds!

Instead of erupting in a geyser of frozen ice, this book vomited a spray of goopy, black ink which crawled over the Mage's body in fits and starts, gumming his arms and legs to his sides, preventing the young Mage from performing the body and hand gestures necessary to cast even the most basic spells. Too bad it only lasted half a second. At least it was enough to freak the kid out. Luckily, he had been coated in a now-damaged Mage Armor, or that Book Bomb may have killed him off.

"Show yourselves," the second Mage shrieked, lifting her hands in defense. Purple-tinged darkness pooled around her like a malevolent living shadow, which was something Sam hadn't seen before. Kai, dressed in a sleeveless judogi, stepped from a narrow alcove adjacent Sam.

"Dudette, I'll be your huckleberry," his words were intentionally confusing, and he wore a grin was on his face as he charged, flowing from stance to stance.

"I don't know who you are, but you just made a *very* bad choice," the Mage snarled, thrusting one hand outward. A small forest of razor-sharp spikes exploded from nearby shadows, all trying to skewer Kai like a piece of tasty meat.

The Monk was having absolutely *none* of it. Kai effortlessly avoided each spike as fast as she could conjure them, flowing between the lances of shadow, closing the distance in an instant. Shock and fear flickered across her face as Kai invaded her guard, lashing out with a flurry of lightning-fast punches, knife hand attacks, and low, sweeping kicks. She was on her heels, desperately trying to bat away his strikes with a gnarled wooden staff that burned with arcane purple light, but Kai was *far* too fast.

Light flared around the woman as her Mage Armor absorbed a fraction of the damage; her health didn't budge at all, but then that was simply because Kai wasn't *trying* to hurt her.

Sam knew he was spamming *Quivering Blow* over and over, hoping to stun her into inaction.

Speaking of stunning enemies into inaction, Sam had to focus on his own fight. After all, the tank, Geffery, and the ink-covered Mage were only *temporarily* subdued. The Ice Orb spell would only hold so long, and his Weak Paralysis had already worn off. Thankfully, he'd come prepared for this encounter. He toggled a new book forward, this one filled with Paper Shurikens that he'd augmented with the *Weak Paralysis* he'd picked up. The spell, though far from perfect, had a twelve-percent chance to paralyze the target.

With a thought, Sam sent folded star after folded star slicing through the air, first peppering Geffery since he was the larger of the two threats. The Shurikens themselves cut into Geffery's health, but the man seemed to have more constitution than you could shake a stick at. That was fine because just like Kai, Sam wasn't going for the kill. Merely the stun. Weak Paralysis triggered with a glimmer of emerald light on the seventh hit, locking up the tank's body for the next half-second. Unable to hold himself upright, Geffery toppled with a splash of murky water, coming to rest on his back in four inches of standing sludge.

Sam immediately turned his power on the struggling Novice Mage. He caught a lucky break, landing *Weak Paralysis* with his first Shuriken, sending the kid into the water beside the armor-clad guard who was struggling to his feet.

<Those spells won't last,> Bill boomed inside his head as Geffery and the enemy Mage collapsed into the muck and mire. <Keep hitting them, and make with the ropes already!>

Sam couldn't disagree with that. He pulled out his flask and retrieved the most essential item any adventurer could ever carry—heavy-duty rope. By the time he looked up, Sphinx was sitting on Geffery with her dagger a hair away from his eyes. That seemed *far* more effective than his paralysis.

Getting Geffery up out of viscous water so that they could bind his arms, hands, and ankles was incredibly difficult since the guard weighed about a *thousand* pounds. Hauling around that much dead weight was nearly impossible for someone with Sam's level of strength and overall lackluster constitution. Despite his difficulties, Sam and the team managed. With a little expert guidance from Bill, he also tied some world-class knots that not even Geffery would be able to tear his way through. Compared to the beefy, metal-suited goon, the Novice Mage was about a thousand times easier to manhandle since he was scrawny and wore only Mage robes.

By the time Sam finished, it was too late for either of them to do anything but grunt, cuss, and wriggle vainly against their bonds. Even better, Kai had finished off the shadow-wielding Mage, somehow knocking her out cold without killing her. She was hogtied like a pig ready to go to market. As agreed upon before starting the fight, Sam and Kai stayed to secure the prisoners while the rest of the group went ahead to the next point. In what felt like next to no time, Sam and Kai had all three loaded into a dry nook, away from the main sewer line where, hopefully, they would go unnoticed until someone came down and launched a proper search for them.

Then just to be safe, Sam fished out the handful of unspent Book Bombs that hadn't activated during their tussle with the guards and carefully laid them out across the entryway to the nook harboring the trio. Should the prisoners get loose, the books wouldn't deter them from escaping, but that wasn't really their purpose. Hopefully those books would fend off any wayward Jellies Sam and company might've missed during their initial sweep of the rancid dungeon.

In theory, the Jellies wouldn't respawn for a day or more, but Sam still didn't relish the idea of Geffery and the two Mages dying a slow death at the merciless hands of the slimy creatures. True, Sam had sided with the monsters fighting humanity, but that didn't mean he had to *act* like a monster. Task complete, the duo set off at a quick double time, heading toward the planned area where—if things had gone well—they would capture Finn.

As the duo trekked in silence, Sam couldn't shake the feeling that the other shoe was going to drop any second. This was the *Mage's College*. Surely it wouldn't be so easy to break in, right? True, he'd robbed the Sage's Section of the library and gotten away scot-free, but that had to be a fluke. Right? The Mage's College was one of the most powerful and dastardly organizations in Eternium. After what had happened in the library, Sam *had* to imagine they would be on high alert. Yet he found no traps, no extra patrols, no alarms bells shrieking... *nothing* out of the ordinary.

<What's wrong, kid?> Bill demanded. <All of a sudden, you seem wound tighter than a pocket watch. What's on your mind?>

<This just seems... I dunno, too easy, I guess?> Sam sent back, eyes trained on the pockets of shadow all around them which could be concealing countless enemies. Except they *weren't*, for reasons Sam couldn't quite grasp. <I mean, they've sent bounty hunters after us. They *know* we're out there, so why wouldn't they post extra security all over the College? Don't get me wrong, I'm glad they *didn't*. There was just some part of me that was sure—like absolutely *positive*—it wouldn't go down according to plan.>

<Nah. Makes total sense to me. The Mages are full of themselves. They think they're better than everyone and for

good reason—they *are* better than everyone else. They have power, money, and influence second only to the King himself. No one would *ever* think to attack the College. It's a suicide mission for just about everyone, but that gives us an advantage.>

<This plan is so daringly reckless that they'll never see it coming. *No one* would be stupid enough to challenge the Mages in their seat of power. The last place they'll be looking for you—a Warlock on the run from the Mage's College—is *here*. This is the very *last* place you would ever come. Assuming you were a sane, rational, normal human being. Which you're not, and I say that as the highest praise.>

The rest of the trek was made in contemplative silence. They found Dizzy and the others waiting at the rendezvous, no sign of Karren the Blade—Geffery's counterpart—or the other enemy Mage, but Sam broke out into a manic grin when he caught sight of one new addition to the party—a gangly boy with a wiry frame, an unruly head of corn-silk hair, and a set of glasses perched on a hawkish nose. Finn! The other boy had his back turned toward Sam, hands folded behind him as he talked with Dizzy. He was none the wiser when Sam sacked him from behind like a linebacker, then lifted him up, squeezing him in a bearhug.

"*Gah!* I'm being attacked! Someone help me!" The ice Mage flapped and flailed his legs wildly. Sam set him down and spun him around, his grin widening.

"Sam! I can't believe it's really you!" Finn yelled, a smile, equal parts shock and joy, working its way across his face. "I mean... when Dizzy told me you were here, I just couldn't believe it. I'm touched, truly, that you'd come back for me. But I have to ask—are you *mad?* Honestly, you shouldn't be in a ten-mile radius of this place or even in the city if you have *any* sense at all. Instead, I find out you're waging a personal war against the

College itself. It's certainly *bold*, I'll give you that, but what would possess you to do something like this? What are you thinking? You can't go against the College! I... I can't let you."

"What am I *thinking*?" Sam stepped back, holding Finn at arm's length. He studied the other boy's face. This close in, it was easy to see the puffy, purple bags hanging like plums beneath Finn's eyes. The crack splitting his bottom lip. How pale and waxy his skin was. "I'm thinking that I don't leave friends behind. I'm thinking that I don't let bullies walk all over me. Not anymore. Back before Eternium, there was a guy I knew... He was a petty jerk, a bully who treated me like a welcome mat for most of my life. I didn't stand up to him, but I've decided that I won't let anyone treat me that way again. What is the Mage's College if not a giant, institutionalized version of a bully?"

"I'm done letting them have their way. I might lose, but I'm going to fight back no matter what. I also happen to think that *you're* thinking too small, Finn. Me? I'm not just waging war against the College. I'm waging war against humanity itself. The College didn't get this way without a lot of other people being complicit, allowing it to happen under their noses. There's a war coming—if it's not already here—and me and the rest of the Wolf Pack have decided we're going to be on team Wolfman."

"The *Wolfmen*?" Finn visibly blanched. He muttered under his breath while running a grimy hand through his hair. "But that's *treason*, Sam. Do you understand? *Treason*. With a capital 'T'. We could all be executed for even having this conversation."

"You're right. Which is why *you* still have a choice, Finn. You didn't agree to this. Not to any of it. Eternium is your home, your world, your life. So, if you don't want to join us, I'll tie you up with the others. You'll get another slap on the wrist for failing to stop us, but you won't hang by the neck in the town square."

Finn faltered, pondering. "But why? Why the *Wolfmen* of all people?"

Sam smiled. "Why *not*? I mean, they showed me more mercy than the College ever has, and all they're trying to do is survive. They don't want to subjugate us; they want to be free. That's something I can get on board with. Plus, they've offered us a place, Finn. A guild. A charter. Access to books, knowledge, and resources that not even the Mage's College can get their dirty hands on. Best of all, no Accords. It's a risk, but one that lets us be on the ground floor of something epic."

Finn stepped away, crossing his arms across his chest. Clearly, Finn was uncomfortable with this, and Sam couldn't blame him. He was asking Finn to throw everything away, not just to stand up to a bully but to turn his back on his whole life.

"You mentioned The Accords," Finn spoke after a time. "Even if the Wolfmen don't have The Accords, I've already signed them once. I can't just leave the College. The Accords give us reason, structure. We can't just throw them away. I can't let that happen."

"It's a non-issue, Finn. Joining the Wolfmen also has one added benefit—it annuls all previous contracts and bonds with other human organizations. The mechanic for mutiny is literally baked into the system. If you join, you get a second chance. A fresh start."

"I *can't*. The Accords are everything to..." Finn hesitated, his eyes not fixed on Sam but rather on Dizzy. Finally, he sighed. "The crest of House Laustsen *is* a rearing wolf on a field of gold and black... Perhaps it was a sign all along."

"My family never really did get over losing the war against King Henry. If I'm going to die anyway, might as well be doing what it is my family does best—fomenting insurrection. So, what exactly is the plan here, if I may be so bold to ask? As long as I don't do anything to betray The Accords..."

Finn started to cough but waved Sam on to continue.

"Simple. Not necessarily *easy*, but *simple*," Sam informed his friend, even as the coughing continued. "I need to get to the Annex and bust out a Wolfman Scout who's being held against his will. Bill and I will do that on our own, while you guide the rest of the crew to the library. We need to get Octavius' research so we can figure out how to throw a monkey wrench into the new spell he's been working on."

"Oh no." Finn's face paled further. In a muted hush, he added, "Sam, you may already be too late. I was working with Octavius last night. He was putting the final touches on the project. He's preparing to cast it *today*. He might already be starting."

"No, no, no!" Sam's chest tightened. Constricted. He broke into a nervous pace, his boots slapping the ground with wet *splooshes*. They were *so* close! This couldn't be happening! "Do you know where Octavius is? We need to get to him, Finn. We need to do it fast."

"What do you mean, Sam? Octavius is *here*. He's *launching* the spell from the library!" Sam stopped cold.

"What do you mean he's 'here'?" Dizzy stole the words before Sam could get them out. "I thought he had to go somewhere to perform the spell. Like line of sight to the Wolfman Outpost or something?"

"Not quite." Finn shook his head, the coughing subsiding. "Turns out that Octavius wasn't just working on a new *spell*, he was working to build a *weapon*. I've been helping him with it for the past week. It's called a Long-range Amplification Weapon or LAW. It's a portable siege tower of sorts, which utilizes spatial magic to link with a Mage, allowing them to cast devastating spells from almost anywhere in Eternium. When Mages go to war, they're almost always targeted first by the enemy. With the LAW, they could lay down deadly spell cover without ever leaving the safety of the College walls. Even worse, the device dramatically *amplifies* any given spell almost a hundred-fold."

"So where is this siege tower? Maybe we can get there and bust it before Octavius has a chance to act."

Finn blew out his cheeks. "It's far too late for that, I'm afraid. Assuming we leave now, it'll take us at least a half a day to get to the site, and by then I doubt there will be a Wolfman Outpost to partner with. But the LAW is twinned to the caster. Octavius calls it *Sympathetic Magic.* He's performing a small version of the spell here, safe and sound with a smaller-scale replica of the siege tower. The LAW resonates, casting the same spell, only bigger. Amplified."

"But wait! That means if we can stop Octavius here, the whole spellform will implode on itself," Bill boomed, causing Finn to jump half a foot into the air. "Kill the root, destroy the tree."

"Err, um, yes," Finn offered tentatively. "That's right. Also, did that floating book just talk?"

"Name's Bill," the book told him courteously. "Yeah. I talk. It's a whole thing, Mageling. We can discuss it later. For now, we need to stop that spell."

"He's right." Dizzy seemed calm, level-headed, and not at *all* panicked. She was the team leader for a reason. "What's the play here, Sam? This is your operation. You just give the word."

Originally, they were supposed to split at this point—Sam and Bill going after the Wolfman Scout, while the others beelined toward the library with Finn. Considering the urgency of the situation, it made sense for them to abandon the Wolfman altogether. Saving Velkan was an optional quest, and there would be no penalty for failure. Yet... if Sam didn't go after him now, he would never have another chance. Moreover, now that he knew more about the Wolfmen, the idea of abandoning Velkan to the tender mercies of the College didn't sit right with him.

He didn't know Velkan, not really, but he knew no one deserved to be locked in a cage like that. Tortured. Experimented on. Wheeled out for the amusement and benefit of others. Plus, this was a game, and the reward for completing a quest like that for a woman like The O'Baba? That had to be worth something *seriously* cool. The gamer in him just couldn't pass up the opportunity, even if it did increase the risk of the mission. Besides, getting into the Annex would only take a few minutes at most, and if they *did* have to square off against Octavius... having an angry Wolfman on their team would be a big help.

Sam nodded; mind made up. Yep. Definitely worth the risk, *and* it was the right thing to do. "No change. Bill and I will go after Velkan on our own. Everyone else is with Finn. Get to the library, don't get caught, and don't do anything until I get there. Not unless there's no other choice. Just try to hold off Octavius long enough for me to get back. Time to go earn our place with the *real* wolfpack."

Chapter Thirty-Six

<This is risky, ground-walker,> Bill grumbled in Sam's head. <I don't like it. You may have had a point earlier.>

Sam could certainly understand the book's sentiment. Getting from the sewers and into the College proper had been... surprisingly easy.

After agreeing to the plan, Dizzy and the others had donned the counterfeit guard outfits that Sphinx had procured through her connections with the Upright Men. Dizzy played the role of Karren the Blade—going so far as to strap a gleaming sword to her hip—while Kai took on the role of Geffery the Red. Kai didn't really *look* much like Geffery, but in Sam's experience, the Mages didn't pay much attention to anyone they considered to be 'the help'. Arrow and Sphinx both stowed their gear, shrugging into lumpy, brown Novice robes equipped with deep cowls to help conceal their faces.

Sam had done likewise, reluctantly stripping out of his gear to blend in, then slipping a specialty item on over his face. It *would* have cost a pretty penny if Sam had been anyone other than Sam. Bill had been right all along; with Coreless Spell Infusion under his belt, he really did have a license to print money. He'd simply churned out three Ice Orb and a pair of Weak Paralysis spells, less than half an hour of work for all the Novice-ranked single-use items, and then he walked away with the specialty item from the deep Vaults of the Upright Men—an odd, clear mask that depicted the historic figure 'the Gray Fawkes', the infamous Thieves' Guild Leader.

It was a rare item that once applied blended seamlessly with the wearer's face, though it gave the wearer—whether man or woman—a telltale set of rosy cheeks, a rakish mustache and a razor-thin soul patch, which Sam hadn't been even *remotely* prepared for in any way. Honestly, Sam thought the overall effect gave him a very punchable face—which was rather unfortunate—but the mask had properties that made it more than worthwhile. Once on, the mask gave him a random name and replaced any negative status with a neutral status for up to one hour; the effect could be reused but only after a twelve-hour cooldown.

Mask of the Plucky Rebel. Leading an insurgency? Grand plans to take on a tyrant? Just want to crash into your friend Aaron without getting found out? Well, never fear, the Mask of the Plucky Rebel has you covered—quite literally! With this bad boy, you can be someone else, at least for a little while. But great power comes at a great price; I hope you like facial hair and an air of smirking smugness because you'll have that in spades.

By activating the effect, the wearer receives a randomly generated username, and any negative status tags are replaced with neutral status tags for the duration of the effect. Moreover, any bounties you may receive while wearing the mask with the effect activated will disappear when the mask's effect lapses. +2 Charisma while worn, +1 Wisdom, +1 Luck, Active Effect 'Social Chameleon' can be activated once every twelve hours with a duration of one hour. Side effect: Regardless of gender, while wearing the mask, you assume the distinguished facial hair of the Gray Fawkes himself.

Facial hair aside, the mask was absolutely perfect. Sam strutted through the halls without attracting even a curious glance from any of the other Mages scurrying about the hallways. Once Sam got to the Annex proper, he managed to navigate the backways with Bill's help. They hadn't seen another living soul.

Until now, that was. They'd made it to the dungeoneering classroom, only to find that the instructor was in. Sir Tomas—the adventurer-turned-anthropologist who'd seen his best years a century ago—was snoozing at his desk, heels kicked up, a cloth cap pulled down over his face as he snored softly. The tips of his white mustache fluttered with each exhale. Resting on the desk beside him was his massive mace, a weapon which seemed far too large for the frail fellow.

In Eternium, Sam *knew* appearances could be deeply deceptive, and he also knew he didn't want to be on the business end of the mace. After going toe-to-toe with Geffery and coming out on top, Sam fully expected that he could take the instructor in a brawl, but he *couldn't* do so without alerting every Mage in the College that something was amiss.

Even in a place as strange as the College, someone was bound to notice an old adventurer hollering at the top of his lungs while chasing a 'Novice' with an enormous mace. But they'd already come this far, and Sam wasn't about to turn back—not when the prize was so close at hand.

<It'll be fine, Bill. Like you said back in the sewer, no one would ever think to invade the College. That goes double for sneaking into the Annex to release a potentially bloodthirsty Wolfman. We just need to keep our heads down and stay quiet. This will all be fine. It *has* to be."

Feeling a fresh surge of jittery excitement, Sam padded forward, inching his way along the edges of the room, then slipping down the stairs slowly, *slowly*, testing each step with the tip of his boot. Even a single squeaking floorboard could be his undoing. Sam thought his heart might well explode through his chest like an alien hatchling as he crept past the desk, mere feet away from the dozing professor... but the man was out like a light. He didn't so much as shift in his chair.

After what felt like an eternity—even though it was actually only a matter of seconds—Sam was in front of the heavy door that stood guard over the storage room. He licked his lips, stole one look over his shoulder, then slipped in as silently as a ghost, letting the door swing shut behind him with a whisper. Sam found himself in a storage room filled with shelves and shelves of classroom supplies, as well as adventuring equipment— everything from ropes and pickaxes to torches and dull-edged practice swords.

The real prize was tucked away in the far corner of the room—a massive cage built onto a wooden platform. Huddled in the cage was a lump of fur and lean muscle that reeked like week-old death. Sam's breath caught at the smell, and he thought for a second that he was too late... that Velkan of the Redmane Tribe had given up the ghost. But then the lump of fur stirred, and the creature sprung to its feet, letting out a guttural roar that shook a metal-faced shield from the wall. It clattered on the ground like a struck gong. All Sam could do was wince.

<Yes. *Perfect*,> Bill sent in a fury. <So *glad* we were so *careful* sneaking in here. Maybe you can tell me again why we decided to risk our *lives* breaking this guy out?>

<You were held captive by the Mages for three-hundred years,> Sam shot back. <I feel like you of *all* people would be the most sympathetic. Now *stow* it!>

"Come to torture me some more?" Velkan snarled, throwing himself against the cage, rattling the bars as he thrust his claw-tipped hands through the gaps. Straining for freedom... or maybe just to murder someone. *"Torture me all you want. I'll never betray my tribe or my people. Do your worst, human."*

Sam curved his back and dropped his eyes. *"I'm not here hurt you, Velkan. I'm here make freedom."*

The Wolfmen crouched down on his haunches, eyes narrowed to thin slits as he weighed and measured Sam. His ears flicked in uncertainty. *"This is an interesting ploy, at the very least. Changing it up? Why should I believe you, human scum?"*

"I have none of time for this," Sam snarled in his broken Wolfman language, raising his gaze and baring his teeth, asserting his dominance over the Scout. *"The O'Baba sent me. She calls you kin. I'm let you out, fulfill my side of deal. You do what you want, but you want make it out of the Mage training house* alive? *You come with me. Understand?"*

Shock flickered through Velkan's golden eyes. Just like that, Sam had managed to do what Sir Tomas had failed to accomplish for weeks—get Velkan's cooperation.

"Understood," the beast grumbled as Sam worked to get the cage open.

Sam half expected the Wolfman to lunge at him as soon as the heavy steel door swung free, but no. Which is when Sam realized the furry Scout was little more than skin and bones at this point. The Wolfman was emaciated beyond belief, as though he hadn't had anything to eat in days or—more likely—weeks.

His muzzle was gaunt, almost skeletal, and though he was still fiery enough in *spirit*, there wasn't much fight left in his body. He'd been badly mistreated, and it showed. Sam pulled out a spare set of frumpy, brown Novice robes from his spatial container and tossed them at the Wolfman Scout. They wouldn't do anything to properly disguise him, but if Velkan put the hood up and kept his head down, maybe he could pass muster if no one looked *too* closely. Or from a short distance... or a long distance.

With the robes in place, the Wolfman also took a minute to snag a leather belt along with a short sword that he strapped to his side. Sam just hoped the blade wouldn't be necessary. Done, Sam, Bill, and Velkan snuck from the storeroom.

Naturally, Sir Tomas was waiting for them. The old-timey adventurer was on his feet, his heavy mace leaning almost casually against one shoulder, his other hand resting against a cocked-out hip.

"Well, what is *this* here?" his mustache was bobbing as he spoke. "If I didn't *know* any better, I'd say someone was attempting a jailbreak, hmm? Now, explain yourself, *cur*, or prepare to eat steel. Have you had your daily allotment of *iron?*"

Truthfully, Sir Tomas sounded positively *excited* about the notion of a brawl, which was probably a bad sign. What were the chances that the old guy was quite a bit tougher than he looked? Sam licked his lips, preparing to summon his Orbital Tomes and unleash magical hell on the old codger.

<Don't, kid. I got this,> Bill sent to him, surprising the young Bibliomancer. The book floated up, the cover burning with preternatural light.

"How *dare* you! Who are *you* to question us? You withered, *replaceable* adjunct professor! Do you know who I am? *Hmm?* Why, I, Sir William the Bravi," Bill continued, not giving the sputtering professor a chance to answer, "Master of Library Magics, Dean of Discipline, and Tenured Professor of Bibliomancy should *incinerate* you on the spot for your insolence!"

"*Bu-but-but,*" Sir Tomas stuttered, withering under Bill's relentless onslaught. "Well, I thought..."

"Your place is *not* to think. Which of us wields an oversized club, and which of us is a magical talking book? Leave the thinking to me, *adventurer!*" Bill thundered, the glow around him intensifying.

"Of course, m'lord. Of course. A thousand apologies."
Sir Tomas doffed his cap and bowed nearly double at the waist.
"Is there anything I can do to help?"

"Nothing at *all*. Now, if you want to keep your little job
here, move out of my way and keep this encounter to yourself."
Bill hovered closer, dropping his voice to a conspiratorial
whisper, as though letting the professor in on something of the
utmost secrecy, "I need this specimen for a very *confidential*
spell, the first step in wiping the bloody Wolfmen off the face of
the map, and your captive here is going to help us. Look, he is
obviously already in my control."

Bill paused, ruffling his pages as though thinking. "You
know, if everything goes well, I might even put in a good word
for you. After all, you *are* the one who captured this creature..."

Sir Tomas seemed to brighten noticeably at that. "Oy,
thank you, Sir William. Thank you a thousand times over. You
can expect the utmost discretion from me. Best of luck with your
spell. About *time* someone fired a shot across the bow at those
mangy dogs!"

"Just so." Bill bobbed in the air. Before Sir Tomas could
probe into their story any deeper, Sam and Bill slipped from the
room and into the Annex proper with Velkan trailing a few
paces behind them.

<That was *incredible*!> Sam sent as they ghosted along
the hall. <How did you know that would work?>

<Eh. Simple, Legs. Sometimes all you need to win a
battle is a stick and a carrot. Real power isn't always about
hurting people; it's about convincing them that you can do *more*
than hurt them. That poor sad sack back there, he just wants to
keep his job and revel in the little bit of power he has here at the
College. That means more to that sort of guy than anything else.
So, imply that you can take that tiny bit of power away, and

you've already won the war. Now let's move it; the *real* battle is still ahead of us. Well, frankly, I don't think we'll be able to talk our way out of that one.>

CHAPTER THIRTY-SEVEN

Compared to busting the Wolfman Scout out of the clink, the trip from the Annex to the back entrance of the library was a cakewalk. The little-known corridor that no one used was completely empty. There was *one* moment of heart-wrenching tension where Sam heard the heavy footfalls of some unseen Mage, but with a little quick insight from Bill, they managed to find an even *lesser*-used passageway that got them to their destination, free and clear. Yes, Sam, Bill, and Velkan had to endure waves of vertigo, abrupt gravitation eddies that felt like they might crush Sam's insides, and moments where time seemed to slow to a snail's pace, but it was totally worth it.

The library foyer was devoid of life, which Sam found disconcerting. The big desk in the entry hall *always* had someone on duty. At this hour, Mage Solis should've been lounging around sipping health potions like a normal person drank tea or at least getting ready to *start* his shift. Sam spotted Solis' battered copy of *The Riveting Adventures of D.K. Esquire: Dungeon Delver* laying out on the desktop, confirming his suspicions, but there was no sign of the man. Sam wasn't sure what that meant, but he hoped against hope that nothing had happened to the old man. Although Solis was an exalted member of the College, he'd always been a gentle, kind-hearted soul.

Sam hoped nothing had happened to him. Roughly shoving his fear and doubt to the back of his mind, Sam reached out to Bill and conjured his Orbital Tomes with the slightest effort of will. Six books sprang to life around him, rotating in a lazy circle. He'd brought *everything*. There were three volumes all chock-full of Paper Shurikens in different varieties—one book dedicated to Fireball, another to Ice Orb, and a third to Weak Paralysis. His fourth combat text contained Papier-Mache Mage, which he promptly cast, propping his arms out to the sides as a swirl of inked-pages encased his body. The fifth volume held his basic Ink Lance spell, while the sixth and final tome was filled with pages for his Rorschach Test—enough for three casts.

Admittedly, Sam was more than a little worried about using that spell since the target had the possibility of simply ignoring the effects. Though Octavius and his friends were tools one and all, Sam was sure they would have a way to protect their minds. There was nothing he could do about that, so he just had to be ready.

With his Papier-Mache armor firmly in place, Sam pulled out *Bill's Foppish Hat,* home to his enchanted Quill Blade, and slapped it onto his head for good measure. There was no point in trying to hide his identity at this point. If Octavius *was* here, Sam would have to fight him, and he'd need every possible advantage he could get.

"*You know,*" Sam spoke over one shoulder to Velkan in the guttural Wolfman tongue, "*you come with me, there's chance that you no leave. I won't hold grudge, you decide to go your way. Try to get back to tribe and give them know what happened.*"

The Scout considered Sam for a long beat as he parsed the words, then dipped his muzzle, flicked his ears, and shook his shaggy head. He replied in broken human tongue, "Velkan, could not live with shame. Dying with honor, it not such bad thing."

A colossal *boom* rocked the air a second later, the ground quivering beneath Sam's boots.

<Looks like your pals got the party started without you, kiddo! Move your butt unless you want to wind up dying on a sacrificial Wolfman altar for the rest of your days!>

Sam didn't even bother to reply. He kicked it into high gear, sprinting down an aisleway filled to the brim with books, following the well-familiar pathway that led to Octavius' study spot. He flew around corners and tore along straightaways, the raucous sound of battle growing louder and more ominous with every step he took. More thunderous *booms* shook the air, interspersed with the sharp *clang* of steel, cries of pain, and flashes of utter brilliance. Jagged splashes of gold, green, and red tattooed themselves across the floor, shelves, and leather-bound books like a bomb blast made out of confetti and late afternoon sunbeams.

Sam wheeled around a sharp bend and abruptly found himself in Octavius' study, which had been transformed into a magical warzone. The tables and padded leather chairs perfect for a leisurely bout of studying were nowhere to be seen. In their place was an intricate tower of wood, stone, and metal all bolted together with fist-sized bronze rivets and covered with glowing runes that Sam had seen a handful of times before, all courtesy of the notes and blueprints he'd gazed at during long nights attending Octavius.

A crystal the size of Sam's fist *floated* at the top of the odd tower, hanging in the air, unsuspended while it burned with amethyst power. That *had* to be a monster Core, and considering its size and radiance, Sam was guessing it was a *powerful* one. Off to one side was a carved wooden lectern with a beefy book splayed out on top.

Octavius' personal grimoire.

Presumably, the book which contained whatever nasty spell the Peak Student was working to amplify. The rest of the room was chaos and madness. Magic flew through the air in brilliant sprays. Weapons flashed in deadly reply. There were bodies sprawled out across the floor, and Sam was sick to see that one of his friends was already down for the count and that the rest of the Wolf Pack was faring little better.

Arrow lay unmoving just a handful of feet away from the magical tower, his body badly charbroiled. What remained of his face twisted in a grimace of pain. Additionally, a contorted sword made of some unrecognizable metal jutted from his chest like a piece of shrapnel from a car wreck. A brown-robed Mage that Sam didn't recognize lay in a sprawl of limbs nearby, his chest a regular pincushion of feather shafts. Blood pooled around him, glittering in the firelight.

Sphinx danced with Tullus, Octavius' thick-headed, slow-witted thug. Sam had never actually seen Tullus in action, but at a guess, he thought the man must've been some sort of Battle Mage or Spellblade. Instead of the typical robes most Acolytes wore, Tullus had summoned chainmail that flashed gold and silver as he moved. Floating in front of him was a trio of conjured swords that fought of their own accord. Sphinx ducked and dodged the slashing emerald weapons, moving with sinuous grace, but the swords were ungodly fast; she was already hemorrhaging blood from a myriad of minor lacerations.

Tullus, by contrast, looked no worse for the wear. It was a cold, hard, *brutal* reminder of just how overpowered Mages could be in the world of Eternium. Meanwhile, Finn and Dizzy were busy sparring with Elsia, the fire Mage who'd nearly turned Sam into a ball of molten goo during his escape from the library. She looked positively deadly. Her eyes burned like molten gold; her red hair stood straight up, floating like the flickering tongues of a candle. A cloak of *actual* fire trailed down her back, while more flames wreathed her outstretched hands. With a scream—so high-pitched Sam flinched back at the onslaught of noise—she pressed her palms together, hurling a column of magma at Sam's friends.

Dizzy dove right, quickly springing back to her feet as Finn unleashed a counter spell of his own—an equally formidable column of purple-blue ice. The two streams of magic smashed together like sumo wrestlers, both furiously working to push the other from the ring. Arctic power vying against a beam of sunfire, golden sparks and arcs of blue lightning flashed out where the two beams met. It would've been beautiful if not for the potentially deadly consequences.

The battle looked like a draw, right up until Dizzy bolted in on Elsia's flank, bringing her maul around in a wicked arc aimed straight for the fire Mage's vulnerable head. With a growl, Elsia broke off her attack and begrudgingly retreated against the combined power of Finn and Dizzy. As tough as Elsia probably was, Sam felt confident that she was outclassed in this instance.

There was still one other major threat to worry about, though—Octavius. The Earth Mage was standing nearby, not wearing his typical attire but instead sporting a set of colorful robes woven from some sort of silken fabric and studded with a multitude of smaller, glowing gemstones. He also wore an expression of absolute *rage*. Uncontrolled *fury*. "I refuse to let this happen!"

He screamed, face beet red, spittle flying from his lips. "I've worked too hard, spent too many hours on this to fail now! This is finally House Igenitor's chance to earn the honor we've always been due! On the blood of my forebears, I refuse to let some commoner *riffraff* take this away from me."

Octavius thrust his right hand forward, and a javelin of obsidian rock exploded from his palm, screaming toward Kai like a cruise missile. The Monk leaped and twisted in the air, landing on his hands then springing away, narrowly avoiding the stony spear, which *thudded* into a bookcase, but Octavius hardly seemed to care. He whipped his left hand out, and a muddy brown glow shot through with veins of red and gold enveloped his hand. The floor rumbled and groaned in protest as boards buckled, cracked, and broke apart. Sam felt a moment of awe as stone, dirt, and gritty sand surged up in a swirling column, instantly forming itself into an enormous hand seven feet tall and five feet wide which perfectly mimicked Octavius' own hand.

With a snarl, Octavius whipped his arms through the air, and the stony hand responded in kind, blindsiding Kai with bone-breaking force. The Monk was batted across the floor like a baseline drive. In an instant, Kai's health flashed an alarming shade of red. He was still alive, and before Kai could recover or shake off the blow, the enormous hand scooped him up from the floor. Colossal, rocky fingers wrapped around him and clamped down, constricting like a cohort of pythons out for revenge. The life was brutally squeezed out of the struggling Monk an inch at a time.

Time to put an end to *that!* <Bill, we're gonna have to work together on this.>

<What ya thinking, Sam?>

<Sightless casting and Dual casting. I need you to go after that blockhead Tullus. Use the Ice Orb Shuriken to slow him down some. Don't worry about taking him out, just buy Sphinx a little breathing room. I'll see if I can't punch Octavius right in the teeth.>

<On it!> the book sent. The blue-bound Ice Orb tome rotated to the three-o-clock position, covers flying apart as paper stars burst out nearly once a second. Simultaneously, Sam toggled the Fireball tome to the twelve-o-clock position and

unleashed fiery death stars one after the other. Kai was almost dead, so instead of targeting Octavius immediately, Sam focused on the stone hand crushing the life from his friend.

The Shurikens slammed into the wrist-like base of the summoned limb, exploding in a ball of red and gold and gouging huge divots out of the hand, piece by piece. The room shook under the force of each explosion. Unable to hold its shape under the barrage of Fireball spells, the conjured hand simply exploded in a cloud of powdered stone and dust.

Kai wheezed as he pulled himself from the pile of rubble, clutching his chest with one hand. He was in rough shape, his health ridiculously low... but he was alive for the time being. Thankfully, thanks to game physics, the Monk would soon be back on his feet, kicking butt and taking names. Octavius spun, eyes narrowing into feral slits while his lips pulled back in a snarl that would've been befitting for an angry Wolfman.

Speaking of Wolfmen? Where in the world was Velkan? Sam realized the Scout was nowhere to be seen. Had he lost him while running through the stacks, or had the Scout simply changed his mind about almost certain death? Sam wasn't sure, but he couldn't think about that right now. He had Octavius to deal with. If he wasn't entirely present in the moment, he knew the Earth Mage would rip him to pieces without a second thought.

"You," Octavius cursed as his eyes locked on Sam. "*You're* behind this! I should've known. I *mentored* you. Took you under my wing and gave you a chance to succeed. You repaid my *kindness* by stealing a priceless artifact and shaming my whole household. But was that enough for you? Obviously *not.*"

Octavius shook his head. "No, you won't be content until you've utterly destroyed me. I see. Well, I think you'll find I'm not so easily defeated. You won't be escaping this time. You'll be properly tried for your crimes, and my name will be restored."

"I just have one thing to say. When arguing, never throw dirt at your opponent." Sam prepared himself to strike. "All you do is lose ground!"

Without waiting for a reply, Sam swapped Fireball Shuriken for his tome of Ink Lance. The ebony book shot into position, black ropes of goopy ink exploding from the pages, wrapping around Octavius before splattering to the ground.

Damage: 0 (Acid damage resisted!) Slow effect resisted!

"Cute," Octavius snorted, "but I'm afraid you'll have to do better than *that.*"

Octavius curled his hand into a tight fist and sand erupted from the ground, swirling around the Peak Student like a dust devil, momentarily obscuring him from view. When the air settled a second later, Octavius was no longer wearing his elaborate robes but was instead decked out in stone armor. He now stood over seven feet tall and looked more like an earth golem than a man. Only Octavius' smug, self-satisfied face poking out from the suit of earth armor told Sam that the Mage hadn't just summoned an Elemental to fight on his behalf.

Obsidian spikes poked up from blocky earthen pauldrons, and though Octavius wielded no visible weapon, his forearms were *enormous* and capped by fists the size of dinner plates. Each knuckle was studded with a spur of glittering, razor-sharp quartz. One punch would turn Sam's face into road pizza.

"There are *so* many ways I could grind you into topsoil," Octavius stomped forward, the weight of each step shaking the room, "but this, I think, will be the most satisfying way by a fair margin."

Yeah, this was probably bad, but Sam could only grin as two words ran through his mind on repeat.

Boss Fight! Boss Fight! Boss Fight!

Chapter Thirty-Eight

<Bill! *Bill!*> Sam screamed in his mind. <I need your *complete* attention for the next several minutes!>

Octavius stomped forward, moving with preternaturally fast speed for a creature so large and domineering. Sam half expected the suit of earth-based Mage Armor to be sluggishly slow, but if anything, Octavius was even *faster* than he'd been before. That didn't seem even *remotely* fair! Octavius lunged, a fist the size of a dinner ham swinging toward Sam like a wrecking ball.

<Yeah, yeah! I'm on it,> Bill shouted as Sam danced away, keeping his head by an inch.

A huge, rock-covered foot shot out like a battering ram, aimed squarely at chest level. Acting on muscle memory and instinct, Sam threw himself to one side, curling into a ball and quickly rolling back to his feet while thanking his lucky stars for his time spent on the judo mats.

<What do I do here, Bill?> he sent as he circled right, staying low, ready to bolt at a moment's notice. <What the *abyss* is this thing, and how do I stop it?>

With a thought, Sam brought his Weak Paralysis Shuriken tome to the front and fired off a handful of ninja stars, one right after the other. The Shurikens slammed into the encroaching Peak Student... but bounced away uselessly, failing to do any damage or eat away at the stony armor covering Octavius from head to toe.

Damage dealt: 0 (56 damage absorbed.) Paralysis resisted!

<Okay. Yep. I see the issue,> Bill sent along in a strangely unhurried way. <Hard to know *exactly* what Octavius

did... but if I had to guess, I'd say he mashed together Mage Armor, Conjured Weapon, and a Summon Lesser Elemental spell in the Soul Forge. Never seen that *particular* combination before.>

<Great bit of info, but you missed the *important* part. How do I *stop* it?>

<Eh... Fireball? Maybe?> Well, that was completely unhelpful.

Still, with no other leads to go on, Sam brought his Fireball tome racing around to the prime position and hurled a Shuriken at less than three feet out. The ninja star exploded on impact with devastating force—unfortunately, at a mere three feet away, Sam was within the blast radius. A fist of flame sucker-punched Sam in the ribs, knocking him back, singeing his eyebrows but somehow not touching his health.

Damage dealt: 0 (66 damage absorbed.) Fire damage resisted!

*Damage taken: 115.5 (66 Fireball Paper Shuriken * 1.75 bonus fire damage versus Papier-Mache Mage.)*

Papier-Mache Mage: 288.25 durability remaining. Caution: On fire. -10 durability per second until not on fire.

Good thing he had invested nearly his entire Mana pool of four hundred and seventy-five Mana when creating this spell. A black scorch mark stained his chest plate, and thin embers of red and orange crept along the surface of his gauntlets, sending up curls of gray ash. Sam did the only thing he could think of—*stop, drop, and roll.*

<This is *completely* undignified,> Bill scolded as Sam flopped and flailed, smothering the flames before they could spread farther. <Also, unrelated, but based on how that went... I'm going to go out on a limb and say Fireball Shurikens are definitely *not* the best option.>

Bill wasn't wrong. As Sam clambered to his feet—the budding flames extinguished at last—the smoky plume from his latest attack had dissipated, revealing Octavius completely unharmed. There wasn't even so much as a smear of soot marring the rocky surface of his elemental armor.

"Nice try, you *worm*, but I'm a Peak Student on the precipice of *Journeyman* status. You never stood a *chance*... and you never will."

Octavius thrust one rock-covered hand forward, palm up, fingers splayed out, a spell falling from his lips. The ground rumbled, and shafts of razor-sharp earth erupted from beneath Sam's feet, frantically trying to turn him into a human shish kabob. Sam was prepared.

He darted left, rolled right, then promptly backpedaled, avoiding a lethal blow by the skin of his teeth. Sadly, Octavius had used the distraction to close the distance, and now, he was in striking range with his big, blocky fists. Since he was in such close proximity, Sam didn't dare risk using any of his augmented spells; he couldn't afford to set himself on fire again or accidentally coat himself in a layer of paralyzing frost.

No, the fact remained that spellcasting was best done at range, not two feet away from a murderous stone golem. Instead, Sam conjured his Quill Blade with a surge of Mana and a whispered incantation.

The feather from his hat took flight, flipping, twirling, then zipping into Sam's outstretched palm as it shimmered and morphed into the familiar sword with the elegant silver feather blade. Its weight was somehow reassuring. Octavius might send him for respawn, but Sam wouldn't go without a knock-down, drag-out fight. Weapon in hand, Sam struck.

He sidestepped right, avoiding a lumbering front kick that undoubtedly would've caved in his chest cavity and hacked at Octavius' protected left forearm. The feathered blade landed with a sharp *twang*, improbably slicing a narrow furrow into the rock but not penetrating deeply enough to hit the Peak Student's flesh. The fact that he had damaged the armor *at all* gave Sam some small measure of hope—a hope that maybe, just *maybe*, Octavius could be beaten after all. Octavius crowded in, trying to back him into a nearby alcove, but Sam nimbly evaded, refusing to let Octavius pin him down.

<That's the way to do it, Legs! Keep this joker on his toes, and soon, I'll be calling you 'Wrist'! That's some *finger-*fancy swordplay for a Novice! See if you can't open up a little distance from his *body*. We don't want to be in *arms* reach. Use your *brain*!>

<You need to *stop*,> Sam grunted, sweat pouring down his face as he worked the handful of sword forms Sphinx and Bill had taught him. In his mind, he started singing 'head, shoulders, knees, and toes... knees and toes'. Freaking *Bill!*

Sam feinted left and right, executing an arrangement of lunges, thrusts, and flicks all while dutifully countering and avoiding the killer hooks, jabs, and kicks Octavius offered in response. Bill was right; being in close wasn't great, but it did have *one* significant advantage—namely, Octavius was just as restricted as Sam was when it came to spellcasting.

Sure, Sam didn't have the breathing room to throw anything at the Earth Mage, but that was a two-way street. Anytime the Peak Student tried to unleash some new and potentially *life-ending* spell, Sam dashed into his guard. Quill Blade scraped against armor and made Octavius flinch, thereby disrupting even the most basic spells.

Even though Octavius apparently had even less experience fighting hand-to-hand than Sam did, this was a fight Sam couldn't win. Not this way. He was doing a great job of *not* dying horrifically, but he wasn't inflicting any damage. None. *Zero.* Plus, all it would take was Octavius landing *one* solid blow to end things for good.

Sam was a Mage, a spell-slinger! Not a *Fighter.* What he *needed* to do was get his magic into play. He had one hard-hitting spell in his arsenal that would damage Octavius no matter *how* much armor the man was wearing, but to use it, he needed space. A lot of it. So, against his better judgment, Sam charged, screaming as he laid into Octavius with a series of wide, sweeping slashes. That flowed into a relentless onslaught of short, frenzied strikes with his weapon arm fully extended. The sheer ferocity of his attack put Octavius back on his heels for a beat and set the Earth Mage up for what Bill called 'the second intention'.

As Sam's stamina started to fade—he was a Mage, after all, not a warrior—he finally let up, withdrawing his sword and falling into a back stance, his blade raised high overhead as he labored for air. The attack was *so* obvious Sam was *sure* Octavius would know what he was planning. Except, it suddenly occurred to Sam... Octavius probably *didn't.* Sam had to remind himself that Octavius wasn't a Fighter either. Sam doubted the man knew anything but the bare basics when it came to melee combat. He relied totally on magic and was probably expecting Sam to do so as well.

As a result, it wasn't totally surprising when Sam brought the sword down, and the Peak Student took the bait, stepping in to parry the attack with his oversized fist. Sam spun right just before the sword landed, winding up on Octavius' unprotected flank. Instead of lashing out with his sword, he brought his Ink Lance tome to bear, blasting a sticky glob of jet-black ink into Octavius' unprotected face.

Damage dealt: 4/second for 15 seconds! Target slowed by fourteen percent!

The acid bit into both rock and face as the ink spread, but the real perk was that the spell slowed the man down *just* enough for Sam to dart back, putting some space between them—enough room to cast his emergency spell. "Rorschach Test!"

In seconds, pages and ink burst forth in a whirlwind, blurring together and transforming into the familiar, giant scroll that hung unsupported in the air. It took effect, and Sam's concerns that the Mage would have mental defenses were put to rest. Just like when he'd used it the last time, the effects were immediate. Octavius' eyes widened in equal parts shock and terror, his face twisting into a mask of purest horror at whatever he was seeing inked out on the scroll.

The Peak Student spun and screamed, Sam apparently forgotten in the face of his fear. Perfect! Now he had the breathing room he needed to lob Fireball or Ice Orb Shurikens at the Peak Student without fear. No matter *how* tough Octavius or his conjured armor was, he wouldn't be able to stand up to twenty or thirty spammed Fireballs. No way.

Gloating in his moment of victory, Sam brought the tome of Fireball Shuriken spinning to the front. The pages burst open, ready to unleash a storm of paper fury... Before Sam could activate his first spell, something slammed into his shoulder. Something sharp. Something impossibly painful. In mute shock, Sam glanced down and saw a javelin of rock protruding from his arm.

*Damage taken: 46 (550. 504 damage absorbed by Papier-Mache Mage (288.25 * 1.75 earth magic resist).) Bleeding, light. -3 health per second until repaired.*

Health: 84/140

"How... how did that happen?" As Sam stood there staring at the wound, trying to properly formulate a thought, the floor rumbled beneath him, and the same giant fist Octavius had used so effectively against Kai erupted from the ground. Blunt, blocky fingers wrapped around Sam like a straitjacket, pinning Sam's arms to his side and preventing him from doing the basic hand gestures required to cast his spells.

That was *impossible!* The Rorschach Test... it should've kept Octavius occupied for a solid minute. *Unless...* Octavius faced him. The expression of fear Sam had seen splashed across his face just seconds before was gone. Now, he was *laughing.* With a wave of one enormous hand, Octavius dispelled the armor encasing him, returning in an eyeblink to the ornate, flowing robes he'd been sporting before the battle began.

"Did you really think you and your crew of *miscreants* ever had a chance at stopping *me?* Really? I'm Octavius Igenitor of *House* Igenitor, practitioner of the arcane arts, shaper of the elements, herald of knowledge! As for you? *You* are just a commoner. A *nobody* in way over his head. You have lost, and I have won, which is the way things were *destined* to be."

Feeling sick to his stomach, Sam glanced around for the first time since starting his battle against Octavius and realized that his team *had* lost. Thoroughly. Kai lay dead, not far from Arrow, while Dizzy, Finn, and Sphinx had all been captured by Octavius' teammates. The three of them were propped up against a nearby bookcase, unconscious and in terrible shape, yet breathing.

"You were never a match for me," Octavius crowed. "To think you genuinely believed that your taboo mind magic would work against *me?*"

He paused, the epitome of smugness, and pulled a small leather journal from an oversized sleeve. "After you got away with that silly little *book*, I did a little digging. Turns out not *all* records of the infamous 'Bibliomancer' were destroyed after all. This is a first-hand account from the Archmage himself, detailing the most frequently used Bibliomancer spells. When you cast that spell, I knew *exactly* what effect to mimic. You let down your guard, and I took the opportunity to strike."

"Fine. You won," Sam spat out. "Just kill us already."

"Ha. As *if.* You won't escape that way. You and the rest of your friends will have the pleasure of gracing a cell in the dungeon, fueling The Accords for the rest of your foreseeable lives. Before you do, it's only fitting that you should be allowed to watch me finish the very spell you were so eager to destroy. Although." He paused, rubbing at his chin. "Yes, I wouldn't want you trying anything while I work."

With a determined nod, Octavius strode forward, muttering a spell as he walked. There was a flash of muddy-gold light, and suddenly, Octavius had a heavy-headed warhammer in one hand, formed entirely from rose-colored quartz.

"The Rose Hammer ought to do the trick quite nicely, I should think..." Octavius stopped in front of Sam, planted his feet shoulder-width apart, and raised the weapon like a golfer swinging for a hole-in-one. Before Sam could fully process what was about to happen, the hammer's blunt face smashed into his left kneecap with a thunderous *pop* that resonated through the room.

Damage taken: 20 (20 blunt damage). Debuff added: Crippled left leg! Seek a healer.

A wave of indescribable pain washed through Sam; lightning and fire raged inside his bones and screamed inside his head. With a cruel smile, Octavius lifted the hammer and struck again, crushing Sam's *other* knee as easily as someone else might crush a soda can.

Damage taken: 15 (15 blunt damage). Debuff added: Crippled right leg! Seek a healer.

The pain was incredible. Unfathomable. Even more amazing was the fact that Octavius had managed to land both blows without *killing* Sam outright. Sam's health was abysmally low, but incredibly, he was still clinging to the mortal coil. That was... a shame, actually.

Health: 32/140

<Hang in there, Sam,> Bill whispered reassuringly. <You're tougher than this guy. He might win the day, but he can't make you give up. Not unless you give it to him. I'm right here with you. We can always get him another time.>

"Now," Octavius lifted his hand and banished the rock-forged weapon with a flick of his fingers, "I'll put some pressure on that wound so you don't bleed to death."

The stone spike in Sam's arm vanished with a *pop*, and a band of stone wrapped around the hole. Octavius continued, "Let us proceed with the matter at hand. Time to put an end to that pesky Wolfman Outpost and collect our due from the Crown."

Octavius offered his back to Sam. 'You are no threat to me,' the gesture said in no uncertain terms. He leisurely strolled over to the podium where his grimoire waited.

<Please, Bill,> Sam sent, his head swimming from the pain. <I need help. Sightless casting, maybe? Can't you do *something*? There's got to be *something!*>

<I'm sorry, Sam. If you can't cast spells, I can't cast spells either. That's one of the few restrictions on Sightless casting. There's just nothing...> The words faded mid-sentence. <Well... not sure if it'll do any good, but I suppose there is *one* thing we could try.>

<What? Anything!>

<Well, you can't get to a health potion because you would need to drink it, but you have the five Jelly cores in your flask. From the sewer. You're right on the cusp of level seven. If you can wiggle your fingers and open the flask, even just a little, you could get to one of those cores. Mostly people use them for ingredients, but if you burn 'em for experience... it could put you over the edge. Magic can be a finicky thing, and the power released from leveling up might disrupt the construct he built on you. It's *dirt*, and leveling *cleans* you. It's a long shot, but even if it doesn't set you free, maybe it'll give you a chance to do... I dunno, *something*, I guess?"

Bill sounded terribly uncertain, but Sam didn't see any other options, and his father had a saying that went back for *ages*, 'A drowning man will grab even for the point of a sword'. Seriously, what did he have to lose?

Sam focused his thoughts, desperately trying to block out the pain radiating up from his legs like heat from a dumpster fire, and carefully inched his fingers toward the Unending Flask. With short, precise movements, he unscrewed the metal lid, accessing the space inside it. He couldn't see, but with a little groping around, he quickly found what he was searching for.

A slickly smooth stone, almost like a piece of polished glass that pulsed with just the slightest hint of warmth. Like a stone that had sat out in the sun on a warm summer day. There were five of the Cores in the flask, but there was no way to access them all at once. Hopefully, he would be able to get at them fast enough because they were running out of time.

Chapter Thirty-Nine

Sam focused on the stone in his hand, and a prompt appeared in the corner of his vision.

Trash-tier monster Core found! Would you like to convert this into experience points? Current worth: Three hundred experience points. Yes / No

Sam nearly choked as he looked at the total. Three hundred points! That was almost two days' worth of experience if he were out casually grinding. No wonder the Mages were so powerful! They were sitting on a gold mine of experience—also *actual* gold since the Cores each went for a small fortune. Right now, money was the least of Sam's concerns. Without missing a beat, he accepted 'Yes.'

The slight heat emanating from the stone intensified, and the stone dissolved; energy soaked into Sam's palm, then sprinted along his arm, beelining for his Core. The power rushed into his Center, and as it did, a new feeling surged through him. *Energy.* Raw, undiluted *power.* It was like a spring breeze. Like the light of a new day. Like the rising of a full moon on a cloudless night. It was primal, wonderful... *addictive.*

He fed that addiction, taking in all five Cores and gaining fifteen hundred experience in under ten seconds. Finally, an inferno exploded through him in a surge that he'd come to associate with leveling up. Golden light flared around him like a sunburst, banishing dirt and grime and filling him with a sense of well-being.

Even better, wild arcs of golden energy surged out like the flailing tentacles of some monstrous kraken, and though his friends weren't close enough to reap the benefits, the power disrupted the enormous spell-conjured fist wrapped around him in a death grip. Bill had been right. The conjured hand fell to pieces. Stone fingers disintegrated before Sam's eyes, turning into a pile of dust that cushioned his tumble to the ground.

"Octavius," Tullus Adventus shouted, "*problem!*"

"What is it *now?*" Octavius snarled, stealing a look over one shoulder. "How in the–"

He never finished his words. A roar ripped at the air, and a blurry shape leaped from the top of a nearby bookcase, dropping onto Octavius like an anvil made of flesh and fangs. Velkan! The Wolfman hadn't bailed on them after all! He'd just been biding his time, waiting for an opportune moment to strike. Like now, for example.

The Wolfman fought like a hungry tiger, claws raking at Octavius' face and chest, his jaws snapping at vulnerable, exposed flesh. Sam watched in wonder as Octavius and Velkan stumbled away from the podium in a tangle of limbs, sprays of crimson arcing through the air. A shimmering shell of sandy-brown snapped into existence around the Earth Mage–likely his version of Mage Shield–but it didn't do anything to slow Velkan's assault. The Wolfman might not have been able to *hurt* Octavius, but he was sure trying like his life depended on it.

"Don't just *stand there!*" Octavius shrieked. This time his terror wasn't fake. "This thing is mauling me! Help me, you buffoons!"

"But the prisoners?" Tullus waved at Sam and the others.

"We'll deal with them! Help! Me! *Now!*" came Octavius' frantic reply.

Tullus and Elsia shared swift glances with each other, uncertainty etched into the lines of their faces. Elsia shrugged and sighed, "Whatever."

Abandoning Dizzy, Finn, and Sphinx, the two goons charged the tangled whirlwind that was Octavius and Velkan. Neither Tullus nor Elsia could risk casting spells since they might hit Octavius in the process. That meant they were going to have to get physical in order to pry the bloodthirsty Wolfman away.

That *also* meant they weren't paying attention to little ol' Sam. Truthfully, why would they? They'd already mopped the floor with him and his party once; if push came to shove, they could do it again. *Easily.* Especially since the rest of Sam's teammates were beaten within an inch of their collective lives and passed out cold on the floor.

Objectively, Sam *couldn't* beat them in a fair fight. No way. Which is why he needed to *cheat.* His gaze landed on Octavius' spell book, and the seed of a plan blossomed in his mind.

<Oh, that's good, Legs... Oh, sorry to remind you of your shattered kneecaps.> Bill was picking up Sam's thought process. <It could work. Oh. Even better, use a trigger *word,* so that it'll go off right when he's in the middle of casting the spell. Remember what happened to you when you messed up that Fireball scroll?>

Sam grinned and started dragging himself across the floor toward Octavius' ignored spell book. As he reached it, he fished out a simple quill and a bottle of magically infused ink from his spatial flask. While Octavius and his crew of dim-witted thugs wrestled with Velkan, Sam grabbed Octavius' carelessly unguarded grimoire.

Inside the book was a copy of the blueprints for the Long-range Amplification Weapon—Sam took the liberty of slipping those into his flask for later examination—then he quickly thumbed through the pages of the tome until he found the perfect word to use as a trigger. He flipped to the back page in a mad rush, slapped down the simplest spellscript he knew, then added a thin line with a stylized triangle at the end followed by the trigger word.

It took less than ten seconds and fifty Mana to finish—ten seconds that felt like a *lifetime*. Sam was *sure* Octavius and company would dispatch Velkan and bring the hammer down at any moment, literally crushing his plans and probably his hands as well. Somehow, the angry Wolfman Scout managed to hold his ground.

Velkan was one cagey fighter, and though he could never *beat* all three Mages, he *was* doing an excellent job of holding them at bay. In part, it was because he fought smart— always staying on the move, constantly repositioning himself so that the Mages could never surround him. Moreover, Velkan never went for big attacks that exposed him to danger. He would only strike at weak, vulnerable targets—an unprotected arm, a turned back—bleeding the three out one hit at a time.

It was impressive to watch. Assuming Velkan survived, Sam wanted to learn everything the Wolfman had to teach about melee combat. Reluctantly, Sam pulled his attention away from the battle, returned the book to the original spell page so Octavius would be none the wiser, then started dragging himself to his remaining teammates.

All three were *badly* beaten but most certainly alive. On closer inspection, Sam noticed that all three were suffering from broken legs just like he was. Frustrating. This was an awfully brutal, though clearly *effective* method of keeping prisoners from running away. Sam had only one health potion remaining from his time at the College.

He had planned to use it before, but dying had fixed him up. He pulled the vial free, popped the top, and held it up to Dizzy's lips. He forced the tanky fighter to drink the brew down in a few long gulps. The results were instant, reviving her in a flash and returning fifty points of health to her. Over three seconds, she was mended as thoroughly as dying had mended Sam.

Her eyes popped open, roaming around the room in sheer fury. Dizzy wasn't scared. She wasn't hurt. She was *mad*. She sprang to her feet, reaching for her maul, but Sam stopped her, grabbing her wrist in a white-knuckled grip before she could draw the weapon and go berserk.

"No time! Things are about to go south here... in a *big* way." Sam pulled out the crude map he and Bill had made earlier and thrust it into her hands. "You know the way out?"

"Yeah," she replied with a frustrated nod.

"Good. Think you can carry these two out of here?"

"As if you even had to ask," she shot back, bending over and unceremoniously scooping up first Finn, then Sphinx, tossing one over each shoulder like sacks of grain. "But what about you?"

"Don't worry about me, Diz. Bill and I will stay behind and make sure this thing is over. For real. But you? You need to run. Don't stop for *anything*. This place is about to go up like the Fourth of July. If I survive, I'll meet you guys at The Grater Good. Just hunker down there until I show up. I'll get there... one way or the other."

She hesitated for only a moment, her gaze searching his face. Finally, she nodded. With a grunt and a heave, she set off. "I hope you know what you're doing."

"Good luck, Sam," she hollered over one shoulder before disappearing into the stacks of books.

<I like the heroics thing, Sam. I really do. Good on you. Bu~u~t... if we stay here, we're as good as dead. When that thing blows... it's gonna be bad.>

<I need to see it happen, Bill. I need to make sure this really works. We can't leave it to chance, and I can't exactly run for it. I mean, look what happened to us. Octavius and his goon squad thought we were as good as dead when we escaped from the College the first time around, and yet... here we are, alive and getting ready to blow them all to high heaven. I'm not leaving until I see Octavius' crispy body.>

Bill sighed, the sound long, heavy, and reminding Sam of the wind ruffling the pages of a book. Not really a surprise.

<Yeah. Okay. I get it. But if we're gonna stay, we need to be *smart*. We need cover.> Bill floated up, searching the room. It was a hot mess of blood, gore, smoking craters, and scattered books. <None of this will do. If this goes the way I think it will... Well, this is gonna be big.>

<Follow my lead and move quick!> There were several ways into and out of the study chamber, and it only took Bill a handful of seconds to find the one he wanted. <There. That one.>

Taking a deep breath, Sam lifted himself as far as he could and slid across the room like a stealthy gecko, giving the magical siege tower a wide berth and pulling himself into the connecting aisleway. The sounds of battle quickly faded behind him, muted by the shelves of endless books. Sam moved as fast as possible, keeping his head on a swivel as he took one twisting turn after another, searching for any signs of the College guards while simultaneously allowing Bill to navigate him through the confusing warren of shelves, racks, aisles, and display nooks.

<Left here. No, not *that* left—your *other* left!> Bill mocked in Sam's head as the human rounded a corner, panting from the exertion of army crawling as far as he had. Sam froze as he heard the chatter of familiar voices. *Octavius.*

<Good, good, good! We're here, Legs. Uh... sorry again. Hey, we made it! It took some doing, but if I'm not wrong, we should be on the backside of the chamber. Is it as far as I want to be? No. Not even close. But will the books buffer us from the blowback? Also no. Now, slip over there and take a little look-see through that row of books.>

Cautiously, Sam faced the bookshelf lining the left-hand side of the hallway and peaked over the top edge of the books. There was a thin slit of light. It was hard to see, so Sam pulled a single volume free—stowing it in his spatial container for later use—then stole a look through the narrow opening. The breath caught in his throat as he saw a very familiar scene unfolding before him.

Sure enough, Bill had led them to one of the many stacks that ran parallel to the study area Octavius had been using for his spell. Sam was currently staring out from *behind* one of the small study nooks, which looked on to the larger chamber. There was no way Octavius would be able to see him, but he had an almost unobstructed view of the floor, the grimoire, and the mini mystic siege tower positioned in the center of the room.

"What do you want us to do about them?" Tullus' voice was low and raspy.

"Despite your utter *incompetence*," Octavius spat, "there's no way they will get out of the library this time. Elsia, I want you to go alert Mage Solis and the College guard. *Now.* I want them combing over every inch of this library. Every. Single. Inch. Do you hear me? As for you, Tullus, you'll stand here and watch my back while I finish my spell."

"But shouldn't we maybe... you know... *wait?* On the spell that is?" Tullus suggested. "At least until the Warlock is captured?"

"I've wasted enough time with that piece of sentient pond scum. Just make sure another Wolfman doesn't ambush me mid-spell, *again*? Do you think you can manage *that*, you oaf?"

"Of course." Tullus bobbed his head and averted his eyes. Speaking of the Wolfman, Sam was surprised to see there was no sign of Velkan anywhere. Well, that wasn't entirely true. There were claw marks absolutely *everywhere* and more blood than seemed humanly possible, but there was no Wolfman body.

That meant that the Scout had managed to slip away even after tangling with three *powerful* Mages. An impressive feat that made Sam wonder just how exactly Sir Tomas, the dungeoneering professor, had captured the sly creature in the first place.

"Enough dawdling! Move. Both of you!" Octavius snapped, clapping his hands together as though to shoo away a pair of misbehaving hounds. Elsia turned on a heel and set off without a word, though her face was a thunderhead of hate. Tullus merely nodded and posted near the entrance to the study area, his face stony and unreadable. Meanwhile, Octavius headed for the grimoire, his face twisted up in a sneer of absolute hate.

"Attack *me*, will you? You mangy, flea-ridden *dog*," he muttered loudly enough for anyone in earshot to hear. "Well, I may not have been able to kill *you*, but I'll get even yet. Once I do, I'll ascend to Journeyman, and then the *rest* of your kind will pay. *Everyone* who *ever* doubted me will pay!"

Octavius positioned himself in front of the lectern, cracking his neck and placing his palms face down on either side of the grimoire. He closed his eyes for a second, breathing deeply through his nose, his forehead creased in concentration... probably trying to clear his mind for the spell to come. Anything other than crystal-clear concentration and laser-focused intention could *spell* doom when working on a spell of this magnitude. Sam had to lightly slap himself. Bill's tendency to make puns at inappropriate times was rubbing off on him.

Finally, Octavius opened his eyes, nodded to himself, and began to recite the complicated words scrawled so carefully into the book while his hands danced in the air, executing enormously complicated gestures and patterns which had taken *ages* to learn. His chanting grew more fervent as he progressed, his hand movements growing faster yet simultaneously more fluid with each second.

As Octavius intoned sacred words that Sam couldn't even begin to comprehend, the siege tower began to hum with ominous life. A **buzz** like the droning of some great wasp filled the air, while the enormous stone suspended above the machine burned with toxic emerald light. Faster still the words came, flowing from Octavius' tongue like an auctioneer trying to make a commission.

Energy built around the man like a storm cloud as the spell came to a crescendo, coalescing into something elemental and deadly.

Octavius' voice was sure, his pronunciation flawless and exacting. "*Et matrem terræ devorabunt eos.*"

<Hold on to your butt. Here it comes!> Bill squealed with glee. Sam could almost *see* the book rubbing his hands together in eager anticipation.

"*Hostis noster caro et sanguis. Lupus nocte luna profanum!*" As Octavius spoke the last word, *profanum*, the grimoire sprawled across the lectern exploded into a column of blistering fire, mule-kicking Octavius right in the teeth. He staggered back, reeling drunkenly from the blast, though still very much alive.

Book Maker's Book Bomb was a powerful weapon but not powerful enough to take out a Mage of Octavius' level. Luckily, they weren't just depending on the bomb to do the heavy lifting. No, they'd just provided a spark. Now, the powder keg of *Octavius'* magic would finish the job.

The cloud of power that had gathered around Octavius flickered madly, arcs of electricity spitting out and zapping anything that got too close. The siege tower itself was now letting out a tortured shriek as metal rubbed against metal, wood splintering and fracturing under the weight of barely contained Mana.

"What is *happening*!" Octavius screamed into the room, spinning in a slow circle as he fought to control the magic surging through him and threatening to spill out of the strange weapon he'd built. Sam couldn't resist. He pulled free several more volumes, making a large enough gap to poke his head out.

"Hey, Octavius! How's your spell going?"

"You! What have you done?" The Peak Student rounded on him, eyes locking on Sam. His body was shaking under the strain of trying to contain the magic, his lips pulled back in a snarl.

"What? *Me*?" Sam replied with an innocent shrug. "I have no *idea* what you're talking about!"

Maybe Sam wasn't a master of the arcane *yet,* but there was at least one thing he'd learned about spells since coming to Eternium. The bigger they were, the more dangerous they could be. If you interrupted a spell at the wrong moment... Well, that power needed to go *somewhere.* The most likely place to go was back into the caster, who served as a conduit between the spellform and the Mana pool that powered it.

"Surely, there's no way *I* could've done this," Sam sounded completely aghast. "Why, don't you *remember*? I'm just a *commoner*! I can barely comprehend the *sheer* responsibilities and dedication required of a licensed Mage. *You're* the practitioner of the arcane arts, Octavius! You're the one who can shape the elements, the herald of all knowledge. I'm just a pesky nobody in way over his head. You've *got* this!"

Octavius opened his mouth in reply, but whatever he had planned to say never left his lips. Blinding, blue-green lighting erupted from his mouth and eyes, while more bolts of wild energy surged through his arms and legs, lancing outward. For a moment the world inverted... then it turned white.

As white as fresh canvas. No sound, no motion. Just blank *emptiness*. A formless void. The world seemed to shudder uncertainly all around Sam. The ground rumbled; everything spun topsy-turvy. Sam was *sure* he'd died. It was the only plausible explanation... but then sound returned.

A high-pitched squeal filled Sam's head like a buzz-saw slicing into a sheet of metal. Smells came next—the scent of scorched wood, burnt meat, and smoldering paper. Last of all came sight, shapes slowly resolving from the scene of formlessness. Sam blinked several times, grinding his palms into his eye sockets, then shook his head to clear away the purple afterimages seared across his retinas.

The machine, or what was left of it, was scattered across the study chamber in a field of smoldering debris. Where the machine had previously sat was a smoking crater, eight feet deep and five feet wide. Of Octavius... there was no sign at all. Not even a scrap of robe remained.

He'd been wiped out as completely as anyone could be wiped out. Obliterated root and branch. Tullus had fared only a little better. He hadn't survived—he was far too close to the epicenter of the blast for that—but at least there were bits and pieces of him remaining.

Only enough to fill a beach pail, but at least there was *something*. Now... he needed to find a health potion so that he could get on the move again. He just so happened to know where Mage Solis stashed the supply he used to stay mobile. It was a bit of a trek at this pace, so Sam got to crawling.

EPILOGUE

Quest complete: Trust of the Pack. Congratulations!
You've thwarted the plans of the Mage's College to wipe out the
Wolfman Outpost with a deadly new spell. In doing so, you and
the members of the Wolf Pack have openly declared war on the
Mage's College and successfully betrayed humanity! All in
exchange for a permanent place among The People. Is that the
smartest move? Hard to say, but no one will ever be able to
accuse you of commitment issues!

You have earned 10,000 Experience points for
completing this task and gained the favor of the Wolfmen!
Reputation with The People has increased by 2000 points, from
'Neutral' directly to 'Friendly' (bypassing 'Reluctantly friendly').
1000 reputation points remain to reach 'Friend of The People'
status. You have unlocked the secret title 'Racial Traitor', which
will remain hidden during regular gameplay for the time being.

"You have done well," The O'Baba purred, turning her
golden gaze on each member of the Wolf Pack arrayed before
her in a loose half-circle. Sam and the rest of his crew were all
patched up or, in the case of Kai and Arrow, fresh off respawn
after the battle with Octavius. They were finally safe and sound
in Narvik.

Slipping out of the library had been surprisingly easy in
the wake of the chaos that followed the explosion. Elsia had
moved quickly, summoning a hoarde of guards and junior
Mages to the library, but there was *so* much confusion that it was
a piece of cake for Sam to slip out through the secret
passageway, making the rendezvous with the others at The
Grater Good.

Most surprising of all was that *Velkan* had made it! After tangling with the Mages, the Wolfman Scout had broken loose, then disappeared into the stacks... only to pick up Dizzy's scent a short while later. Once he had a nose full of blood to track, it was an easy thing for him to find the emergency passage on his own and meet up with the rest of the party. That warmed Sam's soul. He hadn't spent much time with the Wolfman—knew almost nothing about him, in fact—but Sam knew *one* thing, the only thing that really mattered—when Sam was in trouble, Velkan had come for him when he just as easily could've run.

"In truth, when this whelp here," The O'Baba waved a clawed hand in Sam's direction, drawing him from his thoughts, "came to us, I was sure he was mad as a water-adder nymph. Certainly never thought he would fulfill his word. Yet."

She paused and rose from her seat in the grand lodge, nestled in the heart of the Wolfman Outpost. "Yet here he stands. With him, his own pack. A Wolf Pack in the truest sense of the word. You all may have the faces of mankind, but in your hearts, each of you have proven yourselves to be *wolves.* You have shed blood for our cause, both your own and our enemies. You have bled and even *died* to see the survival of The People, and for that? For that, you shall be *rewarded.*"

Her ears twitched, and Yurij BrightBlood—the Wolfman Shaman who'd nearly sacrificed Sam once upon a time—approached with an intricately carved wooden box that had polished bone inlaid into the lid. The O'Baba jerked her head, and Yurij hunched his shoulders, bending into a deep bow as he lifted the lid and extended the box, revealing the contents.

With delicate care, The O'Baba reached over and pulled out a pendant. It was just a simple leather thong with a golden medallion on the end, studded with a glimmering tiger's eye stone in the center. Etched into the face of the stone was a single runic mark which Sam didn't recognize... the jagged lines and hard angles didn't belong to any language he knew. The O'Baba approached Sam, slipping the pendant over his head, then pulled another less intricate version from the box and approached Dizzy.

"These pendants are tokens of our favor," she crooned softly, almost fondly. "The rune is from the tongue of The People, back in the days before the moon fell and the world shattered. In your language, it roughly translates to *Wolf-Hearted*. These pendants will make you known among The People. For Sam... this will name you a *Lord* among The People. The mere presence of this stone upon your person will be felt by any member of our kind. You may not look as we do, but you are of one heart with us, now and forever."

She fell silent as she made her way down the line, stringing one of the necklaces over each member of the Wolf Pack. When she'd finally finished, she pulled free the last item in the ornate box—a scroll, bound in vellum and tied shut with a blood red strip of fabric.

"This is the other reward you were promised... a Guild Charter. With this, I hereby name the Wolf Pack the first Noble Guild of the Wolfman Race!"

She offered it to Sam, but he pressed his lips into a thin line and shook his head. "No. As much as I'd like to, I'm not the Guild Leader here. Dizzy is. She's the one that brought this group together, she's the one that made this possible, and she deserves to be in charge. I'm happy to do my part, but running a guild is not the role I want to play."

A blush crept into his cheeks. "To be honest, I'm here for fun. That looks like a lot more paperwork than it does adventuring."

He reached down and patted Bill. "Besides, I already have *more* than enough paperwork to handle already."

The O'Baba chuffed, her ears wiggling in what Sam decided was akin to a laugh for the Wolfman. After a moment, the 'laughing fit' subsided, and The O'Baba shuffled over, positioning herself in front of the armor-clad brawler.

"It is not the choice I would have made," she growled, shrugging her shoulders, "but this is the way of our packs as well. It is not for outsiders to decide who should run the hunt. If you have earned his trust, then you have earned my trust as well, Hunt Leader. Do not disappoint us."

She pushed the charter into Dizzy's hand. A brilliant smile broke across the tank's normally serious face. "Now," the she-wolf said, raising her voice, "I would have a moment alone with the Bibliomancer. He and I, we have unfinished business to discuss."

After a polite round of bowing and a wave of respectful 'goodbyes', Yurij showed the rest of the Wolf Pack from the Long House, taking them to their new quarters. Just like that, Sam found himself alone with The O'Baba. The old woman regarded him through hooded eyes, her face unreadable. For the second time since meeting her, Sam felt as though he was being weighed and measured... and he wasn't quite sure if he measured up or not.

<Man, she's kind of intense, isn't she?> Bill whispered in his mind. <Not in a bad way necessarily, just an *intense* way. You don't think she'd gonna try to eat us, right? I mean... she couldn't do that, not after the ceremony? Naming us as a Lord of The People and all that. Sam? Are you listening to me? Sam?>

Sam *wasn't* really listening. He was focused on The O'Baba, refusing to flinch or look away from her dissecting gaze. She was a predator, there was no question about that, but Sam wanted her to know that he was a predator in his own right. Maybe he didn't have fangs and fur, but he was a fighter. He'd stood up for himself, faced down his fears, confronted the bully, and walked away victorious with a band of real friends at his back. Sam didn't want to be disrespectful—she was the leader of this group—but he also wouldn't be disrespected.

Finally, she snorted and flickered her ears. "I had a feeling about you, you know. I think you are destined for great things, Sam_K. Undermining the College was an impressive feat, but perhaps even more impressive to me is that you saved my kin. Velkan, he has met with me, you know. Told me of your battle with the one called Octavius. You have proven yourself a hundred times over, and for this, you have my deepest thanks and my blessing."

She was on him in a second, pressing one callused hand against his shoulder, her claws digging effortlessly through his leather armor and puncturing the skin below. It hurt, but after having both his kneecaps shattered, it didn't seem like nearly such a big deal. Sometimes, perspective mattered.

"For your faithful service to a People not your own, I call you *my* friend. I name you Sam_K Magebane, the first Wolfman Warlock." She squeezed down even tighter, driving her claws farther as she muttered a short, wordless chant under her breath.

Power built in the air around her like a cloak, seeping out through her claws and into Sam's arm. Tendrils of primal force snaked their way *up,* momentarily wrapping around his throat—making it hard to breathe—before finally migrating to his head. Sam's scalp began to itch and crawl, almost as though something was wriggling just underneath his skin. After a beat, the itching subsided. As it did, Sam's short-cropped hair began to grow; cascading down to his shoulders in a mass of dark, bouncy curls.

The O'Baba finally withdrew her claws, and a message appeared.

Quest complete: Blood Runs Deep. Wow! Look at you. Against all odds, you saved Velkan of the Redmane Tribe, blood-kin to The O'Baba, Mother of Wolves. Didn't see that coming. As a result, your personal reputation with The People has increased by 1000 points. Current reputation: Friend of The People. Nice! Furthermore, The O'Baba was so impressed with you that she has given you a new name: Sam_K Magebane. With the swanky title comes The O'Baba's Blessing: Hair of the Dog I (Upgradeable)!

Effect: Hair of the Dog gives you the most luscious locks in all the land. You'll be the envy of everyone! Just look at how silky smooth that fancy do is! Wow! You cannot change or alter your hair. Any attempts to hide your hair will fail—aside from regular head coverings such as hats—but why would you want to cover such beauty anyway? +5 Charisma because hey, you're <u>always</u> having a great hair day! Additionally, your hair can be plucked and used as an alchemic ingredient in book-bindings in place of infused twine and waxed thread!

Be warned, this kind of power always comes with a cost! Since a Shamanic Blessing has gone out into the world, so too has a Shamanic Curse been released. Dark power waits, ready to strike like a cobra. Someday, somewhere, some unlucky soul will make me grumpy, and when that happens... they will be cursed with irrevocable baldness for all their days. But what are the chances that will matter to you? You'll probably never meet that person anyway! It's not like this is some kind of ominous portent, guaranteeing you will have a nemesis for life or anything. Don't look a gift Shaman in the mouth is basically what I'm saying!

"Now, with blessings and rewards out of the way," The O'Baba waved to a seat, "why don't we talk about something else my kin Velkan mentioned. The weapon Octavius was building to use against us. The Long-range Amplification Weapon. What can you tell me of it and how it works? How to defend against it?"

"What can I tell you about the LAW? I can do more than tell you... I can show you." He pulled the blueprints he'd snagged from Octavius' grimoire.

The O'Baba grinned as her golden eyes skipped over the precise drawings and carefully scribbled notes. "Yes... destined for great things indeed..."

"Of course, I am." Sam pulled his hat off and bowed, allowing his flowing hair to tumble around his shoulders. "After all..."

"I *am* a Bibliomancer."

AFTERWORD

We hope you enjoyed Bibliomancer! Since reviews are the lifeblood of indie publishing, we'd love it if you could leave a positive review on Amazon! Please use this link to go to the Wolfman Warlock: Bibliomancer Amazon product page to leave your review: geni.us/Bibliomancer.

As always, thank you for your support! You are the reason we're able to bring these stories to life.

ABOUT JAMES HUNTER

Hey all, my name is James Hunter and I'm a writer, among other things. So just a little about me: I'm a former Marine Corps Sergeant, combat veteran, and pirate hunter (seriously). I'm also a member of The Royal Order of the Shellback–'cause that's a real thing. I've also been a missionary and international aid worker in Bangkok, Thailand. And, a space-ship captain, can't forget that.

Okay ... the last one is only in my imagination.

Currently, I'm a stay at home Dad–taking care of my two kids– while also writing full time, making up absurd stories that I hope people will continue to buy. When I'm not working, writing, or spending time with family, I occasionally eat and sleep.

Connect with James:
AuthorJamesAHunter.com
Facebook.com/WriterJamesAHunter
Patreon.com/JamesAHunter
Twitter.com/WriterJAHunter

ABOUT DAKOTA KROUT

I live in a 'pretty much Canada' Minnesota city with my wife and daughter. I started writing The Divine Dungeon series because I enjoy reading and wanted to create a world all my own. To my surprise and great pleasure, I found like-minded people who enjoy the contents of my mind. Publishing my stories has been an incredible blessing thus far, and I hope to keep you entertained for years to come!

Connect with Dakota:
Patreon.com/DakotaKrout
Facebook.com/TheDivineDungeon
Twitter.com/DakotaKrout

ABOUT MOUNTAINDALE PRESS

Dakota and Danielle Krout, a husband and wife team, strive to create as well as publish excellent fantasy and science fiction novels. Self-publishing *The Divine Dungeon: Dungeon Born* in 2016 transformed their careers from Dakota's military and programming background and Danielle's Ph.D. in pharmacology to President and CEO, respectively, of a small press. Their goal is to share their success with other authors and provide captivating fiction to readers with the purpose of solidifying Mountaindale Press as the place 'Where Fantasy Transforms Reality.'

Connect with Mountaindale Press:
MountaindalePress.com
Facebook.com/MountaindalePress
Krout@MountaindalePress.com

MOUNTAINDALE PRESS TITLES

GAMELIT AND LITRPG

The Divine Dungeon Series
The Completionist Chronicles Series
By: DAKOTA KROUT

A Touch of Power: Series
By: JAY BOYCE

Red Mage: Advent
By: XANDER BOYCE

Ether Collapse: Equalize
By: RYAN DEBRUYN

Axe Druid Series
By: CHRISTOPHER JOHNS

Skeleton in Space: Histaff
By: ANDRIES LOUWS

Pixel Dust Series
By: DAVID PETRIE

Made in the USA
Monee, IL
25 May 2020